GABRIEL'S LEGACY

GABRIEL'S LEGACY

ROBERT LEITERMAN

Gabriel's Legacy

Copyright 2022 by Robert Leiterman

All rights reserved. No part of this book may be used or reproduced by any means, graphic, electronic or mechanical, including photocopying, recording, taping or by any information storage retrieval system without the written permission of the publisher except in the case of brief quotations embodied in critical articles and reviews.

Though inspired by life this is mostly a work of fiction. All of the characters, names, organizations, incidents, and dialog in this book are for the most part a product of the author's imagination.

First Printing by Robert Leiterman

Cover design and art work by April Leiterman

ISBN#-9798712001101

TABLE OF CONTENTS

LIST OF ILLUSTRATIONS: 9
ACKNOWLEDGEMENTS: 11
INTRODUCTION: 13
ACT-ONE: FROM THE DARKNESS..15
CHAPTER ONE: SO IT BEGINS..17
CHAPTER TWO: GHOSTS..31
CHAPTER THREE: AWAKINING-A Not So Understanding............37
CHAPTER FOUR: THE JOURNAL..55
CHAPTER FIVE: THE HEALING BEGINS..69
CHAPTER SIX: DESPERATION..83
CHAPTER SEVEN: GOD PARENT...89
CHAPTER EIGHT: OBLIGATION...95
CHAPTER NINE: REUNITED..109
CHAPTER TEN: THEY WALK AMONG US..119
CHAPTER ELEVEN: MENTORING THROUGH UNDERSTANDING
....135
CHAPTER TWELVE: PREPARATION-BACK TO SCHOOL.............143
CHAPTER THIRTEEN: SEEING IS BELIEVING-A Test of Faith
....149
CHAPTER FOURTEEN: BEYOND DOUBT...159
CHAPTER FIFTEEN: ANOTHER'S BLESSING...................................177
CHAPTER SIXTEEN: SCHOOL NURSE..183
CHAPTER SEVENTEEN: HEART TO HEART....................................195
CHAPTER EIGHTEEN: SHRINKAGE...201
CHAPTER NINTEEN: SOLITUDE AT LAST.......................................213

ACT-TWO: AMONG THE ANCIENT TREES..........................221
CHAPTER TWENTY: AROUND THE CAMPFIRE..........................223
CHAPTER TWENT-ONE: FROM THE DARKNESS..........................233
CHAPTER TWENTY-TWO: THE BRIEFING..........................239
CHAPTER TWENTY-THREE: A ZONE TO SEARCH..........................253
CHAPTER TWENTY-FOUR: NAVIGATING THE MOUNTAIN ROADS 263
CHAPTER TWENTY-FIVE: INTO THE WILDERNESS..........................281
ACT-THREE: ENLIGHTENMENT..........................297
CHAPTER TWENTY-SIX: THE VOICE OF PRAYER..........................299
CHAPTER TWENTY-SEVEN: THE MEDALLION..........................315
CHAPTER TWENTY-EIGHT: ON TASK..........................333
CHAPTER TWENTY-NINE: ABOVE AND BEYOND..........................347
CHAPTER THIRTY: WE DO WHAT WE MUST!..........................361
CHAPTER THIRTY-ONE: NEITHER HERE NOR THERE!..........................375
CHAPTER THIRTY-TWO: MONSIGNOR..........................391
CHAPTER THIRTY-THREE: AN AIR OF CHANCE..........................421
CHAPTER THIRTY-FOUR: THE ULTIMATE SACRIFICE..........................437
CHAPTER THIRTY-FIVE: INNER STRENGTH..........................447
CHAPTER THIRTY-SIX: LOVING STRENGTH..........................459
CHAPTER THIRTY-SEVEN: REPRIEVE..........................471
ACT-FOUR: THE AFTERMATH..........................485
CHAPTER THIRTY-EIGHT: THE BEGINNING..........................487
ABOUT THE AUTHOR / ILLUSTRATOR
FATHER AND DAUGHTER PROJECT..........................495
BOOKS BY AUTHOR..........................496

LIST OF ILLUSTRATIONS

By: April Leiterman

1	Front Cover: Gabriel's Legacy...............................
2	Back Cover: ....
3	"The Locker Room": 16
4	"Ghosts": 31
5	"In the garden of Saint Francis": 213
6	"A Conspiracy of Ravens": 222
7	"The Messenger": 253
8	"Steven of the Redwoods": 298
9	"Alex": 359

ACKNOWLEDGEMENTS

I would like to thank the following family and friends for their support of this project over the last 12 years. Steven Streufert for the many late night hours he had spent reviewing, supporting and editing the later stages of the manuscript. My very creative and talented daughter April who artistically designed the cover and other pieces of art displayed throughout this and other literary projects. The unyielding support of my big brother James for all of my literary works. For Butch and Shirley Russel, Erick Rowland, Nancye Kirtly and Rick Dowd for their support and input during the developing stages of the manuscript. And for Father Manning of the Saint Joseph's Parish in Fortuna, who took the time out of his busy schedule to review the rough draft. Not to forget the numerous others who were either a willing or an unwilling audience to my numerous revisions and storytelling rants. And I would also like to give a warm hearted thank you for those that I have neglected to mention. I would also like to thank my wife Regina for her patient support on this and many of my other literary journeys over the years, for without her patience this project and others would have never happened. And lastly, I would also like to acknowledge the forest mysteries that have inspired me over the years of living and working in the outdoors. May their secrets remain so.

INTRODUCTION

Why do some good people fall short of a lengthy life while others, live long unforgiving ones?
Inspired by those struggling thoughts, I flashed back to my earlier years of my Catholic upbringing. I was always taught to turn the other cheek and to forgive those who have trespassed against myself and others. With a career in public safety, I was taught to protect and to serve.

At first I learned that turning the other cheek, clashed with enforcing the rules and regulations. It took me a fair amount of thought and struggle to find a mutual understanding, to realize that both served a purpose.

I strive to live the life I was taught, and follow the examples of those who inspire me while being fair and impartial.

I had spent more than 30 years as a park ranger serving the people and protecting public lands with these three guidelines in mind... Protect the *park from the people*, the *people from the park*, and the *people from the people*.

Growing up as a teen I had always wanted to be a park ranger. *Was I to blame that silly notion on the family summer vacations we took across the western United States as a youth?*

I often wondered if my choices were predetermined by powers greater than I could understand. So, what is the difference between a good choice and a bad choice? Is it the outcome of our actions? Are the voices we hear really the debate between the two, each with their own job?

I was one of the lucky ones to obtain a career in the field that I had grown up wanting, dreaming about, and had gone to college for.

Am I following my path? Was I divinely guided by powers greater than myself? Was that part of my legacy?

The story:

So, what really happened to Gabriel Wilson, a park ranger, who was said to have followed the mysterious voices that directed him to be in the right place and the right time? Against all the odds, he pulled off the impossible. That was until one stormy day, in the park he swore an oath to protect, his luck had finally run out. *Was he following his legacy?*

Ten years later, when almost all was conveniently forgotten, strange things began to happen to his fifteen year old son, Gabe. He too began to hear the voices, see the shadows, and smell the unusual. Frightened and confused by what he couldn't explain or understand He embarked on a journey, guided by family and a series of choices that would either bring closure to the family curse or an end to the Wilson legacy once and for all.

Enjoy,

Robert Leiterman

Act 1:
From the Darkness

"The Locker Room" by April Leiterman

CHAPTER ONE
SO IT BEGINS
(WEDNESDAY AFTER SCHOOL)
MARCH 9TH 2000

Gabe stopped abruptly in his stride. His oversized canvas duffel bag fell to the waxed tile floor of the aging gym. Gabe spun to his right as he squinted down the narrow, dimly lit hallway. His spine tingled; his trembling hands clinched in fists, his labored breaths were deep and rapid. His eyes cautiously searched for anything that shouldn't be there.

There it is again!

His thoughts raced, his toes tingled. The unnerving feeling was back.

Am I being followed? But how can that be? I'm the last person here!

He hated the pathetic lighting. Dimly lit bulbs hung from the tall dingy ceiling and cast long shadows down the darkened hallway. The earth-tone bricks absorbed the light. This place made many of the other students feel uncomfortable. His peers believed the gym was haunted by the student who committed suicide in the boy's locker room a few cars back. As a fifteen-year-old, he didn't believe in ghosts, but with that said, he really didn't care for the hallway much himself.

If it isn't the ghosts then what is it?

The thought made him shiver.

This was the most frightened he had ever been. Well, almost.

He took a deep breath and tried to force the disturbing thoughts from his mind.

He hated being the last person out of the eerie locker room, but today it couldn't be helped. Karate practice had ran over. And, well, Coach Moats' rules were quite clear: 'The last one out turned off the lights'. This afternoon it was him. He could kick himself for not following his friend Erick out of the place five minutes earlier, but Erick had left in a hurry. His thoughts told him to stay.

"Who are you... what do you want?" he yelled towards the darkness. The pitched fear in his voice echoed down the long cave-like hallway. He continued to clinch his fists as he stared in the direction of the noise. He could feel the presence of something or someone out there in the darkness. He strained his ears to listen, his eyes peering into the void. His mind tried to make sense of it all. He fought the fear that welled up from within. He couldn't believe that he was afraid of something he could not see or hear. It was the unknown that brought the tightness to his chest and fear to his heart. The uncontrolled chill made his skin crawl. And this unfortunately wasn't the first time either. His thoughts flooded in as he remembered the other day...

It was two weeks ago, around sunset on one of the back alleys in the small town of Springville. He had been walking home. Despite his mother's earnest protest and his better judgment, he had taken a shortcut through one of the dingy, dark alleys in town.

The concerned voice in his head stopped him in his tracks, causing him to turn and look behind him. To his surprise, there wasn't anyone there. He shrugged it off as a fragment of his over active imagination, and entered the alley anyway.

Though it was late, there was plenty of ambient light from the distant street lights. He was halfway through when two scruffy looking, college aged males stepped out of the shadows and around the corner blocking the exit. Their scraggly faces and tattered clothing screamed of trouble...

The cautious little voice had been right!

Their stares, their whispers... he knew they meant him harm. Without missing a step he turned around as if he had forgotten something and headed back the way he had come. But to his dismay a third individual, bigger and more intimidating than the others stepped out from the shadows, into the alley and blocked his exit.

He felt his heart sink as a strange fear overtook him. He looked in vain for a way out. The walls seemed even taller. His vision narrowed, time slowed, and the sounds went with it. The ends of the alley seemed to stretch farther out of his reach, the safety of the light ever so distant. He was trapped, in trouble, and he knew it. The troublemakers had chosen their ambush well. The fear welled up from within as he backed himself into the closest wall. His senses were working overtime.

The thugs seemed to relish in his fear as they moved slowly towards him, taking their time, savoring the moment. Even their words, as they talked amongst themselves, seemed slowed. He could barely follow their actions, the laughing, and the expressions of satisfaction in their sinister-looking eyes.

His thoughts all garbled together, his mom's last words, the warning, was the clearest of them all.

'I told you to stay away from the alley!'
Their loud, sarcastic laughter echoed off the canyon-like walls. He felt their hate, their sarcasm. He heard it in their voices, saw it in their body language. He felt it in the air. They approached slowly as if time was on their side, bathing in his fear. The smells of body odor, cheap cologne, and stale cigarettes grabbed harshly at his nose. Gabe balled up his fists even tighter and waited for the inevitable. He couldn't believe this was happening to him.

If only he had listened to my mother!

However, suddenly, their laughter ceased, their sarcastic anger replaced with fear. The air around Gabe felt electrified. The two smaller thugs abruptly stopped and stared past him. Their confidence gone, concern streaked across their faces. Their eyes glazed over with fear.
What?
Gabe followed the strange gazes of the two young men toward the third. The bigger one picked up his pace as he swaggered towards him. The individual's confidence faded noticeably with their every step. Gabe flattened his back against the wall and braced himself for the inevitable clash. They were done playing with him, he felt it. Now they were getting down to business. He locked his eyes on the approaching giant, his strength draining.

The big thug glanced nervously over his shoulder. His pace increased. Gabe saw fear in those pathetic looking eyes as the brute turned his head to cheat a quick glance over his shoulder. The giant was no longer in control. He moved like he was escaping a fright of his own.
What was he looking at? What did he see?

The giant increased his gait, hugged the opposite wall as he grazed past. He shot Gabe a pathetic glance before he snapped another quick look over his shoulder again. Gabe saw an apologetic sorrow in the giant's eyes. Confused, he gazed in the direction the giant had come, in the direction they all seemed to stare.

Gabe saw nothing...

But someone had to have been approaching, it was the only thing that could have frightened those three bullies, and saved me from what was about to happen!

Gabe flushed with a welcome feeling of triumph and relief, his eyes shot back to the thugs in time to see the two of them stumble backwards over each other in an all-out panic. They turned and ran in the direction they had come, their bravado gone, arms flailing disjointedly as they each shot a terrified glance over their shoulders.

"Let's get the hell out of here!" a desperate voice crackled, each drove the other to move faster with frantic shoves.

What the heck?

The alley suddenly seemed unusually brighter. His own huge shadow now stretched the length and width of the asphalt, giving him the height and girth of a giant himself. The panicked expressions on the thugs' faces illuminated in the brightness.

The biggest of the thugs quickly overtook the others in an all-out sprint. There was ultimate fear and the look of a sincere apology in the big man's eyes as he shot Gabe a departing glance as he passed by. It was the last thing Gabe remembered seeing just before the trio disappeared, pushing and shoving their way around the corner.

Gabe had instinctively taken several steps backward along the wall, away from the approaching bluish light. He stopped, cupped his hands around his eyes and squinted into its direction. The sudden brightness from the opening of the alley was blinding.

'Had it been the spotlight from a vehicle, possibly a police cruiser that had stumbled upon my rescue?

Thinking about it again made his heart race.

The warmth on his face! The strange comforting tingle! The bizarre feeling that generated from within his soul radiated out to his extremities. He shivered, not from cold, but from joy. His fear was gone, he felt protected, and loved. He could have stayed there in that very spot forever.

Then there was the eerie silence, the faint ringing in his ears, the smell of sweetness that immediately followed; but a moment later, the light vanished as quickly as it had appeared submerging the entire alley, once again into an uncomfortable darkness. With it went the warmth, and the tranquil feeling that embraced him. To his dismay, there wasn't a vehicle anywhere to be seen. He heard the distant hum of their motors, the muffled barking of the neighborhood dogs. It was as if he had been transported off to another place and time, and then abruptly returned. He missed that incredible feeling; he closed his eyes wishing for the magical blue light to reappear. He stood there confused, waiting for his eyes to adjust to the uncomfortable, dimly lit alley. He waited in vain for it all to make sense. He shivered, this time from the cool breeze that crept down the back of his neck. The strange warmth within him was gone....

There was that soft, discouraging voice again, telling him to leave, that he didn't need to be brave.
But why now, why here of all places?
His thoughts came crashing back to the pit of his stomach, back to the shadows in the room. He felt his skin crawl, his heart race. He shivered as the air temperature continued to drop. He didn't like the way he felt. For a moment, he could almost see the outline of his warm breath.
It wasn't totally his fault. Many of the students talked about the locker room being haunted.
Humorous talk to scare the freshmen? But, why am I feeling this way?
He felt confused at first it all seemed quiet, but as his ears adjusted, the sounds of the old building became more noticeable. He cupped his hand behind his ears to magnify the sound. There was the familiar hum of the gym lights behind him that played off the walls.
Are these creaks and pops of the old foundation?
He hoped there was the steady, rhythmic, dripping of one of the leaky shower heads, the one that the custodian, Mr. Jenkins could never fix.
Then there was that strange familiar feeling of being followed, being watched. He shuddered uncontrollably. He hated the fact that his sense of fear continued to dominate. His imagination was beginning to run away. He forced a few deep breaths in a futile attempt to calm himself.
Just turn around... just turn around and walk the other way!
His mind told his body.
"I'm not playing around, show yourself!" he screamed, on the verge of panic. Suddenly, to his disbelief, the locker room immediately became uncomfortably quiet. The walls and the floor no longer creaked and popped. The shower no longer dripped.
The shower?

Said the little voice in his head.

"No way, this can't be happening!" his whisper echoed in the darkness. A strange eeriness emanated from down the hall.

The shower has never done this before!

His thoughts raced. Part of him wanted to turn and run screaming down the hallway, through the gym, and then out into the parking lot. Never to look back, never to speak a word of it ever, to nobody. The other part of him wanted to prove that it was all nothing, that his imagination had gotten the better of him. At that moment he understood why, in horror movies, the victims always put themselves in harm's way, the moths always managed to find the flames. They say it was the curiosity that killed the cat, being drawn to the wrong place at the wrong time. But this he had to do.

He gave out a deep sigh and tried to swallow, but his throat was too dry. He balled his hands even tighter. His fists began to shake. Despite his mental protest, he cautiously moved down the hallway in the direction of the boy's locker room. The squeak of his carefully placed shoes on the waxed floors was barely audible over the sounds of his thundering heart. He was going to get to the bottom of this even if it took every bit of his strength, courage, and willpower he could muster.

There are no such things as ghosts... there are no such things as ghosts!

He kept telling himself.

Someone is having fun at my expense!

He tried to force his mind to listen to his echoing thoughts, but his instincts favored his inner voice, the one that seemed to speak from the depth of his soul.

He counted his steps and when he reached *ten* he stopped and listened again.

"Drip, drip, please... drip!" he pleaded. Silence filled the void from beyond the open door to the locker room that stood in the darkness only ten feet away. To his amazement, the leaky shower head appeared to have fixed itself.

He wiped away the beads of sweat that tickled his face. He took a deep breath and cautiously closed the distance. He stopped to conceal himself behind one of the closed double doors to the shower room. He took a couple of deep breaths and listened, hesitant to peek around the edge of the door to the showers. The air was dominated by the hum of the distant gym and hallway lights.

"This is ridiculous!" he grumbled under his breath. He crept to the edge of the open doorway and eased one of his eyes beyond the opening. The droning hum of the light faded into a void of darkness. He remembered the light switch off to his right, and struggled with the desire to flick them on. To his surprise, his eyes had begun to adjust. The faint rays of hallway light stretched into the locker room, illuminating the first row of benches. Reluctantly, he continued his journey among the shadows, edged on by an inexplicable desire to know. He knew there was a second light switch on the back wall of the locker room by the coach's office, immersed in darkness.

As he edged himself onward, the movement of a dark shadow froze him in his tracks. He struggled with the urge to turn and run. He forced a muffled laugh when he realized that the frightening shadow was his own, silhouetted by the back lighting from the hallway. This realization gave him strength to continue. He took a couple of deep breaths and moved farther into the locker room, farther into the shadows, willing the leaky shower faucet to drip again. He was answered by the creaking of the ancient foundation, the dull droning of the lights, and the growing desire to make it to the showers.

He took another deep breath and willed himself forward, his eyes never leaving his dancing shadow on the distant wall. To his surprise, his feet shuffled blindly down the familiar path, right past his friend, Erick's and his own lockers. The hum of the lights faded behind him. The squeak of the floor and the pounding of his heart filled the soundless void. He traced his nervous fingers along the edge of the chipped and flaking paint of the aging bench, guiding himself past the battered metal lockers. He wanted to stop and listen, but his nervous momentum carried him forward.

A couple dozen steps more would take him to the back wall and eventually to the light switch next to the coach's door. From there he could illuminate the entire locker/shower room complex with a flick of a switch, putting an end to the world of shadows. The thought made him quicken his pace. Still, to his dismay, a drop of water hadn't fallen from the faucet onto the tile floor.

Once clear of the bench he reached out, open-handed, into the void, as he stepped towards the wall. Misjudging the distance, he stumbled noisily into the bricks, slapping the palms of his hands painfully hard against the solid wall for balance. The sound echoed in the darkness. He winced in pain from the sting as he tried to push the numbness out of his mind. He shook out his hand with a grunt and then hastily slid the palms of both of his hands along the wall towards the light switch that he knew was there. The coldness of the wall made him shudder. The shadows were now indistinguishable from the darkness, the distant hum of the lights faint, his rapid breathing echoed in the eerie silence. He slid his hands more quickly along the wall.

"Where's the door?" he heard the fear in his own hollow whisper. Now on the verge of panic, his hands slid off the wall as he stumbled noisily forward into the locked door of the coach's office, and then clumsily onto the floor.

"Je-e-e-e-e-z!" he exclaimed as he quickly pulled himself back up to his feet with the help of the wall. His eyes instinctively shot back down the long hallway to the distant source of light. His hands guided him up the doorframe and back onto his trembling legs. During any other time the situation would have been hilarious, but now he felt pathetic. With nothing injured but his ego, he wasted no time continuing his frantic search for the light switch.

Come on... shoulder height!

He scolded his inner self. He found the switch seconds later and flicked it on with a loud *'click'*. The caged lights all began to buzz loudly at once. Instead of the sudden flood of light he expected, the bulbs glowed dimly as they slowly built up their intensity. It would take at least two more minutes for the yellow florescent lights to reach their full brightness.

His back sought the comfort of the wall as his lungs struggled for their every breath.

What's that?

An old familiar smell caught his attention.

He watched multiple shadows appear and then fade away as if they were never there at all. With the vanishing silhouette went his fear. The buzzing no longer seemed so loud and obvious. His 'need to know' pulled him off the wall and on toward the showers. He strained his ears as he closed in on the shower entrance that lay ten yards away. It was then that it hit him.

Why am I even her drawn to the eerie silence of a shower... the legend of a ghost?

The thought made his skin crawl.

When he reached the edge he stopped, took a couple of deep breaths, and listened with strained ears. He coughed and shuddered at the sudden smell that filled his nostrils.

Sulfur?

The rhythm of his breath, the pounding of his heart and the faint humming of the lights were the only sounds he heard.

Here we go!

The thoughts echoed in his mind.

Just one more step, lean and focus. You can do it!

Just as he was about to peek around the edge of the wall a distant, familiar sound pulled his attention back up the hall way.

Footsteps?

He flattened his back against the wall, his eyes focused in the direction from where he had just come. Footsteps on the hard floor were moving his way at a hurried gate. Each step growing louder and more determined. They entered the locker room and abruptly stopped. Gabe felt his heart pounding in his chest, he was sure the sound of his heart was bouncing off of the walls.

"Gabe... is that you?" the concerned voice echoed. It was Erick Adams, Gabe's friend, a 15-year-old fellow freshman. He had come back. Gabe felt a comforting lump appear in his throat, making it difficult to swallow. He was very glad his friend had returned.

Erick came back?

The sounds of the footsteps made their way in his direction. With renewed strength and added courage, Gabe focused once again on the interior of the shower. Still not knowing what to expect, he forced himself through the open archway with a big step and stopped. He narrowed his eyes and strained his ears. The smell of sulfur still drifted in the air. He struggled to understand the reason why he was even there.

What was it?

The lighting brightly illuminated the aging tile.

Everything appeared to be as it should. At first, he didn't notice it, but to the far left, in the direction of the questionable showerhead, the floor seemed dull and shaded.

A shadow?

The very thought made his heart skip a couple of beats.

Unsure if he was imagining it or not, a sweet, sickening smell pulled at his nostrils and pushed noticeably against his chest, instantly replacing the rancid smell. He sneezed loudly and blinked. When he looked up, the shadow was gone.

Did I imagine it?

He felt the goose bumps race from the tips of his fingers, down the length of his spine. There was no doubt about it; he felt a presence of something in the room other than, his friend.

"What are you doing?" Erick's concerned voice thundered immediately behind him.

The sudden surprise made Gabe jump and turn on his feet to meet Erick's curious gaze.

"I thought I heard something, in the showers!" Gabe said, his excited voice squeezed embarrassingly higher than normal.

Erick smiled at the sound of his friend's voice. He diverted his eyes, but the damage was already done. He failed to hold back a smirk. It was a short moment before their eyes met again. Gabe could read the laughter in his friend's curious expression.

"The showers are empty," Erick's voice echoed as he gestured with both of his arms into the open space. "They have been since we left them." He looked down at his watch, "almost twenty minutes ago." He wrinkled his eyebrows, but failed to hold back his smile. "If you're afraid of the dark, then why didn't you just say so?"

Erick's playful grin only seemed to infuriate Gabe.

"No, I'm not!" he started to yell defensively, but suddenly remembered the bizarreness of the leaky showerhead. "But, the shower... listen, it's not leaking!"

Erick looked past his friend again as if reexamining the room. "You mean that one?" he pointed to the well-known shower in the corner and cupped a hand against his ear. "Looks and sounds like it still leaks to me!"

Gabe jerked his frustrated gaze towards the corner of the room. His mouth fell open when he heard the rhythmic sound of dripping water, steadily falling onto the tile floor.

No way!

The shower was working again. Gabe shuddered as he gave his friend a confused glance. All he could do was point, as his mouth hung freely open, speechless.

How could this be? It'd stopped!

"Yep, that there is a big waste of water," Erick nodded. "So," he refocused his attention back to his friend, "did you call me all the way back here just to tell me that the shower still works?" he gave him an inquisitive grin. "I mean... if you were—"

"I didn't call you—" Gabe protested. He had finally found his voice. "I was just getting ready to leave when I heard...." he nodded towards the faucet. He stopped when he saw his friend's look of disbelief.

"I only came back because you asked me to!" Erick exclaimed defensively.

"Because I asked you to?" Gabe shook his head. He read the confusion in his friend's face. "I didn't call you back... why would I do that?"

Erick pointed towards the hallway. "Your friend, what's his name. The new kid you've been hanging around with a lot lately said that you wanted—"

"Who?" Gabe interrupted, dumbfounded.

"That cool, slender blond dude with the curly hair, you know... the one who never says much and always smiles. You and he were the last two people left in this room."

"What?" Gabe crossed his arms and shuddered noticeably. He felt his skin crawl as a chill radiated through his body. "You're the only blond guy I hang out with!"

"You're kidding right?" Erick looked angry.

Gabe just shook his head in disbelief. There was no other guy; Erick was the last person he had seen in the locker room. He wanted to ask more questions, but it was as if he could no longer speak. He felt his energy draining from his body; his arms and legs were suddenly weak. He leaned back against the wall for support and dropped his arms uselessly along his sides.

Was this the ghost of locker room fame?

He flashed back to the alley... the bright light... the looks on the muggers' faces.

He suddenly didn't like the way his fingers tingled, or how his stomach seemed to tighten. The whole room had begun to spin. He leaned back against the wall for balance and gave out a heavy sigh.

"The kid told me to hurry back." Erick gave him a strange look. "Hey, are you feeling okay, you're looking kind of pale!"

"Ghosts" by April Leiterman

CHAPTER TWO
GHOSTS
(WEDNESDAY AFTERNOON)
MARCH 9TH 2000

Gabe suddenly felt sick; it was as if his insides were moving all on their own. It was hard to believe that just moments ago he was feeling fine.

Now this?

He felt his friend's firm grip on his biceps and himself being pulled weightlessly back up onto his feet. For a quick second, out of the corner of his eye, he thought he had seen another blond teen standing next to them. Then the figure was gone. Gabe turned his head and tensed, but only his friend remained standing, his face in his. When the light-headedness cleared, he saw Erick's curious eyes peering into his own. He could read the concern across his face.

"What in the heck is wrong with you?" Erick's accusatory voice quivered.

Gabe looked around and regained his balance, he felt the strength returning to his weary limbs. They tingled and throbbed as if asleep.

Adrenaline?

He instinctively pushed his back against the wall and twisted clear of his friend's grip.

Erick let him go, then crossed his arms. He narrowed his eyes as he patiently waited for Gabe's explanation.

When Gabe regained his balance, he stepped out away from the wall and his friend. He stared silently at him for a moment before he cleared his throat. He wanted to tell Erick everything, but there was a slight problem, he didn't know how or where to begin. There was no way to explain something that he himself didn't even understand. They both had questions and obviously they both needed answers.

"To be honest with you," Gabe shrugged, "I really don't know." He thought he detected a sickening whine in his own unsure voice.

Erick re-crossed his arms, repositioned his feet in response. "To be honest!" he shook his head, the confusion obvious, "as if you haven't been telling me the truth from the beginning. And if you haven't a clue, how am I supposed to figure it out." Erick pointed towards the gym. "Let me see if I can help jump start your memory. First, I leave *you* and what's his name here alone in the locker room." Erick exaggerated his look up toward the ceiling, and nervously tapped the tip of his chin with his fingers as if he were thinking. "Apparently someone *you* claim, *you* don't even know—"

"I don't!" Gabe cut him off as he shrugged his shoulders. He moved another half step farther away distancing himself. The thought that his friend didn't believe him hurt.

You don't believe me!

Erick held up a hand to stop Gabe from interrupting.

"He, this mysterious friend of yours, tells me to hurry back here to the gym to meet up with *you*... says it's important. The whole time I'm wonderin' *what could've been so darn important anyway!*" Erick releases his chin and thrusts his index finger accusingly towards Gabe's chest. "So I did, and I find *you*, cowering against this wall—"

"I wasn't cowering!" Gabe snaps back defensively. "I wasn't—"

"Afraid to go into the shower! I'm thinking, why on earth did *you* need to go back to the showers?" The annoyance in Erick's voice was still prevalent. His voice now replaced with concern.

"I thought I heard something." Gabe shrugged.

"Something like..."

"Oh, I don't know, like things or—" Gabe mumbled.

"Things?" Erick quizzed, his eyes opened wide at hearing the words. He gave his friend a mischievous grin. "I thought you didn't believe in ghosts!" He moved closer, spoke softer like he was trying to hide his nervousness. He glanced over his shoulder, shifting his gaze back and forth in between Gabe and the showers. The ghost stories were starting to take effect.

"Well, I don't. At least I thought I didn't," Gabe spoke softly as he gave a quick glance back to the showers. Erick's gaze followed.

"Then, what was that you said about the showers?" Erick demanded.

"The strange noises seemed to come from the showers, but when I got closer, well, you know... the one that always leaks?"

"Yeah," Erick's eyes lit up, "the one on the far left, the one that the kid hung himself from?" his voice enthusiastic.

"Allegedly hung himself... anyway, why did you have to bring that up?" Gabe complained, at that moment it was the last thing he wanted to hear.

"Because it's true!" Erick shrugged. "Big Mike and that nerdy guy, Andrew, they both saw him too! Hanging off that same freaking shower head," he pointed to the shower head, "the one right there!" he shuddered noticeably, excited. "I can hardly wait to tell the guys."

"No! Erick, you can't!" Gabe protested, noted panic in his eyes "I didn't see anything! Seriously I didn't!" Gabe complained. He wanted to keep things quiet. If he told Big Mike, he might as well have told the whole school, or the rest of the town for that matter. Big Mike couldn't keep a secret even if you bribed or threatened him.

"I know you don't want to believe in ghosts, but..." he pointed to the showers. "There is some history here, you aren't the first you know, and you probably won't be the last... This is cool!" he smiled nervously and shot another cautious glance toward the showers. He cleared his throat. "So, now about this blond kid?" he quizzed.

"Yes, about this blond kid! I honestly don't know who the heck you're talking about!" Gabe protested.

"Ugh, you're kidding right?" Erick silently looked him up and down in disbelief.

Gabe shook his head and shrugged his shoulders. He hadn't a clue. "How long have you been seeing this, kid, around me?" Gabe's voice crackled with emotion.

"Since last week, I think... he's a new kid. He doesn't say much, really," Erick gave it some thought as he went on to explain. "Come to think of it, he said more to me today than he has all week. I got the impression that he wanted me to catch up with you right away, there was a bit of urgency to his voice."

Urgency in his voice!

Gabe could read the confusion on his friend's face.

"Seen him with you at least twice now," continued Erick. "I've been waiting for you to introduce us, but by the time I think of getting around to it, he's usually gone." Erick clicked his fingers. "Just like that." He stopped talking for a moment as if he were in deep thought, again. Then he grinned. "Maybe he's a ghost!"

Gabe hesitated at first, but then decided to share what had been bothering him for the last couple of days. He cleared his throat. "If I tell you, anything, you have to promise me you'll keep it a secret."

Erick's eyes brightened at the word *secret*.

"I mean it, it's very important that you promise!" Gabe's eyes pleading for his friend to agree. The whole strange mess was bubbling up from inside and ready to burst; he needed to tell someone, a friend he could trust.

They stared into each other's eyes.

"Okay, I promise. I cross my heart, hope to die, even if they stick a needle in my eye!" Erick went through the ritual of enacting their secret oath.

"This is serious!" Gabe exclaimed, he nodded to his friend. "Come on!"

"Alright, alright!" Erick fought back a smile. "If I breathe a word of what I've been told, I'll spend eternity in a box filled with mold!"

Gabe joined in. He whispered the oath alongside his friend as they clasped their hands together in their special handshake.

"Buried deep beneath the land," their voices joined in unison, "banished forever below the sand."

"Okay, okay, let's have it then." Erick exclaimed. He looked on wantonly.

Gabe took a deep sigh, cleared his throat, and began. He described in detail everything that happened to him that day in the alley. The expressions on the faces of the older boys, when the bright warm light changed everything.

Erick silently stared back at him, politely nodding his head as he carefully listened to every word.

Encouraged, Gabe continued. Without missing a stride, he jumped to what happened to him in the gym as well. He shared every thought that came to mind.

"This stuff is all so weird," his friend exclaimed, "if the voices sounded like they weren't so nice, then why did you follow 'em?"

Gabe paused a moment before he answered. "I don't know!" He shrugged, he looked confused. "Curiosity, I guess. I had to prove to myself that they were all just in my head. I'm still not convinced that what I heard was a ghost!" Gabe wasn't totally convinced by the sound of his own voice, and didn't think his friend was either.

"Gees, what do they have to do, come right up and introduce themselves?"

"I sure hope not!" Gabe's voice crackled with nervous energy. The very thought made him uneasy.

"Do you feel or hear anything now?" Erick nervously looked over his shoulder.

Gabe followed his friend's gaze back to the showers. Things were different now. With the lights on and having Erick standing there next to him, made all of the difference in the world.

"Are you sure?" Erick was looking for reassurance.

"Yeah, now that you're here, it feels like it never happened." Gabe forced a smile, he wanted his friend to change the subject. He wanted to leave the gym and hurry home by the way of a busy, well-lit street. Gabe didn't want to admit it, but something was happening to him and it started almost two weeks ago. Even though he wanted to, he wasn't too sure he could come right out and tell his mother anything. Every time he tried to talk with her about the strange things that had happened, she would either silently look away or change the subject. He could almost hear the caution in her voice and see the panic in her eyes. He knew there was more to the subject than she was willing to talk about. For now, he would just have to confide in his friend.

"The light, the dripping faucet, the voices, that's all pretty weird." Erick shook his head and paused for a moment. "Man, how come this weird stuff never happens to me? It's always the big mouths like Big Mike and the nerds like Andrew who get all of the action!" he sighed heavily before he spoke again. "And then there's the subject of that blond kid!" He studied Gabe's face. "Yes, the blond kid, remember!"

"I'm not the one seeing the blond kid, remember!" Gabe whispered, shrugged and pointed, "You are!" He read the excitement in Erick's face and heard the uncertainty in his own voice.

"Evidently, you're the only one who's not!" countered Erick.

CHAPTER THREE
AWAKINING
A NOT SO UNDERSTANDING
(THURSDAY EVENING)
MARCH 10TH 2000

Gabe sat quietly across the antique oak dinner table from his mother, Lydia Wilson. It was just the two of them. He stared down at his half empty plate as he nonchalantly pushed the remaining peas around it with his fork, just as he had done as a youth when he was tired of eating. His half-eaten mashed potatoes were no longer warm, his appetite long gone. His thoughts drifted in-between his earlier episode in the high school locker room and his mom's re-cap of her busy day at the bank. He grunted, forced a smile and nodded to let his mother know that he was still half-listening. He had given up trying to follow along. Her story sounded like all of the others. Sometimes they were about the men and woman she worked with, other times they were about the customers that walked into the bank, the very same boring bank that she had worked at for the last 10 years. His focus was on how to tell his mother about the latest unexplainable.

Looking young for 52, Lydia used her delicate hands to tell her story; her wedding band periodically flashing gold when the light hit it just right. She refused to take it off. *Sentimental reasons*, she would always say. It was hard not to stare as she demonstrated the beautiful, dimpled smile of hers. Her wavy brown hair graced the shoulders of her white, lacy buttoned up top. To Gabe's delight, her librarian-like, thick rim glasses, sat on the kitchen counter where they belonged. He never liked those glasses; it was the final piece of her wardrobe that made her look like the typical, boring banker that she pretended to be. He called it her *disguise*.

Despite his coaxing, Lydia seldom went out on dates. When she did, she always came back feeling guilty. No matter how hard he prayed for someone new to show up at their doorstep or bump into her at the bank, there never was an answer. Some things never seemed to change. It had been years, two thirds of his life and she had never gotten over his father's, her husband's death.

The table they sat at was big enough to comfortably seat six, but like always, she set the table for three. Whenever he asked her about the extra place setting, Lydia always said it was for the unexpected guest. No matter how many guests showed up, *unexpected* or otherwise, there always seemed to be an extra plate tucked off to the side. She was still waiting for that *unexpected* guest to make their appearance. Deep down inside he knew she went through all the extra trouble for his dad. Despite the excuses she gave, she had never truly gotten over his *unexpected* death almost 10 years ago.

Gabe had also struggled, but with every day of his father's passing, so went his memories of him as well. The anniversary of his father's death, was only six days away. The event of his passing had forever destroyed their St. Patrick's Day. Every year about this time his mom would go through the progressive stages of her crazy depression. It would always begin two weeks before March 16th, the anniversary of his father's death. The mood swings, the endless bouts of crying, and strange behavior. He hated it. He was told that time would eventually heal, but in this case, time seemed to be working against them both. Nearly two weeks ago, bizarre things began to happen to him, crazy things that he didn't understand, or begin to explain. He wished March 16th would just come and go. The cycle needed to end, his mother needed to change. Things needed to return to normal.

Normal... why couldn't things have been different? Why didn't my mother stop my dad from leaving that day?

Despite being five, he still remembered something about the evening that it all changed... the day the world started to spin faster.

> *March 16th 1990, he was five, he vaguely remembered his grieving mother trying to explain to him that his father would never be coming home again, a concept a five year old boy would never truly understand. That God had taken his father with him up to heaven and that someday they would be together again....*

The thought of that day still made him shiver.

All he had to do was look up from the table to see the influence of his father. To his right was their wedding picture. There was a young couple, Lydia in a formal white lacy dress, and Gabriel, his father, in a well fitted black tux. They were each holding the other in a loving embrace as they shared their vows.

There was another photograph along the hallway to the bathroom, the one that his mother seemed to cherish the most. Framed and covered with protective glass, was a picture of his father in his park ranger uniform. A strong looking man leaned casually against the fibrous bark of a massive redwood tree with folded arms across his badged chest; the wide brimmed felt Stetson graced his head and partially shaded a well-tanned face. He smiled confidently at the camera like a man who either feared nothing or knew something he wasn't about to tell.

Gabe often stared at that picture trying to understand more about the man that stared back, wondering what his dad might have been thinking at that very moment.

Did he know he would soon be dead?

His own words surprised him.

As strange as it might have sounded, they said it was the last known photograph ever taken of his dad. Gabe always thought there was a strange eeriness to those kinds of pictures. It was taken three days before his father passed doing what he loved, protecting the resources, and saving the lives of others.

If he only knew!

The eerie thought made him shudder again.

The photograph was the very same one that graced the church altar during the funeral.

In loving memory of a husband, father, son, brother, and friend. To best display the spirit of the man that lived... they had sincerely said. He remembered the looks of pity... the fact that his father wasn't there. There wasn't a body to place into the casket, nor was there a casket to be laid into the ground.

They said his body was never recovered after the *accident*, the very same *accident* that no one was willing to talk about. Nor was his mother willing to take him to the place where his father died. Its message was still unclear. They said a picture was worth a thousand words, but it only made him think of a thousand questions, a thousand reasons why things weren't right in his world.

There was another photograph of his father and his uncle that hung on the wall above his bed for the last five years, complements of his Uncle Dan, his dad's surviving brother.

'*Thought you should have it*', he remembered his uncle's emotional voice.

In the photograph, both Dan and his dad are standing together, side by side. Uncle Dan was a head and shoulder taller and to the right of his father's stocky figure. Like his father, Dan was also a park ranger, fighting crime and saving the resources in the Southern California Mountains. A '*calling*' he had always put it.

With his broad shoulders, rugged complexion and friendly demeanor, his uncle fit the ranger persona. Despite his uncle's size, he was amazed how similar the two brothers had looked. The picture had been taken back when they were both new rangers. Two young uniformed men standing side-by-side, sporting tough expressions. Seeing the photograph had always made Gabe smile, but today, he had to work a little harder at it.

Gabe had always looked forward to his uncle's visits; with them came the relentless stories of drama and adventures. He called them *Dan's Adventures*. When he was out of ear shot of his mother he relentlessly quizzed him about his father's adventures as well. Those were the stories that he looked forward to hearing. Whenever he pulled together enough courage to ask about his father's death, the mood would change....

> *"Be patient, I promised your mother."* Dan would clear his throat, force the emotion from his eyes. *"She'll be the one to tell you when she's ready."* Dan would hold him at arm's length, take a quick glance in the direction of his mother and force a smile. *"Right now, all you need to know is that your dad was a hero!"*

Was a Hero!
Those words alone used to make him smile, but on days like today, they weren't enough. He was no longer that little boy, who was so eager to please.

A Hero?
He thought about whenever he asked his mother how his father had died, her response was always the same. She would take a moment to wipe away the tears from her sorrowful eyes, clear her throat and say, *'He passed doing the things he loved'*. That he *'devoted his life to family, and protecting the park'*, that the *'rest would come with time'*.

Come with time? Why isn't now the time?
Every time he asked about his father it was like he had hit a nerve, dug up an unmentionable past. His desire to know had now burned deeper into his heart; he knew it wouldn't be long before he would demand his right to hear the forgotten stories about his father before they were permanently forgotten. He needed to understand.

Strangely, Gabe felt as if somehow, he was running out of time. A strong desire burned within him to know more about that part of his father's life.

He refocused on his mother. She was still staring past him out the window as she talked, oblivious to the fact that his own thoughts had drifted off once again.

His mom always sat facing the picture window, her eyes forever scanning the tranquil pond just outside. Its creation was another item added to the life list of his deceased father's accomplishments. Evidently, it was he who had hand excavated and designed the whole project himself. Right down to the odd looking statue that, Gabe thought looked out of place.

He turned and followed her gaze out into the direction of the pond that had once been a section of the lawn. He was told his father had hated to mow the grass and his mom loved large spacious lawns surrounded by mixed forest. The thought had made Gabe smile. He too had hated to mow what was left of the grass. He sometimes wished that his mom had let his father turn the rest of the lawn into a forest as well. When some of the other kids at school talked about their swimming pools; he proudly talked about the pond that his father had made by hand.

Gabe loved that pond, he had always felt at peace there. He listened to the birds and frogs that also sought its sanctuary. He was mesmerized by the huge school of koi that flashed in the sun light among the pond lilies. A life sized statuary of St. Francis of Assisi overlooked the pond. It seconded as a bird feeder for their Catholic household. He could see why a man named St. Francis enjoyed the garden so much.

One day, curious about the statue he asked his mom....

"Why St. Francis?"
"He was the one your dad wanted to reside over the garden." *She said so matter of fact as she planted the starter asters into the ground beneath the statue.* *"In life, Francis had a way with animals, in death, his caring spirit lived on."*
Gabe just nodded, his eyes studying the statue closely.

Unsatisfied with her answer, Gabe looked it up for himself. To his surprise, his mother was right.

The statuary of St. Francis of Assisi - The Founder of the Friars, the Patron Saint of Ecologists and Ecology, graced their yard for a reason. Based on his uncle's exciting stories, his dad had worked as a park ranger in the local mountains before his passing. Prior to her being a boring loan officer, his mom had studied ornithology, the study of birds, in college, and had done a little field research of her own. It was inevitable that the two would meet.

So, why St. Francis? Why not Buda or a gnome like so many other gardens?

The thought burned from within.

The answers were in the man's history.

St. Francis was born at Assisi in Umbria, Italy in 1182 A.D. and canonized as a saint two years after his death in October 3rd of 1226. Dead at 44! Gabe's father also died at 44 years of age that was odd!

It wasn't until 1939 that Pope Pius XII declared Francis the patron saint of Italy, an example to the people of his time, for teaching them the standards of Catholic behavior. A model citizen! He thought, even 700 years after his death.

In February of 1958, ironically, the same birth month but by then his dad was age 12 when the Pope's declaration was confirmed by the Italian parliament. In an Apostolic Letter of November 29th. 1979, when his dad was about age 33, John Paul II proclaimed Francis of Assisi the patron saint of ecology and ecologists.

That part made sense, his mom was into things like ecology and wildlife and his dad did those things at the park.

Earlier, he hadn't given that history stuff much thought, just things they made him learn at school. But recently he was finding these things, to be a bit more interesting. The more he learned, the more he knew and well, the more he knew the more he understood. It made perfect sense. The statue had something to do with his father and he was determined to find out what!

St. Francis was imprisoned for a year at age 20. Once he was released he became dangerously ill. No sooner he recovered from that illness, he became ill again. He was determined to fight in a war in Southern Italy, but he never made it there. Someone or something prevented him from reaching his destination. While on his journey, Francis was so impressed by a man's passion that he traded his new armor for the man's tattered clothing.

Gabe could never see himself trading clothes with anyone.

Twice Francis heard what he described as Heavenly Voices. The first was while in the town of Spoleto, where he fell extremely ill while still in route to the fighting. While he lay there in sickness, a heavenly voice told him to turn back, to serve the master rather than the man, so he did. The second time was while praying in the church of St. Damian, outside the walls of Assisi. He heard a voice from the crucifix asking him to repair God's house that was falling down. So, over time he slowly rebuilt the old church, one brick at a time. It took him a while to realize that it was the peoples' faith, not the building that needed to be rebuilt.

Gabe was beginning to understand the meaning behind the story.

He grew up Catholic, he was well aware of what they described as the power of prayer.

You prayed for help. You prayed for forgiveness. You prayed for understanding.

To hear voices in return? Now that would be freaky! Was Saint Francis followed by people he couldn't see?

The thought made him shudder.

He forced his thoughts back to his father. Through the labor of love, his father had turned the openness of the lawn back into the heart of the forest, the watering hole for almost every wild bird, animal, insect, and curious teen in the neighborhood. He couldn't help but wonder if his father's actions were guided by heavenly requests or a desire to surround him with the environment that he swore to protect. So, instead of a swimming pool like everyone else, they ended up with a….

"Gabe, you're awfully quiet," Lydia's voice squeaked with concern. "This isn't like you. Are you feeling alright?"

He heard the noticeable change in his mother's voice and turned to meet her inquisitive eyes. He stared momentarily, searching for understanding, waiting for his thoughts to organize into words and words into sentences. Her sudden concern caught him by surprise. All he could do was nod, force a smile and diverted his gaze out the window. He knew his eyes would give himself away.

His thoughts automatically flashed back to his encounter in the alley, how he rushed back home to tell her what happened, hoping she would be able to help him find a better understanding. Instead, he watched the color fade from her face, and the tears well up in her eyes. The anger and disappointment reflected in her voice. His encounter scared her; she knew something that she wasn't telling him. Instead, she scolded him for disobeying, for taking the short cut through the alley against her wishes and his better judgment. She rambled on about not wanting to lose her only child. She was hiding something, he could feel it.

His actions frightened her, and her actions frightened him.

What is she really saying?

He had never seen her like that before. In the midst of her sorrowful embrace, he could sense that it had something to do with the passing of his father. He felt the burning need to talk with his uncle, to get to the bottom of her turmoil.

Soon the feelings faded, drained away to nothing. He never got around to making the phone call to his uncle. It was as if the whole situation had been conveniently forgotten.

Should I tell her about what happened in the school shower today? How would she react to that?

His thoughts wandered.

"Gabe, what's wrong?" she quizzed again.

He looked back up at her. Their eyes met, each shielding their own secrets. He could feel her probing his thoughts. He needed to run interference.

Lydia set her coffee cup carefully down on the table without taking her eyes off of his. Her mouth opened slightly as if to say something, but then silently closed. It was her eyes and facial expressions that were now speaking clearly. It was as if she wanted to know, but was afraid to ask. She knew what he was going to say, but didn't want to hear. It was as if a ghost of the past had finally caught up with her.

She hadn't stopped him yet; she hadn't said no. Maybe this time would be different. He had to try again. He noisily set his fork down onto his plate; the clanking echoed in the strange silence. He saw his mom twitch nervously at the irritating sound. It reminded him of a bell sounding before an important announcement.

"Mom," he fought the quiver in his own voice, but it was still noticeable. "Something strange happened to me today in the school locker room."

The sound of her fork connecting with her plate echoed in the silence. She stared at him, her eyes filling with tears.

Gabe diverted his eyes.

She allowed him to reach over and gently caressed one of her hands. Hers were surprisingly cold. He cleared his throat and struggled on; forcing himself to be brave, hoping to get it all out before she stopped him.

"I heard voices..." he found himself speaking quickly, his thoughts were stumbling out all at once. He felt her hand tense up. "The faucet stopped dripping and then started up again. One moment the room smelled sweet and then of sulfur, then... there was this blond kid that, well, everyone else sees but me." He waved one of his arms and shrugged his shoulders, trying to liven up the conversation. It didn't work.

He felt his body shiver, his eyes searched his mom's for answers... understanding. Hers just stared blankly back, tears rolling down the corners of her cheeks. He quickly pressed on feeling his window of opportunity closing.

Gabe spoke faster, "Erick said a blond kid sent him back into the gym to check on me." He felt the tears building in his own eyes. He dared not wipe them now. "It was really strange, Erick showed up just as I saw a figure moving away from the shower. He thinks it's the school ghost that hangs out in the locker room. Some say the schools haunted, but—"

"No, no, no!" Lydia screamed as she slammed her fist noisily onto the table. She pulled her hand away from his and covered her face. Tears flowed, her breathing erratic.

Her scream made him jump, sent chills down his back. He found himself sitting back in his chair, his hands gripping the table, creating space between him and his mom. He watched his mother's body shake in convulsing sobs. He suddenly regretted bringing up the whole thing, for pushing it as far as he had. He didn't know what to do; he just sat back hopelessly and stared.

***

Lydia felt the weight of sorrow press down heavily upon her shoulders. The lump in her throat seemed to grow, her breaths shortened, her fingers tingled; the room was spinning. She felt light headed, nauseous, and weak. She leaned on her elbows for balance, hoping he wouldn't notice. But he did.

This isn't good. Not again!
The thought made him shiver.
She was revisiting a time she wished was long forgotten.

Gabriel's Legacy

At first she saw spots, then streaks of white and then a sudden bright flash....

Lydia's eyes first focused on a young child in a booster seat, to her immediate left. The little boy had discarded his silverware and was happily pushing his mashed potatoes around his plate with his little fingers. The child's eyes brightened with recognition as he looked up at her. He smiled at the attention. She recognized the little boy right away. It was her son, a familiar scene of Gabe at age five, playing with his food. She reached up and gently touched the end of his nose with her index finger, something she had stopped doing when he turned seven.

"Lydia, I just don't know how to explain it," the man's familiar voice mumbled under his breath. "It's all like, you know, déjà vu'." He raised one arm to emphasize his point.

She snapped a look to her right in time to see her husband Gabriel, hastily shovel another fork full of dinner into his mouth, with a somewhat serious expression. He was still on duty that day, taking a quick dinner break at home as he traveled in between the district office and the park unit he worked at. Though they lived on a few acres on the outskirts of town for convenience, she missed the fact that they no longer lived in the mountains, tucked away in the redwoods, surrounded by the wilds of the forest.

He wore his park ranger uniform: green pants, khaki shirt, and black boots. His gun belt and radio sat coiled on the edge of the counter as he satisfied his voracious appetite. It was good that they were still able to occasionally eat dinner together as a family on the evenings he worked. So there he sat, eating as quickly as he could, enjoying a quick meal with his family.

"You know you're supposed to chew your food don't you. You'll get indigestion, choke on your food, or worse yet," Lydia nodded playfully to little Gabe in a hushed tone, "set a bad example at the dinner table for you know who," she lectured.

Gabe grinned playfully at his father, showing off his mouth full of mashed potatoes.

Gabriel couldn't help it; he appeared to be struggling to keep from spitting a mouth full of supper back onto the dining room table. He stopped chewing as he shot an inquisitive nod over to his son. "I'm afraid, it's, too late..." he forced a brief smile as he chewed, "damage, may be... irreversible." He shrugged as he spoke, his mouth full, his voice hardly understandable.

"Gabriel, be careful what you end up teaching him," she lectured. "Heaven forbid he grow up to be just like you," she laughed tenderly. "And believe me, I just don't think the world is ready for another Gabriel!"

He swallowed. "That's why we call him Gabe," he smiled.

Her two boys joined her in a snorting, spitting laughter. It was a messy sight. She remembered thinking that she could have killed them both. It was a good thing that they were at home and not at some restaurant, for they would have been kicked out for sure.

The laughter was addicting, her eyes watered. She couldn't stop if she tried; it was a struggle just to stay in her own chair. The laughter felt good.

It was hard to believe that such joyous laughter could be immediately followed by such sorrow. She thought it strange how life tried to balance itself, to find equilibrium. Water would flow downhill, warm air would rise up, and cold air would always settle in the hearts of change. It was the way.

She remembered watching the happy expression on Gabriel's face slowly fade as she caught him staring at her.

"What?" she remembered saying as she wiped the food from her cheeks.

His distant stare burned right through her. His eyes reflected disappointment and fear. It was a strange hollow, timeless stare. It was like the thousand-yard stare, she had heard about from the victims of post-traumatic stress. It was as if he struggled with a deep dark secret.

The atmosphere felt dark.

"Since this morning," he looked her in the eyes and gently shook his head; "everything is familiar. It's like ground hog day. I've seen this day before. From the laughter, right down to the desperate radio call I'm going to get before we've finished our meal." He nodded to his park radio on the counter.

"Honey, you know it's just the nature of the job. After a while, it all begins to look and feel the same." She heard her voice squeak and strain, unconvincingly.

Gabriel stared at his son, he forced a reassuring smile.

Gabe smiled back on cue, oblivious to the sudden turmoil.

"No Lydia," he continued, his voice very solemn. "It's different this time." He was so matter of fact. "All those rescues, all those situations? Have you ever stopped to wonder how I was able to pull them off?" He shook his

head. "They were impossible, but yet, I did it! I knew I could do it! Have you ever wondered why that is?"

She remembered the eerie chill that flowed down her spine, the numbness in her fingers, the stubborn lump that suddenly appeared in her throat and prevented her from swallowing. Then there was the incredible thirst that followed. He was right, he had to be the luckiest man alive, but it was more than that; he had to have been blessed...

Yes, blessed. It was as if he had been protected by a guardian angel.

The thought confused her.
Are there really such things as guardian angels?
She squeezed one of her hands into a fist until her knuckles turned white.
She had been raised Catholic, brainwashed into believing that *angels* were there to guide and protect humans, but still, many people died in accidents that they hadn't caused. Good people, people that went to church, people that devoted their lives to their God and followed *his* ways. People that help others...

"Guardian angels?" was all she could ask.
He looked back at her, smiled, nodded, and forced a laugh. His eyes teared in the corners. "Yes, they appear to have been working overtime." He stopped eating and sat back in his chair as if he had suddenly lost interest in eating. He wiped his face with the napkin "Have you ever believed that we were all put here on earth for a reason? Prodded, protected, guided until it was our turn to either shine, or implode?"
His words moved her, caught her off guard. They were very unlike his. Then she saw it; the

look was there for a moment, and then, just like that, it was gone. She thought she saw a glow of blue light about his face. He looked at peace. It was like he had something very deep and personal to share, and then...

It was the squelch of the park radio that brought an end to their trance. Just like he said. It was incredible, she thought, how people in the business could hear their radio call sign come to life amongst a noisy conversation, or in the middle of a rock concert.

He gave out a heavy sigh. "Duty calls!" he tried to make light of the situation. He hesitantly pushed away from the table and reached for his radio and gun belt.

It all happened as if the whole scene moved in slow motion. He called in, the dispatcher responded. The dispatcher's tone sounded urgent. Strangely, she couldn't remember the exact words, but his actions were still visible. He wiped his face clean with his napkin, noisily slid away from the table and tossed the napkin onto his unfinished plate. His eyes never left hers. She broke the trance and looked down at her folded hands. She remembered the red faded napkin. It landed with the embroidered, purple Douglas iris face up. She silently watched him secure the leather keepers to his gun belt one by one, with a practiced hand, the sound of each individual snaps echoed loudly in her ears. He placed his radio back into its holster that was attached to his belt.

She stared down at the radio, her throat tight, her hands tingling, her breathing shallow. She suddenly hated that radio, she hated the park that always seemed to take him away. It was all just like he had said. He was being called away. Her eyes filled with tears. A strange *sadness overwhelmed her that she couldn't shake.*

He lingered as he hugged his son; he kissed him on the top of his head and then hugged him again. "See you kido!"

Gabe seemed oblivious to the meaning of his father's affection, returning the hug with a giggle, mash potatoes and all.

Gabriel's eyes were filled with tears when he looked back at Lydia. She felt paralyzed in her chair, her arms and legs unable to move. He leaned over her, they embraced. Only her arms seemed to move freely. She squeezed him tightly. She knew something was different, that her life was about to change. "Don't go, you don't have to go!" she whispered hysterically through sudden tears.

He leaned back and held her at arm's length, stared into her eyes, shifting his gaze in between hers and their son's as if searching for what to say, for an answer that was nowhere to be found.

"It's why I am here!" he spoke softy back. He released one of her shoulders long enough to wipe the tears out of his own eyes. "It's what I'm supposed to do!"

"But why you, for heaven sake... why you?" she screamed, finding her voice as she pushed away from the table and quickly rose to her feet.

Gabe stopped whatever he was doing, he shifted his worried gaze between the both of them confused.

Gabriel reached over and hugged her again, releasing her. "It is not up to us to ask why, but to serve! Lydia, I love you, you know I will always love you!" He grabbed her and pulled her tightly against his chest, kissing her gently on the lips. She closed her eyes, returned the embrace, accepting his tender kiss and pulling him closer. They pressed their lips harder together. They lingered for a moment before they slowly released.

And just like that, Gabriel's frown morphed into a delicate smile.

She let his arms slowly slip from her grip. He stood there, staring at her for a moment before he turned to leave the room.

"Gabriel, is this going to be the time you don't return?" her concerned eyes flowing with tears, her angry voice shook with emotion.

He stopped and turned back towards her. His eyes filled with tears. He opened his mouth, but nothing came out. He tried to force a smile but couldn't and then, without saying another word, he let out a long deep breath, turned and left the room.

"Gabriel?" she yelled.

She wanted to follow him out to his patrol vehicle, but her legs wouldn't move. She reached over and grabbed her son instead and pulled him in close.

"Gabriel!" she screamed. She began to sob.

Gabe looked up at her strangely.

She listened to the door slam, the engine start and the vehicle speed away. Moments later, she heard the wail of the siren in the distance.

That was the last time she or her son had seen him alive.

CHAPTER FOUR
THE JOURNAL
(THURSDAY EVENING)
MARCH 10TH 2000

As Gabe walked past the open door to his mom's study, a warm breeze pushed against his face from the direction of the room. The water droplets from his recent shower tickled his face.

He brushed them away with the back of his hand and abruptly stopped at the open door. It was almost as if someone or something was trying to get his attention.

What?

He looked past the open door.

The shower was supposed to wash it all away!

"Now what?" he whispered.

Something on the desk of the study caught his attention. A book he hadn't seen before.

Keep walking.

He forced a thought as he started to keep walking down the hallway but hesitated. Instead, he gave a heavy sigh, turned towards the room, walked inside and stopped at the desk. On it sat an old looking dusty book.

His eyes locked onto it, he couldn't look away.

"Pick it up!" the strange little voice in his head encouraged.

He quickly glanced around the room confirming he was the only one there before he hesitantly picked up the book.

It felt odd but yet familiar in his hands.

He stood there staring down at the book, caressing it gently in his trembling hands as if it were a priceless artifact. The unique smell of aged, dust-covered leather gave the book a special quality of its own. The cover on the hardbound book was well worn, like the book had taken many travels of its own. He could imagine the book faithfully taken to every place its owner had gone. When he blew the dust from the cover, a fine layer had drifted around the dimly lit room. It made him sneeze.

He shot a guilty look over his shoulder and squinted towards the lit hallway. He was in his mom's study, located half way between the kitchen and her bedroom. He fought the desire to flip open the book and page through it.

Was this put here for me to find.

It was strange; he had never felt that way about anything before, especially a book. He was unsure if his mom had left it there for him or placed it there so she could look upon it later. But either way, there it sat, beckoning.

Did this have anything to do with tonight's hysterical dinner discussion, about leaving my father's past safely hidden in the closet or the dusty attic, to be rediscovered when mom says the time was right?

His thoughts raced.

Is now the right time?

Judging by the layer of dust that encrusted the journal, it had been recently taken out of storage from a place seldom visited.

Relieved to find that he was still alone in the small study, his quest uninterrupted, he refocused his thoughts on the book. As he gently ran his fingers across the tooled impressions in the leather, he was surprised to find a detailed forest scene, painstakingly etched into the dark brown, canvas-like leather. The art work lay hidden under an accumulation of old dust.

His interest in the book suddenly grew stronger. His fingers moved systematically along the grooves of the tooled designs. He brought the book closer, observing every detail as he continued to slowly slide his fingers across the face of the book like he were reading brail, absorbing the details that his eyes had missed.

Fighting to restrain his excitement, not wanting to miss anything, he gently started, again, first at the binding in the upper left and moved towards the bottom right. The tips of his sensitive fingers interpreted the raised symbols, shapes and patterns as he inhaled the fragrant odor of dust and leather. Strangely, they seemed to work together, increasing his anticipation, the importance of his discovery building in his every thought.

He muffled another cough with the sleeve of his shirt.

Almost to the bottom, his sensitive fingers came to an abrupt stop as they drifted across the impression of a name delicately tooled across the cover in cursive.

He sighed deeply as he ran his fingers over the name twice more and squinted his eyes to read. His breathing abruptly stopped with a startled inhale. A strange chill ran down his spine causing his fingers to tingle and his body to shudder. He gave another quick glance over his shoulder before he spit on the book and hurriedly rubbed the dust from around the name with the bottom edge of his shirt. What he found caused him to involuntarily gasp. A strange energy seized his every muscle. **Gabriel Wilson** was engraved on the bottom corner of the leather cover. He just about dropped the book in the excitement.

"Gabriel Wilson... that's, my dad," he whispered loudly. "How could this be? This belonged to my dad?" The journal fell from his tingling fingers and landed noisily onto the edge of the desk. He staggered backward away from the desk, back towards the doorway, his eyes never leaving the mysterious book. He froze in his tracks when he bumped into the nightstand adjacent to the doorframe. The stand rattled and some of the objects fell to the carpeted floor. He cursed himself for being so clumsy, but thankful that the carpet had muffled the noise. He could now only hope that his mom hadn't heard anything.

He peeked over his shoulder and down the hallway. He listened a moment to insure that he was alone. The distant sounds of the television continued to creep down the hall. He was still in the clear.

He picked the knickknacks and small framed pictures off of the floor without thinking and abruptly started standing them back up on the night stand. It was the last item, an old family portrait of his mom, dad and himself that froze him in his tracks.
Dad!
His eyes began to tear.
He held it gently in his hands, studying its every detail. They were all happy back then. A much younger mom and dad stood arm in arm, in front of them they held a baby, not more than two years old by the looks of it. He easily recognized the infant; it was him, Gabe Wilson Jr., the last to carry on the family sur name. The family photo was a reminder of a time that was lost forever, haunted by an event that refused to release them from its grasp. He had forgotten all about that picture. It had found its way to the least visited room in the house, his mom's study. He gently placed the framed photo onto the nightstand face down, but then almost as if an afterthought, he propped it upright for all to see. Wiping the tears from his eyes, he turned towards the doorway and abruptly stopped. He needed to be as far away from that room as he could possibly get.

Once at the doorway, it was like his legs had ceased to move, his feet momentarily stuck to the floor like flypaper. He felt his heart pounding in his ears, his chest expanding and contracting with every rapid breath. He strained his ears as he again cautiously looked down both sides of the hallway.

A mischievous expression spread across his face.

The coast was clear; he still had time to pull off a clean getaway.

But now if I could only get my feet to move!

He looked down at his feet wondering what could possibly be holding them in place, preventing him from taking a step. There he stood, obstructed by nothing he could see. The faint sounds of the television drifted down the hallway from the den, the last place he had seen his mother, staring blankly at the screen.

The coast is still clear, but for how long?
He was running out of time.

All he wanted to do was rejoin his mother in the den.
I should ask her about the leather book. Did she leave it for me to find?

He looked back over his shoulder, his thoughts drawn towards the book. It sat there in the shadows, illuminated, alone in the darkness, awaiting his company.

He stood there frozen, deciding what to do.

Should I join my mother in the den and wait for her to talk about the book, or should I open the journal and see what it's all about?

The pull of the book was strong.

A few more seconds drifted by, he shifted his weight from one foot to the next as he tried to decide.

"What should I do?" he quietly whispered.

His voice sounded strange to his own ears. The question was almost like a prayer in itself, asking for an answer that he was sure would never come. That's when he felt a subtle brush of warmer air, like on a warm sunny day. It tickled his face and ears as it blew past the doorway behind him and into the small study, pulling his thoughts back to the mysterious leather bound journal. He brushed the hair out of his face.

To his amazement, the streamers to the heater vents hung motionless, perpendicular to the floor.

If it's not the heater... then from where?

The tingle first started in his fingers and then quickly worked its way down to his toes. He stared back towards the leather-bound book, his eyes transfixed, drawn by an unimaginable force that held his every thought.

Is this because of the book? But how?

He leaned towards the interior of the room. His feet were free, no longer held in place. To his surprise, his feet worked their way back towards the edge of the desk. He slid his trembling hands alongside the journal until he touched the cold, dusty leather. He paused for a moment, expecting to feel something special, but disappointingly there was nothing. He pushed beyond, gently sliding his fingers along the edge of the tattered pages. It felt good to touch them.

The familiar essence of dust and leather calmed his nerves. He snatched the journal off the table and held it loosely in his sweating hands. Strangely enough, the book felt as if it belonged there in his possession. Within the binding lay the legacy of his father awaiting his discovery. The thought made him shudder. He slid his fingers, Braille-like, over his father's stenciled name one more time to reassure him of his intentions. The situation was indeed strange, stumbling upon the journal like that, especially after the frightful conversation he had with his mother only a couple of hours before.

A nervous shudder jolted his body when he couldn't remember why he had gone into his mother's study in the first place. There he was again, doing things and going places he had no reason to do or be.

He closed his eyes for a moment, took a deep breath before he opened them. Now with sufficient nerve, he gently opened the cover, exposing the first page. He trembled with excitement. There was an opening paragraph, the writing clearly his father's.

Gabe spoke the words softly; he wanted to hear them with his ears as well. Hearing them from his own lips seemed to give the words more meaning, to make them real.

It was the date that caused him discomfort and his throat to go dry. It was today's date; the only difference was the year. He quickly did the math. He was three years old when his dad decided to make his first journal entry into this book, almost 12 years ago, that he kept so well hidden. He wondered if his father was trying to hide his thoughts from others or his family.

How alone he must have felt.

A strange sadness overwhelmed him. He coughed to clear his throat; he couldn't bear the excitement anymore. He needed to hear his father's words in his ears... in his heart. He softly began:

May 19 1988

Others have written their thoughts, so I will do the same.

Anne Frank treated her journal as a friend, poured out her feelings, searched her soul for answers to questions that very few could solve. Though not hiding in an attic from the Nazis, in war-torn Europe, sequestered from everything around me, I too feel alone. Sequestered from the very reason... why me? Dealing with things I can't comprehend, surrounded by people who would be quick to judge, quick to accuse and never to understand.

Surrounded by things that I can't explain. I know now that I am a pawn in a war between good and evil. A battle that has been building since the crusades and may continue for generations to come. This I know, even though, I am sorry to say, I couldn't tell you who was winning or for that matter who was losing. Maybe there were never meant to be winners, just losers, all outcomes determined by choice. Good or bad choices don't really seem to matter.

Despite what I hear myself say, I do believe in God, always have. I will serve him as I have sworn to, evidently until my ultimate death, which I am frightened to say may be knocking on my door tomorrow.

What do I say to my wife? I see the way she looks at me every time I walk out of the front door. It's in her eyes; it's in her manner.

I can't blame her. I feel the same. It's like I will not be coming home this time. But, when I stumble back in at the end of my shift, I see relief and disappointment wrapped up in an intricate knot, the inevitable postponed yet until another day.

Another day of worry, another day of the unknown.
I am free of regret. It is what I have been put here on earth to do. I know that now. I hope to understand why I have been chosen. Curse or a gift, only God knows, but he isn't telling.

His dad's words pulled at his throat. Sorrow hit his chest like a brick.
Did my dad know he would be dead within two years?
Gabe's fingers tingled as he glanced quickly over his shoulder. He felt the presence of someone else in the room. He strained his ears, but heard nothing. All was clear. He was still alone. The pull of the journal was stronger than ever. He anxiously continued to read.

I am compelled to write, to place my thoughts with no intention of ever reading them again. It seems a bit strange to painstakingly collect them, along with my innermost feelings, and write them into a leather-bound book. For safe keeping?
For a release? I fear that others may someday discover my inner-most thoughts which were supposed to be personal. But then, sometimes I don't care. I don't know how to explain it, but despite the fact that God has placed my welfare into the care of his capable angels, I still feel my days are numbered. Set in stone.
God must know that even writing this depresses me. He must know how I feel or what I know, but still, he remains silent trusting my welfare to his winged warriors that I have yet to see myself. As it is now, I don't even know if they are even winged.

Oh, yes, they have been described to me in the utmost detail, by those select few who have seen them, like my devout brother.

Seen by others?

The words made him shiver.
"Was he talking about Uncle Dan?" Gabe's voice crackled with emotion, his hand began to tremble nervously. He anxiously read on.

They tell of their beautiful eyes, magnificent physiques, their immaculate hair and the ominous confidence that they exude.
Created in the likeness of God. A fairy tale kind of encounter....

'Who was your friend?'
Erick's voice reverberated in his mind.
'When are you going to introduce us?'
Gabe shook off a chill that rattled down the length of his spine. His thoughts flashed back to the gym, the school campus and then to the alley.
Is there a presence with me right now?
He glanced quickly around the room, then forced himself to read on.

I have only heard their confident, caring voices. It is what I follow; it is what guides me. I would like to see more, but I guess it isn't in God's plan.
When I am finished, I will close the book. Hopefully with it my worries and anxieties will be put to rest. God must know

that I didn't ask for this... I didn't ask for any of it to be this way!

Why do I do this? I have tried running away, but it's of no use.

It finds me, they find me, seek me out and hunt me down.

Ignoring it didn't make it go away, they are relentless.

Evidently, it is 'my destiny' they say. Mine alone to bare.

My greatest fear is not dying. No, we all die eventually.

I'm doing what I was meant to do, that for which I was chosen.

No, my greatest fear is that my son, Gabe, will one day have to carry on where I have failed?

Gabe just about flipped the book out of his hands. He couldn't believe what he was reading.

What was my dad trying to say? What did he mean?

"To carry on where I have failed?" he whispered.

His heart pounded in his chest. He forced a breath, looked nervously over his shoulder for a second, and continued to read. His thoughts were so tunneled, his senses so preoccupied, that even if there were a crowd behind him looking over his shoulder, he probably wouldn't have noticed. There was no turning back, no putting down the journal now. His eyes burned into the pages, searching for their hidden meaning.

Like father, like son. God, I hope that isn't true.

But yet, I know I am not alone.

I struggle with the thought. But, then again, who else would understand. By doing this, I am hoping that I will someday come to grips with all that has happened to me... Or for that matter, what it is that I am really supposed to do with this... what many others call, a GIFT. I have found that there is a fine line between a gift, and a curse. It comes down to a matter of interpretation... theirs vs. yours. If you have been through what I have gone through, with what you graciously call my GIFT, would you not think there was something very wrong with me? A friendship at a distance.

But, if you were I, a freak in the world I work and live, it may very well be seen as a CURSE. Someday I pray to know. It all started at a bus stop with my brother... and where will it end? The only person who seems to understand is my brother Dan, though I don't know what he really thinks. He keeps his cards well-hidden and his poker face fine-tuned. There is comfort knowing that he has promised to take care of my family's needs in the event that I might... when, I perish.

A brother's love... a father's regret.

Gabe felt a sudden rage build within himself. All of this time his uncle knew and refused to say anything about all of it.

How could he?

He slammed his fist on the desk.

His thoughts echoed loudly in his mind. He asked several times but his uncle only refused to share, said he didn't know anything more.

'Your dad passed away doing the things he loved. He was a hero!' Dan had raved, 'He gave his life to save another. You should be very proud of that.' The affectionate and understanding hugs from his uncle had always seemed to make it better. It was what a young boy needed to hear, needed to feel.

Didn't my dad love my mom and me more than the strangers that he served?

Gabe smashed the desktop with a heavy fist.

He wasn't a young, gullible boy any more. He was almost a man. He needed to know the answers that his uncle had kept from him and he needed them now.

This is so unfair!

"How could you?" his voice squeaked through the dryness of his throat, but his ears could no longer hear. There were his answers, bound in leather, written with his father's very hand. The book in his hand suddenly seemed too heavy to hold. He let it fall from his grasp along with his thoughts, back to the smooth surface of the desk. His eyes never left the words, his hand pressed them down onto the book.

I have prayed to make it all go away, but these days it seems that my prayers don't get answered. Why is that, God? Why can't you give me a simple answer? With all due respect, for all that I have done for you, you at least owe me that much!

"G-a-b-e!" Lydia's voice thundered in his ears. The shrilling scream jerked him out of his trance.

He snapped the book shut as he spun around to face the sad frantic eyes of his mother. She shifted her glances back and forth in between him and the leather bound book, surprise and devastation filled her eyes, the weight of the book still beneath his hands.

He silently stared back at her, wanting to speak, wanting to explain how he found the book. How it called to him, the similarities in both he and his father's lives, but he couldn't find the words.

Instead, Gabe felt shame; guilt and sadness rip through his thoughts. He didn't know whether to be angry or sympathetic with his mother for keeping this important secret from him for so long. It was she who carried the lone burden during the last few months of his father's life, and then the last ten years after his death. At five, he hardly knew his father, but she had to know that he too was carrying a burden.

She must know that? The burden of not knowing the truth, the truth that was being hidden from me. I had a right to know everything. Surely my mother could see that? This is my legacy my birth right too. Whether she wants to believe it or not, I am the legacy of my father Gabriel!

"What are you doing with, that?" her sobbing shrieks pulled him back further. Her eyes focused as they narrowed on his. Her arm extended to what he grasped in his. The suddenness of it all made him flinch and step back away from the desk, away from the book. The life once again returned to his legs.

His mother rushed forward and snatched the book off of the desk and held it close to her chest before Gabe could even react.

"I found it sitting there—" he tried to explain but his tongue had stuck to the roof of his dry mouth.

"Get out!" she screamed.

"But, mom—"

"I said get out... please!" she begged, her voice struggling to remain calm, her teary eyes pleading with his.

Without saying another word, he reached up and gently rested a hand on one of her shoulders. She looked so vulnerable, so week and frail. She no longer appeared as the strong, sturdy rock he had depended on his whole life.

She turned and dropped her face away from his. He felt her whole body shudder in tearful bouts. The sight of her sadness made him feel depressed and weak. He never liked seeing her this way.

"Please get out!" she whispered. Her voice sounded weak.

He allowed his hand to slide effortlessly from her shoulder. He wiped the tears from his eyes. Instead of standing there by her side, he turned and silently walked out of the room, gently closing the door behind him. He paused for a moment and leaned his back against the edge of the door frame. His legs again felt week. He heard the room suddenly fill with sorrowful rage. It made him sad.

"God, please help!" The words squeaked out of his dry throat, words he hadn't spoken as long as he could remember. He forced a swallow as he looked hopefully up towards the streamers that hung from the vent. They still hung lifelessly, not a breeze anywhere to be found.

CHAPTER FIVE
THE HEALING BEGINS
(THURSDAY EVENING)
MARCH 10TH 2000

Lydia didn't know whether to scream, cry or just hug Gabe for having the journal. It was the tears that seemed to be the right thing to do. They flowed as freely as her emotions. Her body convulsed into uncontrollable, shivering sobs. She had felt Gabe's arm slip limply from her shoulder and his presence fade from the room. Her eyes didn't follow, they couldn't follow. She didn't even hear the sound of the door being pulled shut behind her. She had to lean upon the edge of the desk to catch her balance, to keep herself from collapsing into a babbling mess on the floor. With her elbows planted firmly on the edge of the desk, the leather-bound book in her embrace; she fought to retain her last bit of energy to hold herself together.

She wanted to call Gabe back into the room and apologize for her harsh words. To tell him everything, to explain to him why she behaved the way she did, but her throat was dry, like she had swallowed a tablespoon of sand. The fits of sadness convulsed throughout her entirely, making her fingers tingle and her body shudder.

What was I supposed to say? What was I supposed to do?

If only her mind would allow her to speak. For ten years she had withheld what he now sought. Time was supposed to heal what her mind could not. She couldn't ignore any longer what she now faced.

Lydia turned her eyes to the ceiling. "Why have you forsaken?" she sobbed. What was meant to be a passionate scream only turned out to be a loud harsh whisper. Time was supposed to explain why they suffered. She squeezed the journal tighter into her chest, hoping the answers would squeeze their way out of the book of secrets.

The journal!

Her eyes were drawn to the weight in her trembling arms, her fingers gripping the raised ridges and patterns of the leather. She had originally given the journal to Gabriel as a gift, a place for him to share his most personal thoughts. A way of coping.

She looked back toward the closed door. "How did you get it?" she whispered to the shadows. The thought was directed at Gabe, the meaning meant for her. The book had been locked away in the attic, she with the only key. She saw to it.

How did I even forget about the journal?

A flash of anger clashed with her sobs of self-pity. Her thoughts flashed back to the book. Strangely, the anger faded as quickly as it had arrived.

I gave him that journal... I encouraged him to write in it!

"And he did!" she whispered.

There it sat hidden in the attic, on a high shelf in the back untouched by anyone for years, until now. She had flipped through it once in search of answers days after his passing, but her tears blurred the words and her mind refused to focus. So away the book went, waiting for another day, another time when she would be ready. Never once since then had she cracked it open to read a word. A strange thought made the hairs on the back of her neck pull at their roots.

Did he write this for himself, did he write it for others?

She felt the book weighing her down; its burden again pulling her under, drawing her arms to the table. She was too tired to resist; too exhausted to fight that over which she had no control.

The journal hit the desk top with an audible "thud". Her attempt to control the book's descent only made it louder. The abrupt noise rang in her ears. The book hit with such force that it bounced and lay half-open, the words on the page staring back up at her.

The whole action startled her. The sight of his very words written in cursive made her fingers tingle. She turned away and tried to step back from the edge of the desk, but her elbows held her fast. She dared not move them; she didn't have the strength to keep herself upright or to fight the pull of the book.

She forced her eyes to refocus on the page. There in clear words printed in large letters across the top of the page was her name.

Lydia.

Her heart felt like it skipped a couple of beats.

Was this message truly for me?

Her shoulders drooped, her arms still affixed to the desk as she leaned to support herself, her legs practically useless. Her sorrowful tears dripped onto the page. She tried to wipe them off but her effort only caused the ink to smear. She leaned farther onto the desk, dragged the chair out from under it and then plopped noisily down onto the seat. She slid the journal safely away. Her tears now flowed freely onto the desk, away from the book. She stared at the pages. Her eyes slowly focused.

He left me a message!

She pulled the soggy tissue out of her pocket and dabbed the corners of her eyes, smearing what little makeup she had.

The message had sat, hidden in the attic.

Why did I wait so long?

She tried to hold back the tears, as the anxiety welled up from within. She never dreamed that there would have been a personal message for her in the journal. The thought caused her to shudder.

Was it a message from the grave? Why hadn't I read the journal earlier?

As she read his memories she heard the words as if he were still alive.

August 7th 1988

Lydia, sweetheart, I have not been fair to you. The guardians say a husband should not keep secrets from his wife, for she will eventually find out sooner than he thinks. Well, as you read this, you have probably known all along that something was amiss. That I was no longer a person that you knew. A stranger in your husband's shell. I am still Gabriel, your husband and the father of our three year old son. Even when my time comes, I will always be the husband and the father, and you will always be known as my wife.

 I will just say it, let the words pour from my heart and hope that you will understand. I have not asked for what they say is a GIFT. It has been imposed upon me, it has been imposed upon us. And I have no option but to accept no matter the outcome. I fear and bleed like everyone else and that alone will bring me to my demise. I believe that they forget that fact, when they ask me to carry out God's will.

 I am a soldier of God, a pawn in the fight between good and evil. The moment you said I DO you signed on for a terrible turn. But in all fairness, I could not have warned you of something I didn't myself understand.

 I still don't, fully, but I think for the first time, I am beginning to do so. Just like you, I'm fulfilling a pre-determined life-plan. Me as the ranger, and you as the mother of our child... my wife.

 All essential for the next series of truths that will unfold....

"The next series of truths?" her voice hacked and scratched with confusion as she pressed the pad of her finger into the page below the last word she read until her nail bed turned white. Saving her place until her thoughts could catch up. Her eyes scrolled back to the top of the page.

"August 7th 1988, that was his last two summers!"

Her mind raced.

Lydia felt her energy drain away with every shiver, glad she had sat down when she did. Her thoughts flashed back in time, back in life. The journal entry was a year and seven months before his passing, before he was taken away from her, stolen away from them!

Did he know? He must have known!

Her thoughts echoed loudly in her mind.

She stared down at the book, her mouth open, her throat dry. His voice echoed passionately in her mind. It was as if he were standing right there, reading the journal out loud to her. She shot a quick glance about the room. Nothing but dimly lit shadows stared back. She turned and let her eyes fall onto the picture on the nightstand sitting by the door. The three of them smiling back at the camera.

How happy we were. So long ago that was. Now this?

She sighed in disappointment, whether it was the familiarity of the situation or not, it was there. His presence was still there in the room. The thought of being watched suddenly made her feel uncomfortable. She forced her eyes back to the book, swallowed and then continued, focusing on his every word and the intent in which they were written.

You have accused me of being unemotional. Not caring enough, but that is not true. Things are not always as they appear, you of all people should know that by now. I struggle with understanding every day. I struggle to bring it all together. My work has taught me to separate myself from

> the situation, to buffer my emotions, to accomplish the job, to hold it together to not make the issue my problem.
> I have gotten good at it, so good, I can no longer release my emotions to cry. Almost as if I have forgotten how. I find myself spending more and more time alone, away from the problems of others, away from their needs. Unfortunately... away from my family as well. I'm finding it harder to communicate with those for whom I care.
> I fear that something will happen to them and I will be forced to make it all better, but I will fail. A price to pay for saving others? So I busy myself in the garden, creating, giving life. Making a sanctuary for my soul....

Lydia no longer took the effort to wipe away her tears. They were her release.

They were for Gabriel, they were for Gabe, and they were for herself. She would allow what Gabriel could not. Strangely, she felt his presence in the room grow stronger. She looked up expecting to see him stumble into the room at any moment; nothing else in the world seemed to matter except what he had meant for her to read.

> I am here to do my job; to rectify the problem as best as I can, to do what is only humanly possible. But, as it turns out, in my case, I have gone a bit beyond. They have seen to that. By doing the impossible somehow I have defied God to protect me. Because, with these abilities comes a price which I know I will soon have to pay.
> I can feel it. Where I used to hesitate, I now immediately respond to the situation. I

now follow the voice in my head, instead of my heart. They guide me, advise me what to do. I, in turn, don't question. I do as they say no matter the outcome, no matter the consequences. The voices have never wronged me. Because, I am here to serve, guided by angels. Yes angels. I know you felt them too.... The guardian angels, the watchers, the protectors...

As she read, she could feel the excitement and dread in his voice. She became more disturbed by what she was reading.

What on earth was he saying? What was he trying to tell me? Had he finally lost it?

"Guardian angels?" she murmured, her voice crackled in disbelief. Her eyes read on, drawn to the pages.

You are probably feeling their presence as you read this very journal....

Lydia felt her body shudder as if an icy chill flowed down the back of her neck. She shot a quick glance over her shoulder to confirm that she was still alone in the room. She was, but deep down inside she wished she weren't.

Was it the journal that made me feel the way I did... was that his intent? Did he really believe in guardian angels? Are there really such things? Is there life after death, purgatory for those who sinned, heaven for those who truly repented, and hell for those who discarded it all?

Twelve years of catholic schooling had taught her that. It was what her parents raised her to believe. She wished her son Gabe was still standing there next to her now, that she hadn't chased him off, accused him of lying.

Her slender fingers tingled.

"My god, if I had hidden the book in the attic... and had the only key..."

Her mind raced again.

"Then, how did the journal get here?"

The thought made her skin crawl and the tears stop flowing. Gabe had always told the truth.

She glanced back towards the door.

"Why couldn't you have talked to me?" she screamed. "To write it in a book and hope that I stumble upon it, umpteenth years later?" There was anger and disappointment in her voice.

The Saint Francis of Assisi statue, the patron saint of ecology... the garden in the back.

"Was that part of your message?" she whispered. She read on.

I too felt something I couldn't explain. Oddities at first, periodic in nature, but soon the presence dominated every aspect of my life... our lives. I know, I know. I apologize for not telling you sooner. I guess I'm using this journal to build my nerve. But how was I supposed to explain to you that every aspect of our lives were being watched, scrutinized by angels, the tenders of death. I didn't know how to tell you at first, but now, I do...

Lydia remembered, it had been a few weeks after the very journal entry she was reading when he first tried to explain about the angels. She pushed herself away from the desk top and into the back of the chair. "Why didn't I listen?" Her tears no longer flowed, her thoughts revisiting that day in time....

"What?" Lydia yelled in confusion, "do you know what you are even saying? Have you even listened to yourself lately?"

Gabriel paused for a moment, fidgeting nervously with a pen in his hand. His eyes searching the table for answers.

"Well?" she pressed.

Thinking back, she resented her tone then and even now, eleven plus years later.

"I am protected by angels." he shrugged. "They sit around this table at this very moment." He nodded his head as he shifted his eyes around the room.

She followed his gaze. To her surprise, when their eyes met he smiled. They pleaded for her to understand. She wanted to scream in anger, throw her arms into the air and leave, but she remained in her chair, directly across from his. She could tell he was glad she did.

"They protect me, they protect... us."

"For heaven sakes, Gabriel, protection from what?" This time she chose to toss her arms into the air and looked about the room to emphasize her point.

He raised his eye brows in disapproval. "I wish you wouldn't talk like that—"

"How would you prefer that I talk?" her voice rang with sarcasm. "To act like everything is fine and dandy? When you know darn well it isn't, and you know it!" She jabbed her finger towards his chest. Her own rage caught her by surprise. She saw it in his eyes.

"People in town have been talking, but you wouldn't know that now, would you? No, you're too busy saving everyone else's family but your own!" She pulled her hand to her mouth and looked away as soon as she spoke. The words had pierced his soul. He winced as he fought to hold his caring smile. She resented the moment as soon as the words slipped off her tongue. This wasn't her; those weren't her words. Her anger had dragged them up from somewhere dark. She *loved her husband and knew he cared for her very much.* "I'm sorry," *she blurted out.* "I'm so sorry," *she whispered.*

He reached over and gently took one of her hands and caressed it in both of his as his eyes looked deeply into hers. His warm touch made her hand tingle. His presence made her feel calm and safe. The tingling in her hands grew alarmingly stronger. She thought that she detected a fragrant aroma in the room. She stared down at her hand and thought about pulling it away, but she didn't.

His gaze followed hers to his hands. "Lydia, what's wrong?"

"How do you do that?" *her voice now a faint, meek whisper.*

"Do what?"

"That!" *she whispered,* "Your hands, they make me tingle!" *She shuddered when she spoke.*

He paused as if to let her speak, but she couldn't think of anything else to say. The tingling in her hands increased, starting at her fingers, flowing towards her wrist and past her elbow. The sensation felt as if her hands were recovering from falling asleep. Startled, she pulled her hand clumsily free from his gentle grasp. She felt his grip release without a struggle.

The tingling began to fade the moment her hand was free. She gave him a bizarre look, shifting her gaze in between his and her hands.

"What did you do to my hand?" *she sounded surprised.*

He leaned back to give her some space and spoke as if he read the expression on her face.

"It's not what I do, it's what God allows me to do," *he said in a matter of fact voice.* "It's *what I have been trying to tell you,"* his eyes seemed to be on the verge of tears for the first time in years. *"The angels stand by my side. It is by their grace that I live or die. It is by their choice that someone else does the same."*

She remembered silently staring at him with narrowed eyes, trying to read him, trying to find a flaw in his story. He was telling the truth as he spoke from his heart. He had indeed done some incredible things in an effort to rescue some of the park visitors.

It was then that she saw it out of the corner of her eye, a shadow off to her left. An attractive, fit looking young man smiling deeply at her. His blond curly hair stood out against what looked like a white robe. He reminded her of one of those Greek statues, meticulously carved out of marble.
The figure nodded.
Startled, she turned her head towards the shadow and abruptly stood up from the table, knocking over her chair. When she refocused, it was gone.
Either it had disappeared or never existed... a subliminal thought placed and reinforced by Gabriel?

She remembered the air being heavy in the sweet aroma of incense.

When she shot an inquisitive glance back to Gabriel, he grinned back at her as if he were reading her mind. His eyes saying it all.
"You saw, didn't you? Now do you believe?"

"I was so stupid!" Lydia spoke her thoughts out loud. She looked back down at the journal and slid forward as if she were once again drawn back to the book, beckoned by the message within. She traced the words with her finger and found where she left off, her heart pounding in her chest. The weakness in her arms faded with every quick, shallow breath. The pad of her finger came to rest on the next word. She cleared her throat and took a deep breath. She continued to read softly and out loud, so her ears could hear and her heart absorb. She began again....

There are angels among us who do God's bidding.

They are here to protect us, to see to it that we fulfill our life's plan, good, bad or indifferent. Some people live to a ripe old age, others die in infancy. Some good-hearted people die young while some cold-hearted, selfish people seem to live forever, guided and protected by dark angels of their own. We have trouble understanding how or why it works that way. It is not up to us to ask why, or to judge the decisions made by those who know more than we could ever imagine. I feel much better doing as I was asked, passing the burden on to those whose job it is to deal with those nature of things. I passed them onto God. You should do the same. Have you forgotten what you have learned? The nuns were right, you know! Sounds funny listening to my own thoughts or hearing the words coming out of my own mouth.

She could imagine him smiling as she read on.

We all have guardian angels looking over our shoulders. Some are influenced by the light, others influenced by the dark. You remember that old cartoon, the one where there was the devil on one shoulder and an angel on the other, both whispering, trying to influence the decision that the individual was about to make, both arguing with the other, trying to throw each other off their game?

She laughed. It felt good to laugh.

The one with the best promises wins over the one with the weakest mind.
No, the angels don't change the outcome, you do that, they influence your decision. It's the squeaky wheel. I follow the familiar voice, the familiar thoughts. I do what I know is right, and I know it is right because that is what I have been taught. Growing up catholic, as we did, I know you understand. Look into your heart. Trust what I am telling you, trust your feeling from within. You know what I am telling you is correct. You need to pray for understanding, which is what I did. The burden is no longer on my shoulders. Trust Him!
I love you and Gabe very much. That is why I am doing what I do.
From time to time we have to sacrifice a part for the whole... a part of us like his only son did for you and I... He gave his life so that others may live.

Lydia stared at the last words for a moment, repeating them in her thoughts before she took a deep breath and gently closed the book.

'He gave his life so that others may live.'

"I love you too, honey!" she whispered. The sound of her voice made her smile. It felt good to smile.

She didn't know if it was because she had adjusted to the conditions in her study, but she felt as if the whole room had suddenly become warmer and brighter. She needed that in her life. The strange chill no longer made her shiver. The book seemed to stand out more against the dark surface of the desk. The feeling of being watched was even greater now than it was before. She looked around the room but saw no one else. Just because she didn't see them, whomever or whatever they were, she knew she wasn't alone. She wasn't sure if there really was a presence there in the room, or if it was Gabriel's message that he had written over eleven years ago that had influenced her thoughts and emotions. Either way, it felt good to be there at that very moment.

Was it part of the healing? Was it Gabriel? Was it the guardian angels?

"Gabriel?" she whispered. "Thank you!" She picked up the journal and caressed the book into her arms, pulling it tightly into her chest. It no longer felt heavy, no longer pulled at her soul and arms. Her throat was no longer parched. She closed her eyes and said a little prayer from the heart, for the first time in a very long while. That's when she felt the gentle breeze past her face, the tingle down the back of her neck. When she opened her eyes in surprise, the room was quiet and calm, the door still shut, the tassels on the air vents, motionless.

CHAPTER SIX
DESPERATION
(THURSDAY NIGHT)
MARCH 10TH 2000

Gabe pushed the phone tightly against the side of his face with his quivering hands as his lungs fought bitterly for oxygen. His heart thundered in his ears and hammered in his chest. It was strange, like he could no longer breathe. Despite his willing thoughts and the force on his diaphragm, his breaths momentarily refused to come. The anticipation of hearing the comfort of his uncle's understanding and long awaited voice was leaving his chest tight and his throat dry and scratchy. Somehow he knew the answers all lay with his uncle; he had what he so desperately needed.

The truth!

"If I knew what had happened with my father, I would definitely know what was happening to me over these last two weeks!" he reassured himself with a whisper.

Breathe... breathe!

He filled his lungs and held it a moment before he let the air out slowly, a calming technique he had learned in his martial arts training. He was breathing again.

He felt the tickle about his face and quickly wiped the beads of sweat from his forehead with the back of his free hand. He cupped the mouthpiece of the phone to muffle his voice. He looked down at his watch. It was 11:14 in the evening. It had been at least two hours since his distraught mother had kicked him out of her study and disappeared behind a closed door, the leather back journal pulled tightly into her chest. It broke his heart to see her that way. The weight of the guilt was a burden on his tired shoulders. Somehow he felt the whole thing was his fault, but he didn't know how that was even possible. Everything only seemed to confuse him more. There was a strange guilt that flowed through him, pulling heavily at his heart.

It reminded him of what the Catholics called original sin, a mark on one's soul that could only be eliminated through baptism. As a young child, it was the godparents, usually a close family friend, a fellow Catholic or relative, who accepted the responsibility on your behalf of the family to assist an individual with following the teachings of the church. Uncle Dan was his godparent. He played a bigger role in his life than most. This late evening call to his uncle was of the utmost importance. Things seemed to be getting weirder by the minute.

He sucked in a needed breath. After filling his lungs, he sighed deeply.

The breathing will help calm my nerves.

"What is wrong with me?" His harsh whisper echoed quietly about the vacant kitchen. Strangely, he was almost hoping he would hear an answer. Only the echo of the second hand of the clock that hung over the dining room table accompanied him, with its steady, methodical rhythm. He shook off the uneasy feeling as he cautiously leaned back around the edge of the hallway and glanced down both sides to make sure that he was still alone. To his great relief, so far, he was; and now his plan was working. His mom hadn't left either her bedroom or her study. He wasn't so sure which room she was still in now, for both doors remained closed.

He grimaced as the unanswered rings echoed loudly in his ears. "Come on, pick it up, pick up!" He mumbled into the mouthpiece. His nervousness was growing.

He tried to imagine his uncle's smiling face to calm his nerves, but it wasn't working. The decision to call him hadn't come lightly. Based on some of the entries in his father's journal, his uncle had been aware of some of the things his father was going through. The thought that momentarily angered him also had a calming effect.

My uncle knew and didn't say anything... how could he?

The fact that his uncle knew what had happened to his father over ten years ago was incredibly hard for him to comprehend. There was no denying it now. It had been documented by hand and poured from the heart into a secret leather-bound journal that had fallen into Gabe's hands.

Once he told his uncle what was happening to him, for sure there would be no denying it.

He would have to acknowledge my father's past and my present condition. If there were a connection, he would have to help me understand what's going on!

His uncle would be forced to deal with him. There wasn't anyone else outside of Erick whom he could really trust.

Who else in their right mind would take what is happening to me seriously?

If it weren't happening to him, Gabe wouldn't have believed a word of it himself.

Ghosts in the high school showers, glowing lights in alleyways of town, his dad's journal appearing by itself in his mom's study, the feelings of being watched and followed, and a blond kid that everyone else sees but him.

His mom on the other hand was the woman who took care of him. She was the one person who made sure he had everything he needed and even several things he wanted. The woman he loved dearly, and knew that she loved him, was an emotional mess. He had never seen her behave this way before.

But, why the fuss over the truth of his father's death? Maybe my mom is still protecting him, why?

The sudden sound of his uncle's joyful voice made him jump. He started to speak but quickly realized it was a scratchy sounding recording.

An answering machine!

He felt his lungs tighten and his mouth become dry and sticky. At this hour of his need, his perfect plan had failed. A surge of anger welled up from within. "Where are you? Why couldn't you be home tonight, of all nights?" he whispered desperately into the mouthpiece of the phone that he clenched tightly in his hand.

The message echoed painfully in his ears. "Hey, this is the Wilson's residence, sorry we're not here to receive your call," his uncle's familiar voice was smooth and joyful, "but you know what to do, after the beep. We'll get back to you as soon as we can. Thanks for calling."

Though he expected to hear it, the tone on the answering machine made him jump. That in itself frustrated him. He held the phone silently in his hand trying to quickly formulate a message in his mind. He had not planned for his uncle not being around to talk. That was why he called so late in the evening. He looked down at his watch, 11:15 p.m., only a minute had gone by since he had last checked.

"My uncle couldn't possibly have gone to bed this early!"

He fought the panic that was welling up within. At least if his aunt answered the phone, he could have small talked with her and smoothly given her a message for his uncle. A message that would not have triggered a worried return calls to his mother, ruining his whole plan. He breathed deeply into the phone as the seconds seemed to slowly slip by. As if on cue, he was suddenly able to pull it together.

"Hi this is Gabe..." he tried desperately to calm his voice, but he could still hear the nervous quiver that followed every word. He hoped that they would write it off as a nervous teen doing something he wasn't quite ready to do. After all, he wasn't that far off. "Hi Aunt Betty, I'm calling for Uncle Dan, I wanted to talk to him about a, school project I'm working on. Uh, I have a deadline, so, uh, if he can get back to me as soon as possible, it would be quite... uh, helpful. Well, that's all for now. Hope everyone is doing... okay, hopefully I'll hear from you soon, bye!"

As Gabe quietly hung up the phone he gave out a heavy sigh. He looked down at his hands, his nervous energy flowed through his entire body and out his tingling fingers and toes. He intently listened down the hallway and was pleased to hear only the ticking of the battery-operated clock that sat above the dining room table. If his mother was still asleep in bed, he was still in the game.

CHAPTER SEVEN
GOD PARENT
(FRIDAY MORNING)
MARCH 11TH 2000

The droning seemed to echo in the back of his mind, faint at first but then it began to build. It wasn't the quick, repetitive, irritating drone of the alarm clock that usually awoke him from his restful slumber. It didn't pound relentlessly upon the back of his skull as his alarm clock usually did. No, this was different. This had the quality of bells. His mind raced as his subconscious counted the rings.

The phone!

His thoughts screamed in his mind. He snapped open his eyes and focused them on the clock that sat next to the bed. It was 6:30 in the morning. The more he awoke, the more distant the ringing.

He lay there, eyes open, now staring at the ceiling, hoping the caller would give up. The ring went silent half way through another series.

Thank goodness!

A muffled woman's voice echoed softly down the hall. It was his mom. She couldn't let the ringing go.

Who in their right mind would be calling this early on the morning on a school day, a Friday at that?

It was all followed by his mother's familiar laughter. "I'll get him, he should be up by now." Then quickly followed by. "Gabe, it's for you, it's your uncle!" Lydia's voice echoed down the hall.

"He says he's returning your call?" her voice fluctuated towards the end.

He could hear the curiosity in her inquisitive voice. He had almost forgotten the call he had made out of desperation to his uncle late last night.

"Ugh-oh!" He bolted strait out of bed and jogged over to take the phone from his mother. She stood there impatiently in her plaid pajamas. He tried to read the tone in her voice and the expression on her face.

"It's your uncle." she repeated softly, holding out the phone to him, a curious smile on her face. "I didn't know you had a project due?"

He felt his heart pound heavily in his chest. He struggled for what to say as he stared dumb founded into her face. "Yeah..." he shrugged.

She gestured the phone toward him with an extended hand and nodded. "It's Uncle Dan... don't leave him standing there!"

He reached up and gently took it out of her hand and pulled it to his ear. To his surprise, she kissed him gently on his forehead and walked off.

"Don't be too long, you've got school, remember! I'm getting dressed and then starting breakfast," she said over her shoulder as she walked back down the hall toward her bedroom. Her voice upbeat, totally opposite from the evening before.

He silently followed her with his eyes until he was sure she was out of earshot.

"Uncle Dan?" he heard the excitement in his own voice.

"Yeah, it's me Sport. How's it going?" He rushed through his familiar greeting. "Sorry I had to call you so early this morning. But, aren't you supposed to be getting ready for school by now?" He cleared his throat. "Anyhow, I've got to take care of a few things first this morning. Besides, didn't you say that you needed the goods A.S.A.P."

"What?" Gabe's mind took a moment to break the code.

"As soon as possible!"

"Oh, right!"

"Yeah, so what's up? What's this important project you're working on?" his voice sounded playful.

"Well!" he hem-hawed around for a moment as he struggled for the courage to ask him things he never thought he would ever be asking.

"Lose your tongue? Come out with it."

He heard the impatient tone in his uncle's voice. He bit his lip and forced himself to speak. "It's about my dad...."

A strange silence filled the earpiece. He could almost imagine the bewildered expression on his uncle's face.

Not this again!

"About your dad?" Dan's voice was inquisitive, cautious.

Gabe felt the needed courage kick in. He had to ask the questions before his mother came back to start breakfast. He glanced over his shoulder and down the hallway, he was glad to see that his mom hadn't left her bedroom. He still had time. "You know more about my dad than you've told me," he accused.

"Well yeah," he stumbled along, "we were brothers, you know. We spent a lot of quality time—"

"No, about what happened to him!" he accused. He heard his uncle clear his throat before he answered.

"I promised your mother—"

Gabe interrupted before he was finished. "How am I ever supposed to know anything about my dad if you don't tell me!" he complained, his voice getting louder.

"Your mother—"

"She cries every time I ask her... she won't tell me anything!" Gabe tried to keep his voice down.

"Cries?" Dan's voice reflected his concern.

"Yes, cries like I said! Almost every day now."

"But, I—"

"I found my dad's journal!" Gabe finally blurted out. "It was sitting there on the desk of my mom's study. It was almost like... as if... I was meant to find it!" he struggled to control his excitement.

"Did your mother—"

"No," he interrupted again, the anger noticeable in his voice. "She took it away, kicked me out of her study. I closed the door and she cried for a long time."

Gabe's uncle broke the uneasy silence. He noted his uncle's attempt to calm his own voice. He spoke slower. "Okay... what did she say?"

"She accused me of digging through her things in the attic...."

"Well, did you?"

"Noooo! I swear I didn't! I don't have any idea where it came from. I've never seen it before."

"Okay, okay!" he assured. "You sure it was your dad's?" Concern was noted in his voice. "Can you describe it?"

"Yeah!" Gabe uttered confidently, glancing over his shoulder. "The leather cover had an engraving of the forest, Gabriel Wilson was written below it."

The silence resumed. He could tell his uncle was in deep thought. "Your mom gave that to him." Dan's voice was quiet, contemplative.

"Yes, I know, he also wrote about *you*," Gabe explained, "he said *you* knew about the strange things that were happening to him." He felt his voice crackle; he was on the verge of tears. "*You* knew and *you* didn't tell me!" he said, his voice accusatory.

Though silent on the other end, he could hear Dan's heavy breathing. Gabe swallowed and forced himself to continue. He spoke softly into the receiver. "Those weird things that happened to my dad, well... now they're happening to me too!" Gabe gripped the phone receiver tightly. He felt the fear build as his voice echoed in the silence.

This time it was his uncle that interrupted the uneasy silence.

The words '*Things are happening to me*' rang uneasy in Gabe's thoughts. It was weird, like he was hearing the words for the first time.

"My dear nephew," he spoke tenderly and with great understanding. "I'm so sorry, I should have said something."

Gabe fought back a squeal as he heard his mom noisily exit her bedroom and make her way towards him. "My mom!" he whispered.

"Okay, relax... relax, your secret's safe with me, here's what we're going to do." he spoke quick, as if sensing his panic.

There was a strange calmness to his voice, one spoken by a person who was use to making quick decisions under pressure. "Put your mother back on the phone. We're coming up to visit. We should be up there to Northern California by late Sunday evening."

"You're coming up?" Gabe blurted out excitedly, "what about work?"

"Yes, I'll see you late Sunday evening. Sounds like you and I have a lot of catching up to do."

Gabe felt a surge of energy rush through him as he handed his mother the phone. "Uncle Dan is coming up to visit!" he exclaimed.

Lydia was now dressed in jeans and a t-shirt, her brown hair back in a ponytail. She gave him an inquisitive look as he thrust the receiver into her hand.

He suddenly felt as if a great burden had been lifted from his shoulders. Whatever his mother wouldn't tell him, he was more assured than ever that his uncle would.

He'll know what to do!

CHAPTER EIGHT
OBLIGATION
(FRIDAY MORNING)
MARCH 11TH 2000

Uncle Dan fumbled blindly with the phone receiver in his hand before it came to rest in the holder on the edge of the coffee table. He slid both of his palms across his face before he stared blankly at the wall, his eyes searching for what his mind refused to register. With his throat dry, and a weakness about his legs, he flopped noisily backward onto the couch with an exhausted grunt. He gently rubbed his eyes with the palms of his hands. Just moments ago he had made the call. He couldn't understand why every ounce of his energy had been suddenly drained, stolen from him in an instant. The sound of Gabe's voice had hit a nerve. Stunned, he pressed his body into the couch and focused on the picture of he and his brother hanging from the living room wall. It was an exact duplicate of the one he had given to his nephew Gabe a couple of years back. Dan's tan, rugged complexion accented his athletic, six foot frame. Now the gray was noticeable in his dark, thinning hair. Despite it all, he looked young for his 56 years.

His mind raced back to his brother, Gabriel, back to that moment more than twenty-five years ago. Dressed as park rangers, they both stared defiantly back into the lens of the camera, ready to take on the world. Both young, new at the game of protecting the resources from the legislators, the visiting public and sometimes nature itself.

How foolish and naive we had been. If I had only known what I know now, maybe things would have been different.
He thought.
Sadness tugged at his heart. Visions of his younger brother 40 years earlier forced their way back into his conscious mind.

The strange chill raced through his body. He shivered. His baby brother was forcing his way back into his life.

"Are you checking on me, warning me of something to come?" he whispered.

The dreams usually meant something; he had learned to associate them with either change or disaster. His thoughts ultimately brought him back to his catholic upbringing, what he had learned, and ultimately, what he was still willing to believe. Dealing with his brother's death had shaken his beliefs to their core.

"My brother wasn't a guardian angel," he kept telling himself. "He couldn't have been..."

He had known him all of his life. They grew up like all the other kids in their Southern California neighborhood; but at fourteen, everything began to change.

His body shuddered as his thoughts flashed back to 1960... a bus stop in down-town Long Beach, off of 7th Street, only blocks from the Long Beach Harbor. The reoccurring dream baffled him more now than he remembered.

Brought on by stress or uneasiness?

He wished the whole thing would just simply fade away, be buried in the graveyard of dreams somewhere in his subconscious with the other unwanted, castaways, forever.

Dreaming about it over and over again was pointless!

The thoughts only made his mind regret and his body cower. He was now to a point in his life where he couldn't remember if the situation had really occurred the way he remembered, or if his mind had changed the whole thing, altered the nightmare over time to make it easier to discard and harder to believe.

Was it Self-preservation; A guilty conscience?

The rational side of his brain kicked in. There was always a meaning, there was always a lesson. He likely only needed to figure out what they were and understand their meaning.
But what?
He was there again... he felt the cool breeze dance against his skin, the taste of the ocean. It was dark, well after 9:00 in the evening, and they had a late band practice at the catholic high school just down the street.
Yes, I remember...

Back then life was so much simpler. They were habitually hungry and restless teenagers, full of energy. They had been joking around at the bus stop like they usually did to pass the time. They were doing just what teens did. That's when this whole thing started. That's the moment when their lives changed, forever. His brother slipped, tripped, or fell in front of the approaching bus that was bearing down on them. Gabriel quickly scrambled to his feet and stood there, Dan was frozen, his feet cemented to the sidewalk. He yelled to Gabriel but nothing came out. Seconds later his panic-stricken voice echoed in his ears. Despite the severity of the situation, his brother just stood there dumbfounded, frozen in time, his face turned towards the on-coming bus. As the bizarre scene played out, they were both unable to move as they watched their destiny approach. Then, as if in a delayed response to his scream, Gabriel turned and Dan could read the good-bye in his terror stricken eyes....

Dan looked down at his arms and tried to rub the goose bumps out of his skin as he sat there on the couch in his living room. His thoughts fell into place. Even today, that look in his brother's panic stricken eyes still made him shudder.

A strange helplessness overtook them both. Instead of the squealing of brakes or the honking of the horn into the cool evening, only the piercing roar of the large city bus echoed in his ears. For sure the driver must have seen them, but the bus drove on like they were invisible. It almost sounded like the buss had actually sped up

The interior light illuminated the driver as he stared forward, oblivious to their existence...

"How could he have not seen us?"

The thought of his brother soon becoming a memory, a headline in the local paper, stung his eyes with tears. This would be the way he would remember his brother for the rest of his life. A helpless teen pushed in front of a passing bus by his older brother. A flash of confusion, a cry for help... an action that he could never live down...

Why then, why now?
He couldn't even remember why he did it, or for that matter, why he had dropped a piece of broken cement on top of his brothers head years before.
What could have possibly driven me to do such things?
Growing up he had heard a well-known comedian named Flip Wilson, sum up the actions with a phrase... *'The Devil made me do it!'*
"If Flip only knew how close he really was to the truth." The thought made him shiver again.
"Why did I really grab the front of my brother's shirt and push him in front of the oncoming bus?"

He reacted. He only did what the little voice within his head had told him to do. The bus, he hadn't seen it until it was too late.

> *Then the strangest thing happened; next it was as if everything had taken place in slow motion. His brother's head snapped backward as if strong invisible arms had shoved Gabriel's upper torso forward, and whipped the rest of him in the other direction.*
> *Gabriel's body left the ground and tumbled lifelessly onto the sidewalk next to him, seconds before the bus arrived. A surprised bewildered expression etched across his face. He felt the warm breeze flash by before the bus even arrived....*

Dan held his breath and tightly closed his eyes to remind himself that it was only his recurring dream. He felt a tear trickle down the side of his cheek. Joy or sorrow, he searched his heart to know. It was always the same, the endless loop of emotions that continued to play out in his memory. Triggered by God knows what.

> *His eyes fully fixed on the bus as it roared past, the driver oblivious of the two of them. Blue and black streaks, expressionless faces staring forward like lost souls, their demented looks illuminated by the hue of the strange interior lights. ...The deafening scream of the engine pierced his ear drums; his lungs burned with the fumes of diesel and what strangely smelled like hot, putrid sulfur. ...His eyes stung from the horrid exhaust and swirling dust as they caught sight of a deformed black, white and red banner that covered the side of the bus....*

"Choose!" Dan whispered, he shuddered when he flashed back to that moment.

> There was a huge Celtic cross like the ones carved out of the stones in Ireland, casting a shadow over a weathered leather bound book sitting on an altar, draped in a tattered white linen, the word Choose in stylish blood red cursive blurred as it streaked past. The engines screamed like a fleeing demon. The bus never slowed, oblivious to the near fatal encounter. No horn, no brakes, no recognition... absolutely, mind boggling, crazy...

Dan felt the prickling on the back of his neck as he recalled, standing there that day, watching the bus disappear down the street.

> Illuminated by the shadows of the dimly lit street, he listened to the eerie pitch fade into the night. With the bus went the demon like smells...

If I had only known then what I know now?
He kept reminding himself, he would have melted into the cold sidewalks that night alongside the motionless form of his brother. He was convinced that it was the devil himself who had been the one driving the bus that day.
All those souls aboard were surely going to hell!

> The stirring form of his brother caused him to rush to his side. Relief and the excitement of finding his brother miraculously alive made his hands tingle and shake. The air around him had suddenly become warm, sweet and soothing, the sidewalk lighting substantially brighter. When he reached for his brother, he felt his own fears suddenly fade. The ocean breeze now dominated

the faint sounds of the distant bus. A renewed strength returned. They were safe. But the euphoric feelings faded just as quickly as they had arrived. They stood there once again, lonely and exposed and wanting to be safely home...

"What really happened that day?" he whispered, he still remembered his brothers' confused voice. It chilled him now as it did then.
What was he to say?
He wasn't so sure himself. The devil had come to collect his brother, but the attempt was foiled, something had pushed him out of the way in the nick of time.
"But, why did I push Gabriel in front of the oncoming bus in the first place?"
Who, what had pushed my brother out of the way?

He remembered the moment it hit him like a gust of wind from a furnace. There was a presence; someone was watching. He cautiously searched the shadows from the dull glow of the ambient streetlights. At first there was no one; but there, to his surprise he saw a shadow on the bench across the four lane street. The shadow moved, sat up and then turned to face them. To his horror, it staggered to its feet and clumsily walked with a purpose across the quiet street and in their direction. Its dark cloak concealed all but the face in the shadows.

He couldn't move, the trance held him frozen in a vise of fear until the figure was half way across the street. When he broke free, he quickly helped his brother to his feet.

"Hurry... hurry!" he remembered whispering frantically in his brother's ear. After what he had gone through so far, he wanted nothing else to do with whatever was coming next. His eyes never left the approaching figure as he jerked his

brother to his feet and started dragging him down the sidewalk towards the nearest streetlight...

"Maybe he just wanted to sit at the bus stop?" He remembered trying to convince himself. "But he was already sitting on a bench."

But to his horror and surprise, the figure curved his angle of approach to follow, increasing its gait until it was almost upon them.
"You's boy's okay?" the caring voice grumbled loudly from a short distance away.
Dan stopped and turned toward the figure not knowing what to expect, but no longer fearing the worst. The figure slowed as he closed the distance to within ten yards, the street lights now illuminating an elderly, weather-beaten man's dirty face, aged by time and a hard life. He slowed as he limped towards them.
"You's one, lucky young man!" he exclaimed, his voice breathless from the exertion. He thumbed in the direction the buss had disappeared.
His smile exposed several missing and stained teeth. His red nose and cheeks stood out against his tanned leathery skin and dirty face. He looked like many of the other homeless people Dan had seen on the streets of downtown Long Beach.
Almost as if sensing his discomfort, the man stopped five yards away and closely examined them both, his curious, knowing, blood shot eyes darted unnaturally back and forth between the two of them, and then off to Dan's far left. His head rocking from side to side. Dan pulled his

brother a step backward and a bit farther away. The man's movement frightened them.

He followed the stranger's concerned gaze towards the shadows, but saw nothing.

"Boys, it's not me you's need to worry about!" the man knowingly exclaimed in a hushed voice as he held the tip of one of his dirty fingers to his chapped lips. He leaned forward and winked with wild eyes as if he had a secret to share, then nodded again to their left. The odd gesture made Dan take another step backward, still clinging to his staggering brother. The sight of the man's long dirty fingernails had added to his fright. He could smell the unbathed odor, stench of urine, and the fruity smell of cheap wine permeating the air.

Dan wrinkled his nose.

"Son, someone upstairs, must really like you's!" the homeless man smiled. His voice crackled as if he knew something special. The man pointed his dirty finger off into the shadows and gave a loud, bizarre laugh. "If it wasn't for them, you's would've been on that bus for sure..."

Dan remembered turning and looking wild-eyed back toward the shadows, but saw nothing.

Was that man also crazy?

He was beginning to believe it was so. That late spring evening on that isolated street was anything but normal.

A busy city of a hundred thousand people and where were they that evening? Not a soul to be seen but one... the old man.

It was the thought of the old man's voice that brought it all back.

"Saved again by the grace of God!" The old man tilted his head back and closed his eyes. He

raised both of his dirty hands into the air to give praise. His hood slid back, exposing his receding, matted white hair, and the deep weathered grooves that followed the contours of his face. His long, skinny, aged fingers gave him the appearance of an ancient druid sorcerer. "By God's grace... by God's grace I tell you!" He turned back toward them and opened his eyes. He stepped a little closer.

Not knowing what to expect, he and his brother backed themselves against the wall and resisted the urge to run back into the shadows. But this was where they caught their bus, this was where they needed to be. As strange as they felt the homeless man was, he still remembered feeling a bit comforted by his presence.

The old man lowered his arms. His smile faded and then a serious concern encompassed his presence as if he had an important message to share. He bowed his head and momentarily lowered his gaze.

"We're all here to do his biddin'." The old man looked down the street towards the faint, familiar sound of a diesel engine. They heard it too and followed his gaze. The distant headlights of another approaching bus appeared around a corner. The old man gave another toothless smile as he nodded towards Gabriel. "He has plans for this one he does... big plans! You'll see!"

The droning engine brought the lights of the approaching city bus closer. A strange comfort overwhelmed them. The safety of home would be theirs shortly. When he looked back toward the homeless man he was surprised to see that the man was already halfway back across the street. The man was already heading back

> toward the rock, or rather the bench out from under which he had crawled.
> The man stopped, turned towards them, and yelled through cupped hands, "Oh, does he ever have plans for you!" He pointed towards Gabriel, the surrounding shadows, and then towards the sky as he gave that I know something that you don't laugh again. "They'll make sure of that, they will. Oh, yes, they'll see to God's will!" The man then raised both of his arms towards the sky.
> Dan shifted his gaze, he franticly searched the shadows. To his disappointment, or satisfaction, he saw nothing...

Oh, but they were there that night all right. He could feel them tucked into the shadows watching, obeying, and waiting for the exact moment when they would be called to service.

> They hurried to the bench. The front of the bus slowed to a stop directly alongside them. They both stared, stunned, not sure of what to do. Unlike the first, this one was inviting. Some of the passengers curiously peered at them through the window. It was the setting of the brake and the sliding open of the accordion glass doors that snapped him to attention. He gripped his brother tightly by the arm as he looked into the familiar face of the bus driver.
> "You boys goin' home? Kinda late isn't it?" the elderly black man smiled.
> Dan nodded, then shot a quick glance over his shoulder before he hurried onto the bus, dragging his brother with him.
> "You boys alright?" the bus driver asked as he punched their passes. "You look like you've seen a ghost!"

A ghost!

"Just tired, I guess!" Dan lied. Well, maybe it was only a half lie or a half truth. If the driver only knew how close he actually was. They scrambled onto the bus and hurried toward their usual seats behind the driver. To their surprise, when they looked out the window the homeless man was gone, the bench on the other side of the four lane road was vacant. They looked everywhere, but he was nowhere to be seen, having disappeared just like he had arrived, in a cloak of mystery, shadowed by darkness, a visitor from a strange realm of the unknown....

As Dan's *daydream* ended, he returned to the present thoughts and his familiar living room. He focused again on the picture of his brother.

"No, my brother wasn't just lucky. The homeless man was right! He was being looked after by something that had taken Gabriel years to figure out."

He didn't just survive near disaster after near disaster on his own.

"No, they were keeping him alive. He was protected by guardian angels, used to do God's desires, to keep some people alive and allow others to perish."

It wasn't just the fact that Dan marveled over Gabriel's uncanny ability to be at the right place at the right time, or his incredible ability to pull off rescues that most hardened rescuers would never attempt. He wouldn't have believed it possible if he hadn't known about his brother's gift. Many called his brother fearless, foolhardy, living on the bubble, an adrenaline junkie, and pushing a luck that would soon run out. Dan remembered how angry it made him when someone had jokingly accused Gabriel of having made a pact with the devil.

They were so wrong. If only they could have really known and understood.

Tears filled his eyes and streamed down his cheeks. An aching sadness filled his heart. As much as he thought he had filed away his nightmares, hidden them deep within the recesses of his memory, they refused to stay away. It was almost as if they were drawn to the surface to keep his memory fresh, to keep his mind prepared.

But, for what?

"Like father, like son goes the old adage," the thought made him shudder.

Could I bare this responsibility on my shoulders again?

He knew his sister-in-law hadn't truly survived the first. It was time to set the record straight. There was unfinished business.

'Oh, does he ever have plans for you!' The old man's words still made him shiver. He looked up towards the celling.

"Do you have plans for young Gabe too?"

CHAPTER NINE
REUNITED
(MONDAY MORNING)
MARCH 14TH 2000

The knock on the door echoed loudly in Gabe's mind. He looked down at his watch, it was 7:30 in the morning. Without hesitation, he pushed himself from the couch and tore his way toward the front door, just about knocking his mom over in the excitement.

"Honey, easy does it!" Lydia admonished, shaking her head in disapproval as she caught her balance. "How many times have I told you?"

"I know, I know!" Gabe slowed his pace to a fast walk. He shot her a mischievous look over his shoulder. "It's probably Uncle Dan. He said he'd drop by this morning before I went off to school."

"A few more seconds aren't going to matter one way or the other now, will they?" she forced a smile as she shook her head.

"Sorry!" Gabe shrugged, feeling embarrassed. She was right. He was behaving like a little kid at Christmas, swooping down upon the presents stashed under the tree. His fingers tingled with excitement. When he reached the door he stopped for a moment to pull himself together. He glanced over his shoulder to his mom one last time and forced a smile. She returned it but there was still apprehension in her eyes, uneasiness in the way she stood. He felt the tension momentarily lift from his shoulders like he was being rescued from a sinking ship only to step into a life boat with a slow leak. A rescue, no matter how involved, was still a rescue after all.

He had been counting the seconds until his uncle's arrival and now here he was.

What am I going to say? How am I going to explain it all? Was my uncle really the answer to my problems?

The knock on the door interrupted his thoughts.

"Honey, the door!" his mother exclaimed as she raised an eyebrow towards the door.

The door!

He laughed again. This time it wasn't forced.

His uncle had called yesterday evening to tell them that they would stop at a hotel along the way Sunday night, and meet up with them first thing Monday morning before school.

He must have looked very silly rushing to the door only to stand there, anticipating the moment, letting it savor. He took a deep breath, gripped the door knob, and jerked it open.

Both his uncle Dan and Aunt Betty stood there motionless for a silent moment, their eyes attempting to read his own. Their flash of concern was quickly absorbed into smiles. Despite their attempts to hide their emotions, Gabe still read their anxiety. It scared him. Like a vampire waiting to be offered access into the victim's sanctuary, they stood there waiting. He too stood motionless for a moment before he fought through the strange feelings that anchored him in the doorway; the gateway between two worlds.

"Uncle Dan," Gabe exclaimed as he extended his arms for a familiar embrace, his eyes suddenly filled with tears, his hands started to tremble. Gabe was instantly overwhelmed in emotion. His attempt to fight it off had failed.

This was so bizarre.

It had never happened to him like this before.

As if on cue, both his uncle and aunt stepped forward to embrace them both.

His uncle smothered Gabe with his bear like arms and his aunt embraced with her delicate touch. Gabe felt their tender warmth. Everything suddenly felt like it was supposed to. His fears were for not, and his worries were unfounded. For a strange moment, he also thought he felt the soothing presence of his dad in the doorway. He began to sob, gently at first, but soon his whole body shuddered with emotion. The tears that dribbled down his cheeks weren't for sorrow; they were tears of joy. He couldn't explain the strange comfort that enclosed the moment. For the first time in years he felt safe, protected by their presence and embraced by love and concern.

***

When the door swung open Lydia Wilson felt her heart flutter, her breath shorten. She grabbed the edge of the bookstand in the hallway to catch her balance. The scene overwhelmed her. For a quick second, she thought she saw her deceased husband standing there at the door. When her eyes finally focused and her mind calmed, she saw that it was Dan, her husband's brother, and her sister-in-law, Betty.
How cruel.
It was the timing that bothered her the most. The whole week had made her feel uneasy. Ten years of trying to adjust to a life without Gabriel was all but wasted. She couldn't keep Gabriel out of her thoughts, or his familiar smell out of the house. She didn't know why or how, but the fragrance of bay laurel seemed to permeate every pocket of the house when she would least expect it. It would build and then fade. The fact that Gabe had never seemed to notice the fragrant aroma unnerved her.
It made her shiver to think about it. Two of Gabriel's favorite T-shirts that she had set aside years ago still carried his scent no matter how many times she washed them. Over the last two weeks, to her dismay, Gabriel's smell never faded. In fact, if even possible, the odors had become even stronger. Gabriel always had the strange habit of hiding bay leaves in the pockets, cubbies and drawers '*to mask his human scent*', he had always said. A laughing matter then, but now an unnerving fact that now haunted her subconscious.
It had been nearly ten years since his passing, since he had been taken from their lives. Flash-backs they call them, usually

triggered by objects, dates and smells. Now they all seemed to be working together, building as the tenth anniversary of his passing grew near. These feelings were considered normal for the grieving spouse or child. The solution was textbook, surround oneself with family and friends for support and remove the triggering memories. Easier said than done. She didn't want to forget, she just wanted to understand.

There was a comfort in the fact that Dan and Betty were there. Dan's sudden appearance at the door had also reminded her of the upcoming anniversary of her husband's death, always a tough time for her.

How could she ever forget? How could she ever forgive?

Surrounding oneself with family and friends during these trying times was recommended. But the thought brought tears to her eyes, a lump to her throat. Dan and Betty had on several occasions dropped everything to see them, to help them, to be with them. She felt indebted. They had graciously assisted for ten years and would probably do it for ten more without expecting anything in return. Not having a child of their own, Dan had taken a personal interest in Gabe's future.

Life was suddenly getting harder. Sheltering Gabe from the mysteries of life, from his father's passing, was not going to be easy. There were things Gabe would need to know, some of them right away, before it was too late. She was postponing the inevitable and she knew it. Gabe was coming of age. She cursed the fact that the legacy of his father appeared to be forcing its way into their lives. It had taken her husband, and now it was knocking on their door, again. It now wanted her only son. It was like a family curse.

This can't all be a coincidence!

The thought sent a chill down the length of her back. She felt the tingle in her fingers and toes. She staggered toward the door, toward her brother-and sister-in-law. It was no coincidence that they had driven all day Sunday to arrive at their door-step the next morning because her son had asked them to do so. She shifted her gaze in between Gabe, Dan, Betty, and rested her hand on the shoulder of her grieving son. She saw the tears drifting down his cheeks. She saw his shoulders bow and

felt them tremble as if an incredible burden had been placed upon them. She felt the same burden bare down on hers as well.
What have I done?
Echoed loudly in her thoughts. The sadness welled up within her. She fought the urge to throw up, to double over in self-pity. She didn't know if her heart could take it anymore. "God... why? Please help us!" she whispered. She couldn't control it anymore.
No, not now!
She, too, burst into tears.

***

His mom's sobbing cries jerked Gabe out of his trance. He recognized her trembling touch and turned to face her. He suddenly felt embarrassed. His emotional outburst had affected his mom as well. She began to break down. She wasn't holding it together.
It's my fault.
He had led her down the path which they should have never gone.
"It's okay, it'll be alright!" Gabe heard the strain in his uncle's voice. Gabe turned to face his mother. His uncle pulled her closer. She accepted his caring embrace and buried her face into Dan's coat. Her increased sobs muffled by his uncle's chest. Her narrow shoulders, trembled with every sob. Betty stepped up and gently wrapped her arms around both his consoling uncle and his grieving mom. Gabe took a step back. All Gabe could do was stare as he watched the scene unravel, his mom once again losing control. He was in the thick of it. He watched with empathy as she struggled to regain control of the emotions that now seemed to dominate every day of her life. The lump grew in his own throat, making it difficult to swallow and even harder to speak. There was no question about it, she was getting worse as the week progressed. He hated March 16th, the cursed anniversary date of his father's death. The day before St. Patrick's Day, a holiday forever tainted.

His uncle gave him a playful wink. Gabe forced a smile as he wiped the tears from the corners of his eyes with the back of his hand. He knew what his uncle was thinking. He always joked about how the sensitive guys always get the girls. He admired his uncle's ability to be strong. He felt the need to show him that he could be strong too. That he could keep his emotions in check, take care of and support his mother. His uncle's smile soothed him, gave him strength and inner courage.

"Lydia, how are you holding up?" his uncle asked his mother as he held her at arm's length to better look into her hidden face. She averted his eyes, from beneath her matted hair, as if trying to conceal her thoughts.

Gabe knew that his uncle's genuine concern was for his benefit as well. He watched his mother silently nod her head, her eyes never leaving the floor. He willed her strength with his thoughts.

His uncle gave her an understanding nod and a pat on her shoulder; he knew he had his work cut out for him. His aunt looked on with grave concern, unlike his uncle; she hadn't mastered the art of hiding her emotions. It was usually something guys seemed to be much better at and paid the price for with their health and longevity.

Gabe nodded and forced a bigger smile. He was glad his uncle was there. He felt like things would be different. The more he stared at Dan, the more he couldn't believe how much his uncle looked like his father.

"We came as soon as we could." Dan's voice sounded apologetic, his gestures and mannerism confirmed it. Gabe nodded in appreciation.

Without saying a word, like a well-rehearsed scene, his uncle gently released his mom and slowly stepped away, allowing his aunt to take his place. His aunt took his mother's hand in hers and gently wrapped her other arm around her trembling shoulder. His mom allowed herself to be guided over the threshold and back into the interior of the house. He couldn't help but think that his aunt had unknowingly entered their strange world. He wondered if she really knew what she was getting herself into.

"We had a few errands we needed to clear up first, but, the important thing is we're here, we're all together now. Better late than never, they always say!" Betty forced a smile. "Things will be alright, you'll see." Her tender, understanding voice faded as they moved farther into the house. She patted Lydia's shoulder as she guided her down the hall, confusion and uneasiness slipping farther away with every step.

When Gabe looked back up at his uncle, he found him with hands on his hips, staring guiltily back towards his mother. His mind appeared to be deeper in thought.

After an uncomfortable moment, Betty's voice faded into the distance. His uncle turned back toward him and stared, his mask of confidence and understanding removed. His expressive blue eyes no longer pretended to be happy; his face carried a heavy burden.

They both silently stared at each other as if they were waiting for the other to speak. It was Gabe who tried to break the uncomfortable stillness first. He opened his mouth, but it was like it no longer worked. His throat was so dry, he could hardly swallow.

***

Dan had to fight the lump that wedged itself in the back of his throat. A strange guilt weighed heavily on his shoulders, pressing down upon his spine, a guilt that he had created and nurtured himself.

This time we will not fail! I will not fail!

He willed himself to believe. He screamed it into his mind, forcing the words into his subconscious. There was not going to be a repeat if he had any say about it.

God help me, Lydia is not going to suffer through this ordeal again on my watch.

These words echoed in his mind.

The thoughts seemed to give him strength. He pictured his brother's face smiling, nodding in support and encouragement. He held the image in his mind until it faded, pulled away from his grasp, until only the expressive green eyes remained, staring questioningly back into his own. When he refocused, he caught his breath. He was staring back into the eyes of his nephew. It surprised him, up until that point, he hadn't realized how similar father and son really were.

***

"It's not you," his uncle broke the solemn silence. He nodded as if he read Gabe's thoughts, then turned and looked in the direction the others had gone. "I'm your dad's brother, I remind her of him." He dropped his head and slumped his powerful shoulders as if taking on another burden. "You remind me of him." His uncle's comment had caught him by surprise. Dan raised his blue eyes to meet Gabe's and released a heavy sigh. He narrowed his eyes as he looked past Gabe towards the open door. Gabe saw his whole demeanor change in seconds. He had surprised him again. His uncle was a bit more complicated than he thought.

Gabe looked on. He felt the excitement welling up within himself. He tried to read Dan's emotions but fell short. His uncle had kept his thoughts to himself.

What's he trying to say?

Gabe struggled to piece together the last few minutes. There was something strangely familiar about the whole scene unfolding in front of him.

"The anniversary of your father's death is in a few days." his uncle's voice crinkled, laced with emotion. He nodded without taking his eyes from the doorway. "I haven't seen her like this, since...," he said, his voice tapering off.

Gabe nodded, he understood exactly what he meant. "Since my father's death."

Dan nodded in agreement.

Something was definitely happening. It now involved him, the son of the man that nobody wanted to really talk about.

Gabe felt like he'd been jolted by lightning. His senses were running wild. At first he felt relief because it wasn't just he who was making his mother upset. It was related to the passing of his father. She couldn't let him go. But then his feelings began to change, a building hollowness burned from within. It was then that he felt the cold breeze, a tickle along the back of his neck, a tingle in the tips of his fingers. He turned to face the morning light that played upon the overcast skies. The sun was struggling to chase away the wispy clouds that clung desperately to the surrounding hillside. The battle was for nothing; in this Monday morning of March the sun would inevitably win. Gabe took in a deep breath and gave out a loud sigh. Today, he wondered which side the sun was on.

CHAPTER TEN
THEY WALK AMONG US
(MONDAY MORNING)
MARCH 14TH2000

The young, blond curly haired man studied the flock of little house sparrows that congregated not more than half a stone's throw away. He saw them clearly from the wooden bench where he sat. They hopped and fluttered nervously around the life-size statue of Saint Francis of Assisi that graced the edge of the lily-covered pond. At first, they seemed oblivious to his presence. They pecked and fluttered nervously like birds at a feeder, their little dark eyes searching in his direction, looking beyond him.

He smiled back, pleased with himself for he knew they couldn't see him. He was all but invisible to most. His thoughts wandered as freely as he moved back and forth between heaven and earth. The birds were like children. These simple creatures lacked the ability to focus. Unlike humans, animals learned to trust their instincts, their genetic make-up to help them survive.

But humans, on the other hand!

He sighed deeply. Most of the humans he walked among no longer seemed to know that the gift of instinct ever existed. Yes, he would admit there was a handful that still did; that made things a bit more interesting. But all in all, if things didn't change, if humans didn't focus on those fading skills, they would soon lose those skills forever. And in turn, much like the word of dinosaurs barely hinted upon by the bible, they would become another incomplete layer in the fossil record.

He stretched his arm into the air, mirroring the hand position of the bronze statue. He knew Francis, the incarnation of a man whom the humans declared a saint, a behavior to imitate. He witnessed his struggle through life and on several occasions, assisted during difficult times on behalf of the creator. In the end, he escorted him to the heavens when he passed. The likeness of the statue was all wrong. A mistake magnified over the centuries. The part they did get right though was his love for God, love for people, and his understanding of animals.

The hair cut!

The young man willed the birds to himself. They came one by one until the flock surrounded his translucent figure. Them, not knowing why, but feeling the need to do as requested. Drawn to where he sat, they spread around his feet and onto the bench, some seeking nervous refuge in the surrounding shrubbery. They bobbed and tilted their heads, searching with their little eyes for what drew them there. He willed them closer yet, letting his thoughts run free as well. The animals of earth had a common thread; they were always searching, always following the ones next to them.

He wondered about touch, pain and pleasure, the very senses that directed human choice. The very same that influenced the decision between right and wrong.

Choice.

He watched generations of suffering, mostly at the hands of the Devil, but sometimes by the will of God. A few martyrs suffered for so many. It was the way of things. The rules were written by those who didn't have to follow them, a process the humans quickly accepted as a way of life and were therefore too easily lead astray.

The morning sunlight played against his shoulder length, blond curly hair. His young handsome smile glowed with tender confidence and understanding. His slender hands blended well with his white, well-fitting robe that accented his masculine physique. The robe moved as if it were alive, pulsing in a breeze of its own.

Magnificent!

He couldn't always control his robe, sometimes when the angle of sunlight hit it just right, the light refracted, separating the rays of light into the colors of the rainbow. It was beautiful. Sometimes he did it on purpose just to enjoy its beauty. And occasionally, like now, his robe sought out the beauty from the sun itself.

A flash of light caused some of the birds to jump and fly to the safety of the surrounding brush, while others drew in closer, mesmerized by the scene, the feel of the warmth against their feathers. He noted how animals and humans were so different, but yet so very similar when it came to situations like this. Regretfully, he moved slowly to extinguish the prism so as to not scare the birds or give away his position. He consciously looked around, wishing to remain undetected. To his satisfaction, only the birds had seen. He again remained still once the light had faded to from whence it had come.

He was immortal, created in heaven, given names like *Trons*, *Dominions*, *Principalities*, *Powers*, and *Authority*. He was from the ranks of angels, created from the image and likeness of God. They were human-like in a way in that they were all individuals, but all different like the intricate pattern of every snowflake. The prophets through the centuries had called them *Stars*, *Princes*; *Sons of God*, *The Holy Ones*, and even *God!* He wasn't arrogant enough to embrace the title of the Creator, like his brother, but others of his kind had. Much like humans, they exercised free will, they made a choice. Fallen Angels, they had been called. *Demons... God's Monkeys.* They battle for the dominion over the earth to influence choice. Good versus evil... to win favor with God.

Angels, fallen or not, act as messengers and prevent humans from doing some things while allowing them to do others. They have the power to control the elements of nature. They are watchers and protectors. Upon his command, they become God's executioners. They tend to sickness and deaths of creatures here on earth; guide their souls to their maker. God sends his angels to do his bidding.

And such is the reason why I am here now!

He is watching, protecting, mirroring Gabe's every move and when the time is right, when God allows him to step in and do his bidding with his mercy, only then will he act.

When he looked again, he found the chirping birds now perched on his arms again. No longer cautious and fearful, their imaginary perch stretched down the length of his robe, across his shoulders, arms and legs. Though they couldn't see him, they gripped his robe and hands with their tiny feet. He looked over to the statue of Francis and smiled. He and the friar were now the same. Much like the statue, he could only imagine the painful and pleasurable sensation of touch. He held still and savored the moment.

To experience what it would be like to be human, but yet for only a minute moment in time.

The translucent figure caught the squeak of the back door first before the birds.

They are here!

He turned his head to see Gabe and Dan step out of the doorway and onto the porch. Gabe's head was down; he was in deep thought, oblivious to what was around him. Dan was looking around the yard, his eyes searching, his mind trying to understand. Dan first glanced over to the statue and then to the bench. He then looked away, but only for a second. Dan's gaze immediately returned. He tilted his head. He appeared to be silently searching for an explanation for something he might have noticed.

The angel moved from under the weight of the birds. Startled, they fluttered noisily in every direction, matching the movement of the approaching humans. Gabe looked up but was oblivious to anything unusual. Dan, on the other hand narrowed his eyes, stepped around Gabe and stared as he moved closer. The angel's action didn't go unnoticed. The angel wasn't that concerned. He knew Dan and his abilities. He respected the fact that he wasn't like most other humans and, had proved it many times before. Though he didn't possess the abilities of his younger brother, Gabriel, he would serve nicely as a guide for his nephew until the time was right. Unknown to Dan, he had taken on an incredible responsibility. Much rested on his ability

to prepare his nephew for his journey. He had very little time. The angel slowly rose to his feet amongst the confused birds, his eyes never leaving those of Dan. He knew the moment when he was seen. He read it in Dan's expression; he read it in his body language. He nodded and smiled like he had done several times before. He projected a thought and then words. He installed a blessing and then he disappeared from sight. Though he wasn't seen, his presence was felt.
Dan can't afford to fail.

***

Dan just about pushed Gabe out of his way when he brushed past him. He wanted to blink and pinch his side to reassure himself of what he thought he saw, but he knew there wasn't enough time. It was just like the times before, when you think you see something, but by the time what you have seen registers in your thoughts, it's all gone, the moment has passed. A figment of one's imagination... just another hallucination brought on by stress and wishful thinking.
Yeah, that's what it is!
A second ago their going out back had spooked the birds that were perched on something that was no longer there.
A silhouette of a man... no, more like the outline of brightness shaped in human form.
His skin prickled at the thought. He had seen many things he couldn't explain. So far, he found that the best way to deal with it was to ignore it, pretend like it never happened. It helped him retain a bit of the sanity that he recently had felt slipping through his fingers during these days of doubt and confusion.
The birds scattered, but for a moment the light remained motionless, almost as if staring back. It had a strange familiarity about it. His mind momentarily flashed back to his brother, back to Gabriel's smiling, knowing face, that expression he had when a secret was burning in his thoughts. A strong warmth flushed Dan's cheeks and neck. It ran down the length of his fingers, tingled his toes. His gaze followed the length of his arms to his

fingers. He fought the tears building in his eyes; but it was useless. His emotions weren't superficial. They ran deep.

His legs stumbled to a stop as his eyes locked onto the bench. He scanned its length and then back to what had drawn his thoughts. Then for a moment, he saw the outline of soothing eyes looking back. They reflected caring words. He searched his thoughts.

I've seen those before.

This time he intentionally blinked to clear his mind. Despite his best effort, tears slid down the sides of his cheeks.

'Don't be afraid!' echoed in his thoughts and between his ears. It made him jump in surprise. He didn't quite understand why, but he grinned back at the empty bench. The feelings were coming back quickly. He had indeed experienced this before, but so had his brother. His heartbeats increased along with his breathing.

His body shuddered uncontrollably, for a moment. He stumbled to catch his balance, and tried to control his breathing. It was so very much unlike him, to be so easily overcome by a thought, a feeling.

I had seen so much and built my protective wall so thick and high. How and why do I see this?

He suddenly felt safe and that everything was going to be all right. That despite how it might have looked or how he might have felt, God hadn't abandoned him or his family. He had not abandoned his brother. Unlike his sister in-law, he fought hard against blaming God for all that had happened.

When he focused again it was all gone. Though he didn't see it as he searched the yard with his eyes, he still felt the divine presence. It was watching, guiding, inspiring. He was not to carry this burden alone. It was his job to see that Gabe understood the importance of the next couple of days. The anniversary of his brother's death was more than just a date to try to forget. He could feel it. The strange uneasy feeling was once again growing in his soul.

Was it Gabe's responsibility to take up the torch? Was I to continue where my brother left off?

His brother's work wasn't finished, it would never be finished.

Was Gabe to be the hero and was he to be the sidekick?

The thought frightened him.

Was it supposed to be an honor... to relive the horrors? Embrace the nightmares?

"Is something wrong?" Gabe's voice broke into his thoughts.

He turned to see his nephew searching his eyes for an understanding. Dan shook his head and forced a smile. "No, no, it's fine... I'm fine!"

He saw the confusion in his nephew's demeanor. Gabe new things weren't *fine.*

"Do you believe in guardian angels?" Dan asked, seemingly out of the blue.

Dan felt his trademark blank expression return to his own face as he studied Gabe, shifting his gaze from one eye to the next. Gabe appeared to be unaware of the visitor who Dan had been sure was there.

Gabe just stared at him.

Just like Gabe's father, it would take him a while to understand, what was to be asked of him. With the anniversary in the next couple of days, there wasn't much time to make the connection.

Gabe slowly nodded. Dan saw the confusion on his nephew's face.

"Alright, that's good for starters!" Dan agreed, and then gazed about the yard. He heard the pride in his own voice. He refocused on Gabe, "Because they believe in you!"

To Dan's surprise, Gabe looked back towards the empty bench.

***

"They?" Gabe spoke his thoughts out loud as he stared inquisitively at his uncle. It was as if Uncle Dan had shifted gears in mid conversation.

Do you believe in guardian angels?

His uncle's words echoed in his thoughts.

Yes, there is definitely something going on around here! But guardian angels? The alley, the locker room... my dad's journal, showing up the way it did... falling open to that spot!

"Dan!" he cleared his throat, "how come you haven't told me more about my dad?" his voice was calmer than it had been all week. He was being careful not to set his uncle on edge. Dan was in a talkative mood, the last thing he wanted to do was ruin the flow.

Now if I could just keep him talking!

"I've told you a bit about your dad already... scholarly, landscape gardener extraordinaire." Dan smiled as he gestured his hands towards the backyard. The smile was spontaneous but disappeared as soon as it had arrived. "He was a man of action, a hero, a cool brother, and most importantly a loving husband and father." Dan shrugged his shoulders. His tone ended quickly as if he had either run out of words to say or the unthinkable had forced its way back into his thoughts.

The hero thing again!

It was the fact that Dan had rattled it off with little emotion, like he had repeated the phrase numerous times before; that really ticked off Gabe. He crossed his arms, bit his lip and stared down at the ground as he struggled to remain calm and attentive.

Here we go again...

"I thought you said things were going to be different?" his voice almost sounded cross. He reminded himself that his uncle was also struggling with the strangeness of the whole scene as well.

He followed Dan's eyes as he gazed about the yard.

He's doing it again... always looking for something, or someone?

"Dan, are you sure you're alright?" he studied Dan's face closely, waiting for him to give something up. Just for a moment he thought he saw a crack in the firewall, a chink in his armor, but then, just like that, it was gone.

Dan took a few deep breaths before he spoke. "Gabe, what do you say we take a load off over there on the bench." The softness of his uncle's voice surprised him.

Gabe watched his uncle stroll over to the bench. Though he carried himself with grace and power, there was a troublesome burden on his shoulders. Gabe couldn't possibly imagine what he was thinking.

Dan had already sat down before he got there. Gabe saw his blue eyes studying him, boring holes into his thoughts. Gabe stopped just out of arm's reach. Even with his uncle sitting, he still seemed relatively tall.

"Sit down, please." Dan patted the side of the bench next to him and forced a smile. The gentleness had once again returned to his voice. His eyes were no longer critical.

Gabe sat down noisily next to him, trying to hide the strange fear that lay within himself. He didn't know why, but it was the look that his uncle gave him. *'Be careful what you ask for'* he had often heard people say. Now he knew what they meant.

"You sound a lot heavier than you look!" Dan grinned, patted him affectionately on his shoulder and then looked away. The distant, faraway look had returned.

Gabe grinned and sunk backwards against the seat back of the bench just like he had always done. Now was when he usually got a predictable lecture from his mom about slouching, but not this time. He looked around just in case, to reassure himself. Dan also leaned back against the rest and gave out a heavy sigh.

Gabe smiled.

For a moment they both silently stared at the Saint Francis statue that stood across from them. He didn't know exactly why, but the statue reminded him of his father. The man who created the park-like setting that graced his large back yard that was built for them instead of a swimming pool. He loved to sit there and stare at the pond, watch the turtles poke their cautious heads above the surface and then haul their reptilian bodies onto the logs and rocks to sun themselves. The songbirds echoed in the background. The warmth of the sun felt good against his face and hands. He momentarily closed his eyes to avoid the low-angle morning sunlight.

"What does this statue remind you of?" Dan asked, so matter of fact.

Gabe opened one of his eyes and looked over to Dan, his stare remained on the statue. "The statue?" He knew it was what he meant, but needed comforting reassurance from his uncle.

"Yes, what does *it* remind you of?"

Gabe cleared his throat, and then after a moment's hesitation he answered, "My father." He almost regretted the words as soon as he had spoken them.

"Why is that?" Though Dan continued to eyeball the statue, Gabe could feel his uncle's thoughts boring into his own.

Gabe shrugged as he continued too stared back at the statue. "He was the saint for Ecologists, talked to animals...." Gabe rolled his response back like a pre-planned speech.

Dan nodded as he continued to stare straight ahead.

He felt his uncle's gaze finally shift from the statue to him. This time, when Gabe turned, he was met by Dan's inquisitive smile. For a moment, he thought he had given the wrong answer.

His uncle nodded. "It reminds me of your dad, too."

A sudden relief flowed through Gabe.

"But, the haircut?" Dan shook his head as he squinted back towards the statue. "Your Dad would never have worn it that way," he laughed. "I don't think the Friar Tuck will ever come back into style in my life-time. I remember when your dad first installed that statue." He pointed to the statue and chuckled.

'What's with the St. Francis statue?' I asked him. He said that, *'Outside of Mother Nature, he couldn't imagine any other choice to oversee this place in his absence'*. He was right." Dan narrowed his eyes like he was examining the statue. "It does a bit more than a forest gnome, don't you agree? You know, that chubby, little cone hat wearing little guy." Dan laughed hysterically at his own attempt at humor as he simulated rubbing a large belly with his hands.

"Yeah, well," was all Gabe could say. It was always embarrassing to be the only one laughing at your own Dad joke, but his uncle didn't seem to care. It was obvious that he was stalling, buying himself some time, and warming up for a serious talk. It was his way.

Gabe let him.

"This place is great. He's brought a little wilderness to your back door. Nice!" Dan patted Gabe nervously on his shoulder, his eyes now focused on Gabe's. "Your Dad immersed himself in everything he did—"

"Why did you ask me about angels?" Gabe calmly interrupted.

"Angels... because they're everywhere, you know!" Dan shot a quick glance through the yard before he continued in a quieter tone. "They're even here with us this very moment!"

Gabe raised an eyebrow and gave him a disbelieving grin. "Was that what you were looking for in the yard?" he teased.

"Really!" he pointed towards the back door and nodded. "Didn't you see those birds scatter when we first went outside?"

"Yeah!"

"Did you see what they were perched on?"

"The bench?" Gabe guessed. The truth was, he had no idea. Yes, he saw the birds scatter, they always did when you surprised them. Besides, his thoughts were elsewhere.

"The bench? Oh, you've got to be kidding me!" Dan almost sounded disappointed. "They weren't on the bench; they were on the extended arm and shoulders of something *sitting* on this bench." Dan patted the bench with one arm and raised the other like that of the St. Francis statue. He nodded in the direction of the back door.

Gabe shifted his gaze between the statue, his uncle, and the back door before he raised the other inquisitive eyebrow. He wasn't sure if his uncle were serious or not. He was suddenly becoming too difficult to read, too hard to follow.

Dan chuckled.

"You're about as bad as your dad was when the stuff first started happening around him," his voice squeaked with excitement. "The apple doesn't fall very far from the tree sometimes, no-sir-re!" Dan used the index finger on his right to count the fingers on his left. "One! What about that light in the alley you told me about? It chased those people off, didn't it...

made everything all right? You said it yourself." He paused momentarily before he counted his second finger. "Two! What about your blond friend that, apparently everyone else can see but you? This blond kid, what does he look like? Oh, wait a minute, let me guess! He's close to your age, muscularly built, long wavy blond hair, blue eyes, fair complexion, soft spoken, and well-groomed with an over-powering confidence. He wears a white robe and has this divine essence about him!"

Gabe studied him closely for a moment. Dan's description was pretty close to what his friends had said except...

But how did he know that? I hadn't told him anything about it!

Gabe narrowed his eyes. "They say he wasn't wearing a white robe!" Gabe blurted out defensively.

"Okay, I'll give you that one, maybe he carries a change of clothes. They don't always appear in their purist form, white. The fact is, that they can appear to anyone at any time dressed just like you and me or worse...," Dan paused a moment, "your neighbor, a kind man on the street, maybe even a wino at a bus stop!"

"He wasn't wearing wings!" Gabe snapped back, "all the angel stories have those guys wearing wings—"

"Forget the wings, that's Hollywood! I have yet to see wings!"

Dan's response had caught him by surprise.

Yet to see wings! What is he saying?

"Three!" Dan continued, still using the same dramatic counting method with his finger. His voice was stern and loud. "The sudden appearance of your father's journal, a forgotten book that had been hidden in the attic for nearly ten years, and if it wasn't your mother, then who dug it out of the attic? Who put it there on the desk in your moms study for the both of you to find?"

"I didn't put it there!" his voice defensive.

"I didn't say you did." Dan paused a moment to let his words soak in. His voice was suddenly calm, filled with tenderness. "You told me you were drawn to it, and how it made you feel!"

Gabe's thoughts flashed back to that moment. The feelings of touch, the warmness that flowed throughout, the desire to know more, all were indeed powerful. The power had overcome his mother as well. He suddenly remembered. His dad had talked about his uncle.

Dan knew! He knows more than what he's saying.

"You knew my dad had a journal, but you didn't say anything!" he accused.

Dan just stared at him, his eyes shifting from one eye to the next as if he were looking for more, eyes peering into his soul.

"When were you going to tell me?" Gabe protested. "When were you going to let me know?"

Dan shrugged. "Yes, I knew your dad had been keeping one. He told me, I encouraged it! Your mom encouraged it! Your mom new about the journal, she gave it to him. No, I didn't know what he did with the journal or what he wrote in it. Journals are private affairs! I could only assume that your mom either tossed it out with the garbage or stashed it somewhere." Dan shook his head and threw up his hands. "I had no idea what had happened to the journal. I guess she stashed it! Out of sight, out of mind. Like I said, I had no idea what was written in that thing."

"You mean my dad's journal!" Gabe corrected, his disappointment obvious.

Dan sighed. "Yes, the book in question... the one that holds some of the answers that you're now asking me for," he narrowed his eyes. "The messages that you read, they were for you, weren't they? What are the odds? I'm assuming that the messages your mom found were for her as well. It's beginning to look like your dad wrote those words for the both of you to find. He probably wanted you to understand the importance of what he had been asked to do. He had no choice you know!" Dan took a contemplative moment before the emotions filling his voice again. He cleared his throat and spoke wishfully. "Do you think your dad left me a message in there as well?"

"If you knew so much then, why did you wait until now to tell me?" Gabe burst into tears. It was like he hadn't listened to anything his uncle had said. "Why?"

Dan reached to embrace Gabe but he quickly slid out of arms reach, stood up from the bench and then turned toward the statue. Dan slowly followed him up off of the bench, but kept his distance. Gabe crossed his arms and shivered in the sudden chill. He tried to hide it, but he knew Dan was reading him like a book.

"I'd made a promise, to your mother. I've honored that promise for going on ten years now. It was the right thing to do then, but the times have changed, the rules are different now. You've changed, we've all changed." Dan looked beyond Gabe and rested his hands on his own hips. "Now I'm freed from those promises." Dan spoke softly. He cleared his throat and paused a moment, as if pulling his thoughts together. "It's my job... my responsibility to prepare you, my dear nephew, for a journey that I myself don't know much about. I owe it to my brother. I owe it to you and your mother." Dan gently placed his hand on Gabe's shoulder.

Gabe didn't move.

"It's time to come clean," said Dan. "About the journal, I will have a talk with your mother. I believe it's just as much hers as it is yours."

Gabe gave his uncle a quick glance. He felt himself warming from within. He turned back towards the statue. He squeezed his eyes tight, took a deep breath, and did something he hadn't done in a long time. He prayed quietly to himself.

Dear God, please help me. What am I supposed to do? What do you want me to do? What does this all mean?

That's when he felt it. The chill faded to warmth. Gabe shot a look back over his shoulder. It was then that he thought he saw something standing next to his uncle, with an arm around his waist, a short distance away. It was clad in a white robe that moved as if it had a life of its own. The subject's blond, curly hair moved in the slight breeze that didn't exist. He thought the figure smiled with deep understanding and concern.

"Don't be afraid!" The words filled Gabe's mind. He suddenly felt safe, like nothing could harm him. He returned the smile. A new strength and confidence had bolstered him; he found the strength he needed to go on.

"I think I see him." Gabe whispered. He blinked to reassure himself. But the figure remained smiling back, looking even more elegant than before.

"Who?"

"The young man, in the white robe, with his arm around your waist!" Gabe whispered as he pointed next to Dan. He turned and took a couple of steps towards Dan and the figure.

Dan turned and looked around. His eyes scanned the area a moment before he shook his head. It was obvious that he didn't see it.

"What?" Dan said.

"You don't see? It's right there...!"

"No, I don't see it; are you toying with me?" Dan smiled as he tapped his chest. "I don't need to see it to know it's there! I can feel it in here. They're always there, watching, guiding, looking after the souls that are in their care." Dan took a few steps forward and firmly embraced Gabe with a long big hug. His eyes began to water. He looked nervously down at his watch. "Well, I hate to break this up but, we don't want you to be late for school on account of me!"

Gabe double-checked his own watch.

School!

He had forgotten all about it. He didn't want to be late, but there were a few more things he needed to know. When he looked up again, the figure was gone. He searched the area with his eyes. It was indeed gone. "It's... gone!"

"Only here," Dan pointed to his eyes, "but not in here!" he gently tapped on Gabe's chest. His uncle's words cut into his thoughts.

Gabe could still feel the warmth within. "Why did my father have to die?" Gabe calmly whispered. He threw his question out for whomever could answer. Gabe held his breath as he watched his uncle carefully, searching his body language. Eyeing the garden Gabe searched desperately for clues that would help him find his answers.

Dan exhaled loudly and scratched the back of his head with his hand. He saw confusion, exhaustion, inspiration and determination. "I don't know, but we'll find out soon enough!"

Dan replied as he nodded to the statue. "I've got the feeling that the answers we seek may be closer than we think."

CHAPTER ELEVEN
MENTORING THROUGH UNDERSTANDING
(MONDAY)
MARCH 14TH 2000

Dan watched Gabe walk away with a bit of spring to his step. "So far so good, I think!" he whispered. He had spoken just loud enough for himself and you know whom to hear. He shot a quick look around, but as expected he appeared to be the only person standing there soaking up the morning warmth.

He heard the slam of the back door, but didn't need to look to confirm that it was Gabe's trademark exit.

"Well, I guess you guardians must have other engagements keeping yourselves busy." He spoke a little louder this time. Deep down inside, he was hoping the angel hadn't left. He could have used the company.

Dan felt he was off to a good start with this mentoring thing, but there wasn't any way that he could calculate his effectiveness. He never had any children of his own. It wasn't that he didn't want any. He did. He had thought about it often, especially recently; but no.

The stork always passes overhead but never seems to land.

He had already accepted the fact that they would never have any children that he could probably live with that-but the final decision didn't appear to be theirs.

This mentoring thing obviously wasn't going to be easy; it was anything but that. He envied his brother and Lydia for producing a son like Gabe. He was a good kid. Mom had done well in the absence of Gabriel. Dan couldn't blame Gabe for wanting to know more about his father. It was a shame that he had to wait until now to tell him the real truth about who his father really was, about his passing, about the incredible things the Almighty had asked of him.

To give up one's life to save a stranger? To set aside your family's needs to put others first? To trust the grace of God to care for your family? To believe whole-heartedly that God was acting in your best interest?

"Wow!" he exclaimed. How was he going to explain this concept to Gabe. "God wants you to save people for him, and one day when you least expect it... you will die in the process!" he whispered.

The total devotion to Jesus Christ.

"Live by the sword, die by the sword!" he exclaimed proudly. The thought made his body shudder and his throat go dry. He had chosen a career where he represented authority. He'd armed himself with weapons and foolhardiness and when danger presented itself, he'd hurried off into its addicting grasp while everyone else fled in the opposite direction. He had made his choice.

For better or for worse, but is it the right choice for Gabe?

The thought brought on a bit of anger.

"Do we choose our life's plan before we're born, then try to fulfill it? If we fail, do we get to do it over until we finally get it right like the beliefs in Hinduism? The quest for eternal truth, Veda's ultimate authority, achieving dharma, acquiring an immortal soul, and reaching moksha... liberating the soul from the cycle of birth and death." He exclaimed loudly as he looked up into the sky. "Or do we just get one shot at it?" He continued to stare expectantly for a moment, waiting for an answer. When none came he felt foolish. He forced a laugh.

Who was God to demand?

He wiped the nervous perspiration from his forehead with his sleeve. He suddenly felt very unsure of himself. Finding the need to sit down, he walked the few steps back to the bench. He took a moment to breathe deeply before he plopped noisily back down in the middle of the bench. He felt better after a couple of slow, deep, calming breaths. He then refocused on Gabe.

As an uncle, he played an important role in the upbringing of his nephew. What he was asked to do was commonplace in many cultures. In some cultures it was the job of the aunt and uncles to provide and see to the education of their nieces and nephews, freeing up the parents so they could provide for the rest of the child's needs. He often thought that at a certain age the children stopped listening to the nagging of their parents. The aunts and uncles were like a breath of fresh air. It was like the grandparents spoiling the grandkids and returning them to the parents. Having no children himself, being a mentor, made this responsibility feel that much greater.

The air no longer felt warm. The sunlight was beginning to fade. He looked up into the sky and noticed the low clouds were making their way inland from the coast that lay nearly ten miles to the west. They brought a chill with them that was overwhelming the warmth of the sun. It surprised him; the afternoon forecast of scattered clouds was early. The building fog had once again proved the weatherman wrong. When he slipped his hands into his coat pockets to help take off the chill, he felt something hard tucked in the bottom. Suddenly remembering what it was, he pulled out the baggy of sweet grass. He retrieved a book of matches from his other pocket, then looked up at the statue and smiled. He suddenly remembered why he had brought it.

"Ah, it's me little brother," he spoke affectionately to the statue, with a simulated, Irish brogue. "I brought ye' a little somethin' to ward off the unwanted slugs, snails and pesky beetles," he laughed; it was what his brother had always said every time he tried to use a new product to battle the garden pests. The thought brought Dan a comforting feeling. He dropped to one knee and laid the herb on the cement pavers in front of him. He struck a lit match to the dried organic fibers. He blew it gently through cupped hands to help it along. When the herb crackled and glowed brightly as it ignited, he shook out the match, dropped it on the ground next to it. The flame virtually disappeared and the sweet grass began to smolder. He closed his eyes and fanned the smoke alive and towards his face with his hands before he sat back noisily on the bench. He rested his arms on the back rest. The growing breeze brought the sweet-scented smell of sweet grass up to his nose. He drew the aromatic fragrance into his lungs, coughed, and interlaced his fingers behind his head. He closed his eyes and let his thoughts roam free. He knew it was the properties of organic chemistry that released the aromaticity of the traditional, aboriginal herb, but there was a spiritual cleansing side to the sweet grass as well. As his mind wandered his thoughts drifted from the technical to the spiritual and then off to a place seldom visited.

It was as if someone had flicked on a switch in his mind to an unpleasant memory. His thoughts flashed back to an awkward experience he had to overcome in the earlier years of his career.

The still, lifeless eyes of a deceased victim stared back into the face of the rescuer who had arrived too late. Battered vehicles littered the highway. An overturned vehicle was on fire, muffled screams echoed amongst the chaos, the surrounding brush was ablaze. Voices yelled for him to stay away. He hesitated. A scream for help echoed from within. The heat of the flames scorched his flesh as he attempted to approach, wrapped in a wet rescue blanket only brought temporary relief. His flesh stung as the heat bit through the wool. It was of no use. The scream faded, the percussion from the blast knocked him off his feet. His ears went silent, fingers of fire reached for him... the smell of chaparral, fuel and burning human flesh filled his lungs. His ears began to ring, his vision blurred, his skin tingled. Then there was the smell of sulfur, the sulfur....

He jolted up straight, his eyes wide open, as he glared down at the smoldering herbs. The remains of a beetle lay singed alongside.

He reached over with his foot and kicked the singed beetle away with the tip of his boot. He sat back heavily into the bench. His body tingled, beads of sweat trickled down his face and back. He ran his fingers through his hair as he looked around and gave a sigh of relief thankful that he was still in the garden. That was so long ago, in the first years of his career.

Why dream it now?

He pulled his arms tightly into his chest and crossed his ankles for warmth from the sudden chill, wishing he wasn't alone.

Flashbacks, post-traumatic, that was some pretty serious stuff. He had read that recessed memories resurfaced when stress infiltrated the system. The process reduced the body's ability to heal, to cope. The process that also released the hidden demons, was triggered by smells, taste, hearing, just about anything the senses could receive and interpret.

The beetle! Was it an omen, a sign of things to come?

The next moment also caught him by surprise. The familiar aroma of conifers and burning embers filled his lungs. He abruptly stood up and turned to find its source. He sighed in relief when he saw the plume of gray smoke gently whisking from the house chimney above. The ladies had started a fire to take the edge off of the morning chill. He stared down at his trembling hands and willed them to stop. When that failed, he balled them into fists and then slid them into his coat pocket. He slumped back farther into the bench.

A slight breeze moved about the leaves in the trees.

This is not normal.

This lack of control bothered him.

"I'm better than this."

A deep, eerie laughter was covered by the building breeze. He abruptly sat up straight and looked about.

The wind?

His skin prickled.

"A little jumpy aren't we?" He spoke out loud to help calm himself, a technique he had learned a few years back. He adjusted his shirt collar and forced a smile, closed his eyes, and filled his lungs with the smell of pine and cedar. "Please help me clear my thoughts... help me find calm," he whispered to anyone who was listening. He readjusted himself on the bench. After a couple of slow, deep breaths, he felt his thoughts clear. He allowed his mind to take a better journey...

> *A campfire burned brightly in the night, the wood popped and snapped as it slowly turned itself into ash. The dancing flames illuminated the silent somber faces of him and his brother. The evening sounds of crickets' serenaded the strange eerie silence. Comforting warmth insulated them from the cool, October evening.*
>
> *They were in deep thought, each trying to share their hidden secrets with the other but not wanting to be the one to go first. That day he wished he had gone last. It was the last time he had seen his brother alive.*

He remembered that day, it was more than ten years ago.

> *He carried within himself his brother's concern. It was a strange, unnerving calmness that floated around the fire that night. It was his brother's dreaded predictions that had pushed him into a world that he had wished never existed.*

It was a place that still haunted him today.

Gabriel knew he was going to die, he practically said so... Did he know what was going to be asked of his son?

Strangely, from time to time, he could feel the presence of his brother. He had occasionally caught a whiff of his brother's favorite cologne. When he felt it, he reassured himself that it was just his brother checking up on him; but deep down inside, he wished the feelings were true. He missed his brother very much. This wasn't the first time either. It was too strange to try to explain it to his wife. He felt it was better to leave the moments unmentioned.

She wouldn't understand.

But that wasn't the only presence he felt or the smells he detected. He knew there were two sides to every coin. And if one side stood for everything happy and righteous, then the other had its meaning and purpose as well.

He wasn't so sure he understood it himself. The Bible talked about guardian angels armies of God's soldiers, sent down to even the odds with the Devil. It was a war, if you will to maintain the balance between good and evil. There were several books in print that shared eye-witness accounts of everyday people being saved from the brink of disaster. Physically moved or guided from disasters path, snatched to safety at the last moment. We call them lucky.

Sometimes these Devine entities were seen and other times they were only felt. As strange as it might sound, sometimes they were not even noticed by the people themselves who were saved. This fact alone reminded him of his brother. It wasn't until the very end that he put it all together.

"And you still went through with it, knowing that you would perish. What were you thinking? Brother, what the heck did you think you were doing?" his own sobbing voice echoed in his ears. He wiped the tears from his eyes and then opened them. He stared at the statue with crossed arms.

"I may have failed you the first time brother," he mumbled under his breath, his dry voice croaking with emotion. "But it will not happen a second time, I promise you that," he apologized. "I will see to your son. I will do everything in my power to see to his needs."

A warm breeze blew his bangs across his face. For a moment, he thought he smelled his brother's cologne.

CHAPTER TWELVE
PREPARATION-BACK TO SCHOOL
(MONDAY MORNING)
MARCH 14TH 2000

"So, when did your uncle arrive?" Erick practically yelled over the noisy students, the curiosity rang in his voice as he shot a quick glance around the hordes of students who were making their way up the narrow front steps of the school entrance.

Gabe's cautious eyes followed. To his relief, most of the students seemed pre-occupied with thoughts of their own as they zoomed noisily past them on both sides, some occasionally bumping them as they nudged past. Others bounded up several steps at a time with backpack in toe. He had no idea what motivated them; the weekend was four days away but felt like a lifetime. He had plans. His uncle said he had something special brewing but wasn't going to disclose it until after he had gotten back home from school. The thought brought a smile to his face. "Early this morning," he exclaimed as he fought the excitement in his own voice, "practically woke us out of bed."

"So he drove all night?" Erick's eyes narrowed as if searching for information.

"No, it took them a couple of days to get here!" Gabe nodded to the large tree that stood a pebble's throw away from the edge of the old stone steps. "Let's talk over there!" He glanced down at his watch; they had maybe ten minutes tops until the second bell, or they would be staying after school longer than they intended.

Erick gave him an agreeable nod, then followed him through the incoming crowd and off to the large, lone budding maple tree. It got noticeably quieter almost at once.

"You were saying?" Erick's voice piped up before they reached the tree.

Gabe turned to face his friend. "They arrived early this morning. I called and left a message for him late Thursday and he called me back early Friday like I've already told you." Gabe smiled as he scanned the area with his eyes one last time. They were finally alone, out of earshot of everyone.

Erick narrowed his eyes as he studied his friend's expression. Gabe could only imagine what was running through that imaginative mind of his.

"He's promised to tell me about my father!" Gabe returned the studying gaze.

"But what about your mom? She—"

"Relented," Gabe smiled, "I guess she put her faith into the hands of my uncle." He shrugged. "They'd been talking for a bit early this morning. He and I went outside and then, there you go!"

"There you go huh?" Erick quizzed, "just like that?" The suspicion was notable in his voice.

"Well, maybe not as simple as that, but things are going somewhere fast, I know it!"

"So what did your uncle say?"

Gabe paused for a moment, looking to the ground for inspiration. "That it wasn't my fault, that my mom was just upset, and my asking the questions about my father—"

"Passing away?" Erick's voice was understanding.

"Yeah, didn't help," Gabe nodded. "That's when I started talking about those strange things that were happening to me. It reminded my mom of the strange things that happened to my Dad."

"Really, like what?"

Gabe shook his head and continued to speak, ignoring his question. He didn't have any answers to that as of yet. All he could do was trust that his uncle would bring things to light when the time was right. His friend remained silent almost as if he had sensed his dilemma.

"Evidently, the tenth anniversary of my father's death, March 16th, is this Wednesday!" he exclaimed.

"That's two days from now!" Erick stated.

"Yeah, I know, kinda' strange, it's like you know, everything is building up to something, and then, I'm about to find out why my father died nearly ten years ago to the day. Wow! I tell you, that's kinda' freaky! I really don't know what to think of it."

"I know what you mean. And then there's all of those things that you said was happening to you."

"Yeah!" Gabe nodded in agreement as he stared at the ground in deep thought. He could feel his friend's eyes boring holes into him as Erick patiently stood there waiting for him to continue.

Erick glanced down at his watch, time was ticking away.

"At first I thought it was me that was making my mom upset!" He forced a nervous laugh. He watched his friend out of the corner of his eye and noticed that his expression hadn't changed. "Every time I asked about my dad's death, she would freak, get angry at me and go off crying somewhere. It was getting worse every day." He gave a heavy sigh. "I don't know how much more of that I can take!"

His friend nodded with concern.

"Evidently, something strange happened to my dad before he..." Gabe paused to swallow, he felt the emotions beginning to build.

"Passed away!" Erick completed his thought.

Gabe nodded. "Well, evidently, they are starting to happen to me." He looked directly at his friend and saw his mouth drop open, but forced himself to continue. He pretend like he hadn't noticed. He had gone from hardly being able to control his excitement to regretting he had ever shared his intimate secret with his friend. He pushed himself along. "The seeing of strange things, the guardian angel thing..." he silently stared at his friend a moment.

Erick was studying him closely through narrowed eyes, shifting from one eye to the other as if searching for truth and understanding.

"Do you think that the kid you've been seeing is, well, possibly a guardian angel, sent down here to keep an eye on me, and keep me out of trouble?" Gabe's words just slipped off of his tongue.

Erick gave him a strange look.

He regretted saying them as soon as he had, but it was too late. He watched Erick closely. If his best friend didn't understand, he was doomed. He knew no one else would.

"Who told you that?" inquired Erick.

Gabe could detect the disbelief in his friend's shaky voice. He shrugged his shoulders casually and looked up into the tree in deep thought. But in reality, he was studying his friend carefully out of the corner of his eye. "It's what my uncle thinks."

"Your uncle believes in angels?" he sounded surprised.

"Yeah! Why not?" Gabe's words just about knocked his friend off of his feet.

"Well, for starters, because there isn't any proof!"

"Proof?" Gabe turned towards his friend with a disapproving stare.

The five-minute school bell went off and caused the both of them to flinch. When they looked back over to the entrance steps, the flow of students had reduced to a mere trickle. Those that remained hurried in an effort to beat the clock. He looked down at his watch. They had less than five minutes to be in class. If they were to leave now, it would only take them about three minutes, at most, including their locker stop. He couldn't leave now; he had to make his point, he had to make Erick understand. It was now or never. He looked back up at his friend who hadn't moved a muscle towards class, either. He was still with him, still listening. Maybe there was hope to make him understand in the next two minutes.

"You don't believe in angels? You've heard of guardian angels, haven't you? What kind of proof do you need?"

"Well, for starters..." Erick was at a loss for words.

"For them to walk right up and introduce themselves to you?" said Gabe, "well, according to my uncle they're out there! Following, observing, protecting, and pulling off all of those miracles that we've been hearing about. Who moved the journal?" he threw his hands into the air, "It wasn't my mother... no one else lives there with us! What about that light in the alley? A vehicle that suddenly disappeared?" he quizzed. He felt the anger building in his voice.

"Ghosts?"

Gabe rolled his eyes when he looked over his shoulder. He forced himself to speak more softly. "My uncle said they protected my father and now, evidently, they're supposed to protect me!" He heard the quivering emotion in his voice.

"Protect you from what?" Erick yelled, "The boogie man!" He forced a laugh.

There was a strange silence between the two of them, Gabe's eyes pleading for understanding, Erick's filled with defiance and confusion.

"Gabe," Erick reached up and slapped him on his shoulder. "But, your father is dead, he died! Where were these so called angels when he needed them the most? If they were protecting him, wouldn't he be alive today? I'm just saying, wouldn't he be telling you those stories himself?"

Frustrated, Gabe gripped the front of Erick's shirt and shoved him away from him with all of his might. The force caught Erick by surprise, knocking him off balance and backwards across the ground.

"Hey... what are you doing?" Erick screamed.

Gabe felt a hot flash across his face, his throat dry, and his arms suddenly weak after the quick exertion. He stepped backwards away from his friend, as tears filled his eyes and streaked down his angry face unobstructed. There was a strange bit of truth to those words of his friend. They bit mercilessly into his soul. A truth he couldn't understand, one he refused to understand. He suddenly hated his friend for stating the obvious. He took a couple more staggering steps backwards, turned and ran towards the school. He tripped, caught his balance with his hands and bulleted towards the school entrance.

Erick scrambled to his feet. "What are you doing? I didn't mean it that way!" he yelled as he watched him leave.

At the base of the stairs Gabe skidded to a stop. He momentarily turned in Erick's direction. "What about that kid... whom you say hangs around?" he screamed in between deep breaths, "the one, I never seem to see." He panted heavily. "Well, I think I saw him this morning. How would you explain that? Huh?" Tears flowed freely down the sides of Gabe's face. "How do you explain that?" he screamed even louder. Gabe stared for a moment before he abruptly turned and bounded up the steps and tore off down the hall.

The image of his friend's surprised expression burned into Erick's mind, as his tears slowly tickling down the sides of his cheeks.

CHAPTER THIRTEEN
SEEING IS BELIEVING –
A TEST OF FAITH
(MONDAY) MARCH 14TH 2000

Erick's eyes focused on the empty stairs, as tears trickled down the sides of his own cheeks. His confusing thoughts not making any sense. He kicked at the ground. "Why am I the one freaking crying?" he whispered. He took a deep sigh, wiped the tears from his cheeks and looked down at his watch He knew he was going to be late.

"See if I care!" he screamed back. He rubbed his throbbing shoulders where his pack, loaded with books, was pressed into his shoulder when his best friend pushed him to the ground. It was strange, his shoulder had never bothered him like this before, but as he was recently finding out, there was a first time for just about everything this week. For a fleeting moment, he thought about sprinting up the stairs after Gabe, hollering his name, and demanding that he apologize for actions unbecoming of a friend. Instead, he just stood there stubbornly under the budding bigleaf maple tree, almost too dumbfounded to move.

What's wrong with him? We have never fought like this before.

"What was this ridiculous argument about anyway?" the words squeaked out of his parched throat in a whisper. "Oh yeah, Angels!" he belted out loudly, "ridiculous!"

He heard the school's final tardy bell echo across the grass. He tensed. Though he knew it was coming, it still surprised him nonetheless. The sound meant that he was officially truant, officially in trouble, but at that moment, he didn't care. The annoying bell told them when to start, when to finish, and where they needed to be throughout the day. Like the *Pavlovian* response, his mouth even watered when it rang for lunch. The bell ruled their lives; it felt good to ignore its command for once. He was sure its irritating sound could be heard from several blocks away. It seemed so final, so surreal.

"Let it ring! I don't care!" he crossed his arms. "It's not controlling me today.

His friend was still in his thoughts, his voice still echoed in his head.

Angels? What did he mean by angels anyway?

He refocused, looked around and watched a couple of the passing cars cruise by, their drivers stared straight ahead, busy with thoughts of their own. Oblivious to his plight, uninterested in a lone boy standing beneath a leafless tree instead of sitting in a classroom where he belonged, a place where he knew he should be now.

A gentle breeze caused the buds of the tree to shake like wind chimes again. Erick couldn't help but look up. It was almost as if the tree was talking in a low whisper. He had heard of this phenomenon before by creeks, caused when water flowed over the rocks in a shallow stream, or when the wind forced its way through sticks. He was well aware that in some cultures the noises were credited to the little people whom they believed lived by the water's edge.

Fairytales, more fairytales!

He reminded himself that there wasn't any running water in sight, but it was always windy in the spring.

Every year, the weather patterns were the same, a light breeze in the morning, with wind gusts by the afternoon. Evidently, today wouldn't be any different, except for the cloud cover.

He smiled as he watched the branches sway and quiver under the winds influence. It made him feel warm inside; his worries almost seemed to melt in the rhythmic tempo of the swaying branches. He closed his eyes and let the breeze caress his face, play with his hair. He let his pack fall to the ground, though he never heard it come to rest. He didn't care. The soreness in his shoulder disappeared immediately. He felt lighter on his feet. His smile grew larger. His worries seemed to drain from his extended hands as he reached up towards the upper branches of the tree. He felt the breezes play with the tips of his fingers. He spread them farther apart and raised his hands as high as he could. He wanted this moment to never end.

The voices in the breeze were clear, the whispers were loud enough to hear. He thought nothing of it at first, until he could clearly hear the mention of his name.

"*E-r-i-c-k A-d-a-m-s*" the caring friendly voice echoed sweetly in his ears and warmed his heart. It burned pleasantly, deep in his subconscious. When he heard it again, the voice sounded closer.

"*E-r-i-c-k A-d-a-m-s,*" the voice was no longer cautious, sounding more determined. The strange, caring warmth about his left shoulder radiated towards his hand. He wiggled his fingers.

"*Erick, do not be afraid.*"

The caring voice from his left startled him; it was so very close. Erick opened his eyes and turned to face the familiar-looking, curly long haired blond kid standing next to him, his hand resting gently on his left shoulder.

Erick turned quickly and stepped away in surprise. He turned and faced the boy. "It's you. You scared me. What are you doing out here?" It was the same boy that sent him back into the gym to talk with Gabe. This was the same boy that he had seen several times with Gabe, the very same boy that Gabe claimed he could never see. The thought made him shudder.

The boy smiled and lowered his hand. "*Sorry, I didn't mean to... scare you!*"

"No, no you didn't!" Erick reacted nervously. He quickly tried to hide his feelings, to make like everything was fine.

"*Your first fight?*" the boy asked.

"Are you late for class, too?" Erick's voice crackled as he gestured a hand toward the front steps.

The boy's smile faded. "*No, I've only been late once!*"

Erick thought it strange that the boy's disappointed frown only lasted for a quick moment, a blur in time.

"I guess we're both going to get it big today then!" Erick gestured.

"*Maybe!*" The boy's thoughtful smile returned.

Erick examined the boy's face carefully, trying to read into what he was seeing and hearing. "Do you know something that I don't?"

The boy nodded.

Erick looked surprised. This boy had some information, and judging by the expression on his face, it was probably some pretty good stuff. "And, you're going to share it, right?" he pleaded.

"*Of course!*" The boy forced an even bigger smile.

"Well then, let's have it!" said Erick.

He couldn't help but look around. Somehow he knew that at any moment Principle Jones would come crashing through the front double doors and find them standing there truant, playing hooky under the tree.

The tree!

It was at that very moment that Erick realized that something wasn't quite right. The thought caused a chill to run the length of his back, his hands to tingle. He double-checked, with another quick glance. His observations were right; the other trees didn't sway in the breeze. In fact the tree they stood underneath was the only one swaying. He took a couple of steps out and away from the drip line of the tree to take in its entirety.

The boy intently watched.

Erick raised a hand to feel for a breeze. There wasn't one. He was right; this was the only tree in the neighborhood that was swaying to a breeze of its own. Erick looked over to the boy and pointed at the tree, but no words seemed to escape his lips.

The boy only smiled and bowed gracefully. "*It is for you.*" His voice was calm and graceful. "*The proof you are looking for.*"

"Proof?" Erick quizzed.

"*There is very little time.*" The boy slowly stepped closer.

Erick didn't move, his legs were practically frozen to the ground.

"You have been chosen to help your friend."

"Gabe?" The words squeaked out of his throat. Erick glanced towards the school entrance.

The boy nodded. *"Yes, your friend, Gabe."*

"Who are you?" Erick found his voice. "What are you?"

"Do you believe in angels?" There were confidence, pride and power in his words.

"Not you too!" At that moment Erick felt all of his energy drain from his body, he had no idea what was keeping his knees from buckling.

Guardian angels?

"You can say that!" The boy smiled.

The words echoed in Erick's thoughts.

"What?" exclaimed Erick, "how did you..."

It was what we were arguing about... the locker room...

It suddenly all started to make sense. "You're an Ange—"

"Angel, yes!" he said so matter of fact.

"Then why is it that I can see you and Gabe cannot?" The words slipped through Erick's lips. He looked around the yard, his eyes confirming that the branches of the tree they stood beneath still moved on its own.

"In the locker room, around school... under this tree. You were gifted with sight."

"What?" Erick stared in surprise.

Is this guy for real?

"As real as this tree!" the boy answered.

"How can you—"

"As I said before, we don't have much time. You will be our eyes and ears," the boy's smile faded. *"You will help us protect Gabe."*

"Protect Gabe, but how? From what?" Erick shook his head in confusion. "Why can't he see you!" he demanded again.

"He has," the boy answered, *"he will."*

"Are you really an—"

The thunderous echo of one of the heavy double doors being jarred from its hold-fast with a mighty tug caused Erick to flinch and look towards the school steps. He felt his throat tighten as he recognized the huge, balding figure standing at the top of the steps with one of the doors firmly in his grip.

"Principle Jones! We're dead!" Erick breathlessly warned, but the boy didn't seem at all bothered by that fact.

Shooting intimidating stares and hunting down violators was what Mr. Jones did best. He rewarded them with quality time in detention. He personally oversaw the punishment as if it were an obligation he was committed to see through. Though Erick had never attended any of the sessions, he heard through the grapevine that they were never *fun*. Frankly, from what he heard, he didn't even know if what Principal Jones made them do in detention was actually legal. Evidently, the students were too frightened to have told their parents.

Too afraid?

He could understand why.

Their parents aren't around to protect them at school!

He felt his heart skip a couple of beats when Principle Jones' eyes fell upon his own. It was too late for him and the boy to hide behind the tree. He couldn't have moved a muscle if he had wanted to; he was frozen where he stood.

The scowl that normally seemed to occupy the principal's expression slowly faded to a concerned smile. "Mr. Adams?" His thunderous voice echoed across the grass.

Erick turned back toward the boy, but the boy was gone. He felt a shiver zip through his body, his fingers tingled. He was abandoned. "Thanks!" he mumbled under his breath.

To suffer the principal's wrath on my own!

"You're never alone!" The soft voice tickled his ears.

He twisted his head, looked behind the tree and searched with his eyes. To his surprise and amazement, the boy was gone. "Where—" He mumbled again.

"Mr. Adams, I'm over here!" loudly exclaimed Principle Jones.

Erick turned in his direction.

"Your mother said you'd be out here, and by her grace, there you are!" The principal threw his beefy arms into the air. "It's an uncanny ability that some parents seem to possess.

Know thy prey!" He stood there proudly, puffing his massive chest out for all to see as he took a mental victory lap.

His actions didn't go unnoticed.

My Mom?

It was as if Principle Jones had read Erick's blank stare.

"Yes, your Mom. She said to send you home once you arrived at school." He spoke slowly, like he had always done when talking to students, like he was speaking to someone who was too slow on the uptake. It was what frustrated many of the other students, and staff, alike about the man.

Can he read minds too?

"No, anticipates!" the gentle voice responded from nowhere.

Anticipates?

The principle silently eyed Erick to make sure he understood before he continued. It was that action alone that made the students dread even being around him. "Are you feeling alright Mr. Adams?" he demanded inquisitively. "You're looking rather, pale. Maybe you should hurry home like a good boy." He nodded and wiggled his thumb in the direction of Erick's home.

Erick felt a sudden verge of panic; it was like Principal Jones knew everything, even where he lived. Erick looked in the direction of his house.

Does he really know where I live?

The thought made him feel even more uneasy. Then there was the strange fact that he apparently wasn't in trouble, with the school which made him feel even more strange.

How did that ever happen?

"I'm... I'm fine!" he waved as he blurted out, hoping the principle didn't notice the nervous squeak in his voice, but it was obvious that he did. As if sensing weakness, the Principal's smile turned into a smirk. That look of a predator stalking its prey had returned.

Erick fought the feeling of panic. He needed to know. "Did my mom say why she wanted me home?" He regretted asking the question as soon as the words left his lips.

"Nope, can't help you with that one." he chuckled. "The school nurse got the call about five minutes ago," his voice boomed loudly. "Asked me to hunt you down." As Principal Jones smiled, he thought he heard a prideful matter of fact tone in the man's voice. "And that I did. I found you, informed you, now I'm sending you on your way young man." He nodded again in the direction of Erick's home. "Why are you still standing there? Your mom's waiting. I told her we would send you home straightaway." He wrinkled his eyebrow into an intimidating scowl. "Let's not make liars out of us now Mr. Adams!"

"No sir!" Erick yelled back timidly, "I mean yes sir!"

"Take care Erick, you do be careful!"

Principal Jones' last words caught him off guard. For a split second he thought that he almost cared. Erick's thoughts raced as he strained to decipher the meaning of this odd exchange. They both seemed to stare at each other for a lengthy moment.

Principal Jones raised an eyebrow. "That means *now* Mr. Adams!" His demanding voice echoed across the yard. "Let's get a move on, time waits for no one, especially you!" He pointed a beefy arm at Erick.

Erick turned away and scrambled for his backpack. By the time he heard the loud clank of the second door being pulled free of its holdfasts he was at the edge of the pavement.

He shot a glance back to the steps in time to see the principal give one last look around the steps before he slammed the doors noisily shut, sealing the other students to their fate. The sound echoed across the grass like a starter gun, sending a flock of nearby birds off into the air and Erick on his way.

His feet no longer seemed cemented to the ground. They were free. Something was different; it was more than being free from the custody of the dreaded Principal Jones.

The breeze!

He raised his hands into the air and squinted into the sunlight. The air around the tree was still, the budding leaves hung lifeless, they no longer moved with a life of their own. He looked around, but the boy was still gone. It was like he had never been there at all. "Angels!" Erick blurted out loud, half expecting the boy to materialize out of nowhere to answer. He took a deep sigh and listened for a moment, searching the neighborhood with his eyes. The pack slung over his shoulder felt weightless, the soreness of his shoulder gone.

Angels!

At first the thought made him giggle, but then he remembered his mother.

Is everything alright at home?

He took one more deep breath and turned in the direction of home. His brisk walk soon found a determined run.

CHAPTER FOURTEEN
BEYOND DOUBT
MARCH 14TH 2000

Lydia sat there in her study, her hands resting one on top of the other. Her palms and forearms lying flat as she leaned on the edge of the desk. Her chin resting uncomfortably on the back of one of her hands, her stomach moving in and out with every slow breath. Through her teary eyes she stared at the forest scene tooled into the cover of the leather bound journal, her thoughts, as far as she was concerned, were a lifetime away.

Why did this have to happen to me at all? What did I do to deserve this?

It wasn't the first time she had asked these questions, over the last ten years, and she knew it probably wouldn't be the last. She was always waiting, always listening, and trying to find an understanding of a subject that probably wasn't meant to be understood.

This time of year was always tough for her. Wednesday would be the worst. It was the tenth anniversary of her husband's passing. A *turning point*, they call it. They, being the people who make a living trying to understand people's miseries, probably trying to understand their own at the expense of others. These were people she wouldn't normally share her innermost self with; but she was desperate. Despite the anxiety, the reliving of her husband's passing had caused, she had always told herself she felt better. However, it was this cursed anniversary thing that had turned her life upside down. Year after year the smells, the feelings, they were all getting stronger; and now there was the journal that showed up out of the blue after almost ten years.

Could he be speaking to me through the journal? Could he be speaking through his brother?

The thoughts made her shiver, her throat go dry.

What about my son? What possible role could he play in all of this?

Her head began to throb again. She was thinking too hard.

She refocused her eyes on her watch. It was well after eight in the morning. Erick was already at school. At least he would have some normality to take his mind off the problems at home. Dan and his wife were in the other room.

What would I have ever have done without them?

Her appointment with Dr. O'Toole, the family psychologist, wasn't until nine. She had time just to sit there and wait for the courage to reopen the journal, to dive once again into the secrets of the past.

It suddenly hit her as her thoughts drifted back to the journal; she had known Gabriel longer in death then she had in life. It was a bizarre way to look at it, but she was still finding a way to cope.

Was the good doctor right?

Three weeks ago she had made a decision of her own; the tenth anniversary was going to be it, no more reminding, no more rekindling. She needed to move on, they needed to move on.

But, then this!

"If you are truly there, then help me understand!" she spoke softly. She could hear the delicate tenderness in her quiet whisper, "Help us all understand." She folded her hands and weaved her fingers together in prayer. She closed her eyes and carefully listened to every word she formed in her thoughts.

She had spoken to God every day, but never really knew if he heard, or for that matter if he ever listened to what she was saying or asking.

With billions of people making constant requests at the same time, how could mine ever get through?

As a young girl, she had always imagined a switchboard with angels working as operators, prioritizing the requests based on an ever-changing criteria of needs and wants that was updated every hour. Those requests deemed less important sank to the bottom. Though she believed she had been forgotten by the wayside over the last ten years, she hadn't given up hope. She still believed that someday her prayers would eventually be answered. It was what she had been taught.

Praying was something she did often, more out of the routine she had inherited as a cradle Catholic. She remembered the nuns telling her that *'songs sung from the heart had greater power than words recited from the lips'*. She didn't know why, but she started to hum. It was out of practice and out of tune at first, but after a couple of tries, she was able to blend her notes into a more pleasant sound. She didn't recognize the melody as any particular song she knew, but that didn't seem to matter. The fact that she was humming again made her feel better. It surprised her; she hadn't done this in almost ten years. It was something Gabriel teased her about, but she had known it was something he had liked. When he passed, so had her desire, the joy to hum and sing. She had tried to hum again a few years ago, but it ended in disaster. It just didn't feel right, with bad memories, bouts of depression and tears, in an ugly combination.

Not now, not ever again!

But that was all ancient history. To her surprise, she felt stronger than she had in a very long time. The negative thoughts drained easily away, faded without even a fight. It only added to her strength, to the new power and control that emanated from within. It was an incredible feeling, unstoppable.

Could I accomplish anything?

Yes, today was different; she could feel it from her fingers down through her toes. The strange tingly warmth flowed through to her entire body, a renewed, unfamiliar strength.

She slid her hands until she felt the cold leather touch against her skin. Her body flinched and stopped; the sudden coolness surprised her. The journal had never felt like that before. It was usually warm and inviting. It now seemed to create a whole new feeling of dread and confusion.

She opened her eyes and forced her hands to remain in place as she gazed upon the leather bound book. For a strange moment, she felt as if she were engaging a person in that very room.

But how could that be?

She looked back toward the closed door; it was just as she had left it. The faint conversations of her friends, heard intermittently over the fluctuating volume of the television, leaked beneath the small gap under the door. Her guests were down the hall and in the living room, no doubt deep in conversations about what to do with her. The sound of the television most likely used to cover their words; it was something she would have done, a technique she had herself used in the past. The thought depressed her, but she fought it off with a deep sigh. She turned her attention back to the journal.

Then suddenly, she could smell him, just as she had done periodically throughout the week. The essence was stronger this time. It was Gabriel, she was sure of it! There were certain things that she would never forget and this was one of those. The very thought sent a chilling ripple through her entire body. She fought the urge to pull away from the journal and leave the room. Her feet had decided to stay. The sweet smell of incense had never been so powerful. She thought hard for a moment.

This is new, never to this extent. Was it a message? Was it my imagination?

"Gabriel?" her soft voice squeaked with frightful curiosity. It took her a moment to recognize the voice as her own. The quiet room pressed on a nerve. "Not this time!" her voice cut through the silence. "May God be my witness, today you will tell me your big secret!" She heard the calm confidence in her own voice and felt the unyielding in her demeanor. "It's the tenth anniversary of your passing, your son and I need to know why this is happening." She felt the tears fill her eyes, her throat tighten, the anger well up within her. "You at least owe us that much! I have not forsaken you. Why have you forsaken us?" she let her words linger. "You're in my thoughts. You still dominate my life." She burst into passionate tears, but still fought to keep her voice a whisper. She didn't want the others to hear. "I have tried to move on, but I can't. You were taken from me. You were taken from us, why? I demand to know why!" her last words were louder yet.

Her emotional words cut deeply. She felt them. They were wrong; she knew it as soon as they left her lips. "I am sorry!" she exclaimed, as she closed her eyes, bowed her head and loudly palmed her forehead several times in frustration. "I do not know where they come from."

She gave a deep sigh and folded her hands on top of the journal. She moved her elbows apart and let the side of her cheek rest on the top of the desk. She suddenly thought it silly to be apologizing to an empty room about something that she needed to say to clear her conscience, to settle her soul. Her shrink would have been very proud of her ability to exert herself.

My shrink!

She opened her eyes only long enough to look down at her watch. She still had a good thirty minutes. It felt good to close them again.

Still living by the watch Lydia!

She imagined the doctor's voice. The thought made her smile. She felt better.

The warm feeling began to grow. The love for her brother and sister-in-law burned deeply into her soul. Her love of her son, his understanding and patience for all they had gone through made her thoughts sink deeper. She imagined the smiling face of her husband, his green, caring eyes of understanding looking deep into hers. She imagined the twinkle of anticipation, the look he always had when he could no longer suppress a secret. The tears dribbled down the sides of her cheeks and landed quietly onto the top of the desk. The faint sound echoed in her ears. Her senses were becoming more acute by the minute.

The sweet, aromatic smell suddenly grew stronger. It was almost as if he *were* standing right there, in front of her.

Oh, how I miss you, if only things could have been different. If only you were really here.
"*Lydia,*" the soft, familiar voice echoed in her thoughts.
Is it too late to call the doctor's office and cancel?
She had already made her mind up to make this visit her last. She could have easily made the call, but she needed to end this the right way. They had been together for nearly ten years. Her doctor deserved better... she deserved better.

From now on, I'll leave the journal here on the desk so I can pray and read. Why hadn't I read the journal sooner? Yes, maybe I'll even let Gabe read it, so he can learn about his father. It isn't too late is it?

"*Lydia.*" She heard the voice again, this time it was louder, more determined. It reverberated down her spine and into her subconscious. She felt a cool, gentle touch on her arm. It surprised her. She pulled her arm away, opened her eyes and, let out a muffled scream as she jumped up from the chair, knocking it over as she moved away from what felt like an invisible hand touching her arm.

"Gabriel," she gasped. She just stood there, her mouth open, not able to speak. The same eyes she had just imagined were staring back into her thoughts. A blue, translucent figure materialized just out of arm's reach.

"Gabriel?" She found her voice. "But, you're...."
She felt a confirming thought.
She nodded stiffly. "But how?" She looked towards the door. It was still closed. The room suddenly seemed brighter, a strange warmth emanated from the figure. She squeezed her eyes shut and opened them again. To her surprise the figure was still there.

"*Do not be afraid!*" a steady, comforting voice came from her far left.

She abruptly backed into the desk and faced a well-built young man with blond, long curly hair. His delicate smile, his tender, loving, pale blue eye's; his light colored clothes, almost seemed to give off a radiant light.

"*The messengers have been sent to bring you comfort, to tell you what is to come.*" The figure bowed its head.

"Messengers... what...?" she shifted her confused gaze between the two figures, one a young man, and the other of a glowing blue translucent light. Baffled and at a loss for words, she stood there unable to speak. She only managed to take two cautious steps toward the translucent figure before she abruptly stopped.

Can it be?

"Gabriel?" she froze in place, let her arms fall lifelessly down to her sides. Tears streamed down her cheeks and her body convulsed with every sobbing breath. The light almost seemed too bright.

"*You're so beautiful.*" The figure's gentle voice emanated from the translucent light. The entity drifted towards her, her eyes studying it closely. She backed noisily into the desk again as the blue light engulfed her. At that moment, her body began to shiver. She closed her eyes and remained still. It felt safe and comforting. She felt his touch and immediately desired more; joy bubbled from within. "It's you!" she squeaked.

Is this really happening?

She allowed herself to be taken in by this. She immediately felt his warmth, an energizing tingle that came from the touch, a renewed energy that came from the embrace. A storybook joyfulness filled every muscle, every nerve. It was like every worry she ever had suddenly disappeared. Nothing else in the world seemed to matter.

"Is this really be you?" she whispered.

She kept her eyes closed and breathed in deeply as if processing every thought, testing every clue. It was his smell all right, as if taken right from her memory file.

She opened her eyes again and quickly attempted to return the embrace to the apparition with her trembling arms. To her surprise and disappointment, her reach fell upon emptiness as if attempting to catch mist.

"Is it really you, have you come back?" she regretted the words as soon as she had spoken them. She knew that could never happen. She lowered her arms. "But you're dead!" She felt the shiver rip through her body like an electrical charge.

It was her desire for him that brought him before her now. The feeling of his embrace, his smell, his mere presence, she wanted it all, to never let him go again.

Is this my mind playing tricks with my desires, my emotional needs?

"*I have come here... watching you... watching Gabe.*" a whisper tickled her ear.

Am I dreaming?

"I felt your presence, but I thought it was...." her outstretched hand slipped through the warm, translucent form again. "The journal?" The thought hit her like a brick.

"*The journal... wanted you to understand!*" the voice pleaded as the apparition appeared to dance and drifted at arm's length. "*Wish there was more time... if only more time! Wanted Gabe to understand... wanted you to understand... breaks heart... to see you so sad... love you so much!*"

The bluish mist faded to nothingness. She stepped forward and reached for what was left but still felt nothing.

Lydia's desperate, gaze shifted back and forth until it found the young man.

"Why can't I touch him? Where did he go? Is this some kind of sick trick?" her confused voice on the verge of anger.

The young man's effortless smile now seemed more tired, an unsteady emotion, hidden behind a permanent mask of understanding. "*He has not gone!*"

She watched him nod and then heard Gabriel's voice continue. She felt an uneasiness building within herself.

"*As a family... we have been blessed... given a special gift.*" The tender voice paused as if to let the words sink in. "*God has seen it as important... I have done what I was meant to do... fulfilled my calling.*" the voice crackled with emotion as it spoke quickly, almost as if hurried along. "*The gifts that were bestowed upon me... are to be bestowed upon Gabe.*"

"No, no, no!" she whispered loudly as she shook her head. "You can't!" The words made her shiver, her stomach turn sickly. She couldn't believe what she just either heard or imagined. The uneasiness began to squeeze her from the insides. Her eyes began to water.

"What are you saying? Is Gabe to become... a ghost?"

"*He will be looked after by an army of angels,*" the young man responded calmly and confidently. "*You should not fear the gifts bestowed upon him by the hands of God.*"

His response hit her like a flaming torch.

"What..., how could this even be happening? For ten years virtually ignored. Now this? On the anniversary of Gabriel's death!" her voice exhausted, angered. "This all has to be a dream... a very bad dream! A cruel joke?" expressed Lydia. "Any moment now I'm going to wake up and bring an end to this madness! Angels? Hands of God?" she screamed as she turned towards the young man and stepped back away from where she had last seen the apparition. Disbelief and disappointment flashed in her eyes. She fought through her emotions. "No!"

If this were, indeed, a dream, I could take control of it, redirect it... right?

"The hands of God? Why are you telling me this? I demand to know what is to become of my son?" her words were pointed, demanding. "The same as you've done with my husband?" She stepped forward, accusatory. She moved her hands as if searching for the apparition by touch, to grab. "Where was your army of angels then, huh?" She pointed accusingly to the young man who now stood there silently staring at her. Concern contoured his face. The slight movement of one of his eyebrows was the only outward sign that he was at all affected by what she had said.

"Where were the angels when my husband needed them most? For that matter, where were you?" she pointed. "After all he had done for *you*... you let him die. *You* took him away from his family! Away from us!" she screamed, she felt the rage welling from within. "How can that possibly be the work of *God*?" She quickly filled her lungs and continued. "You get out of here... you get out of my house! You get out of my head!" she grabbed the side of her head with both of her hands. "Get out of our lives!" She covered her ears with the palms of her hands. "And take this damn journal with you, it doesn't belong here. You, don't belong here!" In anger, she swept her trembling hand across the desk and aggressively slid the journal in the direction of the young man and onto the floor. It landed at the foot of the young man, open and face down.

The young man's eyes followed.

This time, to her satisfaction, she saw a noticeable twitch in the young man's eyebrow as he shifted his gaze between her and the journal.

"Take it back! I don't want it anymore." she screamed.

'Now that I finally got your attention.'

"What?" she responded to the voice in her head.

He stared at her in disbelief for a moment before he spoke. *"This is no dream. You have prayed for this very moment. Search your heart, you will see what is taking place today. Put your trust in God, I assure you it is in his plans."*

She started to say something again, but she couldn't speak. It was as if her tongue refused to work.

He slowly raised his hand to silence her. *"Do not let anger and confusion rule your heart. Be strong, look within yourself for the true meaning. And above everything else, do not lose faith."* His voice echoed with tender kindness and understanding. *"Lydia, your husband has always been with you."* The young man gestured his arm towards the corner of the room.

The room suddenly got brighter until a flash of blinding light engulfed it entirely. She immediately felt a strange, comforting warmth return, but only for a moment. Her rage was gone, but her confusion was even greater. Her body felt weak, her mind drained. She stumbled backwards against the edge of the wall to catch her balance. "Gabriel, I'm so, so sorry! What have I done?" she wept.

When she refocused her eyes, all she could see were bright spots in the dark room. A familiar voice was yelling things she could not understand.

The door burst open and in came the large figure of a man. "Gabriel?" she whispered. It only took her a moment to recognize that it was Dan. There were spots of light everywhere she looked. She instinctively sheltered her face from the brightness that poured into the room through the open door. Though it was nothing compared to the blinding light she had just experienced, the light still hurt her eyes.

"Are you alright?" Dan exclaimed as his eyes searched the room. "You were screaming... I heard voices." He fumbled with the light switch on the wall, turning it on and off several times. She knew he had seen something, was investigating. "There was a bright light?" his voice sounded confused.

She felt the room beginning to spin and her balance starting to fail. She called out to her brother in-law, when he reached her, she collapsed in his arms. "I think I have done something very wrong!" she whispered.

"What did you do?" His eyes searched the room.

She pointed to the journal sitting on the floor. His eyes followed.

"It'll be alright." he reassured her as her balance returned. "It doesn't look damaged."

"Thank you!" She squeezed him even tighter. Things would once again be better, now that Dan was there.

"You have been crying!" Betty's voice echoed in the room.

Lydia looked around Dan's broad shoulders towards Betty and nodded. She could just barely make out her concerned features within the glare of the hallway light and the fading spots. "The light was blinding!" Dan stated again.

"Yes," Betty nodded, "what on earth was going on here?" She sounded surprised. "We saw the brightness from under the door... it was almost as if there was a fire in the room, but—"

"It wasn't a fire; the light was bright blue!" Dan exclaimed.

Betty nodded. "And the voices?"

They heard the voices?

It was then that it hit Lydia that, something wasn't right. "It wasn't a dream!" The sound of her own words made her tremble. She looked down at her shaking hand.

My hands!

Dan gripped her tighter. He flared his nostrils as he took a quick look around the room.

It was obvious that he smelled something.

"He was here wasn't he?" his understanding voice whispered in Lydia's ear, his eyes searched her expression.

Lydia slowly nodded as she looked at the journal lying face down on the floor.

His eyes followed. Lydia let him gently pass her off again to his wife and her friend.

"Please take her into the other room." Dan's gentle voice echoed in her ears. She had already gotten her message, now it was time for Dan to get his.

Betty nodded in agreement. "Come on Lydia, let's sit you down on the couch and have some lemon-honey tea. Tell me everything, please. Help me understand."

"Dan, he was here!" Lydia turned and pointed. "They were both standing right there!" she blurted out before she turned and allowed herself to be led away.

"Both?" exclaimed Dan.

"It will be alright!" Betty reassured, as she raised a curious eyebrow to Dan.

After a couple of uneven steps Lydia stopped and faced Dan. "You believe me right?"

"Yes, I do!" Dan answered without any hesitation.

Lydia studied his eyes a moment. Satisfied, she turned and allowed herself to be led away. Her body tingled with a strange excitement. The anniversary had begun.

***

Dan watched them disappear out the doorway and down the hallway, arm in arm.

'He was here!' Her excited voice rattled around in his mind.

Was she talking about Gabriel and an angel?

He returned his curious gaze first back to the room and then the journal that lay face down on the floor. He breathed in deeply and closed his eyes. Outside of the faint smell of Gabriel's cologne, which could be easily explained, nothing appeared to be out of place except for Gabriel's journal.

When he opened his eyes again, the room looked a bit brighter. His eyes had adjusted to the lighting. He walked over to the journal and stood above it for a moment. He took a quick look around the room to confirm that he was alone and then refocused on the book. He was well aware that both Gabe and Lydia had found Gabriel's words directed towards them. It was a one way conversation, written in anticipation of that moment, by a man that had been dead for nearly ten years.

"So brother, have you a message for me?" He heard the curious longing in his own quiet words. He squatted down and gently picked up the journal, slipping his thumb in between the pages so as not to lose the open place. He then turned the book right-side-up. He was about to close the journal and lay it on the top of the desk, but he couldn't resist. He glanced down at the words, paused, and wondered. He had to look. He had to know. He focused on the top of the page.

October 19th 1999

"October 19th 1999?" he said to himself. He took a deep breath and silently began to read.

The countdown has started... I sit by the fire with my brother, near the very spot I will perish. Giving a life to save another! It's against the rescuer's creed. The safety of the rescuer always comes first and foremost the victim is secondary. It's the industry standard... so why am I being asked to violate common sense?

"God... no!" He felt his body shiver. It was like an electrical shock had surged through his entire being. He leaned against the desk for balance and held the journal firmly in his hands.

First Gabe, then Lydia, now me? The message is for me.

He instinctively looked around the room to confirm that he was still alone, and then gazed back down at the journal, took another deep breath and continued reading.

I feel it. I tried to tell Dan the whole story, but thought better of it. He deserves better. He has been with me from the start and, no doubt, he will be with me unto the end. Unbeknownst to him, he will be the one to mentor my son.

Dan felt the energy drain from his legs and tears fill his eyes. He tilted his head back a moment and squeezed the bridge of his nose with his fingers.
How could he have known this?
He felt his body shudder.
He stood up the chair with his free hand and pulled it under him. He let his body flop noisily into it without looking and gave out a deep sigh. He wiped the tears from the corners of his eyes and sniffled his nose before he continued to read.

Is it a gift or curse, for him to take over where I have left off? Only God knows, and he isn't telling. His plan is a mystery to all that serve Him.

The angels will always be there; it is what they do. They exist to merely serve. The angels... the guardian angels!

It is all true.... They are messengers, watchers, protectors, and preventers. They step in to assist only when authorized. They tend to you upon your death.

There is a dark side to them as well. They are God's executioners. Yes, when the orders are given, it is they who carry them all out. Are there good and bad angels? Were they created to serve that very purpose? They, too, have free will and self-determination. The devil... the self-appointed leader of the fallen. He, too, exists by the grace of God. Why does he even allow evil to exist? To allow us to exercise free will?

So this is where it will end. So this is where it should begin. I write this as I hear my brother's deep heavy breaths. He said that he doesn't snore... so says he. This can be debated this quiet evening in the heart of the redwoods. The animals come from miles around to see what is creating the disruption in their wilderness neighborhood.

Dan broke into heart-felt laughter as he ran his fingers through his hair. His tears were no longer from sorrow. He remembered that evening. They had stayed up until the early morning hours, sometimes talking quietly, sometimes silently staring into the crackling fire.

Yes, this is where Gabe's journey will begin. This is where my earthly journey will end. May the medallion of St. Francis be of service to him when he needs it the most. May Dan instill enough wisdom in him. May Lydia forgive me for what I must do. May this journal record, my last wishes. May this journal be the blueprint for the journey of another....

He kept his eyes closed and allowed his thoughts to drift back to that evening around their wilderness campfire, a scene from the journal brought to life... Dan gently leaned back into the chair and rubbed his tired eyes with the palms of his hands.

Is it official? Am I the guardian? There it is in writing... Gabe is to take over where my brother left off.

"As you wish little brother, as you wish!" he laughed nervously. It was all too crazy to make any sense. He couldn't tell anyone that his whole life was about to be turned upside down because of a few words written in the journal of a dead man and the visitation by an angel!

"No, no, this is all too weird. I can't just quit my job in the mountains of Southern California. I really like it down there, Betty likes it down there. What would she say? We don't have any children to uproot. God knows we've tried to have them."

I guess it wasn't in the cards!

He looked at the wall. "We could transfer up this way. They currently have a vacancy, based on my state seniority; I probably have enough to get the position."

He hadn't thought about working and living in the redwoods before.

It could be interesting.

"My sister in-law and nephew do need us!"

His mind drifted back to that day more than ten years ago..

The campfire burned brightly in the night. The wood popped and snapped as it slowly turned itself into ash. The dancing flames illuminated the silent, somber faces of him and his brother. The evening sounds of crickets serenaded the strange eerie silence. Comforting warmth insulated them from the cool, fall evening.

They were in deep thought, trying to share their hidden secrets with each other but not wanting to be the first. That day he wished he had gone last. He carried the concerns of his brother.

It was a strange, unnerving calmness that floated around the fire that night. It was his brother's dreaded predictions then that had pushed him into the world that he now occupied. As he searched his memory, his brother's words once again formed in his thoughts. He opened his eyes and read more from the page in the journal.

I will die very soon, doing what I love. It will not be my choice. I will be doing God's bidding. The angels will have done their job.

It all started at a bus stop in Long Beach, and it will end here in the forested mountains of the North Coast. I will always be here with you, one step behind, looking over your shoulder two steps ahead, waiting for the day when we will all be reunited. Trust your heart, believe. We all serve a purpose, one that you never could have predicted in your wildest dreams. And so are the mysteries of life.

Dan gently closed the journal and slowly slid it farther onto the desk with both of his hands. His gaze searching the room for signs of anyone else. He took in a deep breath and closed his eyes. He was still alone.

From time to time, Dan felt the presence of his brother. He occasionally caught a whiff of his brother's favorite cologne, his natural smells, reassuring him that his brother was indeed checking up on him. He missed his brother more now than ever. He was going to make it a point to read the Bible. As far as he was concerned, angels were real.

He opened his eyes, looked down at the journal and smiled. He felt a great understanding welling up from within. He knew exactly what he had to do, to fulfill his brother's request, his role as the mentor. Tomorrow, Tuesday, they were going camping. They were going to celebrate the anniversary of his brother's death in the mountains. They were going back to their little camp spot in the heart of the redwood wilderness.

He heard the ring of the telephone coming from the other room. He instinctively knew who it was. He sat up, gently slid the journal even farther out of reach toward the top of the desk and tapped the outside cover. "Thank you, brother, you will not be disappointed."

The telephone was picked up during the middle of the third ring and he heard his wife answer it.

"Hello, Gabe?"

Dan felt his heart race as he walked a little faster down the hallway towards the phone.

"Oh, is everything alright?" Betty continued. "Pick you up from school? Okay, we'll be right there!" her voice echoed in the room. She slowly hung up the phone and looked into Lydia's questioning eyes. "Gabe said he isn't feeling well. He asked that we come pick him up."

"So it begins!" Dan mumbled from across the room as he strutted up to them.

They both turned to see his smiling face. They gave him an inquisitive look.

"Gabe's journey, as well as ours, starts today!" Dan felt a strange joy overwhelm him. "I was reading the journal," he glanced over his shoulder towards the study, "Lydia, you're right, it's like it was meant for us." He paused a moment before he continued. He saw Lydia's face flash in agreement. "I know exactly what we need to do!"

CHAPTER FIFTEEN
MOTHER'S BLESSING
(MONDAY)
MARCH 14TH 2000

Erick tripped over the threshold and just about tumbled through the doorway as he burst into the room, panting heavily from his sprint home from school. He had to do everything in his power to keep from bowling over his astonished mother. Her surprised expression would have been comical if it weren't for the fact that he had bumped the lamp from the corner table in an effort to avoid pushing his mom over the edge of the coffee table.

He started to reach for her as soon as she stumbled backwards, but he instinctively turned and grabbed for the lamp instead, just as it wobbled one last time over the edge. Sudden panic welled up as he leaped for the lamp. He knew if he broke the lamp he would never hear the end of it, nor would he ever forgive himself for being so clumsy. It was his mom's favorite porcelain antique. Expensive!

He made a clean save. What a relief! Even better than that, he made it without ever leaving the ground. When he looked proudly back towards his mom, his heart was pounding noticeably in his chest, he was surprised to see her using the edge of the coffee table to pull herself up from the floor.

Did I knock her over?

His stare finally settled, to the surprise on his mom's smiling face.

"Wow! That was different!" she exclaimed as she regained her full height and pressed the invisible wrinkles out of the pant legs of her jeans with her palms.

"Mom?" he finally found his voice.

"I'm fine honey!"

Boy was he relieved. He had just about broken both his mother and her favorite lamp all in one careless move.

What was I doing, barging into the house as if a pack of wolves were after my soul?

"I'm okay, really!" she reassured.

He just stood there, frozen to the floor, unsure of what to say or do next.

She stiffly walked over to him and carefully took the lamp out of his hands and gently placed it back onto the corner table from whence it had come. As if an afterthought, she slid it a couple of inches farther back from the edge. She then turned it on to see if it still worked. They both looked relieved when the rainbow of colors from the octagon lampshade projected its beautiful, stained glass images on the walls and ceiling. The entire scene reminded him of the stained glass elegance of an ancient church.

He let out a heavy sigh of relief. His mom nodded. Evidently, she had felt the same way. He took a couple more deep breaths and then smiled. "That power cord is pretty long isn't it?" He dropped his head and concentrated on controlling his breathing.

All of the things I could have said!

"Yeah, any shorter and it might have been yanked right out of your hands. It's a miracle it wasn't broken!" She quickly crossed herself with her hands.

He tried not to think about it.

"So, what's the big hurry?" she changed the subject.

"Oh yeah, is everything okay? Principal Jones said you wanted me to come straight home, so here I am!" He casually tossed his hands into the air. He felt his pulse rate and breathing increasing again.

"Didn't you want me to come home?"

"Yes, I did, I called the school and asked them to send you home." she said calmly.
Am I in trouble?
"What's going on?" He felt the nervousness building again.
She seemed calmer than usual, especially after the near mishap with the lamp and all, my being late for school.
"Nothing really, it's just, how do I say this!" She took her time casually repositioning the lamp again.
Erick watched the colorful images dance across the walls and ceiling.
She nodded as if finally satisfied and then slowly backed away from the lamp. "There, just like the Notre-Dame de Quebec Basilica cathedral, wouldn't you say?"
Erick followed her eyes around the room and nodded in agreement. She was right, the lighting, well, it was great! The stained glass effect was the best he had ever seen the lamp create. The outside lighting, bleeding through the windows enhanced the whole effect.
"Pretty cool! Mom, you were saying?"
"Yes, like I was saying, it was like there was this little voice in the back of my head that said '*Erick had some important things to do* here at home." Her expressive eyes rested on his face and smiled. "Sweet heart, I think your friend needs you."
Erick wrinkled his eyebrows in surprise. "What?"
"It's almost like a little angel dropped by and said...," she deepened her voice, "Gabe and Erick need to spend some quality time together." She smiled.
Erick widened his eyes. He felt a chill run from the top of his head to the tip of his toes and the energy immediately drain from his body.
"Did they really say that?" He flopped back noisily into the couch.
She gave him a strange stare. "Who?" She slowly walked over to him, reached for his hand and sat down next to him. "Honey, are you okay? You look as if... you had just seen a ghost!" she looked him over closely, then gently placed the back of her hand against his forehead.
He moved away from her touch.

"You're not running a fever are you?" She eyed him carefully.

"Maybe I have seen a ghost today."

"Honey, what's wrong?" Her face twisted into concern.

"You said an angel dropped by... said that Gabe and I should spend some time together!"

She nodded. "Well, yeah, it's a figure of speech honey. I just thought the two of you seemed a little on edge lately. That you needed—"

"No one told you?" he blurted out.

She narrowed her eyes suspiciously. "Well, no one told me what?"

"Anything about angels?"

"Angels! No silly, I just thought it was a good idea for the two of you to get together, work things out!"

He took a deep sigh and reached over and squeezed his mother's hand.

If you only knew!

She returned the affectional hand squeeze and leaned in closer. Her fragrant perfume made him cough.

"It's just that, the weirdest thing happened to me today." Erick tried to explain.

She raised her eyebrows as if asking him to go on.

"Gabe and I had gotten into a ridiculous argument before school even started!" He looked down at his feet.

"Oh, what about? You two normally get along so well. It's just lately..." She stroked the curly hair around his temples a few times with one of her fingers. It usually bothered him, but this time he didn't stop her.

"Yeah, well, it was about angels." He turned and looked into her eyes, trying to read her emotions.

Her second hand joined the other and sandwiched one of his hands. "I could understand you arguing over who is better at this or who is better at that, but for heaven's sake, about angels of all things?" she forced a laugh.

He looked into her eyes and forced a smile. "Yeah, right, I know, but he was so mad at me. He stormed off, but that wasn't the weird thing." He took a deep breath to clear his thoughts.

"There is this blond kid that I have recently been seeing with Gabe, but the strange thing is, Gabe claims he never sees him!" His mom let go of his hand as he continued. "You see, Gabe gives me this strange look every time I talk to him about this guy, the blond kid at school. I guess! I basically called Gabe a liar, ticked him off big time. He pushed me to the ground and ran off to class, left me standing there alone under the big tree out in front of school. Then the tardy bell rang, and before I knew it. I was officially late."

"He pushed you?" She crossed her arms, leaned back into the couch, and watched him closely. "Miss Gertrude, the school nurse hadn't said anything about that!"

"Well, then like out of nowhere, this blond kid, the very same kid I've been seeing with Gabe, the one *he* can't see, starts talking to me. He says more to me today then all of the other times combined. He basically said I needed to stick by my friend Gabe. Said he was an angel and then disappeared just like that, leaving me standing there alone, again—"

"He said Gabe was an angel?" She fought back a smiled.

"No, the kid said *he* was an angel, not Gabe! This dude disappears, vanishes when Principal Jones catches up to us, which really meant just me, and sends me home. This whole thing is pretty weird." He gave a deep sigh to catch his breath. His eyes searched his mom's for answers. "So, you see, when you said an *angel* had dropped by, well, now you know why!" He squinted at her suspiciously. "Why did you have me come home when Gabe is still at school?"

She crossed herself again with her hands and gave him a surprised look.

Erick gave her a curious gaze in return. His thoughts drifted to the porcelain and wooden crosses that hung from the walls of the living room. His mom was somewhat religious, but also a tad bit superstitious.

"Miss Gertrude said something about Gabe going home sick, and don't ask me why or how, but I just got the impression that the two of you needed to get together." She held her palms out casually. "Go ahead and call it mother's intuition, or divine interference if you'd like." She patted Erick gently on his shoulder. He leaned warmly into her touch. "Honey, maybe there is something more to this than we really know. You should go over there right away and patch things up between the two of you. After all, it is only Monday. God willing, you'll have the rest of the week to fix whatever."

Erick reached his arms around her neck and gave her a big hug. "Mom, you're the greatest!"

"Yes, I know, Super Mom!" she shrugged her shoulders. "Leave no chores left unfinished, because what you don't finish today will still be waiting for you tomorrow!" She gave a heavy sigh.

He jumped up off of the couch, but slowed once he saw the lamp in the corner of the room.

Once was luck... twice was skill!

This time he gave the lamp a wide berth. He would snack first, give his friend a moment to settle, and then go see what this was all about.

CHAPTER SIXTEEN
SCHOOL NURSE
MARCH 14TH 2000

Dan stopped at the open wooden door to collect his thoughts. It read, SCHOOL NURSE, in big, bold silver and black letters. The little cover was slid to the side exposing the red and white letters IN. Per the directions given by the school's main office, this was where he was supposed to extract his nephew from the system.

So this is what it's like! Stepping in for my brother, acting on his behalf, the guardian, Gabe's guardian angel.

The thought made him smile. This whole week had been strange. He looked over his shoulder, seeing that he was alone in the hallway. He cleared his throat and firmly knocked twice on the open office door.

"Come in, Mr. Wilson, come in!" A scratchy voice of an elderly woman croaked from far beyond the door.

How?

He cautiously pushed the door the rest of the way open.

Hidden surveillance cameras?

His eyes instinctively searched for answers as soon as he crossed the threshold of the office. A young teen in faded, tight-fitting jeans sat in one of the wooden waiting chairs to his right. She wore an un-tucked, oversized, pinstriped dress shirt with rolled up sleeves, exposing a half dozen wrist bracelets.

Probably borrowed the shirt from her dad.

Her short blonde hair with pink highlights accented the numerous ear-piercing that protruded from her small ears. He couldn't help but stare. He had subconsciously started counting them when she turned and smiled. He lost count at five when he found himself staring into the curious eyes of her pretty face.

My goodness, a human fishing lure!

He thought as he stared in amazement. The young girl had numerous piercings across her face as well. Dan forced a smile and nodded, his lingering eyes taking it all in. The lure-like jewelry hung from her eyebrows, her nose and her cheeks and around her mouth.

Who knows what she's done to her tongue?

A woman cleared her throat. "Over here, Mr. Wilson." The voice jerked his attention back to the distant desk. A tall, slender woman with gray, short hair pulled herself up from behind the desk and made her way towards him. He turned and stepped in her direction. He could still feel the young girl's eyes burning into the back of his head. He was the one who felt out of place.

The elderly woman smiled, it was like she read his thoughts. He felt slightly frustrated; it wasn't like him to feel this way. He had always been the one in control, calling the shots; but over the last week, he felt as if he wasn't in control of anything.

"Hello Mr. Wilson," she smiled confidently. Her jewel framed glasses hung from a silver chain around her neck. Her creased, white blouse and dark slacks made her look even taller. She reminded him more of a librarian than a receptionist. She reached across the counter and shook his outstretched hand. "I'm Miss Gertrude, the school nurse and psychologist."

Dan started to introduce himself, but she interrupted.

"So, you're Dan Wilson, Gabe's uncle!" her voice enthusiastic.

He nodded curiously.

She smiled, showing her big white teeth as she pointed to the open doorway. "Fish eye mirror!"

"The what?"

"The mirror!" she smiled confidently as she nodded towards the open door. "It gives you a clear view of the hallway."

He turned in the direction she pointed and saw the little fish eye mirror tucked away in the corner of the wall.

Why didn't I see that before?
"Gabe filled me in, you see, no magic to it at all. The mirrors, just another one of Principal Jones' well-placed ideas. He feels there shouldn't be any secrets among the students." She didn't sound convinced.

"How do you feel about it?" Dan gestured in the direction of the mirror. If his memory served him correctly, the students weren't very fond of this Principal Jones character.

"Let me say this, I can see down the hallway pretty well. Anyhow, we were expecting you," she teased.

"Alright!" Dan looked back into her smiling face.

Gertrude shrugged her shoulders. "So, you're here to pick up Gabe?"

Dan nodded.

"Where is he?" He glanced around the room.

"So what's it like being a park ranger?"

Dan looked at her, surprised. He wondered what else Gabe had told her. "Ummm, entertaining, most of the time, get to live in the woods, watch the grass grow, play with bears and, oh yeah, rescue picnic baskets!"

She laughed. "I'm sure! Your nephew speaks very highly of you."

"He's a good kid." Dan continued to look around.

"Yes!" she exclaimed, then she lowered her voice, "Very much so. A good kid with a lot on his shoulders right now. We need to talk." She looked past him and over to the young girl in the chair. "Patricia, honey, could you give us a few!"

The young girl looked up, smiled and nodded. "Sure Miss Gertrude. I'll be at the usual bench down the hall." Her pierced tongue clinked against her teeth as she spoke.

"Thank you dear," Gertrude smiled.

Both she and Dan silently watched the young woman pick up her things, casually walk out of the room and pull the door shut behind her after giving them a second look.

Dan raised his eyebrows.

Yep, and a pierced tongue too.

Gertrude spoke again as if she had been reading his mind. "She's also a good kid, though sometimes a little misguided.

"With all the challenges the kids face these days, I believe they have it a bit harder than we did, wouldn't you say, Mr. Wilson?" By the tone of her voice, it was obvious that she cared.

Dan nodded as his thoughts flashed to his nephew. "Yes, kids these days!"

"Now about your nephew, Gabe!"

Dan felt his heart skip a beat as he looked closely into her face.

"He just hasn't been the same lately," she spoke quietly. "There have been some rumors floating around school that your nephew had seen a ghost in the shower—"

"Taking one?" Dan tried to alleviate the building tension with a bit of humor.

She kept a straight face as she wrinkled her forehead in disapproval. His attempt failed.

"Seriously, he wasn't the first, you know; but it has been a while since the last, ugh, *reported* sighting!" she emphasized the word as she looked over her shoulders. "And there have been other things. The mood swings, his lack of appetite, his lack of focus. A boy his age should want to eat everything in sight." She paused a moment and studied Dan's face. "The anniversary of his father's death is some time this weekend, isn't it?"

"It's in the next couple of days. Why do you ask?" Dan looked rather surprised.

"Dan, we care here more than you think! Our student's well-being is important to us. They can't learn to be good citizens of tomorrow if they are too worried about the problems of today."

Greeting card Cliché!

Dan politely nodded. He started to feel a bit uncomfortable "Ten years this week since his dad passed. We have a little trip planned—"

"Where are you guys planning on going, if I may ask?"

"Camping..."

She silently stared at him, studying his face. "No, you're not thinking about taking him back to where his father died are you?" Her face reflected concern.

Dan stared back with his poker face.

"You are, aren't you? Do you think it's the right thing to do to the poor boy?"

"Frankly, with all due respect, I don't think it's any of your business when or where I decide to take my nephew." He fought to hold back his annoyance. "Your right he needs a break and the State Park is a very nice place to get away and...!" He was about to steamroll on, but had to remind himself that she was, after all, just trying to help.

She silently stared at him and him back at her.

He took a deep breath and slowly spoke. "This tenth anniversary is more important than you'll ever know, for everyone."

"Try me, I might know more than you think!" She still managed to keep her side of the conversation to a harsh, respectful whisper, unlike Dan.

Really!

Dan raised an eyebrows. His voice was creeping up in volume. He took a few deep breaths and tried harder to relax. "Obviously, there are things that you aren't aware of!" Bits of anger escaped from his voice.

"Like what Mr. Wilson?" To Dan's surprise, she maintained better control of her emotions than he did.

"There's the journal...," Dan caught himself, but it was too late. He had said too much already.

"The what?" Her expression gave away her excitement.

"The journey?"

"No, Mr. Wilson, you clearly said journal!"

Curse these psychologists!

Dan just stared, her curious eyes probing into his. He had taken the bait and now he was committed. They silently stared at each other until Miss Gertrude made the next move.

"Please come with me." she said in a nurturing voice. She escorted Dan farther away from the door, around the counter, and toward two leather chairs on the far side of the room.

I don't think so!

He stopped halfway there and turned to face her. "Where are we going?"

She stopped and turned towards him. "To see your nephew."

He looked back towards the leather chairs.

Oh God the shrinks chairs

She gestured towards the far office. "There are some colleagues of mine who could be of help to Gabe. They're great with kids and—"

"No, no, you don't understand," Dan interrupted.

"But, these are good people, the best!"

"Wait!" Dan held up his hand to get her attention.

She respectfully paused to hear Dan out.

Dan glanced back at the chairs and took in a slow deep breath before he continued. He felt his stomach tighten, his pulse increase. "That isn't what Gabe needs right now. Things could get worse if the wrong people get involved."

"The wrong people? I don't think I understand—"

"No, I meant that he still has a few more years of high school to stumble through." Dan let out a deep sigh to help him focus, ran his fingers through his hair and then shook his head. "Here's the Reader's Digest version." He forced himself to slow down and speak quietly. "Somehow, the arrival of the tenth anniversary of my brother's passing has stirred up some strange energy around here. Evidently, my brother knew he was going to die."

She gave him an odd look.

Dan continued. "He confirmed it several times in his *journal*, which he had left behind for Gabe, Lydia, and evidently for me, to read. He even talked about it with me before he passed."

"A journal... oh dear God!" her voice a low whisper. "Has Gabe seen the journal?"

He ignored the concerned look she gave him and continued. He was on a roll.

"Some strange things have indeed been happening to Gabe and his mother -some of which you are evidently already familiar with- triggered by the events that I have already mentioned, and some that I have not! Their feelings for Gabriel, his father, have been magnified several times fold. Smells and sounds reminding them, reminding us, of Gabriel are an everyday occurrence. They grow in strength as time goes by. Sometimes it feels like he is here among us... seriously!"

She started to say something but he raised his hand to cut her off. "Please let me finish!"

She nodded in agreement.

"Do you believe in guardian angels, Miss Gertrude? For that matter, do you even believe in God? Well, do you?" He paused expectantly to await her answer, regretting the fact that he had asked it in the challenging manner in which he had, but at that moment he didn't care. His eyes studied her closely.

She returned the gaze and forced a nervous smile; it was obvious that he had hit close to home. He was still on a roll.

"I'm serious, do you believe in the power of a Supreme Being, God Almighty, an entity with the power and grace to decide whether we have the right to live or die? That angels walk this planet wielding powers that we thought to exist only in the Holly Bible and people's imagination? That they are here to guide and protect, and when the time comes, strike us down in a blink of an eye?" He waved his hands around to help express his thoughts. He felt his heart pounding rapidly in his chest. In a strange sort of way, he felt empowered. "Do you believe that we're all here to serve a purpose? That our right to choose dictates the path that we take? Remember, your answer will dictate our next move."

He watched her slowly finger a gold chain that hung from around her neck. She hesitantly pulled a gold medallion out from around her neck and offered it for him to see. He curiously leaned forward.

Now it was her turn.

"Dan, I wear this everywhere I go." she held it by the chain so it dangled in the light. "I ask for his help when things become difficult. It's the symbol of *John of God* the patron saint of the sick, nurses and booksellers."

Dan gave her a strange look as he shifted his gaze in between her and the medallion. His thoughts flashed to a librarian, his first impression of her.

I would have never guessed that she used faith to guide her book selection!

The thought made him smile.

"Now I'm serious." She gave him an odd look before she continued. "*John of God* was declared the patron saint of nurses back in August of 1930," she continued. "I see some similarities between his lives and mine: serving in the military, distributing books, and waiting upon the sick. *Yes*, I believe in God, and the fact that his angels help support his work and that nothing happens without his approval. *Yes*, I believe we are given the right to choose. It is our choice that dictates our life's journey... our determined path."

He nodded.

Bizarre!

She shrugged her shoulders. "Do you think it a coincidence that we are even speaking about the subject at this moment?"

Dan silently stared.

"You see, you are not the only one who cares for your nephew." She slid the medallion back beneath her blouse. "I did not realize that so much was happening. I'm also here to help."

He acknowledged with a nod, "It's my duty to guide my nephew down this path into the unknown. His father perished along the way. Now for his son...." His throat suddenly became dry and tight. He cleared it loudly so he could continue.

She gave him a supportive pat on his shoulder.

He allowed her to share her tender support before he slowly stepped away. "I need to get him back to his mother. She's expecting us."

"He is over here," her voice crackled with emotional understanding as she pointed to the door. "Now, about taking Gabe to where his father died!"

"I'm doing what Gabriel wanted!"

"How do you know what he..." she stared at him strangely, "the journal?" She spoke quietly.

"Yes, the journal..." he started to say more, but abruptly stopped and closed his eyes.

***

The smell of incense filled Gertrude's lungs. She coughed, and glanced around the room. Her mind raced to a distant memory. She briefly closed her eyes.

She was in another room, during another time. She was once again at home, dressed in black, sitting at a desk in her study. In her trembling hands she held a picture of her mother and father. Her eyes were full of tears, her makeup smudged, her heart burdened. They were a devout Catholic family. They were to meet at church that Sunday morning but her parents never arrived. An impaired driver prevented it all from happening.

Why?

Now she was parentless because of the selfish action of one inconsiderate man. She remembered that day, a turning point in her life.

Out of anger she had cursed God for taking them away from her. In desperation she had asked for a sigh of hope and understanding. That's when tenderness filled her lungs, the sweet perfume warmed her soul, gave her hope, understanding, and forgiveness. From that day she knew she would never truly be alone.

She took a deep breath.

The journal!
Now she understood. She opened her eyes.
"Mysterious ways!" She whispered. She turned to Dan. "Doesn't look like I'm going to change your mind am I?"
"Nope!"
"Alright then, this way please!"

∗∗∗

Gabe heard every word. He balled up his fists and kept telling himself that everything was going to be alright, but he knew it wasn't. He couldn't believe that his uncle would tell anyone about their *secret*, especially to that nosey nurse that worked for Principal Jones.

How could you have done that to me? Couldn't you have just picked me up and left it at that! No, you had to tell that nosey nurse everything!

He punched the couch on which he was sitting. A loud, muffled thud echoed in the room.

"Gabe?"

He heard the nurse's voice from behind the closed door.

She was nice enough, but now she knew everything. Things will never be the same!

"Gabe?" She cautiously turned the knob and gently pushed open the door.

When they made eye contact, he could tell right away that she knew that he had heard.

"I'm sorry Gabe," she said as she stepped into the room, followed by an inquisitive Dan. "Your uncle is here to take you home."

"Yeah, I see that!" he snapped.

"Gabe!" Dan scolded, "Now's not the time."

Gabe turned noisily around in his chair and stared at the picture of a waterfall on the wall virtually ignoring them. He wished so much he were there instead.

She doesn't have any right to know!

She cleared her throat, "You have heard our conversation haven't you?"

He shrugged his shoulders. He could tell that she was trying to turn on her sympathetic charm, but that was the last thing he needed.

It's not, going, to work!

"I know more now, thanks to your uncle," she glanced over to Dan. "As I explained to you before, we are here to help."

Gabe gave out a deep sigh as he crossed his arms disapprovingly, his eyes never leaving the security of the picture. "How can you possibly help?" he mumbled. "Because

you wear a medallion with a dead man's face around your neck, like it somehow makes you understand *my* problem?"
"Gabe!" Dan exclaimed loudly. "She deserves your respect!"
"That's alright Mr. Wilson!"
"No, it isn't and he knows that!" Dan scolded.
His uncle was right. He didn't know what had come over him.
The anger... the not knowing... my argument with Erick.
Gabe turned towards the two of them and gave out another deep sigh. "Miss Gertrude, I'm sorry. I know you meant well, but do angels follow *you* around? Do dead people talk to *you* through their old journals?" He paused for a moment, examining her face before he continued. "If you understand any of this and know how to fix this, then tell me what to do!" He stared quietly at her, not believing how weak the conversation had made him feel.
"Pray for understanding." She silently stared back, hope in her eyes.
"Prayer is the best you can do! May I go now?" he sounded disappointed.
"Ah, yes honey!" she spoke softly as she, crossed her arms and also stared at the picture of the waterfall on the wall. Her shoulders helplessly slumped. "Honey, well talk later?" she spoke softly as she nervously fingered the medallion around her neck.
Gabe stood up and placed a hand on her shoulders. She patted it gently with her hand as he walked off.
"Will I see you later, at the vehicle?" Dan asked.
"Yeah!" Gabe said without looking back.
"I'll be there shortly."
"Sure!" Gabe nodded, continued down the hall and out the door. Thoughts of his friend hit him like a warm breeze. Apologizing to Erick was the first thing he was going to do. He sensed that his journey was about to get even crazier. The unknown was now his direct path, and there was so much more to learn.

***

Miss Gertrude sat and slumped down into the couch. "Is he ready for this?" she spoke softly, her eyes remaining focused on the picture.

"Are any of us?" Dan patted her gently on the shoulder and started to leave the room.

She turned and spoke slowly over her shoulder, still fingering her medallion. "I will pray for the both of you! And I suggest that you do the same!"

"Then prayer it is!" was the last thing he said before he disappeared out the door and down the hallway after his nephew.

CHAPTER SEVENTEEN
HEART TO HEART
MARCH 14TH 2000

The short drive back home in Dan's International Scout was made even longer by the uncomfortable silence. Gabe cautiously watched Dan out of the corner of his eye, he was sure that his uncle was doing some critical thinking of his own. At any moment, he expected the lecture to begin. After all, he couldn't blame him. His performance was ruled by juvenile emotions.

Dan just sat there, thinking about who knows what. It was as if he were waiting for the right moment.

It was like neither of them wanted to be the first to bring it up.

Gabe was thankful that it was Dan who finally broke the uneasy silence. "Now that didn't go over so well, did it?" he teased.

Gabe couldn't help but turn to his uncle and smile. Dan smiled back, he had a way of making light of just about anything. It was something Dan had learned to do to protect himself from his own emotions. Smiling was after all contagious. In retaliation, Dan playfully reached over and messed up Gabe's hair with his hand like he had always done.

Gabe tucked his head out of reach and protested. "Dan, I'm not a little kid anymore!"

"Sorry, you're right. I'll try to remember that. But, it's just, you know... *instinctive!*"

Dan reached over again; anticipating his move, Gabe skillfully deflected his hand away. The playful sparring softened the mood. The sudden release of energy had set off a chain reaction. Gabe forced his sulking figure back into his seat and let out a deep breath. "I got into a ridiculous argument with my friend today," Gabe said as he shifted his gaze in between the passing scenery and his uncle.

"Oh?" Dan now gave him a hard stare.

Gabe took another deep sigh to relax and focus. "Yeah, it was about angels, of all things!"

"Isn't he the one who told you about?"

"Yeah, the blond kid that hangs around and never talks to me."

Dan nodded. "Yeah, that guy."

"Erick is the one that you said was probably my guardian angel, hanging around to keep me out of trouble."

Dan forced a smile as if to make light of the situation. He shifted his gaze in between Gabe and the road. "So, why were you guys arguing?"

"He didn't believe me!" Gabe shrugged his shoulders. He then turned and now focused his attention on his uncle, watching his every move, watching his reaction. "He doesn't believe in angels!"

Dan gave him an understanding nod. "He doesn't, well he probably hasn't had to deal with those kind of things before. Most people don't!"

"Yeah, but aren't friends supposed to be understanding... supportive?"

"To a certain degree, yeah, most are, but then put yourself in his shoes. Someone you-think-you-know starts talking angels, messages from the grave. Just what did you think he is going to say? Cool, happens to me all of the time!" He thumbed himself in the chest.

Gabe smiled. After all, his uncle was right, and he knew it. "I guess you're right."

"You guess?" Dan glanced at Gabe.

"Okay, okay, you're right! You're right! Happy now?"

"Better." Dan nodded smugly and returned his gaze to the road. "Now, the question is, what are w-e-e-e-e going to do about it?"

That's a no brainier.
"Once Erick's out of school, I'll call him up and beg for forgiveness and apologize!"
"Apologize!"
"Yeah he's probably cooled off by now."
Dan's eyes flashed, as if he were waiting for more.
"What? Apologizing isn't good enough for you?" Gabe's words were direct.
"I believe your friend deserves a bit more than just an apology. Don't you?" Dan gave him that knowing look.
"More than an apology?" Gabe studied him closely. "You've got to be kidding! It takes two to argue doesn't it?"
"Yeah, one big heart to forgive and one patient man to mediate, I kid the-e-e-e-e-e not!" he chuckled. "I think, for your penance, you should invite him along on our little road trip into the mountains."
"What?" Gabe just stared at him.
"Yeah, sounds like the respectable thing to do in a situation like this! Don't you think?" Dan grinned.

It took Gabe about two seconds for the chill to zip right through him. The feeling started right behind his left ear and then ripped its way down the entire right side of his body. His throat suddenly became tight. He became incredibly thirsty, and his fingers and toes began to tingle. He pulled his arms into his chest to hide the shivering. It was a bit strange for him to react this way to an announcement of a camping trip, but, maybe it was the fact that Dan was planning the trip during the anniversary of his father's death.

Or was it something entirely different?

When he looked over to Dan again, he found him staring intently right at him. Gabe suddenly felt overwhelmed by a strange panic; his uncle was no longer watching the road. "The road!" he yelled.

Dan studied Gabe closely. "We're parked... the engine's off!" His voice forced a controlled calm.

Gabe looked out of his window and, sure enough, they were indeed safely parked in front of his house.

How did I miss that?

Embarrassed, Gabe melted back into his seat and gave out an uneasy sigh. He kept his arms crossed to stay warm in the sudden uneasy chill.

"You alright?" Dan asked, his face reflected his concern.

He nodded. "Just a little cold I guess."

Dan returned the nod. "You're right about that, it's like I pushed the AC button instead of the heat." He looked at the dials on the dash and jokingly tapped it a couple of times. "No, it's turned to heat." He looked kindly at Gabe for a moment before he spoke again. "Would you like me to turn the engine back on?"

"No, it's alright." Gabe just sat there staring straight ahead. His thoughts began to race faster and faster.

Dan smiled, his eyes looked straight ahead as if he were trying not to intrude. "Remember the bus stop story I shared with you earlier about your dad and me?"

Gabe turned to his uncle and nodded. "The bus from hell!"

"Yeah, that's the one" Dan chuckled as he continued to look forward, his mind still in deep thought. *"The bus from hell.* They never looked at us, not once. The smells, the way I felt, it was the beginning!" He turned and looked over to Gabe, his hands still gripping the steering wheel. Tears suddenly appeared in his caring eyes. "If I only knew then what I know now."

Gabe just stared at him as he held his breath. For a moment, he was afraid his uncle was going to break down and start crying.

Then what am I supposed to do? Dan is supposed to be the strong one... he's the rock. I'm just a kid!

He needed Dan to hold everything together.

"It was my job to take care of him," Dan continued. "After all, what are big brothers for?" He forced a laugh, but then became serious again. "I'll be an old man before you know it. I know, I have teased you about your friend...." He took a deep sigh, rubbed his eyes, and then continued. "I read some of your dad's journal this morning. Don't ask me how, but it was addressed to *me*, a mystery in itself I may never solve. I felt his presence there in the room," his voice crackled with emotion, "it was like he was standing there watching me, listening, making sure that I found the exact page, the right paragraph. I knew it!"

He ran his fingers through his hair and then used his hands to finish explaining.

Gabe studied his every movement closely.

"Your aunt and I heard some commotion coming from your mom's study, so we went back there." Dan gave a heavy sigh. "Your mom said she was visited by your *dad* and an *angel*." He spoke so matter of fact.

"What?" Gabe stated.

"In the excitement, your mom had tossed the journal onto the floor. When I went to pick it up, well, it was opened to a page. There was a message left for me!"

Gabe saw his uncle shudder with emotion as he looked on. "My mother saw the guardian angel!" He looked over to the driveway and noticed that his mother's car was gone.

"Maybe more!" Dan chimed in almost as if he were reading his mind. "She went to her doctor's appointment with your aunt."

"Is she okay?" Gabe had to fight the sudden panic.

"Not that kind of doctor, she's fine. They should be back soon." Dan cleared his throat.

"The psychologist!" he whispered.

"Your father, evidently appeared to her. She said she spoke with him. Sounds crazy, I know!" Dan paused again to take a deep breath. It was almost as if he were waiting for Gabe to say something. "Your mother, she seemed different, like she has a better understanding, a better handle on what's going on. It's weird, like a huge burden has been lifted from her shoulders."

Gabe stared in amazement.

Will that be enough to change how my mom's feels about this whole mess, help her find closure?

"Do you think this whole thing will be over by tomorrow?" Gabe asked.

The thought excited him.

Dan continue to stare at him. "Don't know," he shrugged, "Actually, I kind of think we're just getting started. As I was supposed to be your father's... I think your friend... Erick, is supposed to be your guide, your guardian angel in human form." Dan's voice quivered noticeably as he struggled along.

"What are you talking about?"

This is all supposed to be ending, not starting over!

"Dan, are you serious about Erick being a guardian angel? He's just a kid like me. He's my friend!"

"Listen, I know this all sounds pretty silly right now."

"Silly?"

"Yeah, for lack of better words, but it'll all come together before you know it. I don't think I truly understand it myself, but I believe it's what's meant to be, written in the stars if you will, on the pages of a journal in this case. Tomorrow is of great importance, I can feel it."

Gabe started to say something but his uncle cut him off with a wave of his hand.

"Your friend's going with us. He needs to be there for whatever's going to happen tomorrow. It needs to be the three of us. I believe it's the way it's supposed to be! It's just what your father would've wanted!"

"Are you kidding? A camping trip with my best friend and my favorite uncle on the anniversary of my father's death!"

"Yeah, something like that." Dan forced a smile.

As strange as it sounded, it probably couldn't hurt. He still couldn't believe that his mother was okay with letting him go, but she wasn't home to be asked. That would be the next hurdle. Then there was the misunderstanding with his friend.

"So, what do you say we head inside and start packin'?" His enthusiastic voice sounded upbeat.

Gabe turned to his uncle and smiled. He didn't know how it happened, but the shivering became a distant memory, his hands stopped tingling, and his thirst disappeared. His admiration for his uncle had grown even stronger. He threw his arms around his uncle's broad shoulders and squeezed. "It sounds like we're goin' campin' then!" His tone reflected his excited mood.

"Yes, you can bet we're goin' campin'." Dan forced a smile and returned the hug.

CHAPTER EIGHTEEN
SHRINKAGE
MARCH 14TH 2000 (MONDAY)

Lydia and Betty both sat quietly in the immaculate reception area of Doctor O'Toole's refurbished office. They gazed around the room, Gaelic music echoed in their ears, their minds filled with deep thoughts of their own. A moment ago they had checked in with the receptionist at the small front window and now it was their turn to wait for the good doctor to see Lydia. She couldn't help but stare at all the new additions. It didn't even look like the same office, a place she had visited on and off for the last ten years. It felt like a happier, warmer place. It no longer looked and felt like a place to share dark secrets. The thought made her smile.

This could be a good start!

She breathed in deeply, indulging in the newness of the medium-sized room. The smell of fresh paint, new carpet, leather upholstery, and the stone tile tickled her nose. She rubbed it to keep from sneezing as she admired the assortment of beautiful, fragrant flowers. They appeared to glow in contrast with the three silver; medium-sized urns that held them in three corners of the room. The black and gray pinstriped wallpaper held the silver-framed pictures of Irish/Scottish/Welsh castles that were centered on three of the four walls. Three black leather couches were positioned around the edges of the room, funneling the gray-green stone tile walkway down the middle of the green, textured woven carpet. A smoked opaque colored glass covered the three dark oak-framed coffee tables that were within reach of every couch. The Gaelic theme was a success, right down to the colorful, foot tall fairy statuettes that graced the center piece of every table. Lydia liked what Doctor O'Toole had done to her place. It was a far cry from the boring original.

"I'll have to re-evaluate my decision to return for more sessions," she whispered to Betty.

Betty gave her a confused look. On the way over they had both agreed that today was going to be her last appointment.

Lydia smiled. The entire renovated reception area reminded her of a design that she was sure she would be able to find in one of the three stacks of Better Homes and Gardens magazines that graced each glass coffee table with a perfect pile of three. Yes, there was a pattern.

Leave it to a psychologist to work her life's plan into her interior decorations.

"Three leather couches... three pictures of castles, three coffee tables, three statuettes, three silver urn...," Lydia pointed around the room as she spoke softly.

Betty's eyes followed.

"I bet the weave of the fibers in the carpet are even in threes! Wait, but there's more!"

They laughed again.

"That's only the physical aspect. Now for the spiritual ones. The room probably connects to the past, the present and the future—"

"Me, myself and I....," Betty jumped in, "the Holy Trinity-the Father, the Son, and the Holy Spirit!"

"Very good Betty! Yep, some serious thought probably went into all of this."

"It's like being in a library isn't it?" Betty's whisper.

"Yeah! More like a museum. Quite a change from the dungeon, before. No longer has that Confessional feel."

They both laughed.

"Where are all the other patients?" Betty asked as she gestured around the room, her tone suspicious. "It's only been just the two of us sitting here; it's been that way since we arrived five minutes ago—"

"That's one thing she is, very *patient*!" Lydia smiled as she interrupted her sister in-law. "Get it... patient?" using a little humor to throw her off the subject.

Betty shook her head, "really!"

"Over years of appointments at this office, maybe once or twice, I've met up with other patients on my comings and goings. Come to think of it, I would sure hope she has more patients," she forced a laugh. "I'm not going to pay for all of this remodeling!" she cleared her throat and spoke softly. "I guess not letting her loyal subjects compare notes is part of her strategy. Not being recognized in public later by another patient—"

"Priceless!" Betty added.

They both laughed.

"Lives stay private," Betty agreed.

"Yes, secrets stay concealed, besides, when you actually think about it, you might not want some of the patients scaring your other client's away." Lydia shrugged her shoulders. "Just a thought."

"Could happen." Betty nodded and then shifted gears. "So, why the elaborate reception room then?" Betty asked.

All Lydia could do was shrug her shoulders and gaze around the room again.

They both silently did.

The room could easily accommodate nine on a busy day, that's if there ever were one.

It was a good question. The doctor used to have two of those standard waiting room couch-lampstand combinations. Orange, burlap-like material, she remembered. It sat eight customers, four on each side of the couch. Then there was that offal, oval throw rug.

Maybe she's actually downsizing!

The door to the reception room swung open and the young, attractive slender blonde receptionist in the casual black slacks and vest appeared in the doorway with a practiced smile. A preset speech followed, "Good morning Lydia, Dr. O'Toole will see you now. This way please."

As Lydia stood up, Betty grabbed her hand and gave it a gentle squeeze. "Will you be alright?"

Lydia saw the concern in her sister-in-law's eyes. She couldn't help but love her dearly for that.

Oh what a helpful sister she has been.

"I'll be fine, really," she could hear her unconvincing words echo in her own ears. She stood there for a moment and returned the caring squeeze of her hand. She let Betty's fingers slip through her own as she turned and walked toward the open door. She felt Betty's eyes looking right through her, but dared not turn and look back. She knew that she would cry if she did.

The receptionist seemed to smile more, and her effect was spontaneous, Lydia's anguish and worries seemed to melt away.

How does she do that? Tricks of the trade? Magic, honest caring? No matter!

She followed the young woman's gesture toward the door of the office that she knew so well. The door was ajar. There were shadows moving around within. The doctor was, indeed, at her desk.

"She's waiting for you."

"Thanks!"

"You're welcome, have a great session," she said as she turned and then disappeared back to her post.

Lydia stood there for a moment at the door, pooling her thoughts and safely securing her emotions. She didn't want to start crying as soon as she saw O'Toole's deep caring brown eyes.

She knocked lightly on the door.

"Come in, Lydia, come in!" her East Coast accent boomed from behind the door. She pushed the door aside and met her in the doorway with a gentle hug and a warm, sincere smile. "How are we doing today?" Doctor Shannon O'Toole slid her free hand to Lydia's shoulder and patted it gently.

We? Some things hadn't changed.

Shannon looked exactly as Lydia had expected a psychologist to look. She remembered almost laughing the first time that they had met nearly ten years ago. A short, dark hared, caring, energetic woman greeted her with her glasses propped up against the tip of her over-sized nose. She helped make sharing one's inner most thoughts as natural as talking about the weather.

Unlike some people who only asked questions as part of a social greeting, it was as if Shannon actually wanted to know how one was *really feeling*. It was as if she actually cared. She waited for her patients to say something, to do something and then responded accordingly.

The doctor scanned her with thoughtful eyes, and then gently touched Lydia on her shoulder again. Shannon pushed the door shut as she directed Lydia farther into the room and toward the special couch. "Would you like to sit down?"

It sounded as if she had something very exciting to talk about.

Shannon reached over and turned on the sound recorder that sat on the shelf in the corner of the room just as she had always done, to review their conversation later for analysis if needed.

Lydia nodded and sat down in the chair. It was one of the reasons why she had been coming to Dr. O'Toole as long as she had. She had a knack of reading exactly how one felt. She didn't know if it was from years of dealing with people with similar problems, or if she actually had a gift, fulfilling her destiny, so to speak. After what Lydia had gone through lately, she now believed that just about anything was possible.

"Lydia, there is something very different about you today." She seemed pleased with this observation. "I am anxious to find out what it is."

As usual, instead of sitting in the chair behind the security of her desk, she sat next to Lydia in an 'almost love seat' style couch, where the patient and doctor both sat in recliners within arm's reach, both facing each other. At first it took her a while to get used to the special chairs, which were the doctor's pride and joy. She originally thought them too intimate for her liking, but now she had grown to appreciate them. They helped her to become more relaxed, more personal.

Lydia's eyes scanned around the room. Disappointingly, the doctor's office was still the same. She welcomed it with a nod, and fought back the tears that were trying to come forth.

"So Lydia, let's get right down to it. How do you like what we've done with this place?" she said, giving her a great big, proud smile.

"The waiting room looks great!" Lydia exclaimed.

"Doesn't it! That was the problem in the first place-it was a waiting room, by no means a very comfortable, protective environment. Stagnant, would be more like it! It was like waiting in a dungeon for the executioner," she laughed as she gestured her hands towards the other room. "Instead of the parlor of the castle, now it's a receiving room, a reception area, a cozy place for warmer thoughts and mental preparation."

"No, it wasn't that bad!" exclaimed Lydia.

"Well, maybe not, but it was definitely time for a change, right down to the music."

"How did you decide on the theme?"

The doctor looked over her glasses and smiled. "With a name like Shannon O'Toole?" she said, so matter of fact. "I had taken a recent trip to the mother country, and well, it was an inspiring trip I tell you. As you can see...," she gestured towards the front lobby again.

Lydia nodded, "It's wonderful!"

"Finally! Now, with all of that out of the way, let's talk about why we are really here."

We!

Lydia nodded and then swallowed. Trying to explain everything that had taken place over the last week or so wasn't going to be easy. Dealing with the anniversary of her husband's passing was one thing, but her son's strange behavior, the journal, the angels, those were another thing entirely.

"Well?" Lydia didn't know exactly where or how to begin. She just opened her mouth and let her thoughts spill out in the form of words. "Do you believe in God?" she blurted out and then studied the doctor's face closely.

Shannon gave her an even closer look back. "You have never asked me that before."

"You knew I was Catholic, right?"

"Well yes," she nodded, "you told me a while back."

"But you've never told me whether or not you believed in God."

"No, I hadn't. It was never about me!"

"Well, do you... believe in God?"

Shannon narrowed her eyes as she looked over her glasses and upon Lydia's expectant face. "You're serious, aren't you? This is very much not like you now is it? Why the sudden urgency?" It was obvious that she didn't like her patients taking over the sessions, but to her credit, she knew enough that sometimes, for better or worse, she had to let things run their course. "It's about the anniversary, isn't it?"

"It's something I need to know," Lydia pleaded with determined excitement. "Whatever I tell you next will depend on your truthful answer!" Lydia felt Shannon's gaze burning into her subconscious. She stared back, stone-faced and persistent. Neither of them blinked. The few seconds of uneasy silence that passed seemed like minutes. Her thoughts raced; there was so much to tell, so much to ask.

It was Shannon who blinked first. "Okay... yes, I do believe in God."

So far so good.

Lydia nodded. It was now her turn to take the doctor down the path of understanding. She lowered her voice. "Do you believe in angels?"

"Angels?" she sounded surprised, her voice contemplative. "There are about 273 references to them in the Holy Bible."

Her matter of fact response started to anger Lydia. "Yes, but, do you believe?"

"In the literary form?"

"No, in literal form!" she exclaimed. The tone of her voice surprised herself.

Shannon closed her eyes, leaned back in her chair and rubbed her face with the palms of both of her hands. "Are you asking me if I believe in something I can't see?" she gave out a deep sigh, "I was taught to believe in religion, but science demands evidence. I can't put my faith into..." she glanced at the certificates on the wall, "the interpretation of the written word and the superstitions that follow. They both have their moments, one contradicts the other."

When she looked over, Lydia saw the sorrow in her eyes. She felt sympathy build deep within. She got the feeling that the good doctor had been struggling with that very fact, possibly for most of her adult life. It was probably that very fact that led her to the career she had chosen.

"It's the battle between church and state!" Shannon continued, after giving a deep sigh. She focused on Lydia. "Believe me, I want very much to believe in angels, but I have yet to see their work. Oh yeah, there are wishful stories, lots of them!"

She doesn't believe!

Lydia's thoughts echoed in her mind. Her sympathy for Shannon grew.

How lonely she must feel.

Lydia knew exactly how she must have felt; she had recently been there herself. It was strange, she wanted to reach out and hug Shannon, shake her awake. She wanted to reverse the roles of nurturer and recipient. She wanted to assure her that everything would be all right. That if she kept her faith, and reached deep within herself, the understanding that she desired would come.

"No good deed goes unpunished." Shannon raised her hands into the air. "I cannot tell you why good people are allowed to perish and the evil ones are allowed to profit off the backsides of others and live forever, continuing their ways. Freedom of choice, gift or a curse! God only knows and, evidently—"

"He isn't telling!" Lydia mumbled under her breath.

Shannon gave her a surprised look.

That's what Gabriel says!

Lydia gave a quick look around the room.

Lydia suddenly felt chilled. Her pulse increased and her fingers and toes tingled. She looked down at her hands.

They trembled slightly.

Lydia crossed her arms and pulled them closer into her body to hide the fact. Her thoughts flashed back to the journal, back to Gabriel.

God only knows, and evidently he isn't telling!

Those words stung.

"Lydia, what's wrong?" Shannon reached out and held one of Lydia's hands. "Honey, you're trembling!" She slid the both of her hands up to Lydia's wrist and squeezed her fingers to check her circulation. It's what medical doctors instinctively did.

"That phrase you just said, it was exactly what Gabriel wrote in his journal!" She heard the confusion in her own voice.

"Gabriel kept a journal?" Shannon sat up excitedly and leaned forward. "You never told me about that before!"

"I had forgotten all about it just until a few days ago. My son Gabe, said he found it sitting on the desk in my study. I accused him of taking it from its hiding place in the attic, but as it ends up, it wasn't him that brought it down."

Shannon gave her a bizarre look. "Wasn't who?"

"Gabe."

"You said you found it just sitting on the desk?"

"Yes."

"If it wasn't your son, then who else could have taken it down from the attic?"

"That's just it, I don't know!" Lydia fought back the tears.

Shannon gave her a confused look.

Lydia pushed herself to continue. "I tried to read it right after he passed, but I couldn't, so I put it away in the attic... it sat there for almost ten years. How was I supposed to know that he'd left me a message, left us a message?"

"What kind of message?" Her interest peaked even more.

Lydia gave out a deep sigh. Her thoughts jumbled. There was so much to say. Where to begin? "Gabe, myself, and evidently Dan, Gabriel's brother."

Shannon leaned forward on the couch, intrigued, her mouth agape. She no longer interrupted. Lydia took a deep breath and continued, before she lost her train of thought.

What should I tell her? What could I tell her?

"During this last week, incredibly strange things had been building up to the tenth anniversary of Gabriel's death." She took another deep breath and continued, covering everything that had happened in a systematic manner. Again she felt calm and in control of her emotions. "It's about the anniversary!"

She started with Gabe's strange stories of the alley and locker room. She then stumbled through the journal, the arrival of her brother and sister in-law. Then as calmly as could be, she reflected on the alleged visitation from her deceased husband and an angel, that very morning. When she finished, she was out of breath. Her fingers and toes tingled with excitement. Her throat was dry and goose bumps ran the length of her entire body. She felt invigorated, like a huge burden had been lifted from her neck and shoulders.

She found herself sitting up, staring intently into Shannon's pale confused face. She tried to read her emotions, seeing if she actually believed what she was telling her. To her surprise, Shannon's mouth still lay open, her narrow eyes almost peering through her. The ear piece of her removed glasses were shoved into the corner of her slender mouth as she contemplated what she had just heard.

They stared silently at each other for a moment. It was Lydia who could no longer wait. She spoke with quiet concern. "Shannon... Shannon?" It took a moment to get her attention. "Shannon!" This time she spoke loud and direct. "What do you have to say?"

There was a slight delay.

"Well, I don't know... you have been, well, busy. I do need to say that I'm a little concerned—" she seemed confused, disturbed.

"I know what you're thinking," Lydia interrupted, "but it all really did happen. You have to believe me!"

"How can you possibly know what I'm thinking!" she interjected defensively.

Lydia forced a knowing smile. "Because, I know that look, I felt the same way myself a couple of days ago. I wouldn't have believed it myself if I weren't there, living every moment of it. But I was, and it did happen!" Lydia silently studied her face a moment before she leaned forward and abruptly stood up from the couch.

Shannon doesn't understand, she doesn't believe. Maybe in the future she would, but I need her to believe me right now!

Lydia didn't need any more confusion in her life. She needed understanding and support. She took a couple of steps towards the door.

"Where are you going?" Shannon blurted out as she slowly raised herself from the couch. A confused expression embraced her face.

"Home... where I'm needed!" She couldn't believe how incredibly good it felt to say that.

Shannon clumsily slipped her glasses back onto her face as she attempted to pull herself together.

"I've decided," Lydia glanced at the certificates on the wall behind the desk, "this will be my last session. As I see things right now," she refocused on Shannon's face, her voice calm. "I'm not coming back."

"But, why? We aren't through... these things we're feeling! The change in you... we need to re-schedule, revisit! We need to talk about... all of this!" She waved her arm.

"It's obvious to me that you're not going to be able to help me at this point!" Lydia's voice was calm, she felt confident and in control. "Maybe others can help!"

"Others?" Shannon looked stunned.

"Those closer to the source!"

"The source?" the doctor sounded confused.

They both stood there staring at each other for a moment. This was the first time she had seen Shannon speechless.

"It's okay!" Lydia reached over and gave her a big hug.

Shannon stood there frozen.

"Thanks to you, I know what I need now!"

Shannon allowed the emotional hug. "What's that?" She looked rather confused, her voice shaky and distant. Her eyes on the verge of tears.

"My family and my faith," Lydia suddenly felt good. Her negative thoughts seemed to melt away. The chill, the worries, they were all gone. She turned away, opened the door and walked silently out of the room, leaving the door open and never looking back.

***

Shannon just stood there as she watched her patient and friend embark on a journey with newfound confidence. Whether or not it was in the right direction was yet to be determined.

"Lydia!" she whispered.

That was when she felt the presence of someone else in the room and heard the soft faint voice behind her that caught her by surprise.

"Sometimes the student becomes the teacher!"

She abruptly turned and looked behind her. She was still alone. Seconds later a light cool breeze blew past her ears and towards the open door sending a chill down her spine.

"No!" the sound of her own frightened voice gave her the chills.

"In the garden of Saint Francis" by April Leiterman

CHAPTER NINTEEN
SOLITUDE AT LAST
(MONDAY AFTERNOON)
MARCH 14TH 2000

Gabe jumped up when he heard the sharp rap on the front door. It wasn't that his nerves were shot from the roller coaster of emotions he had gone through over the last week or so, no, it was more out of learning what to expect, and adjust to the unexpected.

"I got it!" his excited voice echoed as he rolled off the couch and hurried across the living room and towards the door.

His mom continued to sit at the kitchen table. She excitedly conversed and laughed with his aunt and uncle about her recent doctor visit, as they huddled around her, seemingly oblivious to the activity at the door.

When he flung the door open, he was pleased and surprised to see his friend standing there in front of him. A noticeable smile across his face. "Erick!"

"In the flesh!"

They silently stood there for a moment, squirming uncomfortably from side to side, before they both guiltily blurted out at once.

"I'm sorry—"

"I should've—"

They laughed. It felt good to laugh.

"You go first!" Gabe giggled.

"No, your house, you go first!"

"No, guests first!" Gabe exclaimed not wanting to be outdone on this one. "Common practice in the Wilson household. Besides, you're the one who came all the way out here in the first place to apologize to me!"

"Apologize?" Erick pretended to be offended.

"Are you going to invite your friend inside or are you going to make him stay out there on the front porch?" his mom's voice lectured from across the room. "Besides, you're letting in cold air."

Gabe gave his mom a quick glance over his shoulder and was surprised to see all three of them smiling intently back at him. He suddenly felt embarrassed.

It's tough enough to apologize, but to do it in front of an audience!

"Sorry about that!" Gabe patted his friend on his shoulder and guided him into the house.

"That's okay!" Erick said.

"Not about that... about that!" He pointed over to his family. He loved his family, but there was a time and place, this he found embarrassing.

When Erick looked over, everyone was smiling back at them. He gave them a friendly wave.

They returned it.

Gabe rolled his eyes. "I know where we can go to find some *privacy!*" He emphasized the word with an annoyed stare at his family, and nodded toward the back door.

His friend smiled in agreement. Erick followed his friend towards the back door.

Dan started to get up to join them, but Lydia gently laid a hand on his arm to stop him. She shook her head and smiled. "Maybe later!" she said.

Dan reluctantly sank back down into his chair.

"Thank you." Lydia whispered. She went back to recalling and confirming her office visit without skipping a beat.

Gabe listened to her voice fade as they made their way to the back door. He took one last look over his shoulder to make sure that they weren't followed before he reached for the doorknob. He gave out a deep sigh.

Privacy at last!

***

The translucent young man in white, stared down into the calm water of the pond at his mirror-like reflection. Grace and beauty smiled back among the cottony cumulus clouds that drifted past, accenting his beautiful features. Colorful koi swam casually beneath the water's surface, oblivious to the figure intently staring down upon them.

He knelt down upon one knee, lowered his handsome face to within inches of the water's surface. The divine creature breathed in deeply. He sighed disappointedly, his pleasant smile faded slightly. It's not that there wasn't a smell, the flowers were in full bloom, and it's just that he couldn't smell it. He didn't need to smell or taste it, for that matter, to know of its beauty. He lacked the human ability to stimulate his senses. He had watched other humans recoil to some things and smile at others, wondering what they felt, why they reacted the way they did.

The young man watched his youthful image grow in size until it covered most of the reflection of the pond surface.

As he got closer the fish and gravel grew in detail, but the fish didn't scatter. To them, the giant didn't exist. The translucent figure watched the gills of the fish expand and contract, their mouths open and close in rhythmic patterns, reflecting the natural cycle that ran throughout the universe. Their expressionless eyes stared off into oblivion. His smile returned to the liquid mirror.

"Created in the likeness of God."

His confident voice rolled across the water's surface. The young man looked human in every aspect except one, he wasn't and would probably never be human.

The water striders were oblivious to his steady gaze as they scattered across the waters' surface. They moved quickly away from the fish. Though predators themselves, they knew they were also prey.

"One world within another... one unaware of the next!"

He slowly reached down with his index finger until it disturbed the mirror image. Concentric rings flowed out from their origin. The mirror disrupted. The fish scattered, disappearing beneath the safety of the pond lilies, the insects and detail of the gravel, no longer discernable in the sudden storm.

"But, until they meet and the connection is made... do they realize that they share the same time and space?"

He vocalized his thoughts, lifted his hand from the pond's surface and watched the droplets drip from his finger. He watched the expanding energy rings collide into chaos.

"So easy it is to disrupt, so great is the impact."

He watched the water's surface return back to one of glass, the koi peeking out from the protection of the vegetative cover.

"And so quickly it recovers."

Regrettably, he could only imagine the sensation of touch and taste that humans take for granted. Unlike Christ himself, he has never walked the earth as a human, never experienced the lives of mortals. He often wondered what it would be like to feel, smell, taste, and experience the same sensations of being human.

Maybe only then I would understand them better.

"Let us begin."

He smiled before the back door as it swung noisily open. He knew the two boys had arrived.

He slowly turned his head in their direction.

He didn't fear being seen, for today, he was invisible to all. He was only there to listen, to observe, and if needed, to protect.

"It's my responsibility to see that Gabriel's Legacy will continue."

He sighed deeply as his thoughts raced. In a strange way, Gabe reminded him of the boy's father. He had liked Gabriel; it took all he had to stand there and let him be taken within inches of his life saving touch.

"It was meant to be. It is what I am told." He looked up to the sky. *"I did as you asked. Now, here I am again, dealing with Gabriel in miniature. Father have mercy."*

He looked back to the boys.

"Like the boy's father, he too will have a human to guide and assist. If there was something he couldn't accomplish, under your direction, his friend will be there to help right the wrongs."

He stood up and looked once again into the heavens.

"I understand that I am only here to protect when requested, to guide, to watch, to even manipulate the weather if needed and when the time is to come, to do whatever you ask of me, and then to guide him home."

He looked back at the boys and took a few steps backwards.

He felt the excitement in the air. The energy generated from the love of the garden himself.

"Are these human qualities?"

The thought filled him with tenderness. This was truly a blessed place. Built with love for those whom he loved, protected by angels under the guidance of the Almighty.

He turned to listen.

***

Gabe pushed on the door and held it open for his friend.
"I want to apologize," Erick squeaked.
Gabe pulled it shut behind him and turned to face him.
"I never should've called you a liar, you were right!" Erick rested a hand on his friend's shoulder.
Gabe gave him a surprised look.
"It seems that blond kid is an angel, after all! Who would have thought?" Erick gave out a notable sigh before he continued. "Just because you don't see them, doesn't mean that they aren't there!"
They both smiled.
"That sounds like something my uncle would say."
"Your uncle must be a smart man."
"You know it." Gabe high-fived his friend.
"I saw the blond kid again, this morning. It was after you... left, after our argument. He said I was supposed to help you! What do you think he meant?"
"I think I saw him here at the pond the other day when I was with my uncle!" Gabe exclaimed as he looked around the yard. "Well at least I thought I did."
Erick looked at him surprised. "You saw him... here?" He shot a quick glance around the yard. "Are you sure it was him?"
Gabe shrugged his shoulders and dropped his arms along his side. "I think it was, but now I'm not so sure. He disappeared before I could confirm what I saw. He smiled at me. My uncle said he didn't see him, but took my word for it that he was standing there right next to him."
"Right next to him?"
"Yeah, arm around his waist."
"So far, from what I can figure out, that's how it works. Now you see him, now you don't."

***

The unseen angel smiled.
Yes, that's how it works. Sometimes you see me, sometimes you won't! But by God's grace we are there.

***

Gabe nodded. "Evidently, according to my uncle, my dad didn't see them until the end." He forced a smile.

Erick gave him an odd look.

"Maybe it's actually better that I don't get to see them!" Just the thought of it made his heart race. He could tell his friend knew what he meant. "I do feel them though. In my dad's journal, he said he felt them all the time."

Erick smiled back, he nodded and glanced around the yard.

It was Gabe who broke the uncomfortable silence. "So, Erick, you're guna' help me then?"

"Yeah, every day bro," he smiled.

"That's good, because we're going camping."

"Camping? We?" This time it was Erick's turn to look surprised.

"Yep, we! Uncle Dan, you and me. We're going to the park for the anniversary of my dad's death."

He saw the disbelief in Erick's face. "Is your mom okay with this? Are you okay with this?"

"I think so," his eyes directed to the ground. He understood what his friend was thinking.

Why would anyone put themselves, their mother, or anyone for that matter that they cared about through that whole episode again?

You were supposed to forget things like that, not bring them back to life, not re-live all that sorrow and failures. Lydia had gone to the doctor for years for that very reason; but time was also the teacher, time was the healer. Just as things were created over time, things were ultimately destroyed by it. He knew he needed to meet this challenge. The drive was building, pushing him to the brink.

"Yes, I believe everything has been building up to this. Dan is going to take me, he's going to take us both to the park where my dad passed away." He felt his body shudder at the sound of his words, but he needed to hear them.

Erick's face seemed to be even more concerned than confused.

"It's what needs to be none." Gabe shrugged his shoulders. His own voice seemed calm and controlled. He extended his hand towards his friend. "What do you say, are you going to join us in the mountains? Will you help me through this?"

Erick reached out and grasped Gabe's hand. Their eyes rested on each other's. They both smiled. Gabe knew his answer before he even spoke. When they made contact he felt his arm tingle and his heart thunder in his chest, excited about the adventure to the mountains.

"Ok Gabe, let's do this together," Erick responded with an ear to ear grin.

***

The angel smiled. "Let the journey begin! May two hearts beat as one."

ACT 2:
AMONG THE ANCIENT TREES

"A Conspiracy of Ravens" by April Leiterman

CHAPTER TWENTY
AROUND THE CAMPFIRE
(TUESDAY NIGHT)
MARCH 15TH 2010 (THE DAY BEFORE)

The camp five crackled and popped in the cool, quiet evening as Erick, Dan, and Gabe silently stared into its glowing embers. It was mesmerizing. For Dan it wasn't just the coziness of sitting in the darkness around a warm campfire, surrounded by his only nephew and his nephew's friend, which made the evening special. Nor was it the aroma of burning cedar in the ancient redwoods that triggered the primal experience in them. No, it was the familiarity of the unknown, the déjà vu' that had driven this experience home. Dan had been here before with his brother during the autumn of 1999.

How could I have forget?

There were two of them back then, brothers! He shuddered at the thought and tucked his arms closer into his sides as he glanced over his shoulders into the darkness. He smiled. He had done so that evening as well. It really didn't matter that staring into the glowing embers of the fire had ruined his night vision, or the fact that he couldn't have seen a grizzly bear standing a mere five yards away, if he'd had to.

He had sat right there with his brother in silence, both gazing into the flickering flames in deep thought, as they did now. Both were contemplating what to say to the other, both knowing that something was in the air, something that would forever change their lives. The smell of cedar was strong on the breeze then, as it was now. A distant great horned owl hooted its intermittent calls just like it had back then. He felt his muscles tighten, his fingers tingle after every one he heard.

Was he the messenger of death? Was there any truth to that bit of folklore? If you believed it, did I make it true?

It was a time when one really didn't want to know.

Is ignorance bliss?

The fire popped loudly after every new piece was added. The sound made him flinch even when he expected it. His thoughts suddenly back to the here and now.

"Dan are you okay?" The concern in Gabe's voice was discernable.

Dan looked over at his nephew. The firelight flickered off the whites of his moist eyes. For a moment, he thought he was staring into the face of his deceased younger brother. He forced his smile to hide his surprise. "Did I ever tell you how much you—"

"Look like my father when he was my age? Yeah, several times." Gabe returned the smile; it was obvious that it pleased him.

It's time.

"It's pretty strange, you know. More than ten years ago, I sat here in this very spot, and your dad, well, he sat right where you are now." He nodded as he cleared his throat. He gulped down a couple swallows of soda to satisfy his sudden nervous thirst.

"He sat right there?" Erick piped up.

"Yep, in that very spot," he motioned to everyone with his sloshing soda can before taking another swig, "Much like tonight. We sat here quietly, in deep thought, mesmerized by the fire, listening to the sounds of the forest!" He rolled on as a storyteller. His thoughts were drawn to the popping flames of the cedar, and the smoke that swirled around them.

The shades of red, green, orange, yellow and blue danced among the charred embers.

"Did you know that the spirits of all of the colors of the once-living tree are released to the heavens in the form of smoke, heat, and energy? That the rest are returned to the building blocks of life in another form; ashes to ashes, dust to dust?"

Both Erick and Gabe exchanged odd glances.

Dan took another sip of his drink and shook loose his thoughts to concentrate. "But, it was a little bit different back then. The winds were picking up. The trees were talking among themselves as they creaked and moaned. Then, there was this owl. It seemed to have called for hours. It was pretty cool and strange at the same time." He took another sip of soda.

Gabe looked over his shoulder in the direction the owl had called earlier.

"Do you think there was a message?" Erick cautiously asked. "They say that if you hear an owl—"

"That death is soon to follow… the messenger of someone passing." Dan shrugged his shoulders and fought back a chill. "I've heard of that. So is it folklore or reality? I guess you could take it or leave it!" He shifted his gaze to Erick. "We will all eventually die, so does that mean their right? And we live for another year, does that mean they're wrong?"

"But tonight is quiet!" Gabe piped up wanting to change the subject.

"Yes, quite a contrast to that night." Dan's eyes went back to the mesmerizing flames. He focused on keeping his emotions at bay. "We both had a lot on our minds that night." He let out another deep sigh and forced his gaze into Gabe's curious eyes. "It was that late fall evening that your father informed me of his impending death."

"He knew? How did he?" Gabe exclaimed, he narrowed his eyes as if a disturbing thought had overwhelmed him.

"He said an angel told him, told him exactly when, how and where. I don't think he ever knew why!"

"So you knew, yet you didn't say anything about it to mom or me?" His words were pointed and direct.

Dan shook his head. "Your dad never disclosed anything about the when, where, how and why to me. He wrote about it in his journal. I couldn't have done anything about it if I wanted to. That part he chose to keep privately to himself. I probably wouldn't have believed him anyway if he had. It would've been too farfetched, too difficult to swallow!" Dan took another long swig of his soda.

Both boys stared at him. Only their expressive faces stood out against the flickering darkness.

"I really miss your dad... I miss my brother." He cleared his throat again. The firelight reflected off his moist eyes. "He had a mysterious side to him, you know. He kept his secrets well hidden. I wish I had known that he actually wrote in the journal years ago. I would have had a better understanding of what was going on in his head. I had to wait ten years, as it was, to find a better understanding of what's going on now!" He desperately searched Gabe's expression, and was relieved when Gabe nodded in agreement. "Guardian angels, I would have never believed it if I hadn't experienced them for myself."

"But, at least you've seen them, right?" Gabe widened his eyes as he shifted his gaze between them.

Dan and Erick both looked at each other.

Dan tilted his head back and sucked the last of the soda out of his can. He then reached over and threw a couple more pieces of madrone onto the fire. Sparks shot into the air like shooting stars.

Their eyes followed.

"I hear this blond kid has been pretty busy lately. I wouldn't be surprised if he were hanging around here this very minute." Dan shared.

Both of the boys' eyes shot quick glances around the darkness and into the building brightness of the fire. They nervously moved closer together.

Dan smiled at their reaction. He couldn't help but do the same himself. If the angel was out there he couldn't see him, but he could feel him working 24-7 for Gabe's welfare.

To succeed where I had once failed?

The fire roared to life. The sound of an approaching engine and the glare of vehicle headlights caught their attention. Like a moth attracted to a flame, the two boys silently stared at the approaching vehicle.

"Visitors!" Dan exclaimed.

"Who do you think it is?" Erick asked.

"Friends," Dan smiled.

The vehicle pulled to a stop behind theirs, the engine went silent, and went off with the lights. Dan recognized the vehicle. The light from the glowing flames illuminated the reflective emblem on its side. It was the rangers. He consciously looked down at his watch. It wasn't quite 10:00 p.m., campground quiet time and they definitely weren't noisy in the nearly vacant campground.

"Most likely a social call."

He recognized one of the two men as the park superintendent, a friend.

"Chief Ranger Eddie Mendoza!" Dan was pleasantly surprised; he had known the elderly man for years. He stood up and took a couple of steps toward the two approaching uniformed men. "What brings you all the way out here during this time of night? Are you guys hurting that badly for field rangers to the point where the Chief Ranger actually has to pull shifts in the middle of the off season?" Dan laughed as he reached out to shake Eddie's hand and then gave him a warm embrace.

"Hello Dan. Looks like the rumors are true. The prodigal son has returned! Longtime no see!" Eddie returned the laugh.

"Yes, too long!" Dan responded.

"This is Paul, Paul Behan," Eddie gestured with his hand. "Paul, this is Dan Wilson, the man I've been telling you about. He's one of the wilderness rangers down in the Southern California Mountains.

"Good to meet you," Paul gave Dan a firm handshake.

"Are you up here to check out the ranger vacancy?" the fit-looking ranger in his mid-thirties asked.

"Well, not exactly!" he glanced over to Eddie, "I'm not so sure Eddie here is interested in hiring a 56 year old broken down man."

Eddie gave him an understanding nod. "Yeah, that's pretty ancient."

Dan smiled, he had returned numerous times since his brother's passing in 2000. When they did get around to talking about the past, their conversations always managed to find their way to Gabriel. He had made his mark in the park folklore and in the hearts of those who knew and loved him. Eddie knew it was no coincidence that Dan had stumbled into the campground on the tenth anniversary of his brother's death.

"We could always use another Wilson on staff to make us coffee and take out the garbage." Eddie laughed.

"Ha, ha!" Dan pretended to laugh.

"Don't rule us out yet, Dan. You know as well as I do that this place isn't always as it appears." Eddie looked over his shoulder for effect. "Maybe it's the trees, maybe it's the water, or something entirely different. Maybe it will all make sense once we stumble upon that energy vortex thing the old hippies have been raving about!"

"And constantly looking for!" laughed Paul.

The others joined him.

"The coveted fountain of youth," laughed Eddie.

"Yep, it's definitely the water! No doubt about it." said Dan.

Everyone laughed again, except the boys. They in turn shot each other a strange glance.

Eddie rested his hand lightly on Dan's shoulder for a moment before he diverted his attention towards the two boys. "So, who do we have here?"

"This is my nephew Gabe and his friend, Erick Adams."

Both boys stood up and extended their hands around the fire ring without the usual coaxing.

"So, you're Gabriel's little boy!" Eddie sounded surprised. "Well, not so little anymore, are you? Last time I saw you, you were four or five years old at the time, and I believe about this tall." He held his hand about waist height to emphasize his point as he studied Gabe closely in the fire-light. "He does look a lot like him, doesn't he?"

"Yep, more and more like him every day, and I just don't mean his looks either!"

Eddie nodded in agreement and then looked back over to Gabe. "Your father was a good man. He loved these mountains. He did everything he could to protect them, and all of those who came to visit."

"So I've been told!" Gabe nodded shyly in appreciation.

Eddie turned back to Dan. There was seriousness to the tone of his voice. "Enough small talk for now, let me jump to the other reason we dropped by. We've got a missing juvenile, officially reported missing today at 1800 hours," he nodded to the boys, "six o'clock this evening. Evidently, the kid was last seen some time this morning. We're going to go all-out early tomorrow morning when more of the Sheriff's search and rescue posse shows up before sunrise with the dogs and the like. Hey, if you're looking for something to do, we could use an extra hand or two." He gestured to the boys. "It would be great to have you join us." He paused for a moment, prodding deeper into Dan's thoughts. "You know these mountains almost about as well as I do. So, can we count on you? It'll help take the mind off, you know, the past."

Dan nodded. Eddie was right; they needed something to busy their idle thoughts. There would be plenty of time to talk along the way. He made eye contact with the two boys before he focused back onto Eddie. Dan had taken the boys uncontrolled smiles as a definite yes. "Then, if there's no objection, it looks like a go!"

"Good!" Eddie nodded as he extended his hand to Dan. "Briefing at 0600 hours sharp, dress for an all-day affair." He looked back at the boys, "that would be 6:00 in the morning for you civilian types. The kid's family, staff and I will be very appreciative." The group shook hands all around.

They watched the two rangers return to their vehicle and drive off. They silently listened to the engine fade away.

"Well, looks like we have an exciting first day ahead of us." Dan shared.

Both boys jumped up and high-fived each other in the excitement.

"If we're going to spend the entire day searching, we'd better turn in early." Dan interjected.

The firelight reflected off the boys' excited eyes.

***

"*And so it begins!*"

The curly haired young man whispered as he looked on from the shadows that danced around him, caused by the flickering fire. He knew those weren't just ordinary shadows. He had company, that's why he was there. He did not feel the chill in the air, or the uneasiness that was growing in the hearts of those he now protected. Nor did he fear the unknown that awaited the fate of the group beyond the reaches of the firelight. He knew what lived in the shadows, what thrived in the darkness of people's souls, awaiting the opportunity to deceive and redirect.

"*Do they know what awaits them?*"

But, for the moment, all was well. It would be his job to keep *them* away. Beyond the influence of the firelight, hidden among the shadows, *them* of the forest dwelled. For centuries every religion and every culture had acknowledged their existence. They wait for their opportunity to strike down the unsuspecting, to influence their thoughts and desires. It was the way of things. The safety of the light, the uneasiness of darkness, and runaway imaginations, all worked into their favor.

"*Only if humans knew the subtle difference. Tomorrow will be different. They will traveling into the domain of the unknown. That is unknown to the three of them. They will be helping to search for more than a missing person. They will be searching their own souls. I had failed once, and I'm not planning on failing again.*"

He knew the choice wasn't his to make.

"*But what of my influence?*"

Freedom of choice was a human quality; it was one of the factors that set them aside from the common animal.

"*Humans have a soul. Without it, they just wouldn't be... human; they wouldn't understand the power of choice, the curse of the divine.*"

As he did, he knew the dark angels had their jobs to do as well. Choice was to be influenced, war had to be waged, battles needed to be fought and won, and in some cases lost. A strange, delicate balance must be maintained at all cost. Nothing was really lost or gained in the big picture, just redistributed in the appropriate proportions. Good people would continue to die young, while some evil people seemed to live forever. Good choices, bad choices-their meanings were in the minds and hearts of the beholders, or at the hand of God.

"If I were those humans seeking sanctuary in those tents, what would I be thinking right now? How would I be preparing for tomorrow? If they knew what I knew, would they be on their knees asking the almighty to protect them? To guide them through the right choices, to allow me, the angel assigned, to protect and guide them, the opportunity to do what needs to be done? Will the almighty keep the darkness, and all who call it home, at bay?"

CHAPTER TWENTY-ONE
FROM THE DARKNESS
MARCH 16TH 2000 @ 0300 HOURS
ANNIVERSARY DATE

Erick tossed and turned in his sleeping bag. The ground no longer seemed as comfortable as it did when he first lay down to sleep. The smallest of the rocks they neglected to remove beneath their tent had grown in size, their rounded sides taking on edges, and the flat ground no longer seemed so level. His head now felt lower than his feet. Good for someone in a state of shock, but lousy for someone who needed to pee, like yesterday. The interior of his bag was no longer warm and cozy. All of that could be suffered through for one night, but it was the nightmare of every camper that filled him with dread in the darkness. His bladder was full, which meant he had to leave the warmth and security of the tent and venture into the darkest of the night to answer the call.

He had spent the last fifteen to thirty minutes squirming on the noisy air pad that was supposed to protect him from the cold, rough ground. He didn't have to check it to know that it was obviously low in air. He hoped it was a loose valve, which he could easily fix in minutes with a little extra air and a valve check. An outright leak, however, would mean an uncomfortable, cold, next few nights. After he answered nature's call, he would check into that dilemma as well.

He tried to be quiet in the tight confines of the two-person tent, but it seemed that every sound appeared twice as loud in the stillness of the night. To his amazement, Gabe never stirred; almost as if he were dead to the world. The sound of his slow rhythmic breathing and the rise and fall of his sleeping bag said otherwise.

Oh, so lucky was Gabe, at peace with his thoughts, overtaken by exhaustion.

He looked at his watch again. The indigo light confirmed his fears for the umpteenth time. It was only three o'clock in the morning, five minutes since he had last checked. He could not take the wait much longer. If he didn't go soon, he would have another embarrassing problem on his hands. He pushed on, trying to lose himself in his thoughts as he looked upon the lump of his friend.

He wondered how and where in the park his best friend's father had passed away, or what it would be like to willingly go back to that very spot where he had perished. The thought made his sleeping bag that much colder. It was too bad the rescue had materialized the way it did. In a way it was good to take everyone's mind off of the dreaded anniversary. It was a morbid thing, like slowing down at an accident scene to take a curious glance at the mayhem and chaos, thankful it wasn't you.

Earlier, from the safety of their tent, they had talked softly about everything that had happened thus far, how things had built up until that moment. They only touched upon what was expected of them for the March 16th, anniversary. To dwell on it, to speak of these thoughts, could bring disaster down upon them. The thoughts seemed silly; they seemed unwarranted as they sat happily around the warm cozy fire. They even seemed unfounded as they lay there in their sleeping bags alongside each other, protected from the night by the thin membrane of breathable material, whispering to each other so as to not bother Dan.

He didn't know what it was, but they could feel it. A strange energy drifted through the forest. It came and went throughout the night. It was when he stepped into the trees beyond the edge of their campsite, earlier that evening, to relieve himself, that he first felt it. There was an ever so faint pressure on his chest, tightness about his throat, a chill that started and stayed deep within, almost un-discernable in the night. It was there, and then it was gone. The voices around the campfire helped him find control of his emotions. He said nothing when he returned to the warmth of the fire. It had to be his imagination, the magic of the moment.

So here he was again, building up his nerve to go outside to relieve himself. A faint, peaceful snore was coming from the direction of Dan's dome tent, a deep slow breathing from his friend along his side. Hearing them had a calming effect on his nerves. The whole excitement of tomorrow, which was now officially today, had worked against his ability to sleep, but when he finally did, his bladder thought otherwise. He could wait no longer.

He unzipped his sleeping bag and wiggled out of his cocoon, the squeaky air mattress announced his movement. He confirmed the deflated air mattress with a quick glance and a push off with his hand. The cold air permeated his Capilene underwear. A faint light illuminated the tent's interior. The waning quarter of a moon hadn't quite descended beyond the forested ridge to the west. Fumbling for his headlamp, he would make this quick.

He didn't take the extra time to put on his shoes; his socks would have to do. He wasn't going to chance the darkness, so he turned on his headlamp and left it in his hands. He paused after he un-zipped the tent and threw back the entrance fly. The night was quiet, the intermittent moonlight had made the shadows that much darker. The beam of his headlamp turned the darkness into shades of gray. It was almost better without the light. The moisture in the air glowed brighter, reducing his vision. He looked up into the passing clouds of mist. Droplets of moisture tickled his face. It wasn't rain. The old growth forests were known to create their own weather in the microclimates that they created. He panned the darkness again with his light, searching the shadows for the unknown.

He gave out a deep sigh. From what he could see, to his satisfaction, all appeared safe.

He hurried over to the edge of the trees, 45 feet away and stopped. He looked over his shoulder and then as if an after thought, he took a few more steps even farther away from camp into the shadows of the forest. To free up his hands, he placed the headlamp onto his head and shone it in front of him. He could wait no longer. The closer to the task he had gotten, the stronger was the urge.

As he stood there swiveling his head, shining the beam of the lamp all around, he felt vulnerable, chilled in his long underwear. He tried to push away the thoughts about the uneasiness that he felt earlier that night. He knew the forest was full of predatory animals that did most of their hunting about that time of night. He only feared two, maybe three of them. That's if the legendary Bigfoot even existed.

But if angels exist....

He felt his body tremble.

He forced the thought out of his mind with a deep sigh and a few more quick passes of his head lamp. He still heard Dan's faint snores over the sounds of his business with nature.

"Almost done!" He whispered quietly to himself, longing to hear a human voice even if it was his own.

It was then that he felt it, the presence of something watching him. He turned and shone his light more radically now as he shifting from one side of the forest to the other, and then behind him toward camp. He saw nothing, but he felt it.

Something is out there, somewhere.

He tried to convince himself that it was nothing, but then, he heard it. He held his breath. It was the breaking of twigs under a foot placement, thirty, maybe sixty yards in front of him, maybe off to his left.

Maybe off to my right.

It was dark, almost impossible to judge distance and location in the quiet darkness. He started to back up, but then his legs felt as if they were frozen in place. His arms became weak, his breathing increased, his breath drifted up as steam. Coldness started deep within and then flowed to his fingers and toes. He shivered. It was like an eerie numbness grasped his chest and held him firmly in place.

He opened his mouth to speak, but all he could do was gasp for air. He could no longer talk.
What's happening to me?
He forced his thoughts.
Dan! Gabe!
He tried to call for help, but again nothing happened.
"*They will be of no help!*" the cold voice whispered through the air and echoed in his thoughts. "*They cannot help you! For that matter only you can help yourself by helping me!*"
He felt the goose bumps crawl across his skin, a nausea fill his insides. He wanted to vomit.
Was that from the darkness, or from inside of my own head? Is this really happening?
"*All you have to do is walk away, and things will be as they were,*" the voice threatened. "*Stay, and you will regret your choice!*"
He could feel the bone chilling hatred. He suddenly felt breathless. It was like a set of hands had squeezed about his neck. He clutched his throat, found nothing there, but the pressure continued. He began to panic. He tried to step backwards again, but his legs didn't respond. He felt doomed. His legs gave out. He fell to his trembling knees.
He heard the sound of crushing twigs, this time closer.
Something in the darkness was holding him in place, while something *else* was approaching. He felt it, he heard it. Something sinister was making its way towards him. On the verge of panic, he gasped. His energy drained even more. He collapsed under his own weight, his body tumble helplessly onto the ground. A warm breeze blew leaf litter into his face. The smell of decay filled his lungs. He closed his eyes to protect them from the debris. He struggled to pull in a breath; the smell of putrid sulfur caused him to gag instead. Then he vomited. His stomach wrenched until it hurt. Strange, frightening, angry grunts bombarded his thoughts like painful spears. His skin felt on fire, the ground felt as if it moved beneath him. Devastating images of fire battling water played in his mind, but made no sense. He felt insignificant in this scene that smelled and felt of death and destruction. He could endure no more.

Please make it stop! Make it stop!

"*You can make it stop, you can make a choice!*" the dark voice threatened.

He couldn't tell if his mind had screamed those words out loud or if it was from something sinister in the darkness.

"*Enough!*" The firm, powerful words echoed in his mind. He felt them vibrate from his chest and then pass through his entire body. The crushing pressure on his chest and neck were instantly gone. He now felt the cool mist against his face and the moist ground against his skin. He felt the movement in his fingers and toes as he scrambled to his feet and turned to face the shadows of the forest. His headlamp lay at his feet illuminating the ground. Strangely, just like that, the fear of the darkness was gone. He reached down, snatched up the light, and turned it off. He no longer needed the light. He felt a warm protective energy flow around him. He felt safe. He again heard the light snoring from Dan's tent. He took a couple of steps backward toward the tents and then stopped. The warmth grew stronger. He took a few more.

"Thank you!" he whispered. He felt a hand gently rest on his shoulder and abruptly turned to look. There was nothing that he could see. He took a couple steps backwards, turned and quickly made his way back to the safety of his tent.

CHAPTER TWENTY-TWO
THE BRIEFING
(WEDNESDAY MORNING)
MARCH 16TH 2000

"We need to get a move on, the morning briefing waits for no man or woman!" Dan exclaimed as he tried to hurry the boys along in the dim, morning light. Though the sun had just started to rise somewhere beyond the forested mountains, they probably wouldn't see or feel its warmth for yet another few hours. There was just enough ambient light to recognize items within arm's reach, but beyond that things were still shapeless shadows.

"But what about our packs and everything else?" Gabe quizzed, as he frantically scraped together the rest of his gear. His headlamp still sat unused on his head of matted hair.

"Boys', men, or beast, no matter! They wait not!" Dan shrugged his shoulders, "Don't worry about your personal gear right now, it's just the briefing, not the deployment!" Though he didn't smile, the boys could read the humor in his voice.

"The what?" quizzed Erick.

"We'll pull it all together once we figure out the when, where, and how!" said Dan.

Gabe's thoughts were overwhelming. He did everything he could to calm himself.

We're going on a search!

Gabe couldn't believe how well he had slept last night, dead to the world. It wasn't until this morning that he gave the searching thing some serious thought.
Looking for a missing kid! Wow, this is going to be cool!
"Now Gabe!" Dan exclaimed, his voice a bit more serious. "We needed to be over there like minutes ago." The sudden change in Dan's voice startled him. Almost on cue, both boys dropped everything and headed for the pavement with Dan right on their tail.
"Which way do we go?" Erick asked.
"That way, toward the glow of lights." Dan encouraged them along with a gentle nudge. They could barely make out his silhouette in the dark.
Sure enough, Dan was right. After a few dozen steps, the distant lights from a well-illuminated campsite became visible from around the curved, vegetative wall that lined the campground roadway. Dozens of four-wheel drive pickups, jeeps and SUV's were parked wherever they could fit; some with quads sticking out of the backs. He thought he saw the glow reflect off a horse trailer near the source of light. There was only enough room for people to squeeze around the vehicles two-abreast. Half of the vehicles were well-marked government units. Half of those were split evenly between the state and county. The rest of the four-wheel drives seemed to possess the winches, roll bars, and floodlights of off-road enthusiasts. It appeared that their owners seemed to take their search and rescue membership responsibilities seriously.
The boys' smiles grew when their eyes met. Gabe knew that they had been thinking the very same thing.
Look at all of that cool stuff!
Those were some pretty cool-looking pickup trucks they had hurried past in the reflective light. Lingering around a couple of them wouldn't have been possible with Dan prodding them along toward the growing brightness of the busy camp. The sound of a not so loud generator rumbled in the distance.
"To be seen and not heard!" Dan panted under his breath as he hurried them along. "Remember, I ask the questions," he panted, "and you do the listening."

He's got to be kidding! Is Uncle Dan doing his Dr. Jekyll and Mr. Hide yourself from the public, routine?
This was indeed a different side to him. He was all business.

As they moved closer, they heard the rumblings of a man's voice off to their far right over the rumble of the motor. A dozen or so men and women stood in a half circle near a well-lit motor home. Most of them looked on attentively while others stood around the outskirts talking quietly amongst themselves. The faint mumblings were now heard clearly as words. They were calm and authoritative.

All he could see were the backs of the heads of people standing and sitting in front of them. The lighting had made everything brighter; the multi-lights that shone from every direction had all but eliminated any shadows. A couple of individuals in camouflage fatigues and bright orange long sleeve shirts raised their coffee mugs towards Dan as they passed by. Dan returned the greeting with a "Good morning!"

A couple of the other rescuers standing on the edge of the semi-circle turned to them and smiled. Woodland camouflage BDU's, blue jeans, boots, ball caps, and bright orange shirts seemed to be the uniform of the day. Some wore packs over their coats, while others wore headlamps still affixed to their heads.

Gabe looked down at his watch, it read 6:35 in the morning.
Boy are we late!

He gazed back towards Dan. He was surprised to see him looking on towards the crowd, his game face in place. Gabe thought it was somewhat strange that everyone there had to get up early to look for a missing person, probably someone they didn't even know. These definitely weren't your normal bunch of every day campers. From Gabe's position in the crowd, he still couldn't see the faceless voice that was addressing the group.

"The latest weather report predicts a 30-50% chance of rain by this evening and we all know what that means in this country!" Chief Ranger Eddie informed the crowd.

"Yeah, rain thirty to fifty percent of the day!" The voice that boomed from the crowd was immediately followed by playful laughter.

"And, if you don't like what nature sends your way at that moment...," a man in the group added.

"Wait a minute for it to change!" Two other voices recited in unison.

There was more laughter from the crowd.

"So it goes without sayin'-bring your rain gear. Well, that's about it. Again, I want to thank you for your time and effort." Chief Ranger Eddie's voice boomed clearly over the multiple conversations that suddenly sprouted. He smiled as he removed his Stetson and wiped the nervous perspiration from his brow of his balding head with the sleeve of his green coat. His kind, old eyes looked tired and appreciative; his uniform looked slept in. "The families and friends of Alex Bradley, as well as the park staff, are very appreciative of your time an' commitment."

A few of them nodded, while others started moving anxiously around. They were getting antsy; some still had preparations of their own to complete before they deployed on their assignments.

"Hey, that's the guy from last night!" said Gabe.

Erick nodded in agreement. "I think you're right!"

"We're working against the clock here, folks. As you know, rain destroys evidence, an' *evidence* is what we use to help safely find our missing person," exclaimed Bud, the large deputy with the salt-and-pepper flat crew cut who was standing next to Chief Ranger Eddie. The man rested his hand on Eddie's shoulder and thanked him with a respectful nod. The deputy in charge of the search and rescue operations looked impressive in his spit-polished boots, pressed woodland camouflage six-pocket fatigue pants, and long sleeve orange shirt, for the collective search-and-rescue team. A .40 caliber Smith & Wesson handgun sat in his shoulder holster over his O.D. green, nylon load-bearing vest. The white letters 'Sheriff' and his silver badge reflected in the lighting.

"Thank you, Eddie. Well, then, if there aren't any more questions...." his voice had a way of quieting down the crowd. "Just to recap, we're goin' to keep communications' simple by monitorin' channels 3, 5 an' 7 for local chatter on the civilian band an' channel 11 for the serious stuff. We will use the sheriff's sub channel for essential local interagency communication. Parks an' the Sheriff's Office have their own repeaters that cover most of this area an' we've got clay mars if we need to bring it all together." He used a laser pointer to circle the search area of the large, topographical map that hung next to the erase board on the side of the motor home. "I'm sorry to say that outside of satellite phones, or direct contact with the Almighty, your cell phone coverage will be limited to about half of the search area's hilltops. Folks, need I remind you this is some rugged country out here."

"Deputy Chet here, our communication officer," Bud gestured towards a tall slender, balding man with glasses that had been standing at the entrance of the mobile home. The man acknowledged with a casual wave of his hand. "He's the closest thing you're goin' to get to a guardian angel when you need somethin', pronto. Notice that he only has two hands an' no wings."

The boys gave each other a knowing glance.

The group laughed as Chet wiggled the fingers of both of his hands and turned to show his back.

"So, be nice!" Bud smiled. "Let's *not* walk over each other on the radio. Communications will be essential durin' the search." He blended smoothly into the next item. "Where are my K-9's? Mike? Tony? " he squinted into the bright lights.

"Over here!" a loud voice rang out from the edge of the roadway. A shaved-headed; well-built, uniformed deputy who looked to be in his mid-30's was working the leashed German shepherd next to him.

"Mike, you guys ready?"

"Affirmative!"

"Did you bring enough food for yourself this time? Don't want you eatin' all of Brutus's grub again!" Bud pretended to be serious.

The group laughed.

"Got it covered Bud! If it's good enough for Brutus, it's good enough for me!" he thumbed his chest.

There was more nervous laughter.

"Fair enough Mike," he placed the tip of his laser pointer into the center of a large hanging map. "You an' Brutus will start A.S.A.P. in the center of Zone 1, the juveniles' campsite." He pointed to Mike. "Find me some leads will you, an' take a couple searchers with you, the clock's tickin'! An' Tony! Are you here with that bloodhound' of yours?" He swiveled his head as he squinted into the lights around the campsite.

"Yeah!" the voice rang out to his far right. "Just got in about five ago."

Almost everyone turned to look.

He directed his gaze towards the man's voice. "Glad you could make it. You an'..." he paused a moment as he clicked his fingers, to recall the dog's name, "Sam, will be on standby. We're goin' to pull four hour shifts an' keep the dogs fresh. We may be dealin' with some rough terrain an' a few unknowns. We might also have to multi-task, work the dogs off in two separate directions. Time an' conditions will dictate."

"Roger that!" the chubby searcher almost sounded disappointed. "We should be ready to go well before then."

"Excellent! An' Peter?"

"Yes, sir!" The voice boomed just off to Gabe's left. His brown ponytail bobbed against the orange shirt of his long torso.

Bud made it a point to exaggerate his surprise. "You still haven't cut that damn thing off the back of your head?"

"No sir!" he smiled as he shook his head. His pony tail bobbed around.

"I keep tellin' you, loose the hair, an' get full time deputy spot."

"No thanks. Field biologists don't have ridiculous grooming standards."

Some light laughter from the milling crowd.

"Is your group ready?"

"Affirmative!"

"Excellent. Your group will work the scenic trail in the outskirts of Zone 1 an' possibly into Zone 2. You will pretty much be workin' the southwest flank." He aimed the laser at the trailhead on the map and wiggled it around for affect. "Evidently, the victim's mother said the kid had been out that way the day before, might have gone back for some reason. Please keep me posted."

"We're 10-8...!" Peter called over to Chet, the communications officer.

"Noted! In service!" Chet nodded in acknowledgement and gave him a thumb up.

Peter headed off into the darkness with five others.

"Billy!" Bud scanned what was left of the crowd.

"Here!" she gently waved her hand. The woman's soothing voice caused both of the boys' heads to turn in her direction.

"It's a girl!" Gabe whispered to Erick in surprise.

Erick nodded.

A slender blonde woman was seated at the far end of the nearby table. Her short hair hung just below the edge of her camouflaged ball cap. She wore the same search-and-rescue uniform as most of the other searchers.

"Thanks for helpin' out!"

She nodded and smiled.

"Were goin' to have you an' your squad do some long-range work in Zone 2. It's goin' to be a bit taxin'. We're goin' to need your group to cut a line along the west flank. It's been about 20 hours since the confirmation of the kid's last known location. An' as you already know, mom didn't report the incident until 1800 hours, 12 hours ago. The rangers initiated the search immediately upon notification an' are thus far unable to locate the party. Could have gotten 10 or could have gotten 30 miles in by now. As you well know, it's all dependin' on terrain, trails, knowledge of the area, conditionin', an' frame of mind. I've learned that our missin' person, Bradley is prone to depression so be safe.

"Radio communications may be intermittent. You may need to commandeer a mountain top or two an' spread out your communications into a picket line. Pack plenty of food, water, an' the usual. Be prepared to bivouac over-night. An' as the good Chief Ranger said, expect some rain." He paused for a moment as he eyed the group. "You're our tough guys... and gals!" he nodded in Billy's direction and wrinkled his forehead, "Why are you people still standin' aroun', go find 'em!"

Bud stood there a moment as he watched most of the parties dispersing noisily throughout the campground. Dogs barked excitedly, people busied themselves around camp, things were loaded in and out of trucks. The sound of engines being turned on echoed in the campground. People shouldered packs. For the most part, everyone seemed upbeat about the task of the search.

Both boys couldn't help but silently watch the controlled chaos. Almost everyone was either gone or busy but them.

"Boy are we in trouble!" said Erick.

Gabe looked on. They were more than late. Any later and they would have missed the meeting entirely. His searching eyes quickly came to rest on Dan, who, to their surprise, was no longer standing behind them; he was up talking privately and shaking hands with both Bud and Eddie. Both men took turns looking back over Dan's shoulder to where they were standing.

"We're so busted." Gabe spoke loudly enough for his friend to hear.

Erick nodded. "He's ratting us out isn't he?"

"Yeah, deservingly we're the only ones standing around lost with stupid looks on our faces."

"Hey, speak for yourself!" said Erick. "So, this is a search?" He piped up excitedly as he looked around. "Cool, I wonder what we're supposed to do."

"We've got the standing around doing nothing part down pretty good!" Gabe felt a sudden surge of disappointment run through his thoughts. The assignments appeared to be all handed out already.

Everyone here probably has something to do except us! Were too late.

He suddenly thought of his dad.

Was my dad ever late for a search? And if he was, did they still let him search anyway?

"Gabe, Erick, over here!" Dan's voice boomed louder than the chaos. He waved them over. "Boy's, over here!"

They both saw Dan waving them over to the table alongside the motor home with Eddie and Bud.

The boys looked at each other.

"We'd better get over there!" whispered Erick.

They hurried over to join them.

Dan, Eddie, and Bud, silently watched them approach. By the looks on their faces, Gabe wondered what had been said. The deputy's eyes seemed to be looking right through him.

"Ah, my sleepy heads!" Eddie smiled.

"Good to have you gentlemen finally join us." Bud cleared his throat. "Better late than never!"

It wasn't the sarcasm Gabe was expecting.

Bud reached over and firmly shook both of the boy's hands. "Erick... Gabe! Yes, I see the resemblance. I knew your father, he was a good man. Didn't need search dogs with him aroun'. A lot quieter too!" He nodded in the direction of the barking dog and smiled as he turned to Eddie. "Looks like good old Brutus has found somethin'. Good show!" Bud turned his attention back towards Gabe.

Gabe could see the caring twinkle in the man's eyes.

"Your father had a special knack for findin' what he was lookin' for."

Gabe nodded, not quite knowing what to think or say. Every time he turned around, someone was talking about his father in past tense.

"So, this will be your first search, huh?" Bud asked, as he patted both boys on their shoulders.

The boys nodded.

"Good deal," Bud smiled.

"We were just discussing the search areas," Dan said, as he looked back toward the map.

Bud walked over and refocused his attention on the huge park map before him. He picked up the laser pointer and aimed it toward the map, the red dot appeared. The radio traffic crackled in the background as he spoke. "So this is what's goin' on. The search areas have been broken down into three distinguishable Zones... Zones 1, 2, and 3, each increasin' in size an' distance as they move away from the center. In this situation, Zone 1 will be about a one-mile radius aroun' our current position, the most probable location. Zone 2 will have a three-mile radius, an' Zone 3 will have a six-mile radius. Each

Zone will slightly overlap so nothin' is missed. We're here," the red dot hovered in place on the map around a grouping of little colored flags, "the incident command, the control center for the search... affectionately called the I.C. We're located in the center of zone 1. We're marked by this pushpin with the black flag marked I.C. This pushpin with the red flag represents the last known location of the victim, were goin' to call it L.K., last known position. That would be site number five in this campground here."

The boys moved closer to the map for a better look.

Gabe raised his eyebrows.

The missing person was camped on the other side of the campground from us. If it could happen to them, it could happen to...."

The thought gave him a chill.

"The campgroun', the service yards an' employee residences, surroundin' roads, the nature trails an' the trailheads of some of the major front country trails are all within the search area of Zone 1, which has been covered pretty well. They're all within a mile of the L.K., you boys follow me?" Bud quizzed.

Both boys looked at each other and nodded.

"What are the green flags over there for?" Erick asked.

"Good eye. We're usin' green for the park staff. Those are the areas already searched by the rangers' yesterday afternoon an' throughout the night. Since the missin' person was reported so late in the afternoon yesterday, the rangers weren't able to get a thorough search off of the ground. They did some preliminary front country work here, here an'... there." Bud followed along on the map with his pointer. "They were able to cover the existin' paved roadways, turnouts, both campgrounds, the shorter nature trails, an' about a couple miles up some of the major trails, all of them within the area of Zone 1 an' a portion of Zone 2. As you can see, the zones increase in size like concentric growth rings on a tree, one encompassin' the other. The roadways an' facilities will continually be checked throughout the search in case the subject doubles back.

"Zone 2 is basically the backcountry, which includes some of the outlyin' paved an' dirt roads, an' a portion of the wilderness trail system startin' from one-mile out an' extendin' for three more from the L.K. location. Zone 3 will be for those individuals who really enjoy hikin' and drivin' the backcountry roads an' trails from four to ten miles out.

"So here is the Reader's Digest version. The placement of the pushpins will map out the searchers' progress. Everythin' red is missin' person-related, like footprints, clothin', an' equipment found, alon' with all of the pertinent items found that relate to the missin' persons whereabouts. The orange flags will map out the progress of the different search-an'-rescue posse elements. The yellow flags will reflect the movements of the K-9 units, the scent dogs. Durin' the search, every movement will be cataloged, graphed, an' charted 24-7. It is essential that we know what is goin' on where an' by whom. Every resource that gets logged in gets logged back out. We have a large area to cover an' we need to keep track of every step, every person, an' every piece of resource. Don't want to lose anyone, or anythin' do we?"

The radio crackled to life again.

Chet popped his head out of the motor home and calmly barked over to the deputy in charge. "Bud, it starts!"

Bud quickly snatched up the lapel mike of his shirt and winked at the boys.

"Go for I.C.!"

"I.C. this is K9-1"

"Go ahead K9-1!"

"I.C. we're on Bradley's trail heading south out of the campground an' down the main road... break!" A bit of confusion was noted in his voice as the barking dog could be heard in the background.

"Excellent work Mike!" Bud said to the others standing around him. "That's some dog!"

The others smiled and silently nodded in agreement.

The radio squelched to life again. "K9-1 continuing, Brutus was favoring a gravel turn out about 100 yards or so north of the campground, behaved a bit strangely. The sent trail ended there, hard to say if the x-ray turned around or hitched a ride... break."

The group silently stared at each other as the radio went silent for a moment. The deputy was using the common practice of not tying up the radio airways by allowing breaks during his extended radio traffic.

"K9-1 continuing... if we end up unable to locate any good sign to the south, we need to consider the hitching option, will keep you posted... clear!"

"Good work, K9-1, I.C. clear!" Bud clipped his lapel mike back onto his collar. He then pulled a red and a couple of yellow pushpin flags out of the plastic bucket. Quietly, he pushed one of each color into the approximate locations of the gravel turnout north of the campground, and a single yellow one on the main road just south of the campground.

"What's an x-ray?" Gabe asked.

"The missing person," Dan said.

"What does that mean?" Erick asked as he pointed to the small flags.

Bud and Eddie exchanged looks before Dan answered.

"It means the victim could have hitched a ride just north of the campground."

Erick gave him a smile. "Then the victim isn't lost in the forest after all? Maybe they hitched a ride back home!"

Bud gave a deep sigh as he shrugged his shoulders and shook his head. "If Bradley's back in town, the kid hasn't taken the time to let anyone else know that. It could be the kid's way of punishin' the mother, for that matter, punishin' the whole family. Based on what we've heard about the kid's personal issues, it could be a possibility. Pissed off today, beggin' for forgiveness tomorrow," he shrugged. "I really wish it were that easy." Bud crossed his arms and shook his head again. "Bradley could have hitched a ride with the wrong guy, been abducted by a serial killer... it wouldn't be the first time. Remember that Fernandez girl," he glanced back over to Eddie.

Eddie nodded. "Last seen hitching a ride from the mall parking lot, never to be seen or heard from again? A tragedy!"

"How often do people go missing around here in the park?" Gabe was almost afraid to ask.

"We conduct about two major searches a year," Eddie explained. "About once every five years, a Bradley-type of situation takes place. Occasionally a park visitor steps into the forest and is never seen again. They get lost, commit suicide, and perish in an accident or something of a criminal element. The forest is huge, filled with wild animals and rugged, unforgiving terrain. For the novice, it isn't hard to become confused, lose their way, panic, head off in the entirely wrong direction, injure oneself, and eventually become lost. Cell phones are no guarantee we'll find you either, but it sure does help. One of these days they'll be able to mark your location with the G.P.S. in your phone after you make your 911 call.'

"Now you're dreaming Eddie!" teased Dan.

"That bit of science is on the way," said Bud, "but until then, if the party doesn't stay put we could zip right past them in a hurry to get somewhere else. Some children will actually try to hide from us, thinkin' we're after them. In a way we are, but not how they see it."

Bud gave Gabe a gentle pat on his shoulder. "Today the missin' kid has got a twenty-four hour head start. It's our job to bring them home safely to their loved ones. Most of the time we're successful, sometimes we're not." He shrugged. "We can only do our best."

"So, on that note, where would you like us to be?" Dan interjected.

"Let's see?" asked Bud as he looked at the map. "Eddie, I was thinkin' about sendin' a group north. If you don't have any objection, I can send these guys instead."

"Okay by me!" Eddie exclaimed. "Dan's fully capable of pulling it off."

"Thanks for the endorsement, Eddie." Dan shared.

"Thanks for the free labor!" Eddie laughed.

"Hey, it's a bushman's holiday!" Dan added.

"Alright then, Dan," Bud continued, "you'll be workin' the inner edge of Zone 3 here." He used the laser pointer to map out the route. "We can have you drive to one of the northern trailheads an' hike south until you meet up with the other trails that eventually connect with Spring Trail. We'll give you a detailed description of Bradley's clothin' an' all the other fundamentals. Be sure to look over that trail head, if Alex did manage to hitch a ride—"

The crackling of the radios interrupted their thoughts.

Bud reached for his lapel mike. "Go for I.C.!"

"Team Alpha is in place along Scenic Trail."

"I.C. to Team Alpha, I copy 10-8 Scenic Trail."

"Affirmative I.C, we have confirmed recent tracks both coming and going, possibly our subjects."

"Excellent Peter!"

"Roger that, we're on task... Team Alpha clear."

"The Messenger" by April Leiterman

CHAPTER TWENTY-THREE
A ZONE TO SEARCH

MARCH 16TH 2000

Bud gave out a contented sigh as he returned his lapel mike to his shirt collar. He fumbled around inside a plastic bucket for an orange and black pushpin labeled Alpha and placed it alongside the existing green and red pins, identifying the Scenic Trail Head location. "They have confirmed that the Bradley kid had recently traveled that way at least twice."

"If I remember rightly," Eddie jumped in, "that substrate isn't the best tracking surface. Frankly, I'm surprised they were even able to find out as much as they did."

"Jealous, are we now, Mr. Outdoorsman? What can I say?" Bud shrugged his shoulders as he teased. "Peter's the best!"

Dan nodded in agreement. "That would definitely take some decent skill!"

"You know it! An' skill that boy has!" Bud boasted.

"We're looking for a kid?" Gabe sounded surprised.

"Yeah, a young kid about your age. Names Alex." Bud nodded to the boys. "Weren't you two payin' attention durin' the briefin'...." He caught himself. "Oh, that's right, you missed that part." He winked teasingly at Dan.

Dan rolled his eyes.

"Well, evidently, Bradley had a fallin' out with the mother yesterday mornin'. Actually, they've been havin' a fallin' out for quite some time now. It came to head durin' their little mini-vacation. Their plan was to go campin' an' leave it all behind, a temporary fix at best." He cleared his throat. "You see, changin' the environment doesn't always change the problems. When you bring the problems with you, sometimes, you just make them worse. They say some of the biggest triggers for emotional problems are weddin's, funerals, movin'; an' startin' new jobs. These folks were recently dealin' with most of those," Bud spoke so matter of factly, he made it sound like the kid was just another predictable problem.

Bud must have read the inquisitive look on Gabe's face and decided to elaborate a bit more. "Accordin' to Bradley's mother, the kid's dad passed away a few years back while they were livin' out of state, somewhere near the coast of Washington State I think. They recently moved back down here to Northern California after she lost her job. I guess to be closer to relatives, to alleviate the buildin' financial burdens that were causin' them hardships. The kid's been havin' some disciplinary an' emotional problems at home that carried over to school. Fifteen's a tough age for an emotional teen anyway. At that age, their brain is still developin', their trying to figure out who they are, or for that matter why they're even here. Then when those hormones kick in... blahm!"

"Sounds like you're familiar with teenagers!" Eddie laughed. Dan and Bud joined in.

Gabe just stared at the three men.

Is this the generation gap I've been hearing about?

Gabe could relate to the teen's rough time. Circumstances dictate direction and the direction isn't always the right one.

Wasn't that the very reason that we are here now in this very spot today? Was it a coincidence that a kid about my same age is lost on the very day that we are here? Was it a coincidence that the kid had also lost their father? Here we are about the same age, in the same campground, on the same day? What are the odds of that?

If there was one thing he was learning, it was that there were no such thing as luck and unusual coincidences. He had a few more questions burning into his soul.

Did this kid have a guardian angel of their own? And if he did, then where is he? If anyone needed one, it is obviously this kid.

"And what did all this have to do with me?" he whispered to himself.

He was working through a situation of his own. This wasn't all just a shift in hormones. No, there was something more to it.

If this were all just the basic teen problem, then why did it involve almost everyone in his household, and even my friend, Erick?

He suddenly felt a strange sort of kinship with this missing juvenile, and a burning desire to know more. "What's his name again?" Gabe blurted out.

"What?" Bud asked sounding somewhat surprised.

"What's the kid's name?"

"Alex, Alex Bradley."

Alex Bradley.

He repeated the name to himself. Now the kid had a name, they were no longer strangers.

Alex Bradley, where are you? Why are we both here?
At that moment, his body shuddered. A chill charged through his fingers and toes. He felt cold, his legs heavy. He bent his knees for balance, crossed his arms, pulling them closer to his body for warmth.

What's going on?
He looked towards the group. They were all conversing among themselves; they didn't appear to notice his sudden change. He diverted his eyes and looked over his shoulder toward the last of the mingling rescuers. None of them gave him a second look. The sounds of the noisy campsite faded away, overtaken by the sound of a slight breeze that blew in from the east and then swirled around from the west.

He strained his ears, and stared up into the pink clouds that were building in the early morning light of the eastern sky.

Red skies in morn, sailors be warned!
The rhyme echoed in his thoughts. The prediction of rain had some merit. There was some truth to this old sailor rhyme.

The gentle whispers in the breeze drew his thoughts. He watched the tree tops sway ever so gently in the rhythmic gusts. It sounded as if a voice were calling to him. He looked at the others around him; they seemed busy in conversations that he could no longer hear. His friend Erick seemed preoccupied. It was like he was no longer there either.

This can't be happening. A voice in the trees, or is it just the breeze?

There is no such thing as coincidence, there are no such thing as luck. Everything has meaning... everything has a purpose!

Gabe kept telling himself. The whisper of a breeze moved around him and tickled the little hairs along the sides of his face, then his ear. A familiar, sweet smell filled his nostrils.

He coughed and brushed the hair away from his face with his shoulder, but the sensation of being touched persisted. There was a presence. He could feel it. But then he heard it.

"*Gabe, do not be afraid... I know of what you seek.*"

The voice sounded like it came from directly behind him. He quickly spun around, only to find the group staring at him strangely. He ignored their confused looks and continued to search for the source of the voice.

"*It is there... you shall find!*"

The whisper filled his ears again.

It was then that he saw the black and yellow swallowtail butterfly out of the corner of his eye approaching lazily from his left. He turned to face it as it fluttered nearer in a circular, carefree pattern on the gentle breeze. He was relieved to see that the others appeared to have seen it, too. They joined him in his silent vigil as it floated closer. It danced around him in a complete circle, as if to get his attention, then it fluttered toward the center of the map. It was the strangest thing, beyond any logical explanation. The beautiful butterfly continued to hover in a tight circle around the center of Zone 1, marked by the little black flags labeled L.K., as if it were navigating around the map. It flew out away from the center in an ever-growing, concentric circle, moving over the air space of the flat topographical range. And then, as if on cue, it landed in the upper left corner of the map, just outside of Zone 3.

Its wings rhythmically pulsed opened and closed a few more times as Gabe slowly walked over to where the butterfly landed. He leaned forward to examine the butterfly closer.

"*It is here you will seek... It is here you shall find.*"

"What?" Gabe whispered.

The thought echoed in his mind. Outside of the rapid beating of his heart, and the deep drawing in and out of his breath, the gentle breeze was the only sound he could hear.

Beneath the butterfly!

The contour lines beneath the butterfly were close together. From what he could see, there appeared to be the makings of a steep canyon beneath its undulating wings. At the moment, he couldn't see much more than that; the insect obstructed his view. The butterfly fluttered from the map seconds later.

Gabe immediately placed his index finger where the butterfly had landed. Without moving his hands, he watched the graceful butterfly flutter away in a chaotic circular pattern, disappearing into the pink dawn of the rising sun.

When he re-focused his attention back to the spot under his finger he was surprised to see the closeness of the contour lines. A fine blue line indicated a water source, by its size, most likely a small creek, maybe even a waterfall. He measured the distance to the edge of a dirt road to the west; it was about two widths of his spread open hand. He compared it with the section lines on the map; as the raven flies, it was approximately three and a half to four miles between the two points. It looked as if a narrow, forested ridge trail snaked east from the edge of the road and descended west down into the canyon an estimated distance of four to six miles from where the road ended.

When he looked back in the direction the butterfly had fluttered off, it had already disappeared.

Was the butterfly a messenger? Did it actually tell me where I could find Alex? Could this even be possible?

When he glanced back toward the map, his fingers still covered the spot on the map above the canyon.

"Are you alright?" Dan's voice pulled him back.

When Gabe's eyes refocused he was surprised to see everyone standing there next to him, staring intently at him.

"Did you guys see the butterfly?" he excitedly asked.

They nodded; it was obvious that they didn't know what to think either.

"Yeah, it was pretty weird!" Erick said. "It was like the Butterfly knew where it was going."

Gabe nodded slowly in agreement. "The missing kid, Alex, I think I know where he is!" he spoke quietly, so matter of fact. "Don't ask me how I know, but I do!" he spoke louder. "This is where we need to go!" He tapped his finger on the map as he forced a smile. "He should be right there!" When he looked up he was unnerved by the concerned looks on everyone's face, his friends included. It was the strange way that Bud and Eddie shifted their confused gazes in between each other, Dan and the map. It all made him nervous. He felt that something wasn't right. He had to ask.

"What's wrong?"

"Why do you want to go there? We already have an assignment," Dan pleaded, as he stepped closer to Gabe and the map. He closely examined the map. "It's not within the boundaries of Zone 3. It's clearly out of the search area. It looks like it would take us a good 15 to 20 miles of driving and trail hiking to get there."

"I know, but... the butterfly, the weird feeling I got...," Gabe pleaded.

"The weird feelings you got?" Dan quizzed. He rested both of his hands on Gabe's shoulders, as he looked deeply into his eyes, the concern notable in his own voice. A strange fear possessed his normally fearless persona. "You sure?"

Gabe nodded as he looked at the other two men who were studying him closely. He lowered his voice. He wasn't sure if they should hear what he had to say or not. He was pleased to see that Dan understood, though by the look on his face, it was like he was hiding secrets of his own. That section of the map had brought an unexplainable nervousness to all of them.

Was it the butterfly, what the butterfly did? Or the location on the map?

"Bud," Dan kept his eyes focused on Gabe, "could we search a bit farther north, about there?" Dan nodded to where the butterfly had landed on the map. His eyes still locked on Gabe's.

"Let's see, that puts it 10 to 12 miles as the raven flies from where we're standing right now." Bud studied the map.

"Wishful thinking!" Dan turned to Bud and forced an embarrassed smile. "I realize its mighty challenging terrain and all!"

"The kid did have over 24 hours to make tracks!" Bud explained, "You an' I both know it's doable for a highly motivated individual. There's a network of some 120 miles worth of trails over some God-awful terrain out there, an' they're all interconnected." Bud noted. "Definitely an all-nighter for the strong-willed an' touched-of-mind. Of all the places to get lost," he wrinkled his forehead. "Why there?" He looked directly into Dan's eyes as if searching for answers.

"Yeah, highly motivated, probably driven by the devil himself!" Dan's own words surprised himself.

Bud raised an eyebrow. "Falcon Canyon?"

"Are you sure, does he know?" Eddie fumbled with his words.

Dan hushed him with a quick wave of his hand. "No, not yet. But he'll find out soon enough!"

"Find out what?" Gabe quizzed. "What secrets are you hiding from me now?" his voice pointed, accusatory. "Everywhere I turn... more secrets. Is this how it's going to be?"

"Bud?" Dan's eyes focused on Gabe's, his grip still holding Gabe's shoulders at arm's length. Gabe still letting him.

Bud pulled a small flag and a permanent marker out of his pocket, gave a deep sigh and strutted over to the huge topographical map. "Dan, I sure hope you know what you are doin'!"

"You and I both Bud." Dan sighed as he and Gabe made room for Bud's broad figure.

Bud drew a big circle connecting the mysterious valley with the nearest section of road just beyond to the northwest corner of Zone 3. He labeled it Zone 4 and pushed a miniature green flag into the map along the squiggly dirt road.

"Zone-4... it's now official!" Bud exclaimed.

"Once you leave the pavement its clear for the first six miles." Eddie ran his finger across the map. "I can't vouch for the road conditions once beyond Durphy's Ridge cut-off. Mother Nature had made quite a nuisance of herself out that way. It could be 25 plus miles of hell as far as I know!" he shrugged his shoulders and shifted his gaze in between Dan and Bud. "We don't drive out there all that much this time of the year. Hell, Dan's probably been out that way more than anyone here."

Bud shot Dan a long look. "When was the last time you were out there?"

"A few years." Dan shrugged.

Gabe caught the secretive exchange. His mind began to race.

Eddie hesitated a moment before he continued to speak, this time focusing more on Dan and the boys. "Make sure you've got enough fuel, chainsaw equipment, tow chain, and some good hand tools. You know the drill."

Dan nodded.

"I see you'll have a couple of gophers to help make you a burrow through the brush if needed!" Bud confirmed.

Dan laughed.

Eddie smiled at the boys. "It's going to take a little extra time having to walk the road in front of the vehicle from time-to-time. I hope you boys are in pretty good shape, 'cause if you're not, you're going to be wishing you were!"

What does he mean by that?

Gabe narrowed his eyes as he focused his attention on both Dan's and Eddie's body language. There were things that they definitely weren't telling him.

"If he's anything like his father—" Eddie piped in.

"I know, we'll have our hands full." Dan refocused on Gabe's face. "I will have much to explain to him along the way."

"Indeed you will, not at all envious of your position," Eddie concluded. "Be safe, and don't let those kids out of your sight, not even for a moment!"

"Yeah, God help me," Dan mumbled under his breath.

CHAPTER TWENTY-FOUR
NAVIGATING THE MOUNTAIN ROADS
(LATE WEDNESDAY AFTERNOON)
MARCH 16TH 2000 ANNIVERSARY DAY

The engine of the older International whined as it struggled up the fire road to the edge of search Zone 4. The four-wheel drive bounced unevenly on the dirt and gravel road as Dan, Gabe and Erick drove their way up the mountain in a northwesterly direction. Dan liked the way his little four-seater handled the curves, jarring to the outside until the knobby tires finally gripped the uneven surface and catapulted them back on course. He wasn't worried about his driving. In fact, the thoughtless action helped him take his mind off of the inevitable: taking his nephew to the conclusion on the anniversary of his brother's passing.

Dan drove a little faster than he probably should have down the fire road. He felt he needed to make up the time they lost carving their way through the mud, rocks and debris that nature left strewn across the roadway. He definitely drove faster than his two passengers wanted to go, but time was working against them. They needed to be well down the ridgeline and in place before the darkness and the rains dominated the scene. The narrow canyons increased the velocity of the water. It was basic physics. It's exactly what waterfalls do, deliver the water to the valley below as quickly as possible. It was written all over the rugged topography. Even the road they were now driving had to be carved into the sides of the mountains by the old timers, back in the 1930's and 1940's to harvest timber before the land became a park.

For a while, it seemed like the entire 25 miles of debris-strewn roadway had a surprise for them around every turn. Instead of a simple one and a half hour trip like it should have been to drive from the ranger office to the trail head, they were looking at almost five hours by the time they reached their turnout. Once there, they would finish the rest of their journey on foot. He lost track of how many hours the boys had to walk point just ahead of his International Scout to shovel, cut, toss and roll rocks, logs and debris out of their way. He stopped several times to chainsaw and winch their way through downed trees and demanding obstacles. They skirted their way around mud puddles as they went. All was done in an attempt to beat the oncoming storm and encroaching nightfall.

Outside of the early morning pink sky, the novice wouldn't have had a clue that the weather was changing. For them it would've been just another beautiful day in the ancient forest. Visitors seemed to forget that lush forests like these needed sixty plus inches of precipitation a year to support their unquenchable thirsts. He could feel the change in pressure, the slight increase in the predicted cool winds and see the ongoing accumulation of high, stratospheric clouds. There was no doubt, the rain was inevitable.

As he gazed down upon the ancient forest, he couldn't help but slip his foot off of the gas and let it hover over the brake. The road straightened and the trees no longer obscured the view of the beautiful valley below. His quick glance through the driver side window soon became an astonished stare. Almost a thousand feet beneath them lay the tops of some of the tallest trees in the world. The matriarchs stuck out unevenly amongst the sea of green. The emerald carpet he gazed down upon was still well over 350 feet above the forested valley floor beneath. The thought was mind-boggling. The forest stretched another couple thousand more feet up the other side of the valley and on towards the surrounding mist-shrouded peaks. The rays' of late afternoon sunlight had illuminated the open prairies that dotted the upper slopes and protruding peaks. Thanks to a warm snap in the weather, light pastels of orange, purple, red and yellow, graced portions of the grass-covered slopes that were bordered by near vertical walls of green. From that distance only the well versed would recognize that the majestic colors were accents of wild flowers at the start of their bloom.

He momentarily glanced down at the road to confirm that their slowing vehicle was still within the safe confines of the roadway. He didn't have to look down at his watch to know that it was well after 2:00 in the afternoon.

Dan looked again into the valley below. Ancient giants shaded the meandering creek that snaked its way down the middle of the dimly-lit valley floor. The emerald green of the water was barely noticeable on the oxbow turns, where the creek turned away from the direction of the road. The dark shadow that ran partially hidden through the middle of the valley drew his attention back up toward the base of the rising mountains. He saw a distant creek join the main one. His eyes instinctively followed the smaller creek back into the darkening shadows of rock and forest. Above it the mountains narrowed and abruptly grew in height, above it the remnants of an old slide. Beyond that was forested darkness. His heart thundered in his ears and a nervous chill made him shudder.

Falcon Canyon.

He forced his gaze forward and stepped on the gas pedal. He felt the International immediately respond. The back end of the vehicle fishtailed, the inertia forcing them back into their seats. Up until now he hadn't felt the need to put the vehicle into four-wheel drive. He half turned in his seat and smiled, expecting complaints, but not a word was said. Through his rearview mirror he watched the little whirlwinds he had kicked up turn into miniature dust devils.

Dust devils... no relation I hope.

He couldn't help but stare, keeping an eye on them, making sure they didn't follow.

How ridiculous. Keep your eyes on the road Dan, eyes on the road.

The approaching rain would put these little devils in their place soon enough.

Up until now small talk had dominated their conversations. Most of the ride was conducted in strange, eerie silence. Both boys stared silently out of their respective windows, burdened with thoughts and emotions of their own. In fact, it had been 15 minutes since the last words had been exchanged, since the last time they had to stop to clear debris from the road. The ball was in his court, so to speak, and he knew their thoughts burned deeply. He could no longer avoid the subject of his brother's death. He had to admit; it was pretty weird the way the butterfly singled Gabe out, even drew his attention toward the map. There was no doubt in his mind that the butterfly was actually looking over the map by the way it started in the middle and then worked its way towards the edge in an ever-growing concentric circle. Then, stopping above Falcon Canyon.

What were the odds of that? Falcon Canyon, of all places!

He shuddered again as he shook his head and sneaked another quick glance at Gabe, who was sitting across from him. He found him staring out of the front passenger window, his eyes burning holes through the late afternoon mountain air.

What was he to say? How was he to explain?

It had been a few years since he'd been back to the canyon. One day, he'd just stopped going, stopped dwelling in the past. He had first gone to find closure, to figure out how and why. Then he went to figure out where.

Was it a freak accident? A natural process for the elements of time?

'Mass wasting' the geologists called it. 'Years of freezing and thawing... expanding and contracting... water cutting away the metamorphic and sedimentary parent material of these Franciscan soils' like a laser through most everything.

Influenced by gravity, squared by time.

In common language; the mountain just gave way with some of the most unstable soils in the region and followed the path of least resistance downhill. Unfortunately for Gabriel, it was a death trap waiting to claim their own.

But you probably knew that didn't you brother?

His body was never found, never recovered from the aftermath. He was buried under tons of rock and debris, imprisoned beneath the mountain he loved so much.

His soul. Where's his soul? Was it also interred within the mountain? Was it Gabe's job to free it, to send his soul on its way? To dodge so many disasters, and then for this to happen? What was the point?

He still struggled to understand.

It was time. He cleared his thoughts and swallowed to moisten his parched throat. His hands trembled. He gripped the leather-covered steering wheel more tightly, until his knuckles shone white.

Lord, give me strength, please help guide me through this one.

He took a deep sigh, and began.

"Gabe, about your father...," he glanced over to his nephew out of the corner of his eye. He needed to read his nephew's emotions to work through what he needed to say, needed to explain. He also needed to safely make up time on the road. There would always be time enough for him to talk on the trail, for his nephew to listen, and hopefully to understand.

***

Gabe shot him a quick look and then returned his staring gaze straight-ahead. His legs, and hands ached from all the walking and debris-moving they had to do to clear the road enough to squeeze through their vehicle. It seemed as if they had done almost all of the work while his uncle Dan got to sit on his backside and drive. At times, the debris just seemed to get heavier and even heavier. He dreaded the drive.

Wouldn't it have been easier to hike up from the other side, just like the lost kid did?

For now, the larger debris on the road had all but disappeared. His body shuddered at the thought; a strange chill ran its entire length and lingered around his chest. He silently sat there in both excited anticipation and fearful dread, almost paralyzed with this strange mix of emotions. He felt Dan's powerful stare projecting through him.

Isn't this what I had been waiting for? Isn't this what I had demanded to know?

It had been ten years of secrecy, hidden in a time capsule waiting to be released on the anniversary of its conception. He crossed his ankles and pulled his arms closer to his body, in reaction to the sudden chill.

Dan shifted, nodded towards the dark canyon. "The place we're going, Falcon Canyon…." His sorrowful voice sounded so distant.

"Why wait until now to tell me?" Gabe stared straight ahead, his voice unusually calm, emotionless. He didn't know how, but he knew the message in Dan's next words before Dan could even get them out. Gabe had been waiting for this moment and now it was finally here.

The truth!

Out of the corner of his eye, he saw his uncle nervously shrug his shoulders. He turned to let his gaze settle on his uncle's face. His chiseled features awkward. Worry lines cast shadows across his neck and saddened face. He looked so much older, aged in a matter of seconds.

"I have dreaded this day." Dan shook his head and shot a quick glance in Gabe's direction before he returned his eyes back to the roadway. The International was moving slower now that the ruts in the road were more noticeable. "I never thought we would actually be going here together." He briefly nodded. "But here we are, a pivotal turning point no doubt." Dan took a deep breath before he continued.

The knowing look unnerved Gabe. He squeezed his fists tightly as he pulled his arms closer into his body in the cooling air. He narrowed his eyes and strained his ears to hear his every word. It wasn't necessarily what was said, it was how it was said. Most communication was hidden within the body language and he wasn't about to miss a single word.

"You can't blame your mom for trying to protect you. Losing your dad was hard on her; it was hard on all of us. Your dad was doing his job. He saved people; he pulled off rescues that didn't seem possible. Some had thought he sold his soul to the devil!" Dan shook his head. "It was so far from the truth. He operated in the no-man's land between good and evil. Doing God's bidding, directed by angels, protected by angels, then unknown as to why, taken by angels." Dan looked up into the air for a quick moment and then yelled out, as he pounded the steering wheel with his fists, angrily projecting his thoughts to the heavens. "He was the good guy for heaven sake!"

Both boys gave him a surprised look as they shifted their gaze nervously in-between each other.

"But why?" Gabe exclaimed, his words stabbing through the air.

Erick looking on attentive from the back seat, shifting his curious stare in between the two of them as they verbally sparred back and forth.

Dan shrugged his shoulders. "God knows, but he isn't telling?"

"Isn't or wont? How convenient!" Gabe mumbled under his breath. He remembered those words from his dad's journal.

"Who are we to question his work?" Dan spoke softly, added a shrug of his shoulders. He looked unconvinced.

"His work?" Gabe exclaimed, tears forming in his eyes. "It makes no sense. You do things he asks you to do, without questioning, and then he thanks you by ruining your lives and the life of everyone else around you! Nobody works that way, nobody except maybe the devil!"

"Let's not bring him into this right now—" Dan spoke nervously as he glanced into his review mirror.

"Why not!" Gabe screamed.

"It's not what you think…."

Gabe noted Dan's strange behavior and looked over his shoulder to see what was concerning him. There was nothing but swirling dust among the trees, stirred up by their passing tires. "Not what I think?" he repeated. "How can you sit there and say that? You have no idea what my dad went through! For that matter you have no idea what I—"

"I beg to differ!" Dan interrupted. "He was about your age when it first started… late one night in down town Long Beach. I was there!" Dan tapped his chest with his fist. "We were waiting at a bus stop, the same stop we'd always waited at to take the bus home after band practice—"

"You were in the band?" Gabe interrupted.

"Yeah I was in the band... to be talked about later. I pushed your dad in front of a passing bus." He shrugged his shoulders as if it were no big deal. "There I said it!"

Gabe stared at him with an open mouth. He didn't know what to say. "You pushed my Dad in front of a passing *bus*?"

"Yeah! I pushed my *brother* in front of a passing bus." Dan forced a smile as he sneaked a quick peek, his hands firmly on the steering wheel. "I don't know why I did it. Just thought it was kind of funny at the time. You know, 14-and 16-year-old brothers communicating in the universal language of sibling rivalry. Ill responsible behavior. It was stupid I know, but it was like a little voice within my head said *just do it*, and so I did. Once my mind engaged, well my arms just followed along with it! The bus was coming so quickly. I tried but couldn't even move my legs, frozen in time and place. You could imagine what I was thinking. I thought I had just killed my younger brother. Then someone, rather *something*, pushed him out of the way just in time as the bus roared by." Dan became quiet for a moment, revisiting the memory as he continued to stare down the road. His eyes began to water.

Gabe and Erick stared at each other, speechless.

"The driver and the people on the bus never slowed, they never looked at us, and they never looked back. It was like, they were all in a daze, staring mindlessly forward. I still remember that bus driver. A big man in all blue, he gripped the steering wheel with both hands and hunched forward as he stared straight ahead as if on a mission. The powerful wind, the dust, the heat, the sounds, the smell of sulfur, and then there was the word Choose inscribed on the side of the bus."

"Sulfur?" Erick exclaimed. He sat strait up in surprise.

"Yeah..." confirmed Dan, "Sulfur, accompanied by the over powering feeling of evil. It was like... the bus from hell was out collecting souls." He forced a nervous laugh and gave a deep sigh. "It almost snagged your dad's soul as well that day." He looked over to Gabe. "I believe it was an angel that saved him, saved us both that day, turned us invisible. I am pretty sure if it weren't for them; we wouldn't be having this conversation today. You wouldn't be here today." Dan pointed to Gabe.

***

Erick's thoughts flashed to the night before when he went out to take a pee. His body shuddered, goose bumps ran the length of his spine. Last night he had smelled the sulfur. Something was out there. Something pulled at his very soul. He was sure of it. Then, something saved him, pulled him back to the safety of his tent, made it go away.

Should I say something? Would they believe me? Maybe I'll talk about it later when things settle down a bit.

***

Gabe tried to visualize a bus streaking by, ablaze with fire, with winged angels in white, shielding his father and his uncle with their fierce, fiery light as they looked on, ready to do battle.

"Then this homeless man just materialized from a bench and staggered across the street...." Dan interjected.

A homeless man?

"He headed directly for us," continued Dan, "started raving about '*By God's grace*', that, he had '*plans for your dad... big plans!*' He had that crazy, *I know something that you don't* laugh. It made me shudder. '*Oh, does he ever have plans for you!*' Yep, those were his words." Dan's voice cracked with eerie emotion. "That crazy old man's voice echoed in my head. It still does today, when I think about that evening." He flashed another knowing glance over to Gabe. "I still smell him too when I think about it, the stench of urine, body odor, spilled alcoholic beverage, soiled clothing, and another smell I still can't place! Shook me up pretty bad. I couldn't explain any of it. And the weirdest thing of it all. He was right! That homeless man was absolutely right!"

"Was he an angel? My mom said that they can take up many forms!" Erick exclaimed.

Dan nodded without taking his eyes off of the road. "Could've very well have been your standard, downtown homeless transient! Either way, that man was the last person on earth I would've expected to be an angel. Since then I've seen the angels come and go, taking on many different forms."

See angels come and go...is he for real? It was exactly what Erick had said. What did those guys really see?

"I'm at a point now where I don't really know if it was an angel," Dan continued, "sent down from heaven, or a Good Samaritan doing his work. I wish I knew then what I know now. At the time, I had no idea that this was the start of something that would forever change my life, forever change *our* lives. They protected your father that day, and many more days that followed. And then one day," his voice became solemn, "when you would least expect it, when the need was the greatest, the magic ended, just as quickly as it had materialized. It was like everything was building up to that one moment. And, when you least expect it, plans change," he clicked two fingers together, "just... like... that!" Deep emotion crackled in Dan's voice. Gabe flinched. He diverted his eyes as if taking a moment to regain his composure.

Gabe could feel Dan's burden of heavy emotion. His own body shuddered. This whole guardian angel thing was the strangest concept he had ever heard. Nobody outside of this vehicle would ever understand any of it to the extent that they did now. Deep down inside, he knew it could only get more, complicated. It was the only word that drifted into his thoughts.

"The first time I saw your dad share some of his gift was in Sequoia National Park... I believe... 1965, before he met your mother," Dan said, forcing a smile.

Both Erick and Gabe silently focused on Dan's every word as they looked on with great interest. He was excited to hear the stories about his dad. His mother had finally lifted the moratorium. It was now up to him to listen and to understand.

"It was Christmas break, while back home from college, we had decided to do some snow camping, to either live in a snow cave or build an igloo around our tents like we had learned. We were going to test ourselves, pit our meager skills against the wilderness. We cross-county skied a mile or so up the trail beyond the edge of the Lodge Pole Campground. We were going to make our temporary home off of the Marble Fork of the

Kaweah River in the Tokopah Valley, well beneath Tokopah Falls. We brought enough winter gear to last a couple of nights. It was our first winter test so to speak; it was us against the elements of a mild winter at 7,200 feet in the Sierra Nevada Mountains." He smiled.

"You guys were going to camp out in the snow?" Erick exclaimed.

"Yeah, we were looking for a challenge, responding to the need to test our metal. There were four of us." Dan stared off down the road, his words retracing his thoughts. "We had skied up the trail for about an hour and had already taken a couple more hours to set up our camp. We packed down the snow with our skis and used an ice saw to carve blocks out of the snow for our retaining walls to insulate us from the cold and winds. In a few hours, we had carved a rather nice place for a handful of rookies. By then the low angle sun had already come and gone and we were waiting for the moonlight to peer down into the darkened forest canyon that surrounded us. You see, during the winter, the sun retires early and when the moon is up its light practically causes the snow to glow." Dan shook his head. "It's one of the most beautiful sights you will ever see, the moonlight reflecting off the snow, turning night into day. The forest was a black and white rendition of Ansel Adams' greatest works."

"Uncle Adams!" exclaimed Erick.

"You wish!" Gabe teased.

"Never know until you check the family tree!" Erick smiled.

"Shadows stretching like dark fingers from behind the trees," Dan continued. "It was like being in a whole other world where, instead of sunlight, we had a frozen world illuminated by moonlight. We were content just sitting there on our tarp draped over mounds of snow, among the warmth and light of our shelter, but it was Gabriel who wanted to go out for a cross-country ski in the moon light that evening. It was Gabriel who said the winter night was calling him. He was so adamant that we leave the warmth of our enclosure and explore the secrets of the moonlit darkness that I had no choice but to reluctantly go." He gave a toothy smile. "But I was glad I did. We spooked an owl from a nearby tree branch that quiet night and followed it towards the river hoping to catch another glance of it."

Gabe flashed to thoughts of the butterfly.

"An owl?" Erick asked.

"I know!" Dan continued. "I have also wondered about its significance myself, whether it was just an owl in the forest looking for something to fill its belly, or if we chased off the messenger, interrupted a process? What a complicated chain of events, this could have been if that were true!" He cleared his throat and continued.

"Gabriel said he needed to go to the river. I balked at the idea. I had visions of falling through the thin crust of snow that lay above the icy waters below, but Gabriel talked me into going anyway." He gave out a deep sigh. "Your father was good at that. Navigating in the canyon that night was rather simple. We just followed our ears to the river. It thundered in the distance of the moonlit silence. We huffed and puffed along through the forest, wove in and out of the lengthy shadows, as we glided our way across the squeaky frozen surface. There was no way we were going to sneak up on anything that night. It was like wet running shoes on a freshly waxed floor. The cold air numbed our faces, froze our perspiration to our exposed skin, cold dry air filling our lungs as we puffed along. Before we knew it we were out of the shadows and in the moon's brightness along the edge of the river. The stronger part of the current flowed noisily past the snow-covered boulders, while the slower water perked along under the snow beneath us. There out in the open, a slight breeze moved with the water down the canyon. Oh, what an incredible sight and feeling we had that night." He shook his head. "I can still remember it as if it were yesterday. The moonlight was the brightest once we made our way out of the shadows and into the clearing; it was like turning on the lights. The brightness faded to shadows on the other side of the river. The forested canyon walls stretched up the mountainside beyond it. We just stood there in silence, absorbing this, gift. Never had I seen anything as beautiful.

"It was then, during that very moment that we both detected movement on the opposite side of the river. It was like swaying branches in the breeze, only the silhouette of a branch was the wrong shape and size. It looked as if a dark shadow lay partially buried within the snow. It looked out of place. We silently exchanged looks between each other. We had both stood there motionless for a moment. The cold bit into our exposed faces, reminding us that sweating and stopping would only make us colder.

"It was Gabriel who waved back first. He didn't know why, but he just did. The little voice in his head told him to go to that very spot, told him to wait to see what would happen. And then, something did happen! The silhouette we were staring at moved. An unsure shadow weakly waved back.

"Startled, Gabriel returned the wave and called out to the dark object buried within the snow on the edge of the forest shadows. We could barely hear a man's voice over the cascading rapids of the river. It scared the hell out of us for a moment. I remembered thinking 'what is that thing doing out *here* in the freezing cold?' It all caught us by surprise.

"I took a couple of stumbling glides backwards, but no, not Gabriel, he glided closer, across the unstable ice and snow, he slushed across the water and debris. Stoked by a strange surprise and primal fear, I followed him toward the shadow. It was then that it all started to make sense. It was then that the silhouette first became a recognizable shadow and then the reality of a human form. I waved and yelled toward the human on the opposite shore. I cupped my gloved hands and yelled with all my might. It waved back again, this time frantically, with both hands. One of his hands was missing a glove. The human form staggered to its feet but then tumbled back to the snow. Something was wrong. The figure couldn't walk, so it began to crawling toward us, crawled toward the icy river.

"We didn't wait. We felt there was no time. We kicked off our skis and scrambled out toward the figure, trying not to get wet. We carefully chose our steps from snow-covered rocks, to boulders, to driftwood. The figure in turn pulled itself along towards us with disregard for its safety and the freezing temperatures of the thigh-deep water. We yelled for the figure to slow down but that didn't seem to matter. The human form was focused on us as if it was afraid to look away. Afraid that we were only a figment of its imagination... a hallucination? The human form was determined to be with us, to be back with others of its kind. Despite its injuries, it splashed through the water to meet us on the other side. The moon light revealed a desperate man in his early 30's, his eyes filled with tears. We pulled the appreciative man into our embrace near the edge of the river. I wanted to cry. It was an emotional scene."

Gabe watched Dan pause for a moment and let out a deep sigh, before their eyes met. He felt his body shudder as he looked. Dan's caring was projecting love and understanding.

"He was hungry and exhausted. He had injured his leg while out Telemark skiing for the day. He had no idea which side of the mountain he was on. He had lost his bearings then most of his gear when he had fallen and broken his leg earlier that morning. He had been crawling around all day trying to make his way downhill to a road. It was there alongside that river that he had given up hope, accepted his fate. He lay there ready to make right with whomever would listen. He thought he would never see his family and friends again.

"He had rested until the moon rose high enough above the mountains to continue his journey to exhaustion in the moon light. Surrounded by the reflective snow, he waited for the end. He kept telling himself that the voices he heard were the sounds of the water moving over the rocks and debris, not from the grim spirits of the forest coming to collect him. When his shivering stopped he closed his eyes to rest. The snow no longer seemed cold. He could no longer feel his fingers in his gloveless hand, but he didn't care. He knew he was succumbing to hypothermia, frost bite. It was then that he reluctantly thought about accepting his fate. He settled down, to pray, to contemplate death.

"He said he had awoke from his stupor and looked across the river to the other side. He thought he saw 'two angels standing there looking at him', but up until that moment, he thought there were no such thing. To him, religion was a figment of someone else's imagination, a cult, an organization developed to control ones choice, an effort to find an understanding in a world that made no sense. By now, he thought he was hallucinating. He was not a religious man, but a desperate man willing to ask for help from whatever or whomever he could get it. Evidently, when it came right down to it, dying was not an option he wanted to acknowledge.

"The confirming wave was a test of his faith, it was a test of our faith. We cried together. It was all so very strange. That day he believed angels were sent down from the heavens to save his backside, that his prayers had been answered. Later, of course, he realized that we weren't actually angels; but he honestly believed that we were sent to find him, to bring him back to his friends and family. He was absolutely positive of it. He also heard the owl right before we arrived. He said it hadn't called his name but called to him. A Coincidence? The man didn't think so. He felt he had been given a second chance at life, a second chance to fix whatever it was in his life that needed fixing."

"What did you guys do with him?" Erick asked.

Dan snickered out loud. "When we told him that help was less than a mile away, he had a sudden burst of energy, a new lease on life. Despite our wanting to exercise our survival skills and make-shift a litter to carry him to safety, he insisted that we support him by his shoulders and allow him to hobble his way back at his own pace. We did as he requested. It took us an hour, sloshing through the snow, extra weight on our skis. We took him to the ranger residence near the trailhead, woke up the grumpy ranger from his warm bed and turned the appreciative man over to him." Dan chuckled. "The ranger showed his gratitude and appreciation by lecturing us on the proper way to transport an injured person. We skied back to our camp, annoyed by the attitude of the ranger. A lesson on how *not* to act. We tossed a new saying around in our heads that night, *No good deed goes unpunished*!" Dan forced a laugh. "We were very thankful that we had possibly saved that man's life."

Gabe stared at his uncle. He felt a cool chill race through him.

"Did you ever see that man again?" Gabe asked.

Dan shook his head as he continued to gaze out the side window toward the valley below. "No! We were from Southern

California, and he was from the Bay Area. We exchanged names and numbers, made promises to call, but neither of us did. We were too busy with college, he..." Dan shrugged his shoulders, "was probably busy enjoying a new lease on life, I guess." Dan looked back over to the boys. "We hadn't done something because we wanted recognition in return. We did it because it was the right thing to do, because it needed to be done." He shook his head. "That was a lifetime ago!"

Just one more step in our journey to Falcon Canyon.

Gabe pulled his arms in closer for warmth as he felt the Scout slow to a stop.

Great, more debris in the road!

Dan turned and gazed back affectionately to both of the boys, his voice serious. "Remember, whether we are guided by angels, directed by owls, or led by butterflies, we're here because we are meant to be. We're here to do a job. Gabe, we're going to the place where your father tragically passed. There may be times along our journey when you'll be overwhelmed by it all. You may feel the need to cry. Remember that we're all on this journey of discovery and healing... together, your mom, your aunt, your best friend, all of us!" Dan silently surveyed the valley below through the side window a moment, before his teary eyes met Gabe's again. "I am glad we are finally here together. This is the beginning of something we will probably never truly understand. This journey will shine some light on the turmoil of the last two weeks. I loved your father, I love your mother, and I love you." He smiled and stepped out of the vehicle.

Gabe slowly followed him out into the ear-ringing silence. He staggered to regain his balance. He had already been working too long and hard. He breathed in the fresh mountain air and the last of the diminishing dust cloud that they had created. The sunlight was struggling through the buildup of clouds as the sun was creeping toward the west. He looked at his watch; it was almost 4:00 in the afternoon.

Where had all of the time gone?

What normally took a couple of hours under summer driving conditions ended up taking them a few hours extra with the slow road navigation and debris removal. With sunset almost upon them, it only left them a few hours to reach the heart of Falcon Canyon. The fingers of fog were gone from the valley bottom, revealing the shadows of the river below. The pockets of fog that once embraced the mountaintops were now being replaced with descending storm clouds. He filled his lungs again with the mountain air. He could smell the rain. They didn't have much time.

CHAPTER TWENTY-FIVE
INTO THE WILDERNESS
MARCH 16TH 2000 ANNIVERSARY DAY

Dan's knees screamed as their group of three descended quickly down the scree-covered ridgeline. He had to keep reminding himself, as he struggled to keep up with the boys, that he had been quite an athlete at one time. He'd been a man who pushed himself beyond most, making his living in and around a rugged landscape much like this. The fact that he was 56 didn't help. The boys on the other hand, whom he probably outweighed by 60 pounds each, weren't helping matters. Despite their miles of walking and bouts of strenuous labor, they still powered down the hillside, driven by a mysterious energy, youth. A source that he would have loved to tap into. He could feel the canyon calling to him, pulling on his inner chest.
Pulling at my soul?
The thought chilled him like a pocket of cool air.
This isn't like me!
He constantly glanced over his shoulders in the fading light, almost half expecting to see someone or something trailing behind them. The wind whistled in his ears. The trees creaked and moaned as they swayed in the building gusts. Though it was late afternoon, the lighting seemed dimmer, a bit eerie. The sky had taken on a strange color. The darker blues silhouetted the purples, which in turn accented the light bluish gray canvas of the sky. The darker, higher clouds took on a life of their own. Another thing that just didn't seem right was the conflicting wind direction in relation to the clouds. The clouds were cruising one

way, and the winds were blowing from another. The gusts were shoving at their backs, driving them steadily downhill toward their very destination, prodding them along at a dangerously fast pace. He couldn't blame the boys for their horrific decent.

Were we being out right pushed, relentlessly, along to our ultimate destination or demise?

The thought gave him another chill.

Then the inevitable happened. He lost his focus and tripped. He gasped, he lunged forward under building energy. He instinctively threw his hands out in front for balance. He tripped over something, a rock, a root, he wasn't sure. At that moment it was like time had slowed to a virtual crawl. His lower body slowed almost to a stop, but his upper torso picked up speed and momentum. Everything moved as if in slow motion. The weight of the pack pulled him forward. The wind pushed like a hand from behind, but no longer whistled in his ears. The voice in his head screamed for him to leap forward.

He obeyed. It seemed like seconds before both of his feet and hands caught the loose surface and dug in with and audible thud. He slid back noisily onto the seat of his pants and the back of his pack, displacing loose rocks as he glissaded down the scree slope until he came to a full stop, staring up at the sky. He had caught up to the two boys in a matter of seconds, almost clipping the back of Erick's heels, who had only been a few steps behind Gabe.

Could've been a disaster.

Dan closed his eyes for a moment, taking a quick inventory. He lay there motionless on his back, his chest rapidly expanding and contracting as he struggled to breathe. The adrenaline made his fingers and toes tingle. When he opened his eyes he was looking up into the boys' worried expressions. He saw the relief flood into their wind-burned faces when he looked up at them with an embarrassing smile.

"Mr. Wilson, are you alright?" Erick managed to squeak out first, concern evident in his voice.

"I'm fine, just a little tired, I guess." He didn't sound convincing. "I think it's time for a break!" He heard the exhaustion and concern in his own voice as he waited for the pain to kick in. "This place looks like it's as good as any!"

He saw the boy's eyes flash up the side of the mountain from where they had come.

"Tripped, I think." He fumbled to explain.

Gabe nodded as his eyes moved from the finger ridge to the surrounding forest and then to the mist-shrouded valley below. "Looks like rain," he stated.

"Yeah, lots of it I'm afraid!" Dan wiggled his fingers and toes for assurance before he sat up. He had lucked out. Nothing appeared injured but his pride. His appendages all moved as he directed.

So far so good, everything seems to be in working order.

His gaze rested again on the two energetic boys. They tried to disguise their nervous anticipation.

"What I would trade for the spirit of youth this very moment, for knees that don't ache. For lungs that process oxygen at a faster rate, and to not have to breathe your dust." Dan grumbled to himself.

"What was that?" asked Gabe.

"Nothing!" Dan shook his head.

It was the very same dust that seemed to stick like plaster to their sweat-dripping bodies in the high humidity.

The two boys plopped down noisily alongside Dan. They pushed loose debris down the hillside with their feet as they wedged their backsides into the side of the slope. They all silently watched the loose, debris roll a couple of yards to a stop.

Dan could barely hear the sliding debris over the building, angry gusts of wind. Within seconds it was like nothing ever happened. The hillside stabilized and reabsorbed the debris-like quicksand.

"How much farther?" Erick asked.

"We're close, I can feel it!" Gabe yelled excitedly into the wind, his eyes gazing out over the valley.

Dan nodded in agreement. "Close!" He wasn't too sure if things were actually starting to look familiar, or if it was just wishful thinking on his part. It had been a few years since he stopped coming back to this spot. The trees were starting to return along the ridge. Up until this weekend, he no longer saw the point of coming back. This journey was more important now than he could ever imagine. The clock was ticking. He felt it in his chest. He felt it in his soul.

He looked down at his watch, it was 6:37 p.m., and it had been less than two hours since they left the International along the shoulder of the road and bailed out down the side of the ridge following a well-used game trail. They were making good time, despite the conditions. They were probably less than a half hour from the edge of the slide, about an hour or so until official sunset. Throw in another 30 minutes and absolute darkness would be a factor to deal with.

"A half hour at this pace, maybe more!" he exclaimed as he massaged his knees with his hands. Dan felt his body shudder as he fumbled with the meshing to pull his water bottle out from the pocket on his pack. He watched the boys out of the corner of his eye, hoping they hadn't noticed. Doubt was an emotion he didn't want to add to the mix, at least not at this time in the game.

To his relief they hadn't noticed. If they had, they didn't let on. He guzzled down about half of the icy cold liquid. He must have been thirsty because the water tasted better than expected. He was unsure if the chill was from a combination of the chilling wind blowing across his sweat drenched body, now that they stopped, or from his unsteady nerves. Then he felt it, the coming on, a brain freeze headache.

Here I am in a building storm, miles from the nearest bowl of sherbet ice-cream. If I only knew where we were really going with this.

Dan waited for the gusts to subside momentarily before he spoke, and like clockwork, they did. "Did I ever tell you that you remind me of your Dad?" he teased. He forced a smile.

Both boys shot him a questioning glance.

Gabe rolled his eyes. He appeared to be done with that particular question.

A story about his brother came to mind; he suddenly remembered it as clearly as ever.

"Strange!" he said loud and clear into the wind.

The boys looked in his direction and leaned in closer to hear what he had to say.

"Out in the woods, your Dad was like the Energizer bunny, he would go forever if you didn't latch onto him, tie him down." Dan shook his head as the boys drew their heads even closer to listen. "On hikes, he would always say... 'Just a little further, almost there!' He prodded me and others along. Yeah, different that man was." Dan grinned as he remembered. "It was spring, fifteen years ago. Two kayakers were lost, more like stranded. They had lost their boats... took a break from paddling and forgot to properly secure them on shore, most likely a factor of fatigue. A couple of college students stumbled upon the abandoned kayaks while they were out for a day hike. They found two kayaks and a paddle bobbing around in an eddy a few miles downstream. It was late afternoon before they got around to reporting it. It was spring and the days were still rather short. By all standards, it was too late in the afternoon to put into the river and float down, but no, not for your Dad. He jumped at the chance to get into the water."

Both boys laughed. Dan waited for the laughing and the windy gusts to subside again before he continued. "The rangers dropped him off at the boater's put-in-spot, and then hauled off to the location where the hikers reported seeing the abandoned kayaks. By the time the rangers arrived, only a single boat bobbed around in the eddy. The other boat and paddle were nowhere to be found.

"Well, your Dad found the kayakers alright. They were huddled together on shore about two miles upriver from the location where their boats were originally reported. Everything they had that went with the boats, maps, food, water, extra clothes-all was gone. Boy, were they happy to see him. He warmed, comforted, fed, and then set them up for the night. It was strange; they said they knew he was coming, a little voice told them. I don't think your Dad ever got used to hearing that." Dan felt that familiar chill again as he looked directly at Gabe. The feeling ran the length of his body. Dan pulled his arms closer into his sides as he looked over his shoulder, his eyes searching the forest.

There it was again, the feeling of being watched, followed. By now he thought he would be used to that.

"The next morning your Dad directed the searchers into their camp, turned them over and, you guessed it, finished his trip down the river unscathed."

Gabe smiled.

When Erick's laughter diminished Dan cleared his throat. The laughter was good for the soul, it was good for the group.

Are they ready for what I'm about to tell them next? Gabe needs to know about his father's death. I need to tell him now before we arrive. He needs to be prepared. We all need to be prepared.

Dan knew they would be pushing it close on the sunlight, but the story had to be told, their minds prepared. His thoughts flashed to the landslide, the scar that ran down the side of the mountain and also through his soul. Nature had her way of healing them both over time, and by the grace of God, hopefully sooner. It had been more than enough time to get over it.

He closed his eyes. He could see it again. An ugly scar stretched as far as he could see, eerie silence dominated by the wind. The earthy smells, the ghostly snags of dead and downed trees littered the mountainside. The dust devils appeared and disappeared up and down the exposed earth mountainside as if they were on patrol.

Guarding Gabriel's imprisoned soul, trapping him in his earthy tomb?

The devastated hillside was now homes for woodpeckers, rodents, hawks, owls, deer, bear and mountain lions. He forced those thoughts out of his mind by merely opening his eyes. When he did, he found the two boys questioning stares peering directly into his face.

It was time. He was ready to tell, ready to explain. The courage came easier now. He was being helped, he could tell. He recognized that feeling now.

Brother, help me through this and I will forever be indebted.

He wasn't superstitious, but there was more to this than he understood.

"Gabe, we're headed into Falcon Canyon, the area where your Dad died," Dan's voice boomed, louder over the wind than he wanted.

Timing!

The winds had died down as he spoke.

'Where your Dad died!' had echoed loudly down the ridge.

It came off as heartless, sounding all wrong. He started to apologize, but thought better of it.

They both gave him a solemn look.

"I'm sorry, I didn't mean to yell it!" he couldn't help but think.

Once we find the missing kid, then what? Is this the end, or is it just the beginning? Are we part of an endless loop just getting ready to start it over again with the next generation?

***

Gabe felt his insides move around. He imagined it was like swallowing a butterfly.

The butterfly!

He had been waiting for this very moment, but didn't have the nerve to ask. He was glad his uncle did. He thought it was strange the way the gusty wind had died down at the moment his uncle had spoken his father's name out loud.

Coincidence? Was the mountain listening... waiting? Are we being followed? Are we safe?

Now was not the time to think about it-miles from nowhere-on their way to see his father's grave for the first time. There was definitely something to this place: the clouds, the colors of the sky, and the gusts of the relentless winds. He could feel it. They were getting closer to something. Goosebumps crawled down his arms, legs and neck. The storm was building, the rain-he could smell the rain. By the looks of it, this was going to be a big one. They were pressed for time; the rain would destroy the evidence they needed to help them with the search. Time was running out.

Gabe shuddered. In a matter of seconds, the air around him felt as if it had dropped ten degrees. No, it wasn't just the wind;

the chill that riveted through his body had started from within. He tucked his chin into his chest and adjusted the collar of his windbreaker to keep the cold wind from biting into his skin. He first looked over one shoulder, them the other. He was relieved to see that it was still just them sitting there on that desolate, lonely mountain ridge. He gazed down into the mist shrouded valley below. In the dim light, the shadows stretched like fingers across the valley floor. The gusts of the wind bowed the tops of the trees under its relentless power. He turned his head to avoid the wind that whistled and screamed angrily into his ears. He was taken aback by how the ceiling of clouds had blended together, growing ever closer to the surrounding peaks. The storm was almost upon them.

The afternoon sun was a write off, it might as well already have set for the evening. It was very much like this place to hide its secrets, letting out just enough to engage the subconscious and then draw one in. There was nothing one could do but follow. A mysterious force prodded him along toward his destiny.

It had to be. It was meant to be.

He was learning about the sudden passing of a man he couldn't remember. A man that had answered the call, similar to what they were doing now.

Was it a coincidence that strange things were happening to me, much like it did my father? Was it a coincidence that we were here on the tenth anniversary of my father's death or, that a butterfly showed me where to look?

Now, as it is in most fairy tales, his father's passing was to be revealed on the stormy slopes of a lonely mountain. They were searching for a missing kid, much like what was going on with his father that day, ten years ago. Then there were the angels.

If they are here right now, why don't they reveal themselves to me? Why the secrecy? Was that an angel that I briefly saw in the garden?

He shivered again at the thought.

Are angels really leading us? Would angels knowingly take us to this place in these questionable conditions?

This place reminded him more of hell than heaven; walking down into the cold swirling darkness of the unknown, instead of walking up the mountain towards the warmth, towards the familiar comfort of the last bit of sunlight for the day. It was a bit more than he liked.

Dan shared his thoughts.

Gabe carefully listened.

"He had been having an early dinner with the family when he got the call..." Dan gave out a deep sigh. It was obvious that it hurt to bring up the past. "Lydia never knew that would be the last time that she would ever see him...

"According to one of his journal entries, he knew something was up, but he went anyway." Dan shook his head in amazement. "It was his destiny to go, to take part, and he knew it. If he were here today, he would have said he was just responding to the call!"

Gabe desperately scanned his own thoughts, searching his forgotten memory, for that moment in time. He found a disappointing nothing.

"I was five... what does anyone remember when they're five!" His voice squeaked in anguish.

He felt a twinge of anger welling up from within and pushed it back with his mind. It was the sound of Dan clearing his throat that pulled Gabe's attention back from the abyss.

"Evidently, it was late afternoon by the time he arrived for the briefing. That day, they said he wasn't a bit surprised. It was like he had already been briefed. As a matter of fact, it was Gabriel who suggested that they search where they did! Sound familiar?" Dan silently gazed off down the finger ridge as if he were either reliving that day or looking for answers in the shadows.

Gabe's thoughts suddenly flashed to the butterfly during the briefing, how the insect had seemed to know exactly where to look.

Oh, my God!

"Sounds familiar!" The words flashed through his head. His body suddenly felt drained. When he glanced over to Erick for reassurance, he was surprised to see his friend staring directly at him with an unnerving look. He could read it in his eyes as Erick's lips mumbled the words "The Butterfly!"

All Gabe could do was nod in agreement.

What did this mean? Was I being sent to my own death just like my father? Why? What did I do to deserve this?

The thought made him feel faint, his throat suddenly dry. He felt the tears forming in his eyes.

I don't want to die!

They were just supposed to be looking for a missing youth.

Dan must have read the expression on his bewildered face, for he suddenly tried to explain as if he had rehearsed for this very moment over and over again. "I can't even remember the number of times that I've been down this ridge, the number of times that I tried to find closure, tried to make sense out of this whole bizarre mess." He gestured down the ridge with his arms and narrowed his eyes. "But I can tell you the exact date and time I gave up hope and stopped coming, it was 6:37 in the evening five years ago... to the day."

Gabe saw Dan look down at his watch and raise his eye brows and shake his head as he looked up into the sky.

"Is this a coincidence, or what? It's darn near that time right now!" Dan shook his head again as he continued, "I tried to step out of the International several times, but I just couldn't do it. I had the heater going, I just sat there perspiring, my butt stuck to the seat! If someone had driven by at that moment, they would have thought that I was crazy. Beating on the steering wheel, tears in my eyes, yelling, *why?* At the top of my lungs." The tears once again slid down the side of Dan's cheeks as he forced a smile.

"I know *why* your Dad went down that mountain even knowing that he might never come back. It was his calling, he chose his destiny!" Dan shrugged his shoulders.

Gabe directed his gaze down the side of the ridge to avoid eye contact with his uncle. As strange as it all sounded, he didn't want his uncle to know that he had also felt the calling.

Was it my destiny to literally follow my father's footsteps?

"A college kid had injured and stranded himself on a rock outcropping on an unstable hillside up above Falcon Canyon, that pathetic winter day," continued Dan. "He had climbed up a ridge draw, un-aided by ropes, slipped, fell, and injured himself. He couldn't move either up or down. On any other day, it would have been your typical climbing rescue, but," Dan gazed up into the clouds as if making a point to someone other than themselves, "For some bizarre reason, it wasn't!" With that said, he refocused on Gabe. "What made this situation dire was the deteriorating weather conditions, the victim's worsening medical complications and the fact that the exposed mountainside was eroding away before their very eyes. The heavy rains had continued to saturate the soil in and around the rocky outcropping. Boulders, trees, root balls, and all, were sliding down the hillside at neck-breaking speeds, past the victim. They said it sounded like thunder, trains and jets, all mixed together. The ground shook with tremors. Hail and brimstone it was, *'snatched from a scene of the Old Testament'* one of the rescuers had said later." Dan fidgeted with a piece of gravel in his hand.

"The kid had fallen, fractured his leg, arm, or something like that. The freezing rains had added to the complications. The victim's bout with hypothermia and his asthmatic conditions didn't help either. The hillside was eroding around him. They told your dad to wait for the hauling and lowering systems to be safely rigged before he ventured out onto the active slide. But your dad told them that there wasn't any time, that if the debris hit the ropes, it wouldn't really matter because it would *'take everything and everyone with it'*. That the soil was behaving like a thick liquid and a rope was the last thing you wanted tied to you in moving water. He said that if they *'waited any longer there wouldn't be a need to rescue anyone'*, that they would probably have *'difficulty recovering the bodies strewn down the mountainside'*. That he *'wasn't going to be the one to tell the family that they just sat there on their hands, and watched their child get taken out by the mountain because they were too afraid!'* Dan tossed a hand full of gravel down the slope.

They all watched the scattered pieces slide to a stop.
Who were they kidding!

There was a little risk in everything they did. Gabe's thoughts spilled forth.

"The top of the slide was too unstable," Dan continued. "Their only choice, outside of a helicopter extraction, which was still a few hours out, was to put a man in the middle of it all with ropes and try to reach the stranded person from the sides." Dan picked up another hand full of gravel and shook it around in his hand. "Gabriel harnessed up, threw extra gear and rope into his pack and reluctantly attached himself to a rope. He had a couple of guy's belay him across the unstable slope for safety. They let out the rope when he needed and held on tight when he didn't. They watched with baited breath as he traversed the face, sloshed through the knee-deep mud, dodging the loose debris, and untangling his rope as if he were navigating a field of active landmines. The sound of the wind and rain, the braking of branches, and falling debris, were constant reminders of the imminent danger which he had willingly put himself into. They said the mountain '*moaned as if it were demented.*' A couple of the guys said they had never experienced anything as scary as that night on the mountain and were happy to say they hadn't since." Dan tossed those gravel pieces down slope as well.

"They didn't stop him?" Erick asked. "They let Gabe's dad go out there, alone?"

"Yes, it was the way he wanted it. He proved time and time again that he had his stuff together. They all talked about the strange luck that he had, pulling off miracles that no one else was able to do and haven't been able to do since. As it was, he had never bit off anything too big to chew before. Despite everything they had learned, everything they had been taught, they threw out their instincts and trusted his judgment on this one. They all wanted the kid safe, but deep down inside they were glad that someone else had stepped up for this one. It was a suicide mission for anyone else, but for Gabriel? It was what was expected of him. So it was he who scrambled from the safety of the ridge to traverse the saturated, unstable slope.

"As it ended up, because of the gauntlet of debris, the tangled rope being too short, and the fight against time, he did what he thought best. Despite protest, he went off belay, he released the rope attached to his climbing harness. He no longer had the strong arms holding the end of his rope to pull him to safety if the mountain gave way, or the ability to recover his body if things went terribly wrong. Everyone just stared. He trusted his life to his gut feeling, the guardian angels that had his back through thick and thin. He successfully free climbed the rest of the way down to the stranded, injured man.

"Incredibly, using the second rope he carried, he reached and stabilized the injured victim. Secured him to a collapsible stokes litter and the end of two secure rescue lines. He triaged the victims ailments, managed to get him attached to a backboard. That in itself was an incredible feat." Dan's prideful voice went sorrowful.

"Then it happened." Dan used his hands to tell the story. "The whole mountainside below Dan and the victim tore away in a thunderous, earth-shaking roar. Cascading debris and mud engulfed the mountain slope. The rope went tight. The rescue team gripped the end of the rope with all of their might against the weight of the mountain and waited. For a moment, they felt as if they were all going to be pulled helplessly from their perches and into the abyss, but they refused to let go. They dug their heels into the mud and clamped down onto the rope against the strain. Others scrambled to secure the rescuers belaying the rescue lines to nearby trees. Just as they thought they were done for, they found the powerful strength and courage to hold on. The burden of failure was no longer overwhelming.

"When the calm was restored, and the mist and debris settled, there was only a single stokes litter suspended in midair, beneath it unrecognizable destruction. The stokes gently swung back and forth in the gentle gusts of wind, its rope above snagged on an entanglement of wood and debris mid-way down the slope. The supporting rope attached to the upper end of the Stokes litter had somehow managed to wrap itself around the roots of an up turned tree. The victim had swung closer to the edge of the slide, and away from the most powerful wave of the mountain's fury. Miraculously, the rope held against all odds. Their celebration was short lived when they realized that Gabriel was gone. The swaying stokes was the only human object recognizable on the debris scarred landscape of Falcon Canyon.

"They stood there in silent amazement. Incredibly, the young man in the portable stokes swayed back and forth like a slowing pendulum. Gabriel was gone, his luck had finally run out. His guardian angel set him out to dry. He had accomplished what he had set out to do," Dan shrugged his shoulders as if he were at a loss for words and understanding. "He saved the kid, but not himself, a tragic loss. He gave his life to save an idiot that shouldn't have been out there in the first place! Why?" He tilted his head back and yelled his disappointment into the wind. "Why? Why save *him*?" Dan looked down at his feet. "He was a Darwin Award candidate, a training aide for the world to see, meant to be an example of what *not* to do!" Dan put his face in his dirty hands. "Brother, why did you risk everything to save *him*? Why did you leave *us*?" He took a deep sigh as if he had regained the control of his emotions. He looked at Gabe and pointed down the mountain. "It was a choice your father made. I'm trying to respect it, but I tell you, it's not easy!" Dan nodded his head. "You, too will have a choice."

Gabe reached over and rested his hand on Dan's shoulder. Dan reached up and gently squeezed it. Gabe knew what that meant.

"You know, the victim apologized for Gabriel's loss. He praised the other rescuers that day out there on the slopes of the devastated muddy mountain, but none would listen."

"Other rescuers?" Erick piped up.

"Besides the ones on the safety rope?" asked Gabe.

"Yeah, they thought the victim delirious, hypothermic, and succumbing to his injuries, weakened by exposure," Dan winked. "But, we know better, don't we! The victim had seen the angels that helped Gabriel secure that young man in the Stokes litter and help haul him the twenty or so yards up the saturated slope and anchored him to the end of the rope. An impossible task for one man, even the legendary Gabriel Wilson. They helped hold the Stokes litter in place while Gabriel tied the secure knot that held against all odds. It was the angels who guided the litter around the tumbling rocks and debris that crushed and buried everything in its path. Who else could it have been? One man couldn't have accomplished the feat by himself. It was the angels who allowed that man to be saved, the same angles that let your father die! Or one of them at least!" Dan's voice rippled with anger. "They left that other man and took your dad! The question we need to ask is why?" pride and disappointment echoed in his shaky, emotional voice. "Why, after all that your father had done, why did they leave him to die out there?" Dan shook his head in confusion as he looked towards the canyon. "It makes no sense." He mumbled under his breath.

Gabe didn't know what to say. All he could do was weakly shrug his shoulders. He, too, was at a loss for words.

"They had their reasons, but what were they!"

Was all he could think of at that moment.

Dan gave out a deep sigh as he looked around, his hand rested on both of the boy's shoulders. "Boys, we're not alone." There was worry in his newfound voice. "There is a struggle between good and evil going on around us. We've been chosen to do what we've been asked, others after us will do the same. I don't know anything about this person we're being asked to find. I don't know how it is that you think that the kid ended up here, but I do know, this place has a history, *this* place has a strange lingering energy. It makes me feel... uncomfortable. It is part of the reason I stopped coming back. While I'm here I feel your father's presence. I feel him in the trees and the air, as I follow your father's footsteps, but I don't feel him in the shadows. I don't feel him in the aggressive winds that push us along." He glanced back over his shoulder and cleared his throat. "To be honest, it scares the crap out of me! We share this mountain with something else who's agendas are not our own." Dan forced a laugh. "But, it's where we need to be. It's where we need to go. Boys, I've wasted enough of our time. We're burning what's left of our daylight. We have a job to do and, by God, not hell or high water is going to stop us."

Gabe quickly rose to his feet and gave his uncle a great big hug. Erick joined him. Dan embarrassed them both. They had all felt the same thing. At first he didn't see it, but there they were. He was right. Now, it was all out in front. The shadows no longer held power in their secrets. The winds pushed them from behind. It was like his sensei had always said, use your opponent's energy against him.

When they push, you pull, when they pull, you push, and when they least expect it, you jerk them off balance and take them down!

ACT: THREE
ENLIGHTENMENT

"Steven of the Redwoods" by April Leiterman

CHAPTER TWENTY-SIX
THE VOICE OF PRAYER
MARCH 16TH 2000

Lydia effortlessly pulled open the wooden back door and stepped around it. She turned the latch of the screen door and then pushed. The door resisted as if someone had been forcing it closed from the other side against her. She leaned with her shoulder this time and pushed harder, squeezing the leather bound book closer into her chest with one hand, grasping the door knob with the other. The door budged a bit. Now caught by the wind, it seemed lighter, less of an obstacle, almost as if it were opening under its own power. She stumbled through the doorway and out into the backyard. She scrambled to catch her balance. A gust of cold air hit her in the chest and noisily slammed the screen door shut behind her. The gunshot-like noise deafened her ears. Startled, she jumped and turned to face the closed door, gripping the leather journal nervously with both hands. Surprisingly, the book felt more comfortable in her hands now than it ever had.

Bizarre, is there ever an end to any of this?

This was the first time she had taken Gabriel's journal out of the house.

"You seem a little resistive today," she spoke to the journal.

Today she was going to read the journal in the garden he loved so much, no matter what!

"This is all so unexpected, right down to the deteriorating weather," she mumbled under her breath, "I am not deterred!"

She spoke loudly as she looked up into the sky as if the message was for those she couldn't see, or for the presence she felt.

The gusts of cold wind whistled through the swaying tops of the creaking, groaning trees. Ground cover pulsed, wave-like, with the winds every breath. Leaf litter and dust swirled down the walkway and past her face, blowing her brown wavy hair off of her shoulders and into her eyes. She turned her head and covered her face with a free hand to prevent the ends of her hair from whipping into her eyes.

She gripped the leather journal tighter in her hands in response to its pages ruffling in the powerful gusts, and then returned her gaze to the surrounding garden. She could smell the rain and the distant river to the south in the cold, moist air. All the major storms approached from the south, just like this one, and all were preceded by winds.

What is that?

Lydia thought as she stopped, pushed the hair from her face and turned her ear in the direction of what sounded like whispering. It was similar to the sounds she remembered hearing near babbling brooks. Maybe it was the water tumbling over rocks and debris, or just….

Maybe?

Strangely, no matter which way she turned and strained her ears to hear, the sounds always seemed to come from the opposite direction. It's source undetermined, a mystery that was never meant to be solved. She spun around into the gusts but the result was always the same. The building winds were playing tricks on her for sure.

For a moment, she thought something was trying to pull the leather bound book from her grasp. She pulled the journal tighter into her chest, subconsciously protecting it, as she continued down the walkway toward the pond and the awaiting bench.

How silly to feel this way!

The gusting wind continued to pelt, batter and pull. There was a strange bit of familiarity to it all.

The wind waves raced across the open surface of the pond, defusing momentarily as they swerved around and rolled the edges of the pond lilies. It rattled the cattails like wind chimes and jostled the aquatic plants and the floating water hyacinth. The pond had a cadence of its own.

She gulped a quick breath and paused for a second when the green, oxidized copper, St. Francis of Assisi statue came into view. She was quite relieved to find that it was only the moving vegetation in the background that made the statue appear as if it had a life of its own. There it stood, one arm extended out above its shoulder and the other lying flat about its waist, holding an empty, matching tarnished green bowl. Both extended arms, unhindered by all that nature was throwing at it, standing at peace amid the brewing storm.

"Oh Gabriel!" her voice crackled with emotion as she forced a smile. She continued towards the statute. It appeared to slowly turn as she made her way around the edge of the pond, an illusion of depth of field. She had been there before. She closed her eyes, her mind drifted back to the birth of the statue, and the presence of Gabriel...

> *She stumbled along blindfolded by a soft, red silk scarf. Her arms were pinned to her side held about the elbows by Gabriel as he guided her from behind. She shuffled along, unsure of her footing, trusting her husband to guide her safely to the surprise that awaited her in the sanctuary of the garden.*

Strangely enough, that day more than fifteen years ago was much like today.

> *They were in between winter storms, the low pressure was settling in, and another front was expected to hit by early morning. It was late afternoon and it was already getting dark. Here, up north, the winter nights are longer and the days get darker sooner. The building clouds had already filled the overcast winter skies. The smell*

of imminent rain was in the air; the scent of the nearby river was even stronger. Though a deep penetrating chill cut into her exposed face and hands, she liked the fact that she was outdoors with the man she loved.

"Is this really necessary?" she whined in her playful sing-song voice.

"Why wouldn't it be?" he laughed. "Holiday gift giving is always left to the discretion of the presenter, you should know that!"

The sureness of his voice made her laugh. "Are you serious? Have you been reading Hallmark cards again?"

"Almost there!" there was relief in his laughter.

She managed to pull one of her arms free and playfully reached for the edge of the blindfold.

"Ugh! Come on now, no peeking. You promised!" he lectured again, "It is supposed to be a surprise!"

He quickly intercepted her hand and held it firmly in his. "Come on honey!" she whined.

She remembered how warm the touch of his hand was...

She opened her eyes and looked around the garden as she reached over and slid one of her hands over the other for human contact even if it was her own. The wind was still in turmoil and the leather book was still firmly in her grip. Disappointingly, there was no Gabriel; she was still alone. Her thoughts had drifted off again, triggered by a familiar setting. She was almost to the bench.

When she reached it she paused and placed a free hand on the rough, wooden backrest. The surface was not smooth like it was back then.

The bench needs to be sanded, another coat of sealer.

Her thoughts, wandered as she surveyed the garden once more before she closed her eyes, again.

It was amazing how similar these two days were despite there being more than fifteen years apart. Both were the precursors to a building storm. Both were significant turning points in her life. Both were bringing hope. Both revolving around the life sized oxidized, copper statue in front of her.

"Why am I drawn out here on this cold, blustering late afternoon?" she whispered to herself.

It would have been easier to review the journal in the warm and comforting sanctuary of the house. She had left her sister-in-law, Betty, alone in the living room so she could challenge the conditions outside by herself. She practically had to demand that Betty trust her on this one, to let her go outside by herself. It was rather strange but she needed to hear from the journal, out in the garden, alone.

If there really was something special to this leather bound book, then now was the time to find out.

Was everything else just coincidence? Was it divinely guided? Should I be on medication?

She forced a smile. Her son and brother-in-law were on the mountain during the tenth anniversary of her husband's passing.

Was I out of my mind to let them talk me into letting Gabe go up there? Does Dan really know what he's doing?

"And am I really here, alone!" she whispered.

This moment had been building, collecting momentum. It had been for years, but everything had finally come together, the stars and planets had finally aligned. She could feel it. There was nothing she could do to stop any of it now.

Or was there?

She shuddered in the coolness. For a moment she could feel him, her husband, Gabe's father, Dan's brother. His presence was there.

Overlooking... guiding?

The thoughts made her shiver even more.

"Is it a warning? Asking me to pray? Asking me to renew my faith?"

She gave out a great big sigh; she was drifting back again...

Her right hand was held within the firm, welcoming embrace of Gabriel's warm hand. The cool wind still howled past her ears, still pulled her long brown hair across her face.

"Almost there." Gabriel's voice boomed in her ear, a bit louder than necessary.

"This is ridiculous!" she protested as she willingly stumbled along, guided by her left elbow.

"Maybe so, but after all; A surprise is a surprise!"

"Yeah, but taking your wife out into a blizzard?"

"A blizzard? It's not snowing!"

"Yet, you mean it's not snowing yet! I kind of miss the warmth of a perfectly good!"

"We're here!" he interrupted in a delicate voice. He stopped prodding her along, released her left elbow, and placed her warm right hand onto the top of the smooth backrest of a wooden bench in front of her. Her first reaction was to flinch and jerk her hand away from the sudden cold in surprise.

She then tilted her head back in an attempt to sneak a peek, and reached up to remove the blindfold, but felt anxious hands already loosening the restraint. She placed a hand on the red scarf just as it fell away from her face...

The whole scene played back slowly in her thoughts. There was a strange grace to it all.

The silk scarf fluttered and snapped in the wind as it floated away from her view. Her eyes came to rest on Gabriel's. His big expectant,

green eyes stared deeply into hers. She leaned into him and embraced.
"I'm not the present," he chuckled and nodded behind her.
"You're not?" she giggled as she turned and looked towards the pond. *Beyond the wooden bench in front of her stood the huge, shiny life-size statue of St. Francis of Assisi, gazing up into the heavens. One arm out stretched into the air, the other holding an empty bowl. Cool swirling winds ruffled the edges of the surrounding ground cover and shrubbery...*

She remembered smelling the rain that day, too. Strangely, the wind had almost unexpectedly sounded like cheering and applause.

An oversized bird feeder?
"My goodness, a life-size bronze statue of a... of a... saint?" she tried to sound enthusiastic, but fell notably short, strangely disappointed. *She had to admit, what stood there in front of her was much unexpected. Apparently, Gabriel was more excited about the oversized statuette than she was.* *"It's so beautiful, and huge!"* she laughed as she grabbed his hand. *He squeezed hers in return, and pulled her closer. She felt his welcome warmth...*

So silly was that special moment.

"It's copper-coated." his smile brightened his face, *"it will take on a character of its own once it starts oxidizing in the elements. It'll turn*

greenish," he nodded. "To look over you, my son, and our Garden of Eden, while I'm gone." He gestured with his hands. "Merry Christmas...!"

To look over you, my son and the garden... while I'm gone? Her thoughts voiced. "Did Gabriel really mean when I'm gone?"

"A son?" she exclaimed, "Do you know something that I don't?"
"Maybe I do!" he smiled, and gave her a playful wink.
She changed the subject. He had been hinting about a son for the last month or so. "Why Saint Francis? Why not a Buddha, or a little forest gnome, like most other gardens?"
He shook his head adamantly. "Its got to be Francis, you'll see." he turned toward the statue. "But, it looks so right, don't you think? I had to have it once I saw it."
"I'll bet. You've always joked about getting one, but—"
"Joked?" he gestured his hand to the statue, "does this look like a joke to you? Now we have one!"
She spun towards him and embraced his neck, kissing him again. "You're crazy, you know that, don't you!"
He nodded. "The statue comes with its own prayer... remember Big Sur? The little chapel in the redwoods we visited?" He reached into his coat pocket, pulled out an envelope, and removed the card. He opened it and slid out an oversized laminated index card.
She curiously watched.

> "*Care to join me in my version of the prayer of St. Francis? We need to christen the statue in the proper way!*"
> "*Your version?*"
> He nodded. "*Yes, my version, no copyright infringements!*" He laughed.

Lydia would never forget the look he gave her, his joyful, knowing smile.

> *She nodded and snuggled up next to him. Arm in arm they smiled as they sang the prayer together, first Gabriel and then she joined in. Their gaze shifted between the statue, the song sheet, and each other. His sweet voice dominated the cold wind that caressed them both....*

"Oh honey, I miss you!" Her eyes filled with tears, her throat suddenly dry despite the cool moist air. A gust of cold wind almost knocked her off of her feet. She firmly gripped the edge of the bench for balance to support her quivering legs. In the process, the leather-bound journal slipped unexpectedly out of her weakened hand and tumbled directly onto the bench. The journal landed spine down, loose pages up towards the sky. She stood there frozen in place as she watched the gusts tear at the open pages, flipping through them in rapid succession. The pages snapped and popped. She was gripped with a sudden panic that the journal would be destroyed, the pages ripped out in front of her eyes before she was able to do anything to stop it, but the pages abruptly stopped turning.

Not again!

The gusty wind continued to noisily pry at the edges of the pages, but it was as if an invisible hand had pressed them down in place. The edges rolled with the wind like the edges of the lily pads on the pond. She stared down in amazement.

How could this be?

She gripped the back support of the bench more tightly as she slowly leaned towards the journal. Like a little girl trying to catch a beautiful butterfly, she cautiously approached.

The trees creaked and moaned around her, and the cold winds cut through the openings in the neck and sleeves of her coat. The water lapped noisily against the shoreline of the pond. The dark clouds moved across the late afternoon sky. The chilling breeze sounded to her like a consoling whispers.

She swept her hair away from the front of her face, gazed around the garden for a moment and then refocused on the journal.

The journal.

The invisible hand still pressed the journal into the bench as the wind still ravaged the edges of the pages. The angry wind seemed to blow even harder, as if in protest of its lack of success in accomplishing the simple task of closing the book. Her hands hovered in a cold pocket of air around the journal before she moved close enough to almost literally pounce upon the book. Once gripped firmly in her hands, she slowly brought the book to her face. She fumbled with the journal to keep from dropping it in her excitement.

Dare I see the words?

Her heart pounded in her chest, and her hands began to tingle. Another chill shot through her.

Is it nerves?

With a heavy sigh, her eyes first focused on the edge of the tattered page. It was discolored from constant use, more tattered than the rest.

A page visited often.

When her eyes focused, she felt her heart skip a beat. There before her, in Gabriel's journal were the words he liked to recite.

The title *My Prayer of St. Francis* was scrolled across the top of the page in cursive, and below were the words to the prayer.

Her body shuddered, a chill surged from her head to her toe, and she gasped for breath.

It is happening again, this is no coincidence.

"Gabriel?" her trembling voice was sucked away in the wind. She closed her eyes for a moment to clear her thoughts. When she opened them, nothing had changed. The edge of the pages still snapped violently in her hands. The wind still whistled in her ears, dancing around the stunned expression on her face. The wind pulled her hair in front of her peering eyes.

"The Prayer of St. Francis!" she cried out, her tears blown about by the wind. "I do remember..." she looked over at the statue and laughed. It wasn't forced. It was almost as if they were laughing together. She felt his presence. Gabriel was there with her again, standing by her side. She felt his warmth. She felt the firmness of his arm around her shoulder. His smell filled her lungs. His warmth filled her heart. She again swept the hair away from the front of her face. "The guardian saint of Ecology you say! The guardian saint of those who protect nature!"

"He's the guardian saint of Gabriel Wilson, the guardian saint of our son," she whispered. "The prayer is to ask for his guidance."

Without another word she began to recite the prayer in the sweetest voice the garden had heard in almost ten years. Two weeks ago she couldn't laugh; one week ago she couldn't sing. The healing had begun. She read on...

Lydia,

The Prayer of St. Francis... a direct line to the guardian angels... to the protector of nature. The prayer was first mentioned in a French, Catholic magazine in 1912, by an unknown author, possibly a French priest named Father Esther Bouguerel. The work wasn't translated into English until 1936. For what it's worth.

I took the liberty to create my own version of the prayer to go along with your statue. In case you didn't know, Saint Francis of Assisi's Italian birth name was

Giovanni di Pietro di Bernardone. Didn't you have a French Ancestor named Bernard?

She laughed. "My Prayer of Saint Francis, by Gabriel Wilson. I haven't sang this in a very, long, time!" she whispered. She cleared her throat, wiped the corner of her eyes and released her sweet sounding voice into the wind.

"Make me the tool of your peace... where there is hatred, teach me to share your Love and faith.
"Help me under-stand the path of my brothers and sisters so I may under-stand how to learn to for-give.
"Help me to learn to for-give others... to be under-stood as to under-stand... to be loved, and to love, with every p-a-r-t of my so-o-oul.
"Teach me to love others, even if theirs beliefs are one sided... to live by example and teach them through your examples.
"Make me the tool of your peace... where there is hatred, teach me to share your love and faith.
"Help me to learn to put my faith in the almighty... to trust the path he has chosen for me... to do my part and to love, with every p-a-r-t of my s-o-o-o-u-l....

Her body shook as she fought back tears.

Enjoy, your loving husband, Gabriel!

***

The young man stood there oblivious to the cold, his glowing white tunic unhampered by the powerful winds that stormed around him. The elements had no power over those who in turn controlled them. The woman, who stood by the bench in conditions from which most would seek shelter, captivated him. Though bundled in clothing the humans wore to protect themselves from the elements of nature, this human, Lydia, was not at all dressed for the cold. He could tell the coolness and the winds were having their way with her, but she refused to abandon what she had started. Despite the increasing turmoil, she refused to give in to the temptation thrown upon her. She protected the book that she held in her hands as if it meant more to her than life itself.

The human who stood there shivering, began to hum in the most beautiful voice. Softly, barely audible at first, but then overtaken by the Holy Spirit, the beautiful lyrics boomed from her soul, and then out through her lungs.

He moved closer, unseen.

Her voice grew in power and intensity, its melody carried beyond the statue and across the pond. Its grace wove through the trees and was channeled to the far reaches by the meandering gusts. The wind failed to steal her voice, it only managed to spread it to every corner finding its path as the heartfelt song weaved its way through the obstacles of jealousy and deceit. For all angels knew, understanding or indifferent, a true prayer of love carried in song from deep within the soul was in a direct line to God. It was true; it was pure. Most angels stopped whatever they were doing to absorb the prayer's grace, its enduring qualities, letting the blessed words pass through them in route to the heavens. The chiming of bells from a distant tower, the haunting sounds of a stringed chorus, legions of organs, and a choir, a million voices strong, joined in, echoing over the wind. This, only the angels could hear.

"It is glorious!"

But he knew that all of the angels did not appreciate the beauty of song, and that they would do whatever they could to interfere with such a blessing.

He moved closer; he needed to be closer.

"The faith of humanity rests within heartfelt songs like these."

These were special, buffered with loving trust, accented with true emotion and, despite the best efforts of the building shadows that loomed on the slopes of the ancient forest, destined to make their mark with God. When the prayers were sincere and filled with righteousness, they could never be stopped. Nothing could stop a prayer of love and understanding.

"*Except!*"

The words slipped from his slender lips.

"*We shall join in the glory. This time, not even the devil himself and his army of sorrow and mistrust will stand in our way.*"

He reached up with his delicate hand to feel the smile on his face. His smooth, unblemished skin had no lines.

"*Someday I will be able to tell!*"

He whispered into the wind.

"*Humans like Lydia will teach me.*"

He hadn't heard Lydia sing like that since prior to Gabriel's passing.

"*She was lost and now she has been found.*"

He could feel the change; a strange new energy radiated from the garden. He watched the journal shake in her trembling hands.

"*Words written in prayer, and sung from her heart, the most powerful form of love ever written by humans is in the form of song. Though the afternoon is getting darker, I feel the strength of good growing ever stronger.*"

Unknown to Lydia, her action alone was building as one of the keys to the boy's success.

"*Did she know she's releasing the power of love, one of humanity's most powerful virtues?*

"*Part of Gabriel's success was his love and passion for his fellow man, his willingness to risk his safety to save others. It is a rare quality, a rare virtue, a gift dormant in most, active in only a few who were willing to take the risk.*

"*Oh, what I would give to experience what she is feeling at this moment, what she is thinking. The human emotions of love and hate intertwined with every thought, within every decision.*"

He moved even closer and leaned inward to watch the words free themselves from her lips, to feel the emotion that emanated from her soul.

"*Don't you know you're not alone?*"

Standing there beside her was the spirit of her loving husband, Gabriel. He stood there proudly beside her, caressing her.

"Can you actually feel the love?"

When Lydia finished singing she closed her eyes, bowed her head, and pulled the journal close to her heart with folded arms. An understanding smile embraced her face. She appeared oblivious to the cold antagonizing winds that encircled her, tugging at her hair and clothing. There was no doubt in the angel's mind that she knew exactly who was standing there next to her in her Garden of Eden, on the tenth anniversary of her husband's passing.

CHAPTER TWENTY-SEVEN
THE MEDALLION
MARCH 16TH 2000

Gabe stopped dead in his tracks as he gasped for a breath, practically skidding to a stop at the edge of a saddle where the forest ended and the devastation began.

"What the..." he stared at the uninviting clearing.

The wind screamed as it moved, sounded like an approaching jet. The trees groaned and popped as the winds whistled through their massive tops and bent them effortlessly in waves. The trail they were following was no longer discernable in the shadows of early evening. The path appeared to terminate in the void.

First there was a crack, then a muffled crash, coming from the shadowy darkness of the ancient forest before him.

He flinched and took a couple of steps backwards. His gaze focused straight ahead. A massive tree no doubt had given up its fight against gravity and relented to the mercy of the storm. Beyond where he stood, the ridge began to climb again. Before him, unseen, lay another heavily timbered mountain cloaked in dark shadows. To their left lay the faint outline of an open clearing. He stood there stunned, transfixed, balanced on a ledge between two worlds, between the past and the present. He was crossing the line between juvenile to adulthood. Nothing he could have done would have prepared him for what he now saw, or for what he was now about to do. He could feel it; it was like a strange energy flowing through his body. It was in the air that he breathed.

Had I been here before? Or, is this only a dream?
He questioned this moment, but at the same time he wouldn't have passed up this opportunity.

He diverted his gaze from the devastation below. By now, his eyes had adjusted to the growing darkness.

The thought that his dad had once stood there in that very spot caused his body to shiver, and a bitter lump to form in his throat. It was like visiting a place he should have never been.

He turned toward what sounded like voices echoing across the clearing. The two dark flashes in the skyline caught his attention. Two large ravens struggled to maintain their positions heading into the wind. They flew low as they followed the denuded hillside, constantly teetering their wings for balance and control in the diminishing light. The heavy gusts of wind pulled and pried at their feathers as they constantly called to each other. They manipulated their bodies for lift as the gusts of wind forced them toward the ground. Their jet-black, glossy bodies almost appeared white as remnants of light danced across them. Gabe could imagine them cawing encouragement back and forth to each other, happy that on a day like today they were not alone.

The ravens let out a startled scream just before they reached the astonished trio. The ravens turned with the wind and let it abruptly drag them up the slope and out of sight. Gabe stared in amazement. Looks of surprise and discovery embraced the birds' intelligent-looking faces. The magnificent ravens probably had it right, but...

What were ravens, the most intelligent bird in the corvid family, doing up here on a day like this? For that matter, they were probably trying to figure out what we were doing!

His two companions had seen the large birds as well and, like him, they silently watched.

Gabe's senses were working overtime, desperately trying to find and understand what lay there before him. It was like every smell, touch and sound had hundreds of individual meanings all crashing into him at once. His rapid heartbeat thundered in his head. He stumbled backward to catch his balance in the cold updraft that slammed into his chest.

Was it pushing me safely back from the edge or was it warning me, sending me back, giving me one last chance to reconsider?

The first of the icy rain stung as it pelted his numbed face and cold hands. The tears suddenly began to form in his eyes. His throat tightened and became dry. His fingers began to tremble. There was no doubt in his mind that the missing kid was somewhere there, but right then he wasn't sure if *there* was where he wanted to be.

As Gabe looked up into the dark sky he wondered.

Am I looking up toward the heavens or just checking the weather?

They were both something people did when they didn't know what else to do.

"But I'm not like everyone else," he reminded himself. "We're here to find the lost kid before it's too late."

He couldn't help but notice the eerie darkness that haunted the early evening sky, or the lumbering clouds that glowed dark purple in the diminishing light. The fine, penetrating mist had infiltrated every square inch, preparing the forest for the expected deluge of rain. It didn't matter that they hadn't seen the sun itself for the last half-hour. They could navigate without it. They had Dan.

Gabe forced a deep breath and turned his gaze once again down onto the silhouette of the devastated hillside in front of him. He could no longer ignore it.

He could smell them; a few wild flowers, irises mostly, in their early stages of spring bloom, dotted the log-and debris-strewn hillside. Giant root balls lay upended; their exposed roots reaching up towards the heavens like mysterious appendages. He was surprised some of the debris managed to stay affixed to the vicariously steep slope. Trees near the edge grew in noticeably curved arcs up towards the evening sky, a result of living a life on a moving mountain.

Were the trees' efforts for nothing?

"Certainly the mountain will eventually take you, as well despite your efforts?" he whispered.

Gabe didn't like the way his thoughts grew so hopeless. He felt the fear deep within rear its ugly head again when the obvious became very apparent. The reason this devastated scar was still here, and looked as if it had just happened yesterday, was because the hillside was still unstable. The whole mountain slope was an active slide. Water, gravity and percent slope in combination were a recipe for disaster. Naturally unstable soils that dominated the area and careless timber harvest practices of the early 20th century had made this area dangerous in bad weather.

Then why are we here again?

Dwelling upon all of this wasn't good, and he knew it. If they were going to do this, they needed to move, and move right now! He sighed deeply to build his courage and started to step forward, down towards the heart of the devastation.

"Hold it!" Dan's exhausted voice startled him, a strong, firm hand grasped his shoulder, preventing him from moving forward. "That place is way too dangerous to be running out there like that."

He turned to see Dan's gaze searching over the devastation. His low voice cut through the weakening winds. "This place has a history, and history has a tendency to repeat itself if forgotten."

Gabe didn't know if it was just him, or the strangeness of the moment, but the crickets sounded louder.

Was it possible that the winds were dying down?

The dying of the winds meant that the front was here. With the storm front came the relentless rains. It was light at first, but then built into a crescendo that would last until the front weakened and the high pressure returned. With minimal vegetative cover to protect them from the elements out on the exposed escarpment, the devastated scar would turn itself into a sticky, unstable trap within the hour.

"He's out there, I know it and there isn't much time!" Gabe demanded as he pointed out towards the devastation. He could tell that Dan didn't quite agree with him, but chose to nod his head instead. They were out of time for debate. It was time to act.

"Then we need to do this safely." Dan looked up toward the darkened sky.

The change in the weather conditions was obvious. Time was working against them. "We'll drop our packs and do this one at a time, with safety ropes," Dan exclaimed as he swung his heavy pack noisily onto the ground. "I know this will take longer, but it will be safer and right now safe is good. We'll be doing this in the beams of our headlamps soon enough!"

Gabe looked over to Erick for reassurance and was pleased to see him smile back. It gave him courage. Almost in unison they both dropped their packs side by side, away from the edge. He felt lighter, almost as if he could float across the clearing like the ravens.

"This is where the trail ends and the adventure begins." Dan winked and forced a smile as he opened his pack and started rifling through his gear.

Gabe nodded and wondered off toward the edge. It had probably been Dan who had kept the trail open. Here was where he had stopped, choosing not to go any farther. Gabe thought of his father as he scanned the devastation.

"Dad, where are you? I'm finally here, but you aren't the only reason I am here," he whispered.

Another cold wind blew up from the bottom, pushing his hair out of his face. This one didn't try to push him backward or pull him down into this inhospitable place. He closed his eyes and extended his hands out toward the exposed mountainside. The wind tickled his face and hands, chilled his fingers.

"Can you boys give me a hand?" Dan's voice interrupted Gabe's thoughts.

A quick glance saw Erick nod and back away to join Dan with the organization of the gear, leaving Gabe standing there alone with his own thoughts.

Erick pointed towards Gabe and started to complain but Dan waved him off, discouraging him. "We've got this!" He heard Dan whispered softly. "He needs that time alone, we'll be fine."

So where could the missing juvenile be?

Gabe opened his thoughts, his eyes were still closed, and his hands extended palms out, fingers open.

Why would this kid have come all the way out here?
It was probably these same thoughts that baffled the search organizers as well.

The faint odor of incense grabbed at his nose and pulled at his lungs. It was there, but then it was gone. It started at the beginning of the gusts and then quickly faded to the earthy smell of the ancient forest. He breathed in and out a few more times, forcing himself to focus on the sounds and smells of the forest. He desperately wanted to smell the incense again, but it was gone. More than six hours of travel had brought them to this moment with approaching darkness and an awaiting storm.

It was shocking, before him a huge escarpment blocked his path. It was a cold and inhospitable place where, for all practical purposes, they might as well, have been on the moon.

By now the winds had practically died down to a slight breeze. The volume of the crickets had increased to a crescendo, now the frogs were joining in, their voices echoing off of the open terrain. A steady mist gently fell upon his face. He filled his lungs again, and to his delight, the odor of the incense was back, now more pronounced than ever. The odor seemed to be coming from up above on the exposed slope. As strange as the thought might have been, it almost felt as if the winds that blew up from the bottom of the canyon were trying to hide a secret from above them.

He opened his eyes and looked back over his shoulder toward the others. Erick was uncoiling a climbing rope out onto the ground; Dan was wrapping nylon safety webbing around the base of a large tree, most likely to be used for an anchoring system. It appeared that they were going to traverse from the side into no-man's land. He thought about telling them what he had just smelled and felt, but they looked busy, buried deep within their own thoughts. He shrugged his shoulders, wondering if they would even understand.

He sniffed the air again; confirming the fragrant incense that drifted across the devastated slope, and then started walking farther uphill along the edge of the slide. There was a strong desire to find the source of the aroma. Even if that meant he had to walk uphill along the edge and into the growing shadows of the ancient forest, he felt the urge to do it.

***

Erick noticed what Gabe was doing and started to yell at him.

Dan stopped him with a gentle grip on his shoulders. "Let him go, were just about done!"

Erick reluctantly went back to assisting while Dan kept watch on Gabe out of the corner of his eye.

***

Within several steps Gabe was stopped by something he had seen. There off to his left, a short stone's throw away, a metallic object hung from an extended, finger-like root of a huge, upturned root ball of an ancient tree that had been upended by the mountain. He was surprised he had seen it, but there it was. The medallion-sized object shimmered and swayed in the gentle breeze. Though the sun had long hid itself behind the clouds, the object still reflected in the dim light. Reflected was an understatement. It flashed on and off like a beacon, drawing his attention to that very spot.

He moved forward toward the object, but was stopped by the unforgiving drop-off, the edge of the slide. The ground had slumped six vertical feet below the edge of the forest. Climbing down into the slide would definitely have its fill of hazards.

Once his gaze had relocated the object, his mind naturally started picking the safest route to it.

The medallion-sized object hung there, attached to an extended root twenty to thirty yards out onto the slide. A natural animal path meandered across the steep, contoured hillside and past the shiny object. Upon closer examination, he noticed another pathway spur that came from father up into the clearing and met with the well-used, game trail that lay before him.

How could I be the only creature in the forest to have noticed it?

He immediately thought of the missing juvenile. *For sure this had something to do with the kid.*

"Dan, Erick!" he yelled out to the group.

"What's up?" Dan's voice quickly echoed across the clearing.

"I think I see something."

"What've you got?" Erick panted as he dropped the gear in his hands and ran the short distance up-slope towards him.

Gabe heard his friend come to an abrupt stop beside him, kicking small, loose rocks over the edge. He instinctively grabbed Erick by his bicep to prevent him from falling off.

"A little paranoid, aren't we?" Erick scolded.

Gabe ignored his remarks. "There!" he loosened his grip but didn't let go. He pointed to the shiny object. "Do you see it?"

Erick looked down his extended arm.

It took his friend only a moment to spot it, something small and golden. His voice sounded excited. "Yeah, how did you notice that? We should go have a look."

Gabe released his friends arm.

"Not until you're roped up!" Dan's concerned voice boomed from behind them. Dan had been watching.

Gabe turned to see Dan walking up to where they were both standing. "There!" he pointed.

Dan squinted a moment in the direction, his eyes searching. "I see it! Pretty bright, whatever it is." Dan acknowledged.

"Do you think it belonged to the missing kid?" Erick was sure of it.

"Possibly," Dan said his eyes instinctively searching the slope. "As far as I can tell from here, these tracks in front of us are deer." He squinted as he looked farther up the slope. "Now, those over there, I'm not so sure. They appear bigger." He nodded to relate the direction. "They seem to head towards that shiny object you've been talking about. They came from farther up the ridge, could belong to either a bear or our victim."

"Do you think we can traverse over and check it out?" Gabe was hoping.

Dan looked back down the hillside and then in the direction of the climbing rope. "Yeah, we'll need to haul our packs farther up slope, over there and change our anchor location... tie off, here." He pointed to a big tree along the edge. "That one will do nicely."

Both boys smiled back at him.

"Gabe will go first, we'll belay him from here."

"But..." Erick looked on disappointed.

"I called discovery rights first!" Gabe laughed as he shrugged his shoulders.

"Maybe so, but I was actually working!" Erick nodded towards the forest.

"So was I!" Gabe pointed towards the devastation. "Scouting!"

"Okay you two, let's get to it. All of us have important jobs to do!"

Both boys took off like a shot downslope toward their gear. It had only taken them a couple of minutes to retrieve their packs and haul their gear back upslope to their new location. And a couple more, to help Dan secure their anchor rope and rig the system, under his direction.

Gabe put on his climbing harness, gloves, and helmet, while the others safety-checked him and the system. He stood there, poised on the edge of the devastation. If he had it his way, he wouldn't have waited for all of the fuss. He would have scrambled his way, hand-over-hand, to his destination.

"Wear this," Dan said, helping him strap on a small daypack. "It's got a little food, water, first aid kit, pocket knife, head lamp, extra batteries, rain poncho, tarp and chord, a space blanket; and here, clipped onto the front of your pack, covered in a small dry-bag, is a portable radio. We're on channel three. Keep it dry! Use it! Tell me everything you do. Are you hearing me? I want to know everything and I mean e-v-e-r-y-t-h-i-n-g!"

Gabe nodded as he gave Dan a strange look.

What's he trying to say?

"This hillside may look easy, but looks can be very deceiving, especially out there." Dan forced a smile as he gently thumped Gabe's helmet with his hand. "We aren't going to take chances are we? All of this...," he nodded down towards the devastation, "could get really bad in a heartbeat."

Visions of his mom and dad flashed in Gabe's mind.

"These radios are supposed to have a seven-mile radius, but overcast skies, rough topography," continued Dan, "these factors severely reduce reception. Right now, I don't think we could get a hold of the cavalry if we really needed them." He pointed back up the mountainside. "I would need to walk half way back up that god-forsaken ridge just to get out on the portable radio. Let's pray that I won't have to."

His uncle's words burned deeply into his soul. He had almost forgotten how isolated they really were.

"Now, let's go over this one more time," Dan encouraged.

Gabe nodded impatiently. He just wanted to go.

"The hillside is 'doable'," Dan continued, "the ropes are for *your* safety. If I didn't think you needed them I wouldn't be making you use them! The helmet is for—"

"Loose rocks," Gabe chimed in, "the gloves are to protect my hands, the rope and harness are to keep me from falling down that way." He pointed down the slope, "Use the radio, tell you e-v-e-r-y-t-h-i-n-g. Keep my eyes *open* for boot prints and other sign."

Dan silently stared at him a moment before he smiled. He nodded, gave Gabe a big hug, and then playfully thumped the top of his helmet with a couple of fingers again. "Hey Bozo if I didn't think you could handle this, I wouldn't have let you go!" He gave Gabe a wink.

Gabe returned the nod.

Erick punched Gabe playfully about his shoulder. "That's for luck."

Gabe reacted. "I'll owe you for that one."

"And I expect to be paid back in full... upon your return.

They embraced, patted shoulders.

"Remember, guardian angels walk with you. They stand by your side. With God's help they will protect you. All you need to do is ask." Dan looked out onto the devastated mountainside. "I know you don't see them right now, but they're out there," Dan tapped his own chest. "And don't forget about *in here* too."

Gabe nodded as his eyes scanned the mountainside.

"If they're out there like you said, then why don't I see them?" Gabe whispered. He took a deep breath and began carefully scrambling down the embankment.

"We will keep a slight tension on the rope until told otherwise!" Dan yelled.

Gabe nodded and raised an arm, indicating that he understood.

They both silently watched Gabe work his way down the six foot embankment, and then to the deer path. He silently followed the path out toward the shiny gold object. The crickets, frogs, and the droplets of rain against his helmet all seemed to be getting louder.

Gabe felt the loose debris slide away beneath his every step. The ground was soft, a lot softer than it looked. Droplets of water were beginning to bead. The ground wasn't absorbing the water like it was supposed to. He wondered how anything could actually grow on the side of this mountain. The danger he had put himself into was now becoming obvious. Reality was setting in.

Where was the water supposed to go once it hit the ground?

He stopped to catch his breath when he reached the spot where another one of the spur trails connected. It surprised him to see that his uncle was right. The tracks coming down weren't the smaller deer tracks he had expected. They were weathered five-clawed, toed impressions, about the size of a smaller human foot. The details were gone, the soil pushed down.

Was that a bear?

Another series of foot impressions caught his eye.

Big cat tracks!

He felt a chill run the length of his back; it caused him to shiver. His eyes immediately began searching the hillside above him, following the tracks up and across the exposed mountain slope.

Not now!

Despite the falling rain, those tracks looked relatively fresh. There was no doubt in his mind that a large mountain lion had recently passed by, but with the soils staying wet he didn't know for how long ago.

The crackling of the radio attached to the front of his pack caused him to jump.

"What've you got?" He heard Erick's voice in stereo as it screeched over the radio and echoed across the open clearing with a slight delay.

Gabe turned towards the group and was about to yell back, but he saw Dan pointing to Erick's radio. They were only about thirty yards apart, but he supposed it was a good time to get used to using it. He reached down, pushed the transmit button and yelled into the mike. "I found what might have been a bear and some mountain lion tracks, they look fresh!" The excitement in his own voice only seemed to make him more nervous.

He watched Dan take the radio away from Erick before he was able to speak. "How big?" Dan's voice boomed across the clearing with a slight delay.

Gabe looked down at them again. "The cat tracks are about four inches." He held up the four fingers of his gloved hand for reference. He couldn't help but notice the surprised look on Erick's face as if he thought he said he had found some Sasquatch tracks. It was almost as if he was thinking, *'better you than me'*.

"It's a medium-sized cat, probably male. No need to worry. You need to stay heads up though, don't be looking down at your feet all of the time, be sure to look around."

"Is he joking?" Gabe mumbled to himself, "so how am I supposed to follow the tracks then if I'm not looking down at my feet? Great! Not only do I have to worry about the unstable slope; now I have to worry about being eaten by a hungry mountain lion too!"

"Sure, right!" Gabe keyed the mike and responded, he didn't sound very convincing.

"Mountain lion attacks are rare," he told himself. "I have a greater chance of being struck by lightning, or being run over by a car, or a bus! I guess it depends on which buss! Good one Gabe!"

He nodded reassuringly to himself for his attempt at humor. He tried to push Dan's bus story out of his thoughts and the fact that it was starting to rain.

Why did I have to bring up the bus! We're hours from any roadway?

He snapped his head and gazed in the direction of the distant flash. He no longer smiled.

Is that what I think it is?

He instinctively counted the seconds until he heard the faint, distant rumble.

"At a thousand feet per second, twelve seconds... at 5,280 feet per mile, it's at least two miles away!" He reassured himself out loud.

He looked out onto the exposed landslide. The escarpment suddenly seemed larger, more desolate than he originally thought.

"Run over by a bus! How about struck by lightning genius!"

It all suddenly seemed more like a real possibility.

"You want to come back and let one of us take a shot at it?" The radio crackled again, bringing him back. It was Erick.

"No way, I got this." He radioed back. The last thing he wanted to do was let Erick take his place. That he could never live down. He gave them thumbs-up and continued traversing up the hillside, following the cat tracks towards his goal. He focused on the gold medallion that he saw dangling from the root of an upturned ancient redwood. It was like it called to him as it gently swung back and forth in the breeze.

"This is the one!" he whispered to himself. He stopped and stared in awe when he reached the base of the root ball. The upper end of the massive tree was buried by an older slide. Only the eight-foot diameter base of the redwood tree protruded out from the sloped mountainside. The top of the root ball extended fifteen feet into the air. Around and beneath it, the soil had eroded away more quickly, carving a deeper crevasse into the side of the slope.

The more he thought about it, the more he realized that there was no way the medallion could have accidentally gotten snagged from the person who passed by.

Yep, to have placed the medallion, the root ball had to have been climbed.

He knew what he needed to do.

He pushed the transmitting button and yelled into the mike. "I'll need to climb these roots to reach the medallion."

He half expected to hear a *no*, but was pleased when he got the okay to retrieve it. He took one last look at the cat tracks and hoped for the best. They had passed closely by the base of the roots but seemed to have come from the upslope portion where the tree was first buried. It appeared the mountain lion had also climbed the tree in its own way.

So, upslope he turned and pushed onward, three steps forward and one step back. The ground was wet, but not saturated. He knew that would soon change. About a dozen steps brought him to the base of the roots. He used that time to pick out his route to the medallion located about two-thirds up the root ball.

Evidence!

"Going up!" he informed them over the radio. He started climbing without waiting for a response. If they had called back, he didn't hear. His focus was totally on his ascent.

The wood was wet and in some places still covered with a fine layer of loose soil. He remembered, from the climbing class, three points of contact, to keep his butt out away from the object he was climbing, and to take his time. Even though there were plenty of roots for foot and hand holds, he felt challenged, he felt heavy. He was struggling.

The pack!

He remembered, and there was the rope. About a third of the way up, he balanced himself and freed a hand. He grabbed the rope and gave it a tug.

"Slack!" he yelled into the mike. Like magic, he felt about twenty pounds lighter. He had been pulling against the safety rope the whole time.

No wonder!

He looked over his shoulder, out over the devastation and then down to the ground below. It was strange-being only six feet higher upslope gave the area a whole new perspective. He turned back towards the root ball, refocused on the medallion. With renewed energy, he continued to climb.

He stopped below the medallion to catch his breath. His goal was now just out of arm's reach. Whoever had placed it there had done so with great effort. The medallion was hanging out over emptiness, its chain securing it in place about two feet from the end. To retrieve it, he would either have to break the chain or pull it all the way up and over one of the wooden root spikes that held it in place.

He held his place, poised 16 feet above the ground. He was cautious. The rains had made the exposed wood slippery, and the loose dirt even more so. If he slipped and fell, his journey wouldn't stop at the base of the root ball. If he were lucky, he would miss being hung up or impaled on the other protruding roots and land onto the sloping mud; but what was there to stop his glissading decent down the hillside? If he failed to self-arrest, to stop his fall by dragging his arms and legs, the rescue rope would do its job, but the pendulum action would include the length of the rope, and all of the objects to snag him along the way. That was definitely not on his list of things to find out about.

He tightly hugged a couple of the extended roots and reached. He was inches from the medallion; but he would have to get closer. It was obvious that whoever had attached the medallion had much longer arms than he. He pulled himself up above the overhanging main root and shimmied out onto it, both his arms and legs tightly wrapped around for balance. He felt his heart pounding in his chest and the pressure of the branch against his stomach. He pressed the side of his cheek against the wet wood; its wet coolness numbed his face. The lingering, slippery silt stuck to his exposed skin and clothes. A couple of slow caterpillar-like scrunches put the medallion about 12 inches, directly below his face. There was an engraving of a figure in a robe. He recognized it right away. It was a St. Francis medallion.

Why would it be here?

The thought flashed for a moment, but then he regained control. There would be time for that later. He needed to snatch the medallion and get down off the extended root ball on his own terms.

He took a deep breath and reached. Strangely, the medallion felt warm to his touch. At that moment, the aroma of the incense became more pronounced.

Now, how to get it off of the extended root?

From his position, it all came easy. He wrapped his legs around a piece of the extended root, gripped it with his right arm, and carefully slid the chain off with his left.

"Piece of cake!"

He looked at it a moment before he stuffed it securely into his pocket. He saw an engraving on the back but didn't take the time to read it. With the medallion secured he backed down the extended root and continued the rest of the climb up to the top.

He felt a welcomed relief when he finally stood up straight, raised his fists up above his head, and gave out a victorious yell into the rain. His attention was immediately drawn to the surrounding devastation. From his perch, in the diminishing light, he could see the full length of the slide; he was only a small portion of the way across. The length of the destruction far exceeded its width. The devastation extended downslope below him in an inverted "V"-shaped arc for almost a quarter mile. The farther down the slope it went the wider it got. At the bottom were piles of debris and trees sticking this way and that. Near the opposite side of the slide were the remnants of what looked like an active creek, carving its way through the scene. Dark, dense, forests lined the sides as far as the eye could see. The dim light gave the whole landscape an eerie, depressing feel. The slope wound around the exposed mountaintops and disappeared into the mist, shadows, and growing darkness below. He could barely make out the timber-covered slope above and beyond the exposed soil. If he were to guess he was closer to the side from which he had started, then the top or the bottom. He could see why the mountain lions and bears chose to come up here, the view was great but it probably wasn't why they did. This was the place to take it all in. Upslope and off to his right there was another overhang, a rocky outcropping that the slide seemed to have missed. Below it, about an acre in size, a long strip of medium-sized trees still stood. Like an island spared from the end. With nothing to stop the rain and the winds, the bad weather suddenly felt like it had increased. He closed his eyes for a moment and let the droplets cleanse the mud from his hands and raingear. "So where are you?" he whispered softly into the building deluge. "You're around here somewhere, I know it!"

CHAPTER TWENTY-EIGHT
ON TASK
MARCH 16TH 2000

Dan felt a burden lift from his shoulders when he saw his nephew safely standing on the exposed log. He looked so small compared to the huge root ball he stood on. He looked so vulnerable amongst the eerie background. For a second he thought he was looking at his younger brother. He smiled. Gabe was becoming more and more like him every day.
How crazy is that?
They were following in each other's footsteps.
"You doing alright?" Dan's voice crackled proudly as he spoke over the radio.
"Yeah, got it. It was a Saint Francis medal. Someone had gone through an awful lot of trouble to put it there. There's no way it could have gotten hung up there by accident." Gabe's voice echoed over the radio.
"Yeah, saw that!" Both he and Erick gripped tighter onto the end of Gabe's climbing rope, knowing that the rope would keep him from tumbling down the hillside. Despite the safety line, Gabe was still at risk if he were to make a mistake.
Gabe dutifully dug into one of his pockets.
"A Saint Francis medal?" Dan spoke out loud, he felt a strange tingle in his fingers and toes.
Could it be?
"Was it cracked, dented, is there anything written on the back?" Dan's voice suddenly strained with nervous emotion. He spoke only loudly enough for Erick to hear. His brother had worn one, a gift from Lydia. The whole thought was ludicrous, but

stranger things have happened. His brother's body was never recovered.

Could he have known, left it there for them to find ten years later? Did it belong to the missing juvenile?

The second made more sense.

Did this mean the kid was nearby?

Dan swiveled his head as he gazed up and down the slide area. The arriving darkness had reduced his visibility to less than 100 yards.

"Who in their right mind would travel this far into the wilderness to hang a medallion from a large upturned root?"

Dan watched his nephew look around the area, he could barely make out his figure proudly holding the medallion up by the chain for all to see.

"Did you see any footprints or other sign up top?" Dan spoke over the radio, trying to play down the medallion and get Gabe to speed up the search.

He watched Gabe shove the gold object back into his front pants pocket.

"Good boy, don't lose that!" he whispered.

Now that the celebration was over, they could all get back to work.

Gabe scanned the ground, shifting his gaze back and forth in a systematic search.

Dan held his breath when Gabe abruptly stopped. Dan could feel the tension cut through the building rain.

"Did he find something?" Erick asked.

"Don't know, let's hope so."

The radio came to life. "More cat tracks. It must have come up here to look around. You can barely make them out now... the rain. I can see why he came up this way though!"

"Keep looking," Dan encouraged. He knew Gabe was well aware of the urgency. "You're high enough up to get a good look around. You might be our only chance to see something. Use your binoculars." He pretended to look through an invisible pair in his hand. "He'll be able to see better in the dark with them." He told Erick before he had a chance to ask.

They saw Gabe slump his shoulders for a moment before he tossed off of the pack and reached into one of the pockets to remove the binoculars. Outside of the saddle where they both stood, Gabe appeared to be standing on one of the only flat spots as far as their eyes could see. He looked back and forth as he scanned the devastated terrain with his binoculars.

"Come on Gabe." Dan whispered to himself. "Find something, anything!" He looked up through the rain and into the heavens. The rain droplets pelted his face as they fell straight down. The winds had all but died. "Any time now. You have yet to make any of this easy!" He turned back toward Erick. "Remember, keep reminding yourself, it's never the destination, it's always the journey!"

***

Erick nodded, not in agreement but to be polite. He felt it was the destination that was important right now. Finding the boy was his focus, taking a journey along the way for some kind of self-enrichment was the last thing on his mind. The medallion was a clue, but what kind of clue was still yet to be determined. At first he was a bit jealous of his friend, but perhaps not so much now. The distant thunderstorm was getting closer, and his friend was exposed along the open landslide. "Come on, come on, move... move!" He mumbled under his breath. His eyes continued to try to follow his friend's movements.

Erick constantly looked over his shoulder toward the growing shadows of the forest. The surrounding ridgeline looked dark and unforgiving. There was the feeling of being watched.

Oh, it was there all right!

He knew the forest was filled with animals, curious intruders like themselves watching from a safe distance. As far as he knew, the mountain lion might have been right up there with them, observing, following. With the amount of deer sign that they had seen thus far, this large clearing must have been an oasis for every grazing creature for miles around. With the prey came the predators, mirroring their every move! He looked up into the sky, into the falling rain.

So, where are the angels? Where are the guardian angels who are supposed to protect us?

Despite what happened around camp the other night, either actual or imagined, he hadn't heard from a single one this whole trip.

"Ask, and they will come!" Erick forced a pathetic laugh. "Now would be a good time."

Are you intimidated by this place as well? Was Gabe's father truly on his own when he ventured out onto this mess ten years ago? I feel so sorry for him!

The thought made him shudder.

***

A bluish white flash illuminated two large birds in the darkening sky, their glossy bodies reflecting back the spark of light. They screeched warnings as they banked and circled around. It was their determined calls that captured Gabe's attention.

Are you talking to me?

Gabe pondered the thought. It was strange but seemingly true.

Ravens are probably one of the smartest birds in the world, sacred to most native cultures. They are given credit for their ingenuity, humor, and affection. They're also known as tricksters, educators, creators, and messengers, recognized and embraced as guiding spirits by some.

Gabe also remembered reading that...

Spiritual healers could join consciousness with the raven and travel, check things out, and in other cases, help those haunted by ghosts.

"They believed that a raven could bring people's souls back from the spirit world." Gabe whispered.

Wow!

He momentarily envisioned his dad's face, before the voice of the *cawing* raven pulled him back from his thoughts. The birds circled around.

This time without the winds, they flew with more grace and control. The falling rain didn't seem to bother them. They blended with the dark sky as if they were an element of the scene. Their eyes, latched onto his and pulled him along, drawing him forward. They hovered for a moment, tilting their wings, lowering their tails, and fluffing up the iridescent feathers on the backs of their necks. They idled effortlessly just above a stall. His eyes followed them across the devastation, towards the rocky outcropping. The remnant grove of forest stood out like an island in a sea of devastation.

A thunderous boom rocked the ground around him. He flinched, almost lost his footing.

The birds squawked excitedly.

He felt the vibration through his core. He didn't count the seconds between the earlier flash and the bone rattling vibration, but he knew it was close. The weather front was passing nearby.

What to do?

The birds squawked loudly again, obviously unnerved by the storm. They slowly moved forward looking over their wings, as if they were coaxing him along. The sudden windy gusts ruffled their feathers. They tilted their bodies to correct.

"They want me to follow!" Gabe hollered into the mike of his radio. "I'm sure of it!"

"Get off of the clearing!" Dan's concerned voice echoed in his ears.

After a couple of steps, he felt the tension of the rope pull against his harness. What was once there to keep him from falling was now slowing him down. "Slack... slack, I need slack!" he hollered into his radio mike. He immediately felt his body move effortlessly against the rope. He started down the other side of the log and out of view of the others. He pulled harder on the rope as he, sloshed through the ankle sucking mud. He wove his way around every obstacle, heading in the direction of the rocky plug that lay fifty yards away. He recognized the fear that was beginning to overwhelm him, and tried to force the thought from his mind.

The birds seemed to scream louder, urgency in their voices. Gabe wasn't so sure, but he thought he heard then holler...

"*Hurry, hurry!*" as their wings whistled in the air.

Another thunderous clap almost immediately followed another blinding flash. The percussion of the blast just about knocked him off of his feet. Gabe forced himself forward. He didn't dare look up any more as he sprinted towards the safety of the isolated forest before him. Fear was winning. Despite the fact that the mud was trying to grab his legs and pull the boots off his feet, he pushed even harder. His momentum was propelling him forward with every step. He no longer slipped backward; there was no time for that. The tension on his harness would come and go;

They must know I'm running with everything I have to cross the clearing.

He was almost there; the ravens were close. His eyes fixed upon the birds that hovered almost just above him now. They were hollering at him again, still encouraging him in the pounding rain.

"*Here! Here! Over here!*" they called out.

Up over another little rise, around another buried log, and then, almost unexpectedly, he fell forward into a ravine that suddenly appeared in the darkness before him. He couldn't stop. He slipped and fell forward. The rope attached to his harness went tight, stopping his forward movement just before he would impact the water-filled ravine. The sudden stop caused his feet to slip out from beneath him and slam him butt first into the muddy bank. Beneath him, the rain-swollen muddy channel appeared out of nowhere as it cascaded noisily over rocks and debris, carving a canyon through the soft soil.

The sudden jolt that forced the breath out of his lungs had also pulled him back against the hillside. Heaving, gasping for breath, he looked down into the moving chocolate creek five feet below. He instinctively grabbed onto the slippery rope and scrambled across the mud to regain his footing. Frustratingly, his feet continued to slip out from under him as if he were trying to climb across melted butter. He was overwhelmed by panic. The storm was directly overhead, and now here he was slipping on clay and pinned against the side of a cascading torrent, a well-known conductor of lightning.

Another blinding flash left him seeing spots. Within seconds, another deafening, ground shaking rumble vibrated through the mud and into his chest. He screamed out in frustration. He screamed out in terror as he groped blindly for the rope attached to his harness.

"*Stay, stay, stay!*" the desperate, bird-like voices screamed from above.

He looked up to see both ravens pacing nervously along the middle of a medium sized log that spanned the entire length of the narrow ravine.

"*Stay, stay, stay!*" they hollered again in unison.

Gabe stared in amazement at the curious birds, his hands still firmly gripped onto the rope. He knew the rope would hold him in place that the others would not let him go, but he still found it difficult to trust.

Do they know what's happening?

He stopped squirming and looked up toward the birds. They sat on a log only ten feet above him. Devoid of vegetation, the water-carved ravine was only twenty feet wide.

Everything turned bluish white with another blinding flash. The ground trembled almost immediately from the deafening, vibrating rumble. The glowing silhouette of the two ravens appeared to jump from side to side in the strange, strobing light. They screeched and screamed in panic in the deafening rumble.

His fingers tingled and his hair pulled away from the back of his neck. Fearing the rope to be a lightning rod, he let go of the rope. The storm was now directly overhead, casting its fury on everything in its path. He lay there in the mud, the end of the rope still attached to his harness, knowing that there was nothing else he could do but wait out the worst of the storm. Strangely, he felt safe in the ravine; it was the thought of the others, the ones who were hanging onto the end of his rope, the lightening rod, which now made him worry. He said a little prayer for their safety and his own. The story of his father tied to a rope, in the very same canyon ten years earlier, racked his nerves.

"Don't let go, no matter what!" he whispered.

The storm cell passed quickly. The flashes of light no longer seemed so bright, the echoes of the following thunder not so intense and immediate. The rain, though not as heavy as before, continued to fall. The sky was dark and unnerving, but there was still enough light to guide him. First, however, he had to get out of the predicament he was in now.

"Thanks guys!" he whispered to his feathered observers.

The birds fluffed out their neck feathers and nodded their heads excitedly as they shed the rain droplets. Their shrill calls echoed noisily through the ravine. It was as if they seemed to understand.

But how could they?

The radio crackled to life. "Gabe... this is Dan, answer, will you?" the worry was evident in his voice. He could barely hear him over the torrential creek.

Gabe scrabbled to return his call. "Wow... that, was incredible!" he screamed.

"Where are you?" the relief was detectable in Dan's voice. "We can't see you from here."

Gabe was relieved to hear his uncle as well. He had almost forgotten that the others were still hanging onto the end of his rope. "I'm in a ravine." He looked around, and the ravens still sat there staring at him with those knowing, intelligent eyes.

"So that's the static I'm hearing. Are you alright?"

"Yeah... the rope kept me from falling head first into a creek. The side of the ditch... is too muddy to climb out... by myself. You'll have to... pull me out!" he screamed, voice breathless.

"So, how are you going to get across?" Dan's voice echoed of nervous tension.

Gabe looked up towards the two birds. The larger of them was pacing back and forth along the length of the log, screeching loudly, ruffling its feathers along the back of its neck, and nodding its head excitedly. He could almost understand the words...,

"Here, here, here!"

I get it!

"Across a log... over the ravine," Gabe said.

"Is that the ravens I hear?" Dan quizzed.

Gabe looked over to the strange behavior of the birds. "Yeah... it's the craziest thing. I was following them to the rock outcropping... when the thunderhead passed over."

There was a silent moment before Dan responded. He could imagine what his uncle must have been thinking: *'ravens showing you the way!'*

"Ravens? Do you think they were the same two that were flying over earlier?" asked Dan.

"Yeah, they might be. I think they... still want me to follow them!"

There was a long silence before Dan spoke. "Be careful!"

A moment later he felt the rope pull tightly against his harness, and his body was hoisted the short distance back up the side of the ravine, one foot at a time. With a half dozen tugs he was at the lip of the ravine.

"I'm up!" he yelled into the mike. A microphone click was the only response he had gotten back. In a way it was good. He didn't want to have to try to explain things he no longer understood himself.

"Slack, I need more rope!" Gabe yelled into the radio.

Seconds later the climbing rope went limp.

The birds lifted up into the air when he reached the log and hovered towards the end of it. He stopped at the edge of the wedged log for a moment, contemplating how he was going to get safely across. Choices, walking heel to toe boldly-like, across the slippery, bark less surface or scrunch cautious-like, drag himself across with both his arms and legs wrapped tightly around the two-foot diameter log. The decision was an easy one. With only two ravens as witnesses, he crawled and scooted his bottom across its entire 20-foot length, suspended 15 feet above the raging creek below. In the dimming light, the angry creek sounded more ominous, the rain made the log feel more slippery, and the other bank seemed that much farther away.

"Help me!" he whispered into the waning darkness and drizzling rain. "Now would be a good time to let us know that you're out here." He dared not look around. He could still see the birds hovering out of the corner of his eye. Their encouraging squawks still filled his ears. His heart thundered in his head as he filled his heaving lungs with the cool, moist air.

Half way across he felt the log start to bounce with his every move. He froze and looked down, despite telling himself not to do so. Things started to spin; the surrounding sounds became distorted and strange. An icy chill stabbed at the back of his heart. The creek beneath him sounded as if it were whispering a final warning, telling him to *turn around while you still have a chance... That he had reached the point of no return.*

Once beyond this very spot, will God still be able to save me?

He shook off the numbing chill that surged through him. Right then, the gentle strain of the roped harness was the only thing that tugged at his perceived reality. He gripped the log tighter with his arms and legs and forced his gaze straight forward as his body trembled in the cold. He tried to clear his thoughts, tried to remove all fears and doubt.

"I can do this!" he whispered softly into the breeze. "I can do this!" He spoke again more loudly, with firmness. He had gone too far, had given up too much, to let anything stop him now.

Are the voices in the creek real, or are they just self-doubt, tugging at my confidence?

At this point he didn't want to know. Things were just too strange. The creek wanted him, was calling for him. The ravens were helping; they were guiding. They wanted him off the log too; and to go to the rocky outcropping. They had to be his guides. They had to be the good ones.

So what did that make the creek? First the butterfly, now the ravens?

It was all too strange to think about.

There will be time to think later.

His eyes focused on the rocky outcropping, almost a stone's throw away.

"That's where I need to be!"

His choices were easy: either slow down, speed up, or sit there with a death grip on the log waiting for something to happen. He knew that the longer he was on the log, the greater the chances were that something, not so good, would happen. It was Murphy's Law: *anything that could, would go wrong.* If he hurried across, he might bounce the log loose and end up in the raging creek. That would be it, show over, held under water while attached to a rope against the pressure of the flood waters or pinned beneath the log. The relentless power of the water is more powerful than the strongest of men. Nothing but gravity was holding the log in place in the soon-to-be saturated mud. It was a recipe for disaster. That's the thing about mud, a little water turns the clay into glue, and a lot more water will dissolves it into quicksand.

Almost as if sensing his dilemma, the ravens sounded off with urgent cries.

"If it wasn't for you guys during the electrical storm..." Gabe mumbled to himself. He refocused his eyes on the end of the log and forced himself forward. He started slowly, but then quickly picked up his pace. When he reached the other side of the log he was gasping for air and his arms and legs burned with fatigue. Despite his exhaustion, he felt his second wind energized, pushing himself along. He panted into the radio for more slack.

He quickly got it and was off again, slipping and sliding along the muddy slope as he followed the ravens. Suddenly the rope on his harness went taut. He was pulled right off his feet and fell onto his backside in the mud with a sickening '*thud*'.

"Slack... slack!" he yelled into the mike.

"That's all of the rope!" Erick's voice echoed through his radio and across the clearing. "You'll have to wait. Dan's attaching another section!"

The ravens circled around and scolded him with dire urgency...

"*Hurry, hurry hurry!*" echoed in the storm.

The words in their calls were very distinct. He tried to get up again, but the rope held him in place. He shoved a hand into the mud to push himself backward, but abruptly stopped.

There, inches away from his hand were the impressions of what looked like a bare human foot a little smaller than his own.

The rains had all but washed it away. Luckily, a small nearby shrub had protected this one from the deluge of rain.

Gabe felt a strange excitement fill his pounding heart. His breathing became rapid, fingers tingled.

"The boy is here!" he yelled excitedly to anyone that was listening, as he searched the ground with his eyes and struggled again to his feet. There, in the direction of rocky outcropping, were tracks in the now soaked soil. Weathered impressions where something had walked before the rains had worked their magic. If he hadn't found the first track if he hadn't reached the end of his rope, he wouldn't have noticed the others.

Oh what luck!

"No, it isn't luck!" echoed in his head.

He gazed up toward the birds that circled overhead. "Thanks!" he forced a smile.

Almost as if on cue, the birds swooped down toward Gabe and squawked intently at him.

"What's wrong with the two of you? We've found the tracks thanks to you guys!" The ravens didn't seem to change their demeanor. If he hadn't known any better, he might have thought he noticed some anger and disappointment in their expressive eyes.

"Dan, Erick, I've found some foot prints... I believe they belong to the missing kid!" he yelled excitedly into the radio.

The air was immediately filled with a response. "Are you sure? Look for others!" Dan said. "Let us get the other line—"

"The ravens... I think they want me to follow..." Gabe yelled into the radio mike.

"What?" he screamed back in return.

"There *are* other tracks... they lead to the rocky outcropping. I think the ravens... really want me to follow them! They seem urgent... I have no choice!" Without giving it another thought, he unclipped the end of the rope from the carabiner at his waist and let the rope fall onto the mud. It felt good to be free.

As soon as he had done that, the ravens turned and continued towards the rocky outcropping, screaming for him to follow.

Evidently, he had done the right thing. He turned and went in pursuit, his eyes carefully noting where the next impression in the mud lay.

The kid had passed this way.

He had gone to the rocky outcropping, the highest point in the devastated clearing. It wasn't all that far from what he would have done himself.

"Maybe the missing juvenile and I aren't so different after all!" Gabe spoke out loud to himself.

"Wait, it will only take a moment." Dan's voice echoed from the radio into the breeze.

"Can't!" Gabe panted back. "I'm already off belay... I've got to go... The kid is up there... probably climbed the rocky outcropping—"

"Gabe! No wait!" The radio crackled with panic, its reception no longer strong and clear.

This time Gabe didn't answer, he didn't want to be talked out of this one. Deep down inside, he knew the urgency of the ravens meant something. He had to trust his heart, he could only hope he wasn't too late.

CHAPTER TWENTY-NINE
ABOVE AND BEYOND
MARCH 16TH 2000

"Gabe!" Erick screamed as he stood there holding the loose climbing rope, his worried gaze shifting back and forth between the dark void and Dan.

The rain poured down his face.

"Haaaaaaaaaa...," Dan angrily screamed as he kicked a piece of a decaying stump over the side of the saddle and onto the exposed slope. He then picked up a rock and tossed it far out into the dark void with a couple of strides. "For Christ sake, what in the world does he think he is doing?" he screamed as he directed his headlamp into the emptiness.

He watched the debris tumbled into the darkness until it stuck solid to the mud and slid with the creeping soil which was getting more saturated by the minute.

"He knows we gave him the safety rope for a reason, right!" Dan also knew that very soon the soil would be too wet for anyone to safely cross without being sucked into the mess or crushed by large moving debris. The fear that raced through him was immediate. Whether he liked it or not, he had to trust his nephew's judgment. At this point, what other choice did they have?

"Gabe, I hope you know what you're doing?" Dan screamed into the darkness. His shoulders sagged with worry as he paced nervously back and forth along the sideline his fingers interlaced nervously on top of his head.

"He's only a kid!" Dan looked up into the night time sky. The droplets of rain streaked through the beam of his headlamp like meteors through a night sky.

Erick shrugged his shoulder, an expression of panic embraced his face. He looked around confused and bewildered.

Dan scrambled to pull his hand-held third generation night vision scope from his pack and started searching the darkness in the direction of the end of the climbing rope.

Not knowing what else to do, Erick tugged on the rope a couple of times... the rope moved easily, he could tell there wasn't anyone attached. His friend was still out there somewhere.

"Leave it, he can always follow the rope back to find us." Dan adjusted the focus. Everything he saw up close had a light green hue, everything else farther away appeared as darker shadows. The device worked by amplifying the ambient star light, the same way a cat was able to see better in the dark. The problem he was encountering was the fact that, the cloud cover had taken away the view of the stars, his source of light. He could barely use the last of the reflective light of the sun that had officially set over an hour ago. He had used the scope successfully many times before on searches and wildlife observing. Though cold rain had zapped the heat from the devastated area, that didn't affect the use of the device. He looked for recognizable shapes and movements to fill in the gaps. With the use of the device came the shadows, there were no shortages of shadows. That was probably the most frustrating part of all that he encountered when he used it. Despite all of that, it was still one of the best tools he had to use in the darkness. With a flick of a button he activated the infrared function of the tool. It shot out a light beam invisible to the human eye, but brightened the darkness through the lens of the device. Like an invisible flashlight, his view shed brightened to a lighter green but his visibility was cut in half. It was a compromise in a low light situation, which he had no control over.

The infrared reflected off the droplets of rain, it seemed to help. A distant moving silhouette appeared, it was an object flying in the air.

"I see a raven, perched on the top of a rocky outcropping. Isn't that the location where Gabe said he was headed?" Dan was pretty sure but he needed reassurance. He could barely make it out. He would have missed it if the bird hadn't moved.

"Yeah, that's what he said!" Erick confirmed.

"Do you think that bird was really encouraging him up to the boulder field? What the... there's a second one flying around in circles above the first one." It was then he heard its distant call over the sound of the crickets, frogs and light rain. His view drifted below the flying object and sure enough. "Bingo, I think I've got him," his voice excited, relieved, "he's really moving, looks like that bird is either following or guiding him."

He watched the faint outline in the viewfinder of his scope as it moved along the terrain. It disappeared and then reappeared amongst the shadows and uneven terrain. He stared in amazement.

"That's got to be him... a man on a mission."

"He's heading for the island outcropping, which must be where the kid is." Erick's voice was excited.

Dan nodded.

What does all of this mean?

Dan spoke out loud to himself. "So, are ravens good or bad? Are they the omen of death or the giver of life? Which ones are we dealing with out here?"

The ravens faded in and out of the increasing darkness. His magic tool was at its maximum range for conditions. Once they all made it to the island, his tool would be useless from where they both stood, that is until the moon raised and the clouds cleared.

"Should we go after him?" Erick asked, his eyes pleading.

"No," Dan shook his head, his response was quick and direct. "That hillside isn't safe. The soil is turning into liquid as we speak. He will be safer on that rocky outcropping than out there on that mess of exposed, unstable hillside." Dan wanted to believe every word he heard himself say, but he knew better.

"I'm sure he will be safer on the island. That God forsaken island." This time he spoke loud enough for Erick to hear.

Erick gave him a worried look.

Dan looked up into the dark sky again. He felt his throat tighten, his hands start to shake. "Is this what you wanted?" he whispered before he took a long look through the scope.

He thought he saw shadows of something unhuman-like scrambling up the boulder field, gracefully hopping from one boulder to the next. A moment later the silhouettes were gone. They moved quickly.

It was then that he got a quick whiff of fragranced incense, a pocket of comforting warmth, then it was gone. Out of the corner of his eye he thought he had seen a young man in a white robe standing there looking on with an expression of indifference. When Dan turned his head to face it, the glowing silhouette was gone.

That was either the beam of my light in the rain or the cavalry is here. With my luck, it's probably just the lone scout, once again, waiting for the final word.

He seemed unsure about the whole mess, nothing of what he had seen really gave him much comfort.

Shouldn't I be over there with Gabe escorting him up that mountain instead of standing here?

Dan refocused the night scope unit in Gabe's direction again.

"Nothing! He's out of range."

The recognizable shapes and silhouettes were gone, all of them. "If that was Gabe that I had seen earlier, then he's probably safely made it to the island." He shared with Erick.

Alone with no safety rope and out of reach of immediate rescue. The odds are not in his favor!

"Be careful!" Dan whispered under his breath. He glanced back over towards the surrounding shadows.

If you are an angel, then why aren't you standing next to Gabe instead of us?

Dan forced himself to take one last look towards the rocky outcropping. He sucked in a quick breath. For a moment, he thought he saw a shadow of a black figure balanced up on top of the outcropping above where Gabe was supposed to be. Thinking he had somehow bumped the device and changed the setting, he waved his hand in front of the viewfinder. His hand glowed light green. The device was still working correctly.

"Then what was that?" he whispered.

He searched towards the island and then along the entire length of the devastating slide. The birds were gone, Gabe was nowhere. He hadn't seen a deer all day, not even a mouse. Outside of windblown debris, there was nothing alive out there on that devastated mountainside that he could see.

His hands started to shake and his body started to tremble.

When he least expected it, there was a bright flash and then the rumbling of thunder. The light seeking device was overwhelmed. Brightness filled his eye piece, it stung his eye.

"This is no way to finish out the day!" Dan whispered. All he heard in return were the frogs, the crickets, and the relentless wind whispering voice-like through the tops of the trees and the droplets of light rain. The rains and the winds had picked up again.

***

The climbing was quick and easy. Though the rocky, sedimentary surface of serpentine and chert were wet and slick by nature, they weren't as slippery as the mud. This outcropping was like an island, miraculously missed by the landslide. He couldn't blame the lost juvenile for wanting to climb the hill. In the daylight, the view was probably well worth the trip. Gabe hurried along with an urgent spring to his sloshing step.

The mating calls of the crickets and frogs, the distant flashes of light, and the belated rumble of the passing storm surrounded him. The constant drenching of the misting rain had all but eliminated every speck of evidence of the young teen's passing; Gabe now had to rely almost entirely on the ravens to guide him along. The large male squawked encouragement from in front as the bird hopped effortlessly from one boulder to the next, all the way up the hillside. The circling female scouted their path from above. Their movement was quick and direct. Just before the top, they veered off to their left, following a natural trail to the edge of an escarpment.

When he reached the edge he could barely see his surroundings, he stopped to catch his breath and survey the destruction before him. It was then that he realized that he couldn't see ten yards beyond his nose. It was time for his headlamp. He slipped off his pack, fished for his headlamp and turned it on. The world around him suddenly changed, it looked surreal. The beam of the head lamp reflected off of the water droplets of the surrounding boulders, and the droplets that fell from the sky. It was then that he noticed that the hillside before him dropped suddenly away to a ledge twenty feet below, which in turn dropped several feet more into the darkened void, the extent of his light beam.

His eyes caught movement within the beam of his light. The larger raven off to his left tilted its head away from the light and stared inquisitively down toward the ledge below.

"Sorry about that." He apologized to the bird, his guide.

The smaller raven from above came into view. It squawked as it descended in an ever-shrinking circle towards the first ledge.

The large raven perched next to him eyed him suspiciously and remained just out of reach. It also screeched, hollered, and nodded his head down toward something that lay in the shadows on the ledge below.

Gabe peered down into the darkness, his eyes following the beam of light.

Was that the kid down there?

The larger of the birds squawked again as if he had heard him.

"What? You know what I'm thinking?"

He grabbed hold of a rock and carefully leaned over the edge.

On the ledge below him, a dark figure was suddenly illuminated by the beam of his headlamp. It stood out against the background of the ledge where it rested. The droplets of rain that streaked by, mixed with the warm mist from his breath, making it more difficult to see in the darkness.

His body chilled, his breaths became short and shallow. The dark object lying motionless below him was indeed the missing teen.

"I found you!" he whispered. His fingers tingled.

He heard the whistle of the wings as the smaller raven landed off to his right. They both squawked loudly, from their perches on the rocks. They raised the feathers on the back of their necks and shook their bodies as if celebrating.

"We found him!" Gage screamed joyfully as he looked towards the ravens. "You found him!" He spoke softly. Both of the birds quietly stared back at him for a moment, their knowing, expressive eyes occasionally blinked. He felt a warm tingling sensation in his chest, a numbness about his fingertips.

"I need to call this in." Gabe fumbled for the radio and screamed into the mike.

"We found the missing kid... I repeat, we found the missing kid!" Gabe flashed a smile to the ravens.

A scratchy response on the radio came back. "You found the kid?" Dan quizzed excitedly. "Where?"

"Yeah, he's on a ledge about 20 feet below me."

"Are you on the island?"

"Yeah."

"Alright, alright, are they moving? Is the kid hurt?"

There was a moment of silence before Gabe spoke. His uncle's question caught him by surprise. The kid lay motionless well below him.

Did he fall? Is he hurt?

Gabe wasn't ready to deal with his emotions.

It isn't supposed to be like this!

"I don't know!" Gabe looked back over his shoulder in the direction of the rest of his group and saw nothing but darkness. Oh, how he wished they were right there beside him.

The ravens squawked again.

"Can you see the upper torso?" Dan's voice was clear and crisp over the radio.

Gabe looked back down over the ledge. He could make out the outline of what looked like the kid's back, face down, with head turned away, arms pinned under the torso which hung partially over the edge. Gabe's fingers tingled with another shot of fear and adrenaline. The kid could very well fall over the edge of the ledge if he didn't do something, and do it quickly. The angle of the hillside suddenly looked steeper.

"Yes." He squeaked into the mike.

"Do you see the chest rise and fall?"

"He's face down, almost hanging over the edge, how am I supposed to—"

"*Climb down! Climb down! Climb down!*" The large raven screeched again, his calls again sounding like words. Gabe readjusted the headlamp on his head and groped through his pack for his binoculars. He shook too much while standing, his nerves keeping him from being steady. He leaned against a boulder and brought the binoculars to his face, hugging the rock with his body.

Better.

"Is he alive?" the radio screamed.

He ignored it as he held his headlamp over the edge and tried to slow his breathing. He focused on the kid's side in the light beam. He squinted into the rain.

The cliff is so close!

He held his breath as he hoped and prayed.

"Let him breathe! Let him be alive!"

The smaller raven fluttered down and landed just out of reach of the motionless human figure and started hollering, moving her head up and down, feathers ruffled. "*Get up! Get up! Get up! Get up! Get up!*"

Then, surprisingly, the figure stirred, moved an elbow, and then a shoulder. Gabe thought he heard a muffled moan coming from the kid's prostrate frame. Startled, the raven quickly took flight and moved away as she continued to holler at the kid. It wasn't until the larger raven said something to the other one that she stopped screeching.

Gabe was glad the smaller one stopped. The last thing he wanted was for the kid to become startled and fall the rest of the way down the Cliffside to his death.

That would be tragic.

"He's alive, he's alive!" Gabe hollered into the radio mike. He couldn't stop smiling.

"Good news. Good news!" filled the airwaves; the relief was evident in Dan's voice. "Can you get to the victim safely?"

Gabe felt another little shiver ripple through him when he looked over the side and down to the boulder field that lay before him. To reach the kid, he would have to navigate the slippery rocks safely.

It looks steep, if I make a mistake....

"Can you get to him safely?" The words rang out again over the airwaves with seriousness. "If you can't then don't! We'll figure some other way."

Some other way!

Gabe wasn't sure. He had never done anything like this before. He palmed the carabineer attached to his harness with his fingers as he looked back in the direction of the rest of his team. They were invisible in the darkness and falling rain. The end of the rope was somewhere out there in that scary place, much too far away to even consider. By the time he would have gone back to retrieve the end of the rope or had his friend risk injury or even death to bring it to him, it would have all been for nothing.

The rope isn't an option.

He stood up and looked back over the side to speed up his thoughts, to clarify a bit. Below him suddenly looked darker, more dangerous. He forced his hand. If he were going to do this he had to go right then, and there.

There's no other way!

He looked at the raven and was surprised to see him looking back. The bird cocked his head from side to side and gazed at him with its intelligent eyes. It was like he, too, was waiting for a decision.

"So what do you think?" Gabe asked the raven, his voice shaking with fear.

The raven only hopped closer to the edge and peered down into the void. The bird cocked its head again, this time as if he were choosing a route.

"Well, it's decided then!" Gabe looked down towards the helpless kid, and then back to the bird. "I think I can do this." He started to climb over the edge.

The raven sounded off again, its tone more urgent.

Gabe stopped, he shook his head. "The kid can't wait. I have to do something, and I have to do it now!" Gabe couldn't believe how confident his voice suddenly sounded. Deep inside, he could feel a renewed energy beginning to build.

"You're going to need to be safe. You can't take any chances!" Dan's voice sounded in his head.

"Yes, I understand." His confidence faltered slightly.

The radio boomed to life again. "What are you going to do?" This time Dan's voice echoed off the rocks.

"I'm going down to help the kid."

"Copy, you're going down to help the kid... use the radio as long as you can." Dan's voice echoed. "Remember that there may be some reception problems once you drop down over the edge. These are line of sight; seven-mile radios designed for the Midwest, not rugged terrain like this! We might get some skip. If you can't get through, don't panic. You might need to move around a bit to improve your reception. Do you understand?"

"Yes," he answered back.

"You will need to stabilize the victim, remember, just like we talked about. Don't move the person around; they're most likely injured from the fall. Warm them up. We need to fight hypothermia. Use the space blankets I gave you. I will get on the horn and call in the Cavalry. Reception on the park radio isn't so good down here, so I will probably have to hike back up the trail a bit to reach them. It may take a little longer to get help, but don't worry. Erick will be monitoring the radio. Just imagine him being down there with you the whole time, alright?"

Gabe hesitated for a moment before he answered. There was a lot running through his mind at that moment-his dad, his mom, his uncle, his friend Erick, the mysterious ravens, the rain, the cold, the darkness, the unknown, and now the kid that lay 20 feet below.

There was a moment of silence before Dan's voice echoed in the rainy darkness.

"Do you copy? Are you okay with this?"

He read the concern in his uncle's voice and forced confidence into his own. "Yeah, piece of cake."

"I thought you didn't like cake?" Erick's playful banter boomed into the looming darkness.

The sound of his friend's voice made him smile. "Maybe I will make an exception today." Gabe could hear them laughing over the radio. It helped.

There was a moment of uncomfortable silence before his uncle spoke again. "You got this... we're proud of you!" His voice squeaked with emotion. "Your dad, he would've been very proud!" He cleared his throat over the radio. "Let us know when you drop over the side, and when you reach the victim."

"Okay!"

"Good luck!"

Gabe felt a tear building in his eyes.

My Dad!

He looked around.

He's still out there somewhere!

His dad had never left, was never given the opportunity.

He wiped the tears and rain out of the corner of his eyes with the back of his hand and looked up into the darkness.

My dad's probably looking down at me right now, watching my every move, my every decision.

"Where were those guardian angels when my dad was looking for that lost college kid back then? Are these ravens my angels now?" he asked the darkness.

He turned and forced a smile at the squawking raven perched on the edge of the cliff a near ten yards away. Strangely he knew exactly what he meant. The large raven was standing over the route he needed to take.

"You must be my guardians?" Gabe spoke to the bird. "You have wings, but you're not glowing figures in white... but when the light hits your feathers just right... you are more beautiful then angels?"

Gabe threw on his pack and hurried in the direction of the large raven. The bird took flight into the darkness just before Gabe reached him. "Cautious, aren't you?" The bird floated effortlessly in the updraft and the rain as he hovered just above Gabe's head, in the beam of the headlamp. The bird tilted its wings skillfully, helping to hold it in place. "No matter, I don't like this place much, either." He looked over the edge and sighed in relief.

"I'm going down," he yelled into the radio mike.

"Copy, going down... be careful!" Erick's voice rang in his ears.

"Here we go!" he whispered to the raven. "Over the edge and into the unknown!"

The raven squawked in return.

"Alex" by April Leiterman

CHAPTER THIRTY
WE DO WHAT WE MUST!
MARCH 16TH 2000

Dan saw the distant glow from Gabe's headlamp through his night vision scope every time his light beam shot up into the sky.

"It's about time!"

Gabe was on the other side of the rocky island, amid a sea of devastation. Though less than a quarter of a mile away, due to the deteriorating conditions, he might as well have been in another time zone.

Dan thrust the small portable radio into Erick's hands and rifled through his pack to find the larger, more powerful park radio. The radio suddenly felt heavy in his wet hands. He gripped it more tightly, so he wouldn't drop it. Incredibly, Gabe was right about the victim's location.

Why am I so surprised? Like father like son!

The thought stunned him for a moment. The similarities in this situation were too grave to consider. Looking back toward the towering redwoods made everything look dangerous and unforgiving. He fumbled through the dark for his pack again, this time for his headlamp. "Erick, find your headlamp while you can still see it," Dan shared his thoughts.

"Already have it," said Erick. "Looking for yours?"

"Yeah."

"It's on your head." Erick smiled.

Dan reached up and touched it then turned it on. He gave out a heavy sigh as he squinted into the bright beam of Erick's head lamp.

"So I have!" Dan shrugged as he lifted the park radio up to his mouth. "Incident Command, this is Zone 4 Search Team. His voice controlled and steady.

The radio silence echoed louder than the orchestra of crickets, falling rain, and the distant croaking frogs together.

Dan attempted the call several more times, moving from one end of the clearing to the other, even holding the antenna high in the air in an attempt to improve his reception. Each time the tone of his voice becoming more and more desperate. Still, there was nothing.

"Gabe is over the side." Erick yelled.

Dan gave Erick thumbs up and nodded then placed the park radio back into his pack.

"Great! What else could go wrong?" Dan mumbled under his breath.

He pulled a few more items out of his pack to lighten the load and hastily tossed them to the ground.

Erick silently stood there watching Dan under the beam of his flash light. The dark sky lit up intermittently with distant flashes following, eerie rumbles several seconds later. Dan couldn't help but notice the look of abandonment etched into Erick's concerned expression.

"Keep an ear out and stay away from that stuff." Dan pointed towards the lightning flash. "And stay away from that too," he gestured out toward the devastated landslide. "That mud will suck the shoes right off your feet and then some, and if that happens, there's no way to get you free. At least in quicksand you can stay afloat." He shook his head. "Here, people have the nasty habit of going missing!" He gave Erick a good stare. He wanted his message to sink in. He might have exaggerated a tad, but he had his reasons, he had his message.

The whole clearing felt like it shook, in the ear piercing rumble. They both stopped what they were doing and looked up.

"I'll be back!" Dan forced himself to sound brave and in control. He made a lousy attempt at imitating the Terminator.

"Not even close!" Erick sounded scared.

"I know! It was a worth a try" Dan forced a smile.

Erick didn't return one.

There was another flash.

Erick quickly glanced in its direction.

Dan tried to ignore it. He fought back a strange sadness and nodded to the surrounding forest. "You'll be fine right here. Use the tarps you set up to stay warm and dry. You have plenty of food and water—"

They both flinched when the rumble vibrated through their chests.

Dan waited for the rumbling to stop before he continued.

"I'll be back in less than an hour, maybe two hours tops!" He forced another smile and nodded up the trail. "I'd be lying if I told you I was looking forward to this."

This time it was Erick's turn to force a smile.

Dan re-secured the straps to his pack and slipped it back onto his back. "There, that's more like it. Keep the lights burning. You've got plenty of batteries, right?"

He saw Erick glancing back down toward the landslide.

"He'll be fine! Do you pray much?"

"What?" Erick gave Dan a confused look.

"Pray much? Remember, we aren't alone!" Dan fought a smile when he saw Erick look nervously toward the forest. He gently tapped him on his shoulder to regain his attention.

When Erick looked back at Dan, he found him staring up toward the sky, his headlamp illuminating the falling mist. Dan shook off the cold droplets that dribbled down his chest and back. He reacted. "Oooo! That's cold! Remind me not to do that again."

Erick smiled.

"The guardian angels we talked about, well, they're here!" Dan explained, "Listen to me, they aren't going to let anything happen to us and for that matter, to Gabe. We're here for a reason and so are they. That's the beauty of it all!"

"But, Gabe's dad?" Erick pointed to the landslide. "He was here for a reason too! Wasn't he?"

Dan nodded and brushed it off; there was no denying the obvious. "Not this time sport. Gabe isn't alone. He has us, and we have him, we have each other. We're a team!" Dan squeezed his shoulder and then pointed up toward the sky without looking up.

"A divided team of three!" said Erick.

Dan brushed it off. "We're here to pull off a difficult rescue from this spot on the mountain. We're the dynamic trio... the awesome threesome, the Zone Four Rescue Team." Dan threw his hands into the air.

When Erick returned an even bigger smile he patted him gently on the shoulder again.

Dan was going to have to hurry. He was going to have to run like he had never run before. He gave Erick a quick hug.

"Wish me luck."

Dan turned and started jogging up the trail. After a few steps he yelled back over his shoulder. "Remember what I said!"

"Yeah!" Erick yelled back. "We're the awesome threesome... yada yada and we're not alone... yada yada yada!"

Dan shot a quick glanced back towards Erick. "That's right, and don't you ever forget it!" he then turned and never looked back. He could feel Erick's eyes trailing him into the darkness.

The awesome threesome!

He knew Erick liked the sound of that.

The beam of Dan's headlamp led the way. He pushed himself along, ignoring the flashes and distant rumbles. As much as he tried, he couldn't shake the look of indifference.

Dan had almost convinced himself that everything was going to work out just as planned, but the problem was that he didn't have a plan, not really. Climb down the mountain, find the missing juvenile, climb back up the mountain to call for the Cavalry, climb back down the mountain again, stabilize the victim and wait to be extracted at the earliest convenience. It was textbook.

How does conducting this rescue on the anniversary of my brother's death, taking my nephew and his friend down into this devastation, during one of the worst storms of the season fit into all of this?

"The angels... the past history... how does all of this add up?" he panted into the darkness illuminated by his headlamp.

Pictures and images flashed in his mind as he struggled up the side of the mountain. He remembered seeing the angel's face.

Did I really see an angel? Or was it all in my head? Wishful thinking? Was this doubt?

It was a bit strange, he hadn't felt this close to his brother since his death.

Was it the mountain? The anniversary, or the fact that Gabriel's son was involved, that made this place feel so crazy?

"Help me brother," he whispered as he panted, "Guide me up this hill and down the next. Keep me safe... keep them safe!"

When Dan glanced down at his watch it was well after 8:00 in the evening. He told himself that he would make his first radio attempt in 15 minutes.

They had averaged about three miles per hour going downhill, with breaks and all, he wondered how quickly he would be able to make it back out? He figured he would be lucky to sustain one and a half to two miles per hour, without the heavy pack, for the next 30 minutes going up. He knew that pushing himself uphill in the dark at that pace was sure to do him in. He hoped it would be enough.

His lungs screamed, and his legs painfully burned. He pushed harder. It only took him two grueling minutes before reality kick in. He quickly reduced his jog to a fast, uphill walk. He pushed on.

"Only 13 minutes to go before my first 15 minute attempt at getting out on the park radio!"

Boy am I out of shape!

***

Erick felt his body shudder in the rain as the glow of Dan's headlamp disappeared into the darkness, absorbed into the misty clearing. Only the sounds of the falling rain and the serenading crickets and frogs filled his ears. He regretted seeing Dan go, but he knew Dan was only doing his job. He stood there, radio in hand, awaiting his friends' call, to confirm that he had safely lowered himself to the ledge and the victim. He forced himself to sit down under the tarp, out of the bone-chilling rain and winds. With the radio held tightly in his grip, he gazed off toward the distant rock outcropping, an island amid the sea of devastation, a miracle in itself. He couldn't help but think about Gabe's dad being buried out there somewhere, left behind, his whereabouts unknown. The thought overwhelmed Erick. It was the not knowing that created the tightness in his throat.

How does Dan do it? How does Gabe do it? It would drive me crazy.

A hooting owl made him jump.

A Great horned owl. Relax, it's only an owl!

He tried to convince himself that it wasn't the messenger of death and tried to focus on the guardian angel thing.

'Do you pray much?' Dan's words burned into his thoughts. Maybe that was what he needed to do.

Yes, I need to pray.

His mother prayed constantly.

The night was getting darker, the air colder, and the rain was relentless. At that moment his friend seemed even farther away.

***

Gabe clung to the rock wall as his hands and feet felt their way backward down the boulders. It was true, it was harder to climb down than it was to climb up. It took him only a couple of methodical minutes to traverse the rocky face down to the first ledge. He lost his grip and slid the last four feet to the next ledge. He stumbled and caught his balance.

"Wow that was a close one!" His heart hammered in his chest.

As soon as he touched the safety of the first ledge, the ravens squawked their goodbye and disappeared into the darkness.

"No, wait, where are you going?" he yelled into the night.

Their wing beats whistled through the moist air, blending into the sounds of the lonely, stormy night. They circled him a few times before they disappeared from sight. Their final cries...

"*Be careful, be careful, be careful,*" echoed into oblivion.

"Thanks!" Gabe mumbled under his breath.

"I'm on the ledge." He whispered cautiously into the mike. He didn't know why, but there on the ledge everything felt so very different. It was like climbing into an alien world.

Is it my imagination or is there really something to all of this?

Moments later the hoot of a nearby owl caused him to jump again. The call was close; it came from a tree somewhere below the rocky plug of an island in the middle of the devastation.

"Dad, is that you?" The words quietly slipped through his lips.

How silly!

He forced his thoughts back to the victim. Now the forest was really dark. He slipped the headlamp off of his head and held it in his hand as he used its powerful halogen beam to illuminate the area. The droplets of falling rain and mist glowed more brightly in the light. The scattered rocks and boulders cast long shadows across the uneven terrain. All was making it more difficult to see farther into the darkness. With virtually no mud, the travel was easier now than through which he had been trudging. He knew the victim was close; the ledge couldn't have been more than ten yards deep and twenty yards across.

"Hello, I'm with the rescue team!" he yelled, his light still scanning the terrain. It took less than ten seconds to locate the victim. Only part of the victim's backside was visible, the dark, soiled clothes helping the kid blend into the surrounding shadows. Gabe stopped in his tracks and stared for a moment. Everything suddenly came together. He wondered if his father had felt the very same emotions every time he stumbled upon a missing person or an injured victim. The moment seemed to give him strength and power. He didn't know why, but a chill ran the length of his spine. He forced himself forward, constantly reminded himself that there was another drop off practically within arm's reach. He held his headlamp up high to reduce the length of the deceiving shadows as he cautiously knelt down within reach of the victim. The outline of the sloped ledge stood out against the darkness. The lighter colored rocks reflected back. Beyond them was an ominous dark void. Before him lay the motionless victim on the verge of slipping over the ledge. Whatever it was that he needed to do, he needed to do it now.

The distant lightning flashed on and off beyond the dark clouds. He paused to count. It seemed to take forever for the faint rumble to reach his ears. Other flashes came from his far right. He would have to wait and see if that storm cell would pass closely enough to be a threat.

He started to reach out to touch the motionless figure, but abruptly stopped. He fought the urge to leap back. Dark matted hair hung past the victim's shoulders.

Was he a she? Do I have the right victim?

Something just didn't feel right. It was then that he heard the whispers from the shadows. Not knowing what to expect, he quickly turned and shone his light into the eerie darkness.

Are the ravens back? They didn't like the darkness any more than I did.

The misting rain danced in the glaring light. The shadows stretched from side to side as he panned with his light. Silhouettes changed shapes, adding motion to the darkness. It almost made him dizzy to watch. His hands shook and goose bumps ran the length of his whole body.

Is there someone out there? How could I even tell?

He took a deep breath and reached deep within, telling himself that it was nothing, that his imagination was getting the best of him on this stormy night. His eyes still tried to cut their way through the mist and darkness. He felt the breeze against his filthy face. "It's the wind," he told himself in a light whisper. The sound of his own voice calmed his nerves. He suddenly remembered that he wasn't alone. Besides the unconscious victim before him, he had his friend Erick and his Uncle Dan.

He fumbled nervously for his radio, remembering what he needed to do.

"I'm with the victim." He heard the nervousness in his somewhat feeble voice.

"Good --b!" Erick's excited voice echoed loudly on the radio, the sound bounced off of the rocks. Gabe felt his heart sink. Dan was right about the radios not working very well below the lip of the rocks. He'd hoped it wouldn't be a problem, but now it was.
Things just aren't getting any better.
"Where's Dan?"
"He took --- up --- trail -- call --- rangers -- said -- would -- back -- thirty minutes -- ------ -- hours."

Gabe was stunned. The team was now down to two and if communications didn't get any better, they would be down to one, himself.

"What --- --- injuries?" The sound interrupted his thoughts.
Injuries!
The thought rocked Gabe back to work.

He turned his back to the darkness and refocused on the figure in front of him in the beam of the headlamp. The lower part of the victim's slender left leg looked deformed. Portions of the victim's wet and soiled clothing appeared darker than he expected.
A Goth!
His mind raced to the dictionary he used in school.

The German people that overran the Roman Empire in the early centuries of the Christian era. The architecture developed in northern France and spread through Western Europe from the 12th to the 16th. Centuries. The 14th century Medieval, East German castles with arched doorways vaulted ceilings. Gargoyles... fiction characterized through desolate and remote settings... violent, mysterious incidents. Uncouth, barbarous lack of taste or elegance... conformity to or practiced the Gothic style.

He knew this all had nothing to do with his classmates. They created a niche to fit in. He had seen them at school, hanging together on campus, never talking much to anyone outside of their inner circle. They wore dark clothes, dark makeup.

Science Fiction buffs.
He actually liked horror and a little Sci-fi himself. Heck, practically every PlayStation 2, X-box, Game Cube, and Game Boy, was Sci-fi.

Both of the victim's arms were tucked beneath the upper torso. From Gabe's position, he couldn't even see the victim's face. He stared down, helpless and confused. He suddenly couldn't remember what to do.

"The left leg, I think is broken," he forced the words out of his lungs.

"-- -- conscious -- he -- - safe --------?" Erick rattled off his questions over the radio, like he knew what he was saying. It was always easier to tell people what to do from a position of safety.

Conscious? Safe?

"Ahh, no, not conscious, but he's ahhh, practically hanging off of the side of the cliff!" Gabe's confidence and voice were coming back.

"You ---- -- make --- safe first --- can't let --- fall!" Erick's voice sounded urgent. "Drag'em back ---- from --- edge --- need -- stop --- bleed--- splint --- leg, keep --- from harm. You're going -- need -- make --- - shelter. ---- worry, --- talk you through --!"

Gabe found himself shaking the radio to improve reception, an action that didn't make a difference. Still he somehow felt it would help.

"Yes... you're coming in broken!"

"-- keep -- posted." After a moment of silence the airwaves came back to life with Erick's voice. "Everything alright!" Surprisingly, the last part of the message was clear and concise.

"No! You're coming in broken... and maybe it's just me, but I don't think I'm alone." Gabe looked back over his shoulder into the darkness. Hearing his own words gave the scene validity. "There is something out there!" He found himself shuddering at the last of his words.

"--- alone?"

"No! It's creepy!"

"Hang -- there!"

"Yeah!"

Gabe gently reached over and shook the victim awake with his free hand. "Hey, you alright? I'm a friend. I'm here to help you!"

The victim groaned painfully in a soft voice.

At first it startled Gabe, but he quickly recovered. "Hey, where are you hurt?" He practically yelled back as he re-secured the headlamp on his head to free his arms, and pulled the hood of his rain parka back over his head. He then firmly grasped the victim's waist, and what appeared to be the good leg, and started to pull the victim back away from the edge. He stopped when he heard muffled cries of pain.

Strange eerie whispers echoed from the shadows around him.

Everything inside of him went tight, his body tingled and his fingers went numb. His skin began to crawl.

Adrenaline, fight or flight.

He fought the urge to run to nowhere, and forced himself to concentrate on the person that lay there. He was spooked enough as it was. Right now ignoring whatever he thought he heard was the best and hardest thing he could do.

Concentrate on the victim in front of me. I needed to get 'em safely away from the edge.

He shook both of his hands to increase the circulation and leaned toward the victim's face to get a better look. He couldn't see the face clearly. The victim still lay face down on the rocks. He could hear the deep, short, quick breaths. The victim was in pain.

Though the victim mumbled, he still thought he heard the unnerving whispering from the shadows. It was ever so faint, but yet distinct.

Voices? No, it has to be the breeze.

He had no choice but to keep telling himself that. He could feel the gentle breeze tickling the little hairs on his face. Without moving his head, he looked right toward the shadows with the corners of his eyes.

Nothing!

The sky flashed again, he counted. Fifteen seconds later a low rumble echoed into the night. He shuddered. Another storm cell was working its way in their direction. The clock was ticking.

He had no time to think, only time to react.

His thought echoed louder this time. Gabe knelt back alongside the victim's head and upper torso.

"Hey, hey, you okay?" he nudged the figure gently before he gripped the victim's hip and shoulder. He held on more tightly to keep the saturated, dirty clothing from slipping out of his hands. He then carefully rolled the victim back toward himself and away from the sloping edge, being careful not to injure the person more. The victim felt lighter than he thought they should. The figure grimaced and moaned under their breath as their body rolled easily toward him. Gabe looked directly into the rain-and-dirt-soaked face of the victim.

C-spine!

The thought echoed in his mind, but there wasn't any time. Soaked, matted hair, dirt and blood obscured almost the entire face. There appeared to be swelling about the side of the forehead. Gabe stared curiously down into the outlines of a pale, slender face. He had to know. Without another thought, he gently tried to slide the hair back away from the victim's face, most was still tangled in what looked like piercings. He gasped. He was actually a she, and she was beautiful. Stunned, he had to force himself along. This was definitely not what he had expected.

We're looking for a guy, did we have the right person?

Gabe sighed in relief. The girl was now farther from the edge, and much closer to being rescued. He thought he saw the light of the headlamp reflect off a portion of the girl's open eyes.

He flinched when he saw that her eyes were barely open.

Gabe felt a moment of joy as he continued. "I'm with the rescue team. We're here to help you."

He saw her eyes flutter momentarily before they closed again.

Gabe smiled. He gently picked up the sleeves of her dark parka and briefly examined her dirty hands. They were slender, cold, wet and lifeless. A silver colored ring graced every finger.

Outside of scratches and the dirt caked around her hands and arms, under her long, dark, chipped fingernails, her hands appeared to be uninjured.

Good!

He carefully laid her arms across her chest and tightly gripped the clothing about her shoulders with the both of his hands.

Bright blue-white light flashed in the dark night sky. An earth-shaking rumble quickly followed. The thunderhead would soon be upon them.

"Let's go!" he yelled and away they went. His fear forced his immediate action, and his adrenaline pushed him along.

She screamed briefly but then immediately stopped as if she had passed out.

He abruptly stopped but another bright blue flash and ground shaking rumble pushed him along. His heart pounded in his chest.

Got to get away from the edge.

He slowly wove around obstacles, dragging her ten yards away from the edge and towards a larger boulder that caught his eye as a windbreak.

"This'll work." He whispered to the victim.

He knew they would soon be safe.

CHAPTER THIRTY-ONE
NEITHER HERE NOR THERE!
MARCH 16TH 2000

Their radio reception suddenly took a dive for the worst. Erick was now hearing every other word. He was hoping he understood things correctly.

"What did Gabe mean by it being creepy and that he wasn't alone?" Erick nervously asked himself.

He stared out into the rain from beneath his tarp, the radio held firmly in his hand, nervously awaiting any words at all. Twice he almost called Gabe but thought better of it. Gabe needed to focus on the victim.

"If Gabe needed help, he would've called, right!"

He tried to convince himself. "But, what if Gabe couldn't get through? What if something was really wrong?"

The words caused him to worry even more. The hardest thing right then and there was to just sit and do nothing. He looked down at his watch. Five minutes had passed, it felt like hours.

"Call me or something, will you! Please!" he whispered.

The owl hooted again, the lightning flashed in the darkness, and the thunder rumbled across the clearing.

Erick flinched, he felt the goose bumps crawl across his skin. He could think of a few hundred other places he would rather have been at that moment.

He remembered what Dan had told him before he left. 'The guardian angles'.

"So, where are you?" He mumbled into the darkness. "I hope you're looking after my friends?" His words were accusatory.

He sat up quickly as the radio crackled to life.

"Erick, - have her in --- shelter ---...." The radio faded off into static.

Her?

"Did you say *her*, in the shelter?" He tried to clarify. "Gabe, Gabe, do you copy me?"

There was some more static and then the radio went silent.

"Gabe!" he screamed into the mike as he dashed out into the drizzling rain. He ran along the edge of the saturated clearing in an attempt to improve his reception. "Gabe, Gabe... do you hear me? Please answer!" he yelled frantically into the radio. He was only answered by radio silence and the gusts of wind whistling through the tree tops.

Another series of blinding blue flashes illuminated the dark cloud. Fingers of white light traversed across the sky to the east. The thunder that followed shook everything around him.

Holy...!

"Please let it pass," he whispered softly, "please let it pass!"

"*Those are not your worry!*" A soft whisper blew past his ears in the building wind.

"Dan?" he turned quickly towards the shelter expecting to find him standing there, telling him that *everything was going to be alright*, that the *rescue crews were on their way*. However, there was nothing but darkness. The eeriness of it all made him shiver. By now the winds seemed to be increasing again.

"Who's out there?" Erick yelled nervously.

He heard nobody in return.

'*I don't think I'm alone*', Gabe's words echoed through his thoughts. He shivered.

What did he mean?

"I have a knife!" he yelled as he rummaged through his pockets for it. Once found he quickly brandished it tightly in his trembling hand.

His thoughts flashed to the shower room... that time in front of the school... those other times on campus, and now, as he cowered outside of his makeshift shelter along the edge of a clearing. His eyes searched the shadows.

Nothing.

He squeezed the radio tightly in one hand, his life line and his pocket knife in the other. The powerful beam of his headlamp illuminating the edge of the clearing.

Still nothing!

He cautiously and reluctantly made his way to the edge of the landslide and let the bright beam of his headlamp illuminate the devastation. The sight and sounds of the moving water and sliding debris gave him the chills. He could barely make out the jumble of huge boulders and trees that made up the island, in the distance. In front of him lay the desolate landscape of mud, debris and upturned trees. The winds continued to whistle through the tops of the trees. The light rain continued to fall. The frogs and crickets continued to do their thing in waves, each taking their turns at the unnerving silence. His thoughts raced as he shone his light everywhere he looked. His emotions were on edge.

"*Good versus Evil appears to be the common theme.*" the soft voice drifted on the wind.

"Who's out there?" Erick yelled as he spun around. "I said, who's out there!" He demanded, even louder as he brandished the blade of his pocket knife in a thrusting motion into the beam of his light.

The trees seemed to creak and moan in the wind even louder in response. The voices of the crickets and frogs quieted for a moment every time he screamed.

That made him nervous, he knew someone was definitely out there.

He flooded his surroundings with the light of his head lamp and tightened the grip on his two lifesaving tools. The radio and his knife.

"Why are you following us?" he demanded, as his voice crackled with fear and anger. "Leave us a-l-o-n-e!" he screamed.

"*Be not afraid!*" the familiar voice of a young man echoed louder.

Erick spun on his feet again, still brandishing his knife, his head lamp illuminating the darkness around him. He appeared to still be alone.

"Where are you? Let me see you," his voice shook with passion. "Please!" he calmly pleaded, "Is Gabe safe?"

"*Your friend needs you at his side,*" the whisper again echoed in his ears.

Erick spun around toward the disembodied voice. This time his eyes caught the outline of a figure standing two arm lengths away. He instinctively backed up, almost falling backwards into the ravine. He struggled to regain his balance and moved away from the edge.

That's when he recognized the young man standing about five yards away. It was the very same young man he had seen several times before it was the very same young man who he had talked with by the big maple tree. He was standing there at the edge, staring off into the darkness, in the direction of the island. The beam of Erick's head lamp passed through his translucent, ghost-like figure. His long robe moved as if it were alive. Despite the rain, he appeared absolutely dry.

"*Erick, I am not going to hurt you.*"

The young man turned, finally looked at him and smiled.

The mere sight of him gave Erick chills. He took a couple of more steps back towards his shelter. "It's you!" his voice a harsh whisper.

The young man nodded, his eyes peering deep into his own. His expression urgent. "*I feel the presence of my brother. He is here, but I'm afraid he is not here to help.*" The young man's gaze turned soft. "*I cannot accompany you into the shadows beyond.*" He nodded towards the island. "*That is forbidden. This, you must do without me.*" The emotion was lost somewhere, hidden in his face.

Erick felt the fear overwhelm him. His hands shook. He took a couple of steps forward, his fear slowly turning into anger. "What do you mean? You're supposed to be helping us!" Erick yelled as he pointed the radio towards the island in the sea of devastation. "Are you abandoning us just like you did Gabe's father? How could you do this a second time?"

"You are not abandoned and neither was his father. We are with you every step you take." the figure whispered back, barely audible over the wind.

"What... how can you be with us every step and let bad things happen..."

Erick strained his ears as he stepped closer.

"Yes, bad things do happen to good people and good thing happen to bad people. What you see as a mystery is not so in the eyes of God. I can only step in to interfere if I am asked to do so." The young man continued to smile. *"That you must understand."*

"Well, consider yourself being asked. Are you saying no?" Erick shivered in the sudden cold. "Why aren't you going down there with me?" Erick pointed with the knife before he lowered it to his waist. "Isn't that why you're here?" His voice grew even angrier and his eyes filled with tears. When he stepped even closer to the figure, he felt his insides warm, his fingers begin to tingle, and his arms grew heavy. "Are you afraid to go down there? You're afraid aren't you!" he narrowed his eyes and lowered his knife.

The young man shook his head. *"I fear no one but the Almighty. I am not the only angel who will accompany you. When the time is right, you will have an army at your side."*

Erick looked at him, confused. "Our army of three?"

"No, a legion of thousands of the finest!"

The young man returned his gaze to the darkness that cloaked the landslide. *"Your friend needs you as we speak. His time is running out."*

Erick felt his insides tighten all at once. A burning fear ripped through his body.

Time is running out!

"I can't go down there, I'll get stuck in the mud, I'll get struck by lightning, or worse. Dan told me to stay here and wait until he comes back with help. I have to wait here!" He pointed to the ground beneath his feet. "But, Dan said—"

"Then you will have been too late," the young man nodded in the direction of the rocky outcropping. *"Thousands will be at your side if you leave now."*

"Thousands of angels you say," Erick laughed. "Then where are they?" Erick made it a point to look around. "Where in the heck are they? All I see is you, standing here giving me lip service. When we ask for action you choke. Is that what happened when Gabriel asked you for help. When he needed you the most, you choked big time!" his angry voice reeked of sarcasm. "You abandoned him to his own fate in his greatest time of need! Didn't you?"

The young man smiled. His smile angered Erick even more.

"*Abandoned? Ye of little faith. Look again. Trust your heart.*" the young man spoke softly.

Erick followed the young man's gaze out into the darkness. Another flash of lightning blinded him with a bright blue warm light. He instinctively covered his eyes and staggered away from the edge. When he looked back the young man was no longer alone. There were hundreds of other young men in white translucent robes surrounding him, along the edge of the clearing, all gazing off into the devastation, dressed in white robes, covered with shiny silver armor and armed with glowing swords and shields. A determined expression embraced their faces. He fell to his knees and dropped both his knife and radio into the mud. This time, when the shock wave hit him he felt the energy pass right through his entire trembling body. His fear was gone, his faith restored. The young man was right, they weren't alone... they were never alone. Everything served a purpose.

***

Though Dan's lungs hurt from deep within, and his sweat stung his eyes, he continued to stumble along with his trembling arms and burning legs.

To slow down would be to admit defeat, to give in to the temptation would mean to quit!

"No, I can do this... Lord, give me... strength!" he spoke into the wind as he pushed himself along. "Focus, focus... focus!" he panted. "You... will not win... this one!" he screamed, with breaths he didn't have to spare. "You... will... not... win!"

He practically crawled up some portions of the hillside, following the trail-flagging he laid out earlier to find his way back in the darkness. The flagging snapped in the breeze. His aching knees constantly reminded him of his age.

This is why I never act my age! It isn't the destination. It is never the destination... it's always the journey!

He forced a smile as he pushed the indigo button on his watch. Seconds later 8:30 p.m. flashed back. Seven minutes had slipped by since he had last checked.

"Six more minutes!" he panted out loud.

He fast-forwarded through his brother's life.

Not a single second of the time we spent together, did I ever regret? Not once did he ever hold back with me. Nor will I!

They indeed had a special bond, one that was never broken. Though his brother was taken, he had never been gone. He was always there in his thoughts, always there in his heart.

Even at that very moment he felt his brother racing him up the hill taunting him, prodding him along.

The radio crackled to life in the wind, startling him, causing him to slip onto all fours, his lungs screamed for air. On hands and knees, he excitedly pulled the park radio from its holster and held the speaker against his ear. He forced his breathing under control. He was surprised he had heard the radio through the pack, the waterproof covering, and the heartless elements around him.

"Zone 4, this is Incident Command, come in!" came the tired voice. "Zone 4, this is Incident Command, do you copy?"

Jumbled static followed.

Dan couldn't believe his luck, his friend was coming in loud and clear. He squeezed the button and panted into the mike. "This is Zone 4... this is Zone 4... priority traffic!"

"This is Incident Command, I copy your request for priority traffic. I repeat, clear for priority traffic." The firm excitement was noted in his voice.

"This is I.C., Dan, is that you?"

Exhausted, Dan rolled onto his back as he gasped for breath. His eyes filled with tears as he pressed the indigo button on his watch again; it was 8:40 in the evening. He had lost track of time, he'd missed his radio check by four minutes. The last ten torturous minutes had screamed by. He felt a sudden joy charge through him. He would have fallen over if he hadn't already been laying face up on the ground.

Was my brother listening? What were the odds?

He forced some more deep breaths and immediately dug his heels into the gravel and mud hillside for balance and support. His wide, grinning face pointed back down the slope, his head lamp illuminated his breath in the mist and darkness. His lungs heaved due to the excess carbon dioxide in his lungs.

For the moment the rains had stopped, but the winds seemed to have increased. The trees around him creaked and moaned. The place still felt unforgiving.

"Zone 4, go with priority traffic." Buds voice followed.

"Yeah... in the flesh!" Dan's voice quivered with exhaustion.

"It's Bud. Where the hell are you? I've been tryin' to reach you for the last hour! Hours of nothin' now it sounds like you're just next door!" his voice transitioned from concerned to scolding.

"Yeah Bud... I wish I were next door!" Dan forced calmness back into his voice. "You're probably not going to believe this, but... we've found the kid... in Falcon Canyon!" He tried to get the important information out before he lost the signal.

"What? Did I copy you correctly? You found the missin' female, Alexandra Bradley in... Falcon Canyon?"

"That's affirmative... one in the same." He heard the pride in his own squeaky voice. "She is injured, trapped on a ledge, on the island... in the middle of the slide. Remember that place?" He looked down at his arm, he felt the goose bumps prickle his skin as he spoke. His hands trembled. He made a fist to make it stop, but his whole body continued to shiver. He nervously looked around to make sure he was still alone.

The wind whispered in the trees, the shadows danced, debris bounced across his chest and legs.

There was an uncomfortable silence on the airwaves. Dan fought through the nervousness of fearing that he had lost reception. He moved the radio around. "No, not now!" he staggered clumsily to his feet. "I repeat... Bud, we've, found, the, kid!" He spoke slower, hoping his message was getting through. "Do you copy?"

"Good news! Good news! Of all places. So, your nephew was right after all!"

Dan let out a big sigh of relief, communications were still working. He heard the congratulatory hoots and hollers in the background at Incident Command. "Affirmative," he shared. He felt the lump in his throat growing, he wanted to say more, but he knew there would be time for that later.

"All the way to the canyon? What's her status?" Bud's confident swagger returned.

Her status?

Dan summed it up as quickly as he could between his struggling breaths. "Alive, but unconscious... Evidently she managed to fall down... the side of the mountain. Exact injuries are unknown. Gabe went over the side... to treat and stabilize. He's been out of radio contact with rest of the crew... for about 30 minutes. Request immediate medical evacuation... had to hump it out to reach you." Finally getting through on the radio had felt emotional.

"Well done! Well done! Been tryin' to get a hold of you guys. There is a bit more on the kid." Bud's voice suddenly took on a notable, no-nonsense concern. "I need to bring you up to speed. Dan, you clear to copy?"

Clear to copy!

Those dreaded words, sent a sudden chill radiating throughout his entire body. He'd heard them numerous times before throughout his career as a State Park Peace Officer. They usually meant the person of concern was either wanted, or had violated some crime somewhere, and the long arm of the law had finally caught up with them. The message he was about to receive was for his ears only. He looked back down the trail and gave out a heavy sigh.

Now what?

"That's affirmative. What've you got?" Dan almost didn't want to know.

"You in cell range?"

"Stand by."

Dan held the radio against his chest as he slipped off his pack and scrambled to find his cell phone with his free hand. He turned it on. The seconds it took to engage felt like minutes. He left it off so he wouldn't drain the battery. It took him only a moment to realize that he was still out of range. He fought back the building pressure on his chest.

No reception!

"Negative on the cell!" Dan's voice squeaked. There was an uncomfortable moment before Bud began again.

"Here it goes, the mom had neglected to advise us that her 15 year old daughter, was off her meds. Evidently, she suffers from a form of bipolar disorder!" His voice was loud and matter of fact.

Bipolar?

The words bipolar disorder, rattled around in Dan's brain. If he remembered correctly, the victim that Gabriel had rescued years back had been diagnosed with a form of it, as well only back then they called it something different. He shuddered noticeably. The similarities of this rescue to that involving his brother were becoming frighteningly apparent.

Déjà vu!

Bud must have realized this as well, because he paused for a moment before he continued. Dan knew why. He was about to disclose personal things about the minor over the air waves, an action greatly frowned upon. Their privacy was protected by law, treated with white gloves, and Bud knew that. Things must have needed to be said.

"Alex was prone to runnin' away when things got a little tough. Lately with a recent relocation of the family, the death of a parent, an' her past drug history, everythin' came to a head. I tried your cell already, but, evidently, you're still in a dead zone!" Bud paused for a moment.

The words *Dead Zone* took on a new meaning. Dan snapped a worried glance back towards the canyon.

Gabe!

Dan could almost imagine him regretting his last words. He had indeed given this some serious thought.

A lot of good these items will do me now! Bud had already given up more information than he should have and probably did so for a reason.

"Sorry for the delay on the intel. My friend. There is one more thing, she has a history of violence!"

Dan felt his innards tighten up all at once. He felt the energy drain from his core as he turned and watched the beam from his headlamp become absorbed in a pocked of misty darkness.

Gabe was alone on a ledge with this girl.

He thought of his brother. His hands began to shake.

"No!" he screamed into the darkness and the building winds.

"She may be petite but evidently she still packs a good wallop." Bud continued, "She's persistent, determined, and stubborn. Much like someone else I know! Accordin' to her mother she's very capable of taking care of herself. I guess that's why she made it all the way to Zone Four... Falcon Canyon!"

A blinding, blueish light streaked across the darkened sky. Within seconds, the sound of rumbling thunder filled his ears and shook the ground beneath him.

Dan dropped to the ground. His eyes filled with spots.

"What was that? Dan, you copy? Dan?" the radio came to life.

"Got it, still here. It's getting crazy out here!" Dan yelled into the radio over the static in his ears.

"I bet, where are you now? Please tell me you're not makin' this call from that finger ridge!"

"About a mile above Falcon... Erick's overlooking the slide... Gabe's down with the victim!" His words sounded so distant.

"Get your backside off that ridge, that's an order. Did you say Gabe is with the victim, alone?" The concern in Bud's voice was evident.

"Affirmative! Got to get back, pronto." He fought back his anxiety.

"Christ!" Bud sounded worried.

"How soon can you send an extraction team?"

"I'll make the rest of this quick so you can get out of the way of Hells Fury. Whirlybird by daylight, sooner if storm subsides. Ground pounders headin' in your direction as we speak. Accordin' to the weather geeks, were still getting' pounded by severe thundershowers an' heavy rains. No surprise there! Your team needs to pull off the stabilization, medical, an' containment, an' then button down the hatches... hold on tight. Avoid all open and high areas and that means you!"

Dan looked around. He had no choice, he was expose the whole way.

"Sorry, my friend, the Cavalry will be there as soon as they can." The radio crackled again, the voice more calm.

"Copy that!" Dan's voice reflected anxiety and disappointment.

"I've got one last thing..."

Now what?

"Been informed that we've got a couple of marathoners double timin' it to your local with some medication, some Ziprasidone... painkillers. I've been informed that it should help. They know the spot. They'll look you up when they're close."

"Good news!" Dan sighed with relief.

"Mean time, patch her up the best you can. I'll relay the information back to the mom. You best get back there to check on things. Move like the wind my friend. History has a strange sort of way of repeatin' itself. Good luck!"

"Roger that, clear!" Dan answered the radio.

No kidding!

The sheets of rain suddenly started to hammer the ridge. The radio produced static before it went dead. Just like that, contact with civilization faded and then it was gone.

"Is that the best you got?" Dan screamed into the chaos.

***

"Christ..." Bud passed the radio receiver back to Chet, the communications officer. "Oh Dan, you have your work cut out for you!" he whispered to himself.

"Chet, are you much of a religious man?" he asked the radio operator.

"Been known to show up at church every now and then!" he responded.

"I'm gettin' an offal bad feelin' about this," grumbled Bud. They both glanced down at Bud's trembling hand. "I think it's time we said a few words to the man upstairs."

"Déjà vu'!" Chet nodded.

"Yeah, big time!" nodded Bud. "History has a very strange way of repeatin' itself."

They both gave each other a concerned look.

"God giveth—" said Chet.

"An' God taketh away, again!" mumbled Budd.

***

"Thank you!" Dan whispered.

The rain suddenly began to dump. He looked up into the darkness, the beam of his headlamp illuminating the cascading rain as it pelted the ground from every direction. The hairs stood out away from the back of his neck. A chill sliced right through him.

"The rains from hell have arrived and the half time show has come to an end. God help us." He took a deep breathe. The air smelled of rain and forest. "Here we go!" He hastily shouldered his pack and let gravity take him through the gauntlet. He headed back down the slippery, uneven trail dotted with loose debris, and well-marked with orange flagging. Not once did he regret the extra time he had taken to flag their earlier route as they descended into the canyon. It made night traveling that much easier. Now it was a race against time.

Maybe the whole bipolar thing isn't as bad as they first thought!

It was long-term, and once diagnosed there was no outgrowing it. They had the rest of their lives to learn to be at peace with it. After all, bipolar disorders bridged the demographics, didn't care if you were rich or poor. Bipolar disorder ran high among poets and writers, usually considered creative people. The disorder could also be found in extremely functional people like doctors, judges, movie stars, lawyers, congress and presidents.

He forced a smile at the thought.

On second thought, maybe I should start worrying!

He could understand why Alex, as well as many others, suddenly stopped taking their meds. He ran off his imaginary list of known side effects as if it were a commercial as he slipped down the trail.

Denial! To admit that they have a manic and depressive problem in a society that's so quick to label and write them off. The side effects alone will drive them crazy. There are the shakes, sweats, hives, headaches, dizziness, nausea, vomiting, diarrhea, dream abnormalities, vision difficulties, loss of appetite, weight gain, itchiness, memory loss, confusion, mental slowness, hair loss, acne, excessive thirst, excessive urination, and that is only a few of the side effects.

Dan shook his head in disappointment.

Then there's dealing with their depression. Despite it all, depression never truly goes away, nor does the stark reality that the individual really needs to take their meds. Even the so called good things have their problems:

The surge of energy, the euphoria, the hallmark mania, irritability, mood swings, depression, and then there's the extreme ups and downs that makes it so destructive to the individuals themselves and their relationship.

To them, sometimes suicide becomes the only viable option, a frightening thought. The medication smooths out the high and lows, and helps them cope.

The television came to mind, the thought of taking a pill despite the frightening list of disclosures filling the airways. They start feeling better, renewed by hope that the cure is within their grasps, if only temporary.

The symptoms in children and teens were different from adults. Added stresses like alcohol and drugs, trouble in school, running away from home, a loss or divorce of a parent, relationship breakups, fighting, leads to suicide! Sometimes antidepressants in teens may even worsen their depression, add to their hostility and anger, and give them suicidal thoughts. Add all of that to the fact that they are an emotional teen whose mind is still developing.

Déjà vu'!

"God help us!" He exclaimed as he pushed himself even harder down the mountain through his pain and fear. His eyes filled with tears, frightening thoughts raced through his head. The wind pushed and pulled, the ground moved under his feet, the lightening blinded, the disorienting thunder knocked him from his feet as the clock continued to wind down. He felt as if he were in a race to save the life of others, a race he couldn't afford to lose.

One step down... two steps further!

CHAPTER THIRTY-TWO
MONSIGNOR
MARCH 16TH 2000

Lydia stood there panting beneath the dim porch light as she noisily hammered her clenched fists against the big, wooden double doors of the mediaeval-looking rectory. The thick wood muffled her strikes and hurt her hands.
    She fought the nauseous feeling that dwelt within her stomach.
    Creepy!
    She cupped her hands, warmed them with her breath and shook off the soreness, momentarily diverting her leery gaze back to the darkness.
    A light rain fell in the gusty winds. Then there were the voices.
    Are they real or in my head?
    "On a second thought, I don't think I really want to know!" she whispered as she refocused on the door.
    She immediately regretted pounding her delicate hands against the big solid wooden door.
    "Ouch, that wasn't too bright!" she felt frustrated with herself when she noticed the antique iron door knocker staring her in the face. The Wrought iron door ornament was an intricate head of a proud lion, mane and all.
    If that was a snake....
    "Slow it down Lydia, how'd you miss that?" she whispered.
    Her tingling fingers still hadn't totally recovered from the white-knuckle drive from her home, ten minutes away. She noted her erratic breath and pounding heart. She wiped the

water droplets from her face and pushed the hair out of her eyes.

Perspiration or rain?

She couldn't tell the difference. At least, at that moment, none of it really mattered.

She shuddered as the wind-driven drizzle dripped down the back of her neck.

The wind... the relentless wind.

She glanced nervously over her shoulder toward her parked vehicle, and then into the shadows. As strange as it sounded, she was sure she had been followed.

If not by a person or a vehicle, then by what...?

The thought caused her to shiver again. She nervously fingered the shoulder strap of her purse, and crushed the purse tighter into her chest.

The face of the knocker took on a life of its own in the dimness. Its deep-set eyes seemed to look beyond her and out into the darkness. It reminded her of *Aslan*, the stately Lion in C.S. Lewis' The Chronicles of Narnia. He was the guardian of the righteous, the protector of everything good.

A silly thought.

"But that was just a story Lydia, get a grip!" she whispered. Today the face watched the shadows over her shoulders as she faced the door.

Why such a knocker on a Catholic rectory then?

It wasn't what she was expecting.

She gripped the face of the lion with the palm of her hand, making sure she didn't cover its eyes and teeth. She then lifted it up and slammed it loudly three times against the heavy wooden door. This time the knocker echoed loud enough to vibrate the door.

Three times for the Trinity.

"Come on, answer!" she whispered to herself, she whispered to the door. She didn't want the shadows to hear.

"Please, Monsignor, for the love of God, please be home."

She shot another quick glance over her shoulder to assure herself that it was only her imagination that made her feel the way she did, but as every second of every day ticked by, she knew better. To her relief, she still appeared to be alone. The dripping rain and the blowing wind dominated the darkness.

To her surprise, the sound of a latch was thrown and the heavy door began to move behind her. She turned back towards the door. A bright light escaped from around its edges casting her shadow into the darkness, the brightness partially blinded her. She narrowed her eyes, sucked in a quick gulp of air and tightened the grip on her purse. She instinctively took a couple steps backward. The large door creaked and moaned as it slowly swung open away from her. It then abruptly stopped leaving a six-inch gap, a small chain prevented it from opening any further. Seconds later the welcomed warmth caressed her face. The silhouetted upper torso of a human form appeared through the gap in the doorway. She squinted into the brightness and divert her eyes. She could barely make out the outline of an elderly woman's face as she cautiously peered out at her through the gap in the door.

The sudden movement surprised Lydia; she wasn't expecting the door to be opened in the manner in which it had been, or for that matter, to be opened at all. It was a bit creepy.

Lydia sheltered her face from the light with a free hand as she spoke, "I would like to talk with Monsignor O'Toole Please."

"Who?" The elderly woman sounded as if she had just woken up.

"Monsignor O' T-o-o-l-e," fighting the urgency, she spoke slowly, clearly so the woman could follow. "He's still the pastor here isn't he? I need to speak with him right away!" Her eyes started to adjust to the lighting so she lowered her hand. She figured that the older woman was a housekeeper.

"Monsignor O'Toole?" the startled woman asked. Both of her hands were still gripped around the inside doorknob and, for a moment, Lydia thought the elderly woman had gripped it more tightly.

"Yes, it is imperative that I speak with him." Lydia tried to maintain her composure.

"Visiting hours are over. The Monsignor," she bowed her head reverently and diverted her eyes down towards the floor as she spoke his name, "has retired for the evening. Would you like to come back tomorrow during office—"

"No!" Lydia cut her off. Her voice appeared to get louder with every word. "I can't come back tomorrow, tomorrow will be too late! What I have to talk to him about can't wait until tomorrow, it can't wait another second," her voice feisty. "Let me make this clear... it's of the utmost importance that I see him *immediately*!" She had to fight back the panic that was building in her voice. "Like I already told you, it's a matter of *life* and *death*!"

"I'm sorry," she stammered, "please come back tomorrow during the monsignor's scheduled office hours," the woman said, her voice on the edge of irritation, "That would be between 9:00 a.m. and 5:00 p.m., minus lunch of course, Monday through—"

"Hey!" Lydia screamed, "You're not listening!" she cut her off.

The woman flinched, her eyes grew twice their size, before she squeezed more behind the door, turning the door into a shield.

Lydia was running out of time and this woman didn't seem to care. She then spoke clearly, loudly, and slowly so there wouldn't be any misunderstanding. "It's imperative that I speak with him right, now, like I already told *you*, it's a matter of *life, and death!*"

"And, I told *you*, the Monsignor, has, gone... to... bed! Come back, t-o-m-o-r-r-o-w!" Annoyed sarcasm and impatience were evident in the older woman's voice. "If it's that *imperative*, then maybe *you* should call the police!"

Lydia looked down at her watch and raised her eyebrows in surprise. "For Christ sake!" Lydia exploded, her patience exhausted.

The woman looked at her surprised.

"Did you think I would come all the way here if it weren't so freaking important? I don't need the *police* I need *Monsignor O'Toole* and I need him right *now*!"

"I'm sorry! But...." The woman raised an offended eyebrow and began to push the door closed in front of her, but Lydia was literally one step ahead of her. She shoved her foot through the gap before the older woman could push the door shut. It clunked painfully against Lydia's ankle.

"Ahhhh" Lydia let out a cry of pain, "that's it!" That pissed her off. "Lady that was a mistake! So, that's the way it's going to be?" Lydia yelled as she gripped the door firmly in her hands and tried to push it open towards the inside of the room. The elderly woman staggered backwards a couple of steps.

"What are you doing?" the woman screamed, excitedly. "You can't just push your way in here like this. This is a private residence, I won't allow it! I was given strict orders not to—"

"I don't care about your *orders*," Lydia interjected, "like I told you, this is a matter of life and death. I want to see—"

"Monsignor O'Toole!" the woman let out, in an ear-piercing scream that echoed off of the tile floor and stone walls of the entry area. "Monsignor!" echoed again even louder.

Lydia instinctually took a step back away from the door and covered her ears to protect them from the woman's piercing, scream. "Good god!" she cried.

"What is the meaning of this?" a man's loud booming voice echoed down the hall.

Monsignor O'Toole!

At that moment everything seemed to move in slow motion. The older lady turned in the direction of the powerful, confident voice.

"This woman... tried to push her way... into the rectory," the older woman's voice crackled hysterically with emotion as she panted. She looked disheveled as if she had been in a heated wrestling match, but in reality, she had only been slightly pushed out of the way by the door. The woman now seemed smaller, more fragile, as she pointed her trembling accusatory finger at Lydia.

Lydia pushed her face in the gap of the door where her face could be seen.

A tall, portly gray hared man in a black shirt and pants strutted into the foyer and stopped between the two ladies like a referee in a prize fight. He towered over the older woman like a mountain. Lydia instantly recognized his features when the light hit his face. Except for the wrinkles on his wise caring face, and more gray hair, his features hadn't changed since she had last seen him ten years ago. She felt his projected kindness, and wondered why she had chosen to leave the church so abruptly that day. She hadn't seen the priest since the funeral. Today, almost ten years seemed so long ago.

She felt the Monsignor's eyes burning right through her, studying her face, her every gesture, with an astonished expression, a recognizing smile. His eyes never left hers.

"Lydia!" Monsignor whispered under his breath, his eyes reflected surprise and recognition. "Is that you?"

"Yes, Monsignor O'Toole!"

"Her name's Lydia." There was a notable Irish accent.

He shifted his gaze in between Lydia and the older woman.

"Mrs. Gertrude, I've got this."

He looked back towards Lydia.

"Lydia, I'm sorry, but ye'll need te' step back so I can open the door. It 'as a chain latch." He spoke softly in his sing song Irish accent.

She nodded and moved back hoping it wasn't a trick to get rid of her.

She watched the door shut, herd the latch and watched with gratitude as the big wooden door swing wide open. Light flooded everywhere.

"Lydia, please come in." he smiled and waved her in.

Lydia gripped her purse even tighter and gave out an instant sigh of relief as she stepped into the warm, well-lit foyer.

The priest stood there staring for a moment before he shut the door and re latched it with the chain.

"The neighborhood these days, ye' never know." Monsignor forced a smile.

Mrs. Gertrude drifted behind Monsignor, distancing herself from Lydia.

Lydia glared at her.

The older woman gave them both a surprised look. Once behind the safety of the Monsignor she appeared to grow in confidence and size, like a lap-dog in pursuit of a stranger who had turned their backs to walk away. "Would you like me... to call the police?" There was almost satisfaction in her desperate tone.

Really?

Lydia suddenly felt sorry for the older woman.

It was almost as if the Monsignor could read the expression on Lydia's face, and knew what she was thinking. He glanced briefly down at the purse Lydia was clutching tightly against her chest, and then back up to Lydia's eyes. "No, no, that won't be necessary," his voice still calm and in control.

"Are you sure, I can—"

"No, I'm sure! That'll be all, Mrs. Gertrude," he warned. "Good night!"

"But—"

"That'll be all, Mrs. Gertrude!" His words sounded final.

"Ohhh, yes, Monsignor. G-g-good n-n-night then!" she sounded subdued and disappointed.

"Good night!" Monsignor's eyes never leaving Lydia's.

Lydia watched the older woman slink off backwards, then turn and quickly disappear down the hall after a long last look. Her eyes never leaving them until she was out of sight.

When Lydia turned back towards Monsignor, he was still standing at the front door smiling at her. She flinched and took a couple of steps backwards.

"Uhh, Monsignor," she spoke quickly, she wanted to say her piece before he had a chance to throw her out. "My name is Lydia—"

"I know..." he interrupted, "Lydia Wilson, yer' deceased husbands name was Gabriel. Ye' 'ave a son named Gabe. What's he now, 15, a young man. It's been a long ten years Lydia." He spoke calmly, his eyes studying her closely. "So what's this matter of life an' death?"

"I really need your help." She looked up into his caring eyes and jumpstarted her thoughts, "There are things going on, strange things. I... I just don't know what to do or where to begin!"

The Monsignor looked up at the ceiling for a moment, as if smelling the air, and when he looked back down. She thought she saw a tear in his eyes.

"Are you okay?" Lydia asked, surprised by the sudden change.

"Yes, yes, I am, thank ye' fer askin'," he forced a laugh. "I knew that someday ye'd return. An' now, here ye' are. Welcome back." He extended his hand to her.

She took it with her free hand, her other arm tucked her purse into her chest even tighter. When done her hand quickly joined the other wrapped around her purse.

He motioned toward the door on the far side of the hallway. "Come, let us sit an' talk." He gestured peaceably towards her with opened arms and cleared his throat. "By the way, Mrs. Gertrude is only tryin' te' do her job. Since her husband passed about a year ago," he spoke with a sincere delicacy, "she 'as gone through a very difficult time. Ye' do understan'... she is very protective, ye' know."

Lydia nodded. She didn't know what to say. She forced her thoughts away from the frail, older woman to the safety of her family. She was now one step closer to finding answers.

He twisted the knob of the wood-paneled door, off to the left and pushed it open. He reached into the darkness. The interior of the small office brightened, making the foyer look dim and uninviting in comparison. He turned toward her and smiled again. "We can talk in my office if ye' would like."

She nodded.

Any place but out here!

He gave her a knowing glance.

God, I sure hoped he couldn't read minds.

Several years of catholic school had elevated the clergy, in her mind, to the point of the nuns and priests being proficient in ESP... Extra Sensory Perception.

The Monsignors, being the Jedi of the order.

Upon her nod, he turned and walked toward the huge, dark mahogany desk located in the center of the room.

She followed. Her first glimpse of Monsignor's office told her she was in the right place. Her eyes were treated to the standard picture of Joseph and the blessed Mary both garnished in halos, looking lovingly down at the also haloed, infant Jesus. It was the standard birth scene of Jesus Christ, except the infant Jesus was a toddler with a full head of hair, and the size to go with it. Then there was the stationary photograph of Pope John Paul II, a seemingly standard requirement in every catholic rectory, household, and work place.

She took a couple of steps, and then abruptly stopped. It was like running into a pocket of sweet, burning incense. The fragrance tickled her nose and made her cough. She searched for its source with her eyes, but surprisingly she couldn't find it.

To her left was a long book case, the same color as the desk, which ran half the length of the wall. It was filled with an assortment of books, many looking old and well used.

Most likely antiques.

She breathed in again, filling her lungs in an attempt to find its source.

Yep, incense-the sweet smelling expensive stuff.

It blended with the aroma of leather and old, musty books.

But, where's its source?

Certificates and diplomas in gold and black frames cluttered the wall like in a professional's office. Framed pictures of a variety of scenes graced the opposite wall. Below them sat another bookcase similar to the first, but most of those books looked newer.

A library to keep up with the growing problems of the modern day parish no doubt!

There seemed to be no shortage of silver and gold, ornate crosses; several hung from every usable space on the wall.

A priceless collection no doubt?

A medium-sized picture on the wall behind her caught her attention. The gold color, based on everything she had seen thus far, might actually have been real gold. The gold frame was a work of art in itself. There in the picture, standing side by side, were a much younger-looking Monsignor and the Holy Father, John Paul II. They were all dressed in red, white and gold religious regalia. By its position on the wall, this was probably the most prized possession in the whole office.

Monsignor cleared his throat. "Would ye' like to sit down?"

She flinched when Monsignor spoke, she had almost forgotten that he was even there. When she looked back toward him, he was standing behind his desk, gesturing with a hand toward one of the four black leather chairs in front of the desk.

"Thank you," she forced a smile, "for seeing me!" She stepped forward and sat down into one of the soft leather chairs. Surprisingly, it didn't squeak or make flatulent noises as she thought it would.

He nodded, satisfied, and then sat down into his own chair behind the desk.

They both quietly sat there staring at each other before either of them spoke, the Monsignor not wanting to rush the moment, and Lydia not knowing exactly how to ask the questions. He casually made the motion of tiding up his already neat desk, so as to not pressure her. She could feel his excited energy. It radiated from his half of the room. She was pretty sure that he felt the same way about her. She scanned his desk; it was surprisingly empty, immaculately clean.

What's wrong with that? A cluttered desk usually meant a cluttered mind.

There was something else that was odd. The smell of incense... it was gone.

She looked about confused.

"I smelled incense, when I first came in, but now I don't know!"

He nodded silently before he spoke, his hands folded as if in prayer, his eyes peering into hers like he was studying her closely.

"It kinda' comes an' goes. A mystery in itself really." He shrugged his shoulders. "Old smells that tend te' linger in an old house."

She politely nodded.

He then pulled open a drawer and pulled out a half bottle of scotch and two eight ounce glasses. "From others before me."

He placed them on coasters, and then filled them a quarter full.

"Care fer' a drink?"

She gave him a disapproving stare.

"Doctor's orders." He shrugged off her gaze and offered her one of the glasses, his hand trembling slightly. A tremble that wasn't there a moment earlier. His confidence seemed to be waning.

She shook her head again disapprovingly.

"Helps me put thin's inte' perspective... relieves stress... settles me' nerves." He tipped one of the glasses towards her and finished it in a couple of swallows. When finished he let out a sigh of approval. "Directly from the mother country, Dublin Ireland. Prepares me' fer' the unusual."

The unusual?

Her thoughts were the opposite. Ten years ago she had become a recluse, and renounced her faith out of frustration. Her world had stopped spinning in one direction and started to spin in the other. Now, with the recent series of events, the world itself seemed to have stopped spinning altogether, and her gravity field was coming loose. The vague details were becoming clear.

He nodded as if he understood and slid the scotch bottle back into the drawer and quietly closed it.

She looked towards the wall past him, avoiding his prying eyes. She didn't want him to read her thoughts about his drinking.

Did he have problems of his own?

She wondered if the stereotype of the overworked priest were true.

It was then that she noticed the painting of what appeared to be, for all practical purposes, an angel, sitting on a rocky outcropping overlooking a mist-shrouded redwood valley below.

The Monsignor smiled as he exaggerated filling his lungs and making an extra effort to noisily exhale. "No, I don't smell any incense!" He shrugged. "All I smell are these leather chairs," he patted his chair. "Old books," he gestured to the book cases, "maybe some paint... a cheap air freshener an' an empty glass of scotch." He shook his head and cleared his throat again. "From time te' time, others 'ave also said they've smelled it, the incense. I guess my sniffer has gone bad!" he said tapping his nose. His free hand still fidgeted nervously with the empty glass.

Denial!

"The figure, the angel in the painting?" she nodded in its direction without looking at him. She slowly stood up from her chair and walked over to the painting for a closer look.

The Monsignor reluctantly turned in his chair and followed her movement with his eyes. "The angel?" The tone of his voice held a hidden knowledge. She could sense it.

"Yes, I know I've seen him before, the figure in the painting. Where did you get it?" She shifted her gaze back to him in time to see him raise an eyebrow. She felt he knew more than he was letting her see. He was starting to look uncomfortable.

"T'was a gift, given te' me after seminary school, years ago." He leaned back in his chair and crossed himself with his arms, "T'was given te' me by one of the Carmelite Sisters, Sister Ann Marguerite. She grew up locally here, passed away several years ago. Bless her soul!" He toasted the ceiling with the second glass, crossed himself with his free hand and took a sip. It was like he was building up the nerve to share a secret. "She said t'was the *Guardian Angel of the Redwoods*." He paused for a moment as if giving what he was about to say next some serious thought. "Steven, yes I believed she called the Guardian Angel of the Redwoods, Steven. She said he liked te' be called Steven. She painted him one day while he was surveying the valley." The Monsignor shrugged his shoulders. "So the story goes." He took another sip of scotch, this one longer. He was starting to perspire.

"While he was overlooking the valley?" she quizzed.

"Tis' what she said, overlooking the redwood valley!"

"That place looks familiar."

"Does it now?" he held the second glass as he continued to examine the painting.

"I think I've seen him!" She leaned in closer as she continued to stare at the painting.

"What?" His eyes were now on her. "all ye' can see is the back of his head."

"I know I've seen that angel you call *Steven*, the same one here in the picture!" She gave him a quick glance and pointed toward the painting. She examined it even closer.

"From where, may I ask?"

She looked him in the eye before she spoke. "In my study at home!" she was matter of fact.

Monsignor coughed. "Yer' study?"

"Yes!" She looked back towards the painting.

He examined her closely through narrow eyes for a moment before he took another sip of the scotch. The shake to his hand had gotten worse. "Ye' wouldn't be the first te' 'ave made such a claim."

She turned directly toward him and without a single fluctuation in her voice or the slightest change in her facial expression, she started the chain reaction that would forever effect how the Monsignor would think.

"I think I've also seen Gabriel!"

The Monsignor sat up in his chair and almost spilled the rest of his drink down the front of his shirt. "Excuse me?"

Now that she had his attention, she could explain to him what had been going on. Her only hope was that he would understand, that he would believe. She needed his help, and she needed it right then and there. Her biggest fear was that she might be too late. Something not so nice was happening on that cursed mountain. She could feel it. It was happening again! She felt a sudden panic attack rip through her entire body. She stepped backwards and gripped the edge of the desk. Her fingers and toes tingled, and then went numb. Her body shivered uncontrollably. Her heart rate increased; a pressure formed against her lungs, her heart pounded in her ears.

Oh God, it was happening again!

***

Did she just say what I thought she said? Gabriel is dead; I recited over his funeral meself'. I issued the Blessed Sacrament, the anointin' of the sick!

Monsignor narrowed his eyes, and roughly set his glass down on the desk. He missed the doily as the glass slipped out of his hand and spilled what was left of his drink on the immaculate desktop. But he didn't care. He shifted his desperate eyes in between Mrs. Wilson and the mess he had just made. He looked for something to wipe it up with, but there wasn't anything. He normally didn't spill his drinks like this. Now he had two messes to clean up. He opened the drawer and pulled out a cloth and started wiping up the spill.

A mess of me' doin' an' the other...? Did this 'ave anything to do with the second?

Mrs. Wilson collapsed into a heap of convulsing misery and tears.

One second I thought I was strong an' in control, an' now this! Lord, give me strength!

"Mrs. Wilson, are ye' alright?" Monsignor quickly rose up from behind his desk and moved around to her other side, to her aid. When he reached her he abruptly stopped. He started to reach out for her, to comfort her, but he hesitated. His eyes searched the open door to his office.

"Where is that Mrs. Gertrude?" he whispered under his breath.

It's durin' times like t'is that she shined, but she was not herself today which was particularly odd. What had gotten into her?

He had sent her away. He was on his own. He looked up toward the ceiling and then back towards the painting on the wall behind his desk.

Had she really seen Gabriel? Had she really seen Steven?

Those thoughts alone gave him chills. He was now entering a realm he had not spent much time in before. It was like being an elite warrior-you train and train for that one day when they actually call you into duty, for the impossible mission.

Dear, Lord, give me strength...

He reached over and gently placed his trembling hand onto her shoulder. He looked down at his hand.

Why am I tremblin'... why am I havin' so much trouble with this?

Instead of pulling away or stepping back from the chair, Lydia turned towards him, wrapped her arms around his waist and cut loose with teary emotion. Her body convulsed as she sobbed uncontrollably.

Her quick movement caught him by surprise, he found his balance and gently place a hand on her shoulder.

"What is tis' all about?" Monsignor spoke softly, with tender understanding.

History had a way of repeating itself. The cycle would continue until it was finally put to rest.

He looked over to the crosses that lined the room.

Are ye' talkin' te' the right man? Who am I te' be dealin' with the likes of all of this?

It caught him by surprise. At first he let go, but then braced himself against the chair and the edge of the desk for balance. A moment later, he again rested a hand on her shoulder to comfort her. As he patted her gently, consoling her, his eyes were drawn to the painting, then to one of the leather chairs. His thoughts were whisked away to another time and place...

"Monsignor, so what am I supposed to make of all of this? I have been asked to believe in my faith, to follow my heart, to do what is asked of me." The young man's expressive eyes burned into his. "But at the same time, I never see the messenger. People think I'm nuts, my wife thinks I'm nuts." He gave out a deep sigh, sank deeply into the leather chair and, in submissive desperation, lowered his gaze to the floor. Stepping down, asking for help, was obviously something that he wasn't used to doing. "Why is this happening to me?"

The confident Monsignor fought to maintain his knowledgeable stare as his insides flip-flopped, making him feel woozy just to think about all of this. If only he could get a dime for every time those questions were asked of him out of desperation.

"What is tis' young man sayin'?"

He was projecting all the signs of a schizophrenic patient who hadn't maintained his self-medication schedule. As it was, more people came to him for help. They got frustrated, thought that they were getting better, and they stopped taking their medication. There were the ones who hadn't been officially diagnosed yet, and then there were the ones who were, out of desperation, turning to God for a cure. Times were changing, and changing fast. The stress of our society was relentlessly crashing down on more and more souls. It was like the end was near.

They all needed help, but it wasn't he who cured them. He was nothing but a messenger. It was God who gave him the power to advise and gave him the power to recommend alternatives. It was through God that he prayed for and with them.

The strange thing about this one, was that there was sincerity to what he was saying. He had seen him in church on most Sundays with his wife and young child. It was obvious there was something going on in this man's life. There was something to be said about greeting someone at the end of every mass. It was one thing to shake their hands, to look them in the eye, but it was very different to have them come to his office and unload their concerns, to drop their tales of bizarreness right into his lap and expect results, expect cures. The man worked in the woods. It was there that he did God's bidding. He kept park visitors safe and educated, protecting a resource for numerous generations to come, so they could see the beauty of God's handiwork. Before seminary school, it was something he had thought about doing as a career, back in Ireland as well; but that wasn't meant to be. God had wanted him to be a priest.

So, what was I supposed te' think? What was I supposed te' do...?

Monsignor cleared his throat. "So, let me see if I be understan'n what yer' sayin'." He was trained to play it back.

The young man nodded expectantly, his eyes burning right through his. Monsignor could see the sparkle of hope. It helped prod him along.

He repeated, 'Voices tell ye' te' save people by puttin' yer' own safety in jeoperdy? Ye' don't see these people that speak te' ye?' Please don't take tis' defensively, but 'ave ye' thought about seekin' professional help?" He saw the young man's body bristle, he had begun to protest so he raised a hand to stop him. "Mr. Wilson, ye' 'ave heard of post-traumatic stress 'ave yer' now?"

Gabriel nodded. "I'm familiar, but what does this have to do with it?"

"Everythin', tis' 'appens in all forms of traumatic employment, even in the priesthood. It's nothin' te' be ashamed of, 'appens te' many. It's the result of repeated stress put on the body an' mind an' with no way te' properly release it. Do ye' 'ave friends ye' can talk too, 'ave ye' talked with yer' wife?"

"It was her idea that I come talk to you!" Gabriel was so matter of fact.

"Good, a supportive wife." Monsignor could tell he was pulling together his thoughts. He braced himself for the rebuttal.

"Fair enough!" Gabriel nodded in agreement, and then gave him that knowing look.

Monsignor felt a strange, uncomfortable chill begin to work its way through the length of his body. He felt something coming.

*"What would you say if I told you that others have seen a guardian angel looking out for me? They've seen a young man standing there next to me during my rescues, a young man who disappears, a young man by the name of **Steven**."*

Monsignor felt the goose bumps crawl up his back as he slowly leaned backwards into his chair and attempted to rub the tingle out of his arms. He turned his head toward the painting that hung on the wall to his right and then back toward Gabriel. He had never talked about the painting with anyone.

"I, could understand that if it were just me hearing voices, I could say that maybe there actually is something to this post traumatic stuff; but been there, done that. I'd say were a bit beyond post and traumatic. We're well on our way to something entirely different." Gabriel sat up straight in his chair and spoke with emotion. *"When you think you hear the voices in the wind as it whistles across the landscape, or when you hear entire conversations coming from a cascading creek and river. Is it the little people that live in the forest that God put there? Is it just the way the acoustics of the sounds play against the topography that God put there? Is it my ears and imagination that God gave me?"* He smiled. *"Is it God speaking to me and you? Were all of the prophets crazy? Taking everything into consideration, if I were indeed crazy as some would insinuate, the fix would be simple, wouldn't it? Take these two pills every six hours and see me in the morning!"* he forced a laugh.

Gabriel's words flowed without hesitation as they passed through his mind and entered his heart. He felt sorrowful, desperation. Gabriel leaned in closer to him, his eyes burning into his own.

"Do I look crazy to you Monsignor?" *Gabriel's voice was calm and direct, his eyes peering.* "I came here for help and understanding, but I don't think that's what I'm getting."

"So, why wait until now te' talk with me on tis' matter?" *the priest asked as he leaned farther back in his chair and folded his hands against the bottom of his chin.*

Gabriel forced a smile and leaned back in his chair as well, creating space between them. "Because, up until now, things were status-quo. The voice tells me where to be, and what to do. I don't understand how it all works," *he shrugs his shoulders,* "But it does. As things have become more and more complicated, I now need to know why!"

"Why?"

Gabriel nodded, his face solemn and serious. He lowered his eyes as they suddenly began to water. "Why? Because I am told that I will soon perish." *The tears began to flow, his breathing erratic, and his body shuddering. Gabriel was fighting it.* "I have done all that has been asked of me. Now to be told this...." *His voice trailed off. He shook his head in disappointment and confusion. His eyes drifted down towards his lap again.*

"Who told ye' this?" *Monsignor narrowed his eyes.*

Gabriel looked back up into his caring face.

"What is to become of my family? What is to become of my son?"

The Monsignor stared at him. It was then that he smelled the burning incense in his office.

Frankincense is it, one of the gifts of the three kings?

His eyes shot around the office, nothing obvious.

How strange!

He remembered hearing once that the arrivals of angels were preceded with aroma of ancient herbs. The thought made his body tremble. He searched the room until his eyes fell upon the painting.

Steven, the angel that protects the ancient redwoods. God? Is tis' a test of me' own faith?

All of the thoughts that he had pulled together to share had vanished. For the first time, he was utterly speechless.

Gabriel had found a calm buried deep beneath the chaotic frenzy he called his life. He wiped the tears from his eyes with the backs of his hands and apologized for his sudden outburst. He told the whole bizarre story from the beginning. He explained how it had all begun, how the strangeness had built up over the years to what it was now. In the end, he asked to receive the sacraments of Confession, Communion, and then the anointing of the sick.

So he did without any further questions. Within a couple of weeks, per his widow's request, he had laid Gabriel's spirit to rest. Or so he thought!

When his thoughts returned, she was still there, her arms still wrapped tightly around his waist. He reached over and pulled one of the chairs next to hers. He gently extricated himself from her grip, and quietly sat her down in one of the chairs. He sat down in the one next to her. He held one of her delicate hands sandwiched carefully between his. Her hands looked so small.

Oh God anytime now!

Now was when he needed to deliver the appropriate message. He felt the urgency; it was all around them. Something was definitely going on. He gazed at all of the crosses that covered the walls of his office. They were more than an expensive collection of ornate porcelain, wood and precious metals. They were like his own special *New Grange*-ancient Winter Solstice archeological, religious site.

A place in Ireland where the first rays of the rising sun were designed to follow the spiral patterns and symbols carved into the stones by an ancient society. On the shortest day of the year the lowest angle of light illuminated the burial chamber at the back of the tomb. The magical place was created well before St Patrick brought Christianity to Ireland in the 5th century.

Like the concentric grove of ancient redwood trees allegedly planted by fairies. He had collected these crosses on his trips around the world, every one of them with a special history, held special meaning. His office was his little chapel, his crosses were his divine batteries to help with his connection with God.

Now is when I need te' test it. Now is when I need it te' work.

"Lydia, ye' said that ye' saw Gabriel?" his voice still sounded surprised. Monsignor couldn't believe that he was even asking that question. He was taught to believe Jesus had risen from the dead, that he visited the apostles to proclaim the truth. Despite all of the miracles he had conducted while he was alive, including raising people from the dead, some of them still didn't believe until the moment they put their fingers into the holes of Christ's hands, feet and side.

Am I that doubting Thomas? Do I need te' put me' fingers into the holes of her stories?

She nodded as she wiped the tears from her eyes.

He just about fell out of his chair.

Did she just answer me' or was it just a coincidence?

"I know this is going to sound crazy," Lydia continued, her eyes still shut, her face pointed towards the floor. "He was in my

study yesterday and I felt his presence again late this afternoon while I was out in the garden." Her voice was so matter-of-fact. "I was reading through his journal."
The garden... the journal?
She nodded again.
How?
He shuddered noticeably. He watched her squeeze her purse tightly to her chest. Her eyes now open and burned into his, begging for him to understand. He could tell that she was trying to determine if he believed her or not. He wasn't so sure at this point, but this had history, a pretty bizarre one at that. He nodded to encourage her, something strange was indeed going on.

"Evidently, he left messages for his family, he left messages for us." She sat back noisily into her chair, hesitated a moment, then pulled the leather bound journal out of her purse and set it on her lap. "He even left a message for you!" Her fingers slid nervously back and forth across its tooled leather cover.

"A message fer' me... how can that be?"
Believe!
The thought made him suddenly feel week. He watched her actions closely.

"Oh, how could I have been so stupid?" she screamed excitedly as she covered her face with the palm of her hand. The pitch in her voice made Monsignor flinched and back away.

How embarrassin', fer' a grown man te' react like that!

She ignored his reaction and continued. "He left me messages and I ended up hiding the book up in the attic for ten years. Then there it was a few days ago, in my son's hands." She dropped her hands and looked into the monsignor's eyes.

It was as if she read the confusion on his face.

"He tried to explain it to me, but... no, I wouldn't listen. He tried to explain everything that was happening to him. But I was too wrapped up in hating the church, hating God for taking Gabriel away from us."

He released her hand and folded his own hands on his lap. He gave her an encouraging nod, forced an understanding smile, and sat back in his chair. The *confusion*, the *anger*, and the *blaming*-he had seen it all before. *Desperation, emotional turmoil*-someone had to be accountable. Someone had to be at fault.

Bad thin's just don't 'appen te' good people!
The naive words rang in his head.
But they do an' they did. They always did an' most likely always will. The chess game of good versus evil.

A humor check? Pushing people te' their breakin' points, just te' break 'em down, only te' build t'em back up again fer' better or fer' worse. Te', make 'em stronger, more durable, preparin' 'em fer' the Rapture? Takin' the good, leavin' the bad. Only God could make that decision. We all 'ave good an' evil tightly intertwined aroun' our souls. Tis' one of those mysteries of faith. Tis' bein' human... Gabriel's message!

He could no longer ignore the words. "Lydia, did he truly 'ave a message for me?" his words were soft, gentle.

She nodded and looked up at him. "Yes, *he* did."

He shifted his gaze in between her face and the journal she held tightly in her arms.

"May I see it, please?" he gently held out his hand.

She shifted her gaze in between him and the journal.

At first he couldn't tell what she was thinking. She gently ran her fingers along the brown leather journal.

"You have a right to its messages just like the rest of us." Her voice was kind and understanding.

His curious eyes followed her every movement. Tooled into the leather cover was a mountain setting, ancient looking trees.

Lydia set her purse onto the floor, opened the journal flat in her lap. She silently paged through it until she found what she was looking for, her eyes never leaving the journal.

She gave out a heavy sigh before she quietly spoke. "Gabriel, now it is your turn to save your son."

She gently passed the open journal to Monsignor O'Toole's awaiting hands. She looked him directly in the eye before she spoke. "His words to you, two weeks before he disappeared... Monsignor O'Toole."

Monsignor nodded a thank you before he accepted the book. He felt his heart race and his respirations increase.

"A message fer' me from a man that 'ad been dead fer' goin' on ten years now. The bible was a message te' me, written by men that 'ave been dead fer' 2,000 years."

The whole thought had given him the chills. His hands shook, his throat parched. He forced his eyes to focus on every word. He turned the journal around and placed it in front of him. He then cleared his throat and forced himself to read it out loud...

"Monsignor O'Toole... If you're readin' this, were probably at a crucial turnin' point in this strange series of events. As I told ye' at me' visit, I never wanted this, I never asked fer' this but here we ar', answerin' the call."

Monsignor shot a glance over to Lydia, she was smiling. He read on out loud, his mind processing.

"Neither me' son or me' wife asked fer' this but 'ere we all ar'. I don't know what it will take te' convince ye', a man of the cloth who's teachin's are buildt on faith an' trust from a book called the Holy Bible. Father, yer' assistance is crucial. Whatever ye'll do will make or break what 'appens next. Maybe ye' didn't believe me or believe in yer'self, but ye' 'ave te' believe me' wife Lydia. She 'as come for yer' help, ye' ar' her last 'ope at changin' the outcome of what 'ill happen on that god forsaken mountain. Blood runs deep in family, ye an' the church, they ar' all family too!"

When he looked over to Lydia again tears were rolling down her cheeks.

"There was somethin' familiar about that paintin' in yer' office. The one with the youn' man overlookin' the redwood forest from his perch on a rock. I think I know who he is now. He's the man me' brother an' others 'ad described as the guardian angel that was seen with me. I guess I will finally get te' meet him very soon.

"I know me' visit was a lot te' swallow. I wouldn't 'ave believed it me'self if I 'adn't breathed it, felt it, an' lived it. Let's try this again. God 'as a plan for ye' too, he 'as plans for all of us. Thanks for the blessin', it wasn't in vain. Yer' beloved servent... Gabriel Wilson."

By the time he was done reading he had tears running down his cheeks as well.

"Thank ye' Gabriel, I believe ye', an' I am very sorry that I didn't." he whispered under his breath as he carefully closed the journal and handed it back to Lydia.

"Thank you." He said to her.

She gently took the book from his hands and slid it back into her purse on the floor.

He silently stared in disbelief as Lydia ran through everything that had happened to them over the last couple of weeks.

Though he had never seen angels, he believed that they existed. He believed that, for better or for worse, they influenced a human's decision to be at the right place at the right time, to make the right choices. Gabriel was a prime example of that. Choice, it is what made humans so special... like with Adam and Eve in the Garden of Eden, and the creation of original sin. Most people are inherently good, a product of their society. But evil is among us. It rears its ugly head every day. Its influences strong among many, violating the Ten Commandments as if they meant nothing. He turned towards the crosses and began to speak out loud.

"When the angels come down te' earth te' escort our souls te' heaven," he continued, "or te' deliver 'em te' hell, we need te' be ready. Tis' murder? Do those laws only apply 'ere on earth? Te' be returned from the dead?" He silently glanced down at the large golden ring he was wearing and gently fondled it with his fingers a moment before he looked down into Lydia's sorrowful eyes.

"Yes, the bible speaks of it. Jesus 'ad brought the dead back te' life te' make a point. Jesus revisited his disciples after his crucifixion, he died fer' the sins of man, te' rally the troops, te' restore hope. But, fer' Gabriel te' come back from the dead te' visit? For words in a journal te' be a message from the grave? That's not the Catholic way!"

He shook his head, keeping his thoughts to himself.

Tis' demonic? Wouldn't God send an angel, not the dead themselves?

He felt a cold chill spread throughout his body. For a moment, he thought he saw his breath in the chilling air. He curiously passed his hand through the pocket of mist. It swirled around his fingers before it disappeared. He backed away from it.

A sign?

Lydia still sat there staring up at him in disbelief, studying his reaction, waiting for him to say something different than the disappointing rambling that left his lips. She had just poured a story from her heart that she dared not share with anyone else.

And that is what I told her!

He saw the urgency in her eyes. He felt the hair stand up on his arms, the chill down his spine.

He pressed his hands more tightly together and intertwined his fingers as he nervously looked over his shoulder. He didn't want to admit that he felt another presence in the room.

They appeared to be alone, but were they really?

This was his sanctuary. Only the likes of God could enter and leave at will. He shivered noticeably at the thought.

There it was in front of him, the war between good and evil had involved the next generation. He didn't like to use the word, cursed, but for all practical purposes and for the lack of a better word, the word seemed to fit. It appeared the Wilson family was indeed, God forbid, cursed. Death was rearing its ugly head again. He knew that God worked in mysterious ways.

But tis'?

Gabriel's confession came crashing back quickly. Each of his rescues became more and more difficult, testing his mind, his body and his faith. No wonder they thought, as he said, that he had sold his soul to the devil. Most likely, if he had, he still would have been alive today. There was no doubt in his mind that he had been guided and protected by angels, right up until the point that he perished in the process of saving yet another.

Was his son Gabe te' take over where the father 'ad left off? Wasn't Gabriel's sacrifice enough?

Monsignor looked down at Lydia's purse where the leather bound journal was sitting.

"What did Gabriel say about goin'... did he say anythin' about goin' back up te' the mountains?"

Lydia looked up at him with her teary eyes. "No, not exactly. He talked about doing what he was being asked to do, fulfilling his destiny." She no longer seemed solid and confident. "Dan, Gabe, and his friend Erick, all felt they needed to go up to the mountains. There was something immediate about their being up there today."

He narrowed his eyes. "Have they gone up there yet?" he fidgeted nervously with his hands. "It isn't too late te' stop 'em, right?"

She shook her head and then looked into his eyes. "They went up yesterday."

"Te' the mountains!" The panic was evident in his voice.

"Yes!" the confusion was noted in hers.

"The very place that took Gabriel's life? On the tenth anniversary of his death, an'... an', you let 'em go?" He stood up abruptly from his chair, and began to pace back and forth in his office, running his hand through his thinning hair.

Lydia's eyes followed. "They thought that was where they needed to...," panic began to build in her face, her eyes burned towards Monsignor. "You don't think they should've gone?"

He interlaced his fingers on the back of his neck, his eyes peering into the painting. "I don't know what te' think." He stopped pacing in front of her chair and looked down into her eyes. He dropped his hands. "They are not there alone. God will send his angels down te' protect 'em," his tone unconvincing.

"Like they did Gabriel!" Her words bit deeply into him. "Where were they when Gabriel needed them? Where were they?" Her eyes began to water. "I have come here asking for your help. I have come here asking for God's help." She shot a glance around the room.

"An' help ye'll receive..."

He first felt it in his hands and fingers. It then wiggled its way down to his toes. His eyes followed. Then the powerful scent of frankincense filled his lungs. His mouth lay agape.

Frankincense... why frankincense? Frankincense is the fragrant gum resin from trees livin' on the sandy coast of Arabia.

He gently shook his head. His linear, analytical thoughts flowed freely as he searched for answers.

The incense resin was used in incence an' perfunes, ancient times in the religious rites, embalmin' the dead by the Egyptians. T'was one of the three gifts bestowed on baby Jesus an' the holy family by the three wise men from afar. Gold, frankincense an' myrrh, gifts te' the new king. King Herod, who believed ther' could only be one king, wanted baby Jesus put to death! Did Herod know that he was attemptin' te' destroy humanity's hope? Was the gift of frankincense or fer' that matter Myrrh a warnin'?

What about the frankincense that I smell now? Am I te' prepare Lydia for Gabe's ultimate end, te' prepare fer' Gabe's death?

His eyes suddenly focused on Lydia's.

She stared frightfully into his.

"Tis' a reminder of the power of prayer... the ultimate power of God?" he sounded surprised at the words he spoke. "Death would eventually encompass us all, but not our souls. Our soul will live forever. By the grace of God an' his army of angels, Jesus had survived Herod's plot. Tis' Gabe te' survive his ordeal, as well? Prayin' is what we'll do then, with our whole heart an' soul. Yes, we will pray."

Monsignor stood proudly, he no longer felt alone inside. There was hope. There was understanding; he knew how Gabriel must have felt, when all seemed lost until that very moment when backup had arrived. Out of the corners of his eyes, he thought he had saw shadows. Only, they weren't shadows in the sense of darkness, but were dark silhouettes lurking in the corners. The room suddenly became brighter, warmer; the crosses seemed to almost glow. A tremendous joy filled his heart with love and understanding. It was time to reassure Lydia of the same; that God was here for her, he was here for them all.

Monsignor knelt onto the floor and nodded towards her to do the same.

At first she stared frightfully up at him, but then he saw the recognition in her face, the eternal love in her eyes. She understood.

Lydia gazed around the room in wonderment before she lowered herself submissively to her knees as well.

He reached down and gently caressed both of her hands in his. "We'll pray." He forced a smile as he looked around the room. His gaze took in every cross, every certificate and every picture, only resting on the painting of Steven, the angel, a moment before they fell to rest back on hers. Her eyes followed as if she knew exactly what he was thinking. He trembled with excitement. "We'll call up a legion of angels te' look after 'em. This time, there'll be so many angels surroundin' 'em that the devil an' his army won't even be able te' get close."

CHAPTER THIRTY-THREE
AN AIR OF CHANCE
MARCH 16ᵀᴴ 2000

The gusty winds pulled, snapped and tugged at the edges of the tarp shelter that Gabe had hastily constructed. He secured it against a group of small boulders about ten yards away from the edge of the drop off. He surprised himself. He still didn't know how he got the bungee and parachute chords to wrap around and hook to the natural edges of the boulder, but despite the tugging of the gusty surges, they held.

First time luck, second time skill?

He hoped he wouldn't have to find out. The time between the blue flashes and the bone-jarring, deafening rumbles had been reduced, which only meant that the lightning was getting closer. He tried not to count the seconds, but his mind had done it automatically. The thunderheads were funneling through the mountains in his direction. Hidden behind the boulders, they were sheltered from a direct assault by the elements. He hoped they were hidden from the powerful lightning that searched for high and lonely objects to wield its power against as well.

With nothing impeding its path, the gusts of wind sounded like an approaching freight train as it pulled and snapped at the tarp. The gusts whistled through the tops of the trees and across the rocks. The rocky outcropping in the middle of the devastation seemed to be the wind's focal point. In combination with the thunderheads, it felt like the end of the world was at hand. Even the frogs and crickets had chosen silence. Gabe had to reach deeply into himself to dissipate his panic. The strange whispers and the hoots of the great horned owl had blended into the demented conversations of the intimidating storm.

He sat there dripping wet, feeling 20 degrees warmer beneath the tarp, and hoping that everything would hold itself together, as he stared down at the face of the girl who lay unconscious in front of him. The light of his headlamp reflected off the shiny foil of the emergency blanket that cocooned her, making the enclosure brighter. Though her dark mascara had smudged and smeared, and her eyebrow ring, lip posts, and nose stud protruded from her delicate face, giving her a scary look amongst the accumulation of blood and dirt, he still found her attractive beneath it all.

She's cute!

The thought surprised him. Her jet-black hair was matted and caked with dirt and debris that the rain hadn't washed free. Evidently her dark clothes held some warmth, most likely because of a blend of synthetics. Her dirt-stained rain parka was frayed along the sleeves, indicating that it was well-used. Instead of hiking boots, she wore only one black and white canvas, high-top basketball shoe. He was surprised he hadn't noticed that before. The shoe and sock were missing from her mud caked, injured left leg. Her foot was dirty beyond recognition, her lower leg, below her knee was noticeably deformed. He would have to wash off the rest of the mud on her lower leg just to examine her injury. She wasn't dressed for the severe conditions they were in. For that matter, neither was he but at least he had prepared for rain and cold. No matter, now all they had to do was wait out the storm and hope the makeshift shelter held. The last part was pretty easy, sit and wait.

But her injuries... I'm not a doctor. He's a she!

He kept telling himself. He hadn't sat this close to a girl for this long before. He was out of his element in more ways than he could understand. Now they were both safe. He still needed to examine and treat her injuries. She lay there peacefully, appeared to be asleep. Surprisingly, she wasn't shaking from the cold. The thought concerned him.

Is she in the later stages of hypothermia?

During the later stages the body stops shaking and the victim actually thinks they're getting warm. In reality, their systems are slowly shutting down, they're slowly dying. Cooling off from the outside in!

He slipped off his leather gloves, reached under the blanket and held her closest hand. He slipped her arm out from under the space blanket to examine it for injuries. Her dirty hand seemed so small. Now only the silver rings on her fingers felt cold to his touch. He gave out a sigh of relief as he gave her finger tips a gentle squeeze to check her capillary refill. Her circulation was good. He wiped most of the dirt from her hands. It was about her wrist that he noticed the older scars that ran perpendicular to the bottom side of her wrist.

Very odd.

He made it a point to carefully avoid snagging on her jewelry.

He gently touched her face with the back of his hand.

"Warm enough."

That was a good start.

He cleared his throat. "Hello, hello!" He timidly yelled over the rain and the wind, as the elements clawed away at the tarp in tandem. He nudged her a bit harder.

She moaned and rolled towards his hand and into the beam of his headlamp. His instinct was to pull his hand away, but he held his ground. He felt his pulse rate quicken. Now she looked even more beautiful.

"Hello... my name's Gabe. I'm here to rescue you!" His voice crackled with nervousness. He squeezed her hand and this time gently shook her shoulder.

To his surprise her eyes first fluttered then opened to slits. She used her free hand to deflect the bright glare out of her eyes.

"Sorry!" Gabe exclaimed. He shifted the beam of his headlamp away from her face and focused it more on her mid torso.

She opened her mouth and gasped, a surprised scowl etched across her face.

"So, I'm still alive?" she softly grumbled.

He looked on curiously as her eyes searched around the tarped enclosure.

"Where... am I?" Her low whisper was barely audible over the noise of the storm outside. Her voice sounded deeper than he expected.

"You're in a shelter. I found you out there," Gabe nodded toward the direction of the cliff and the darkness. The light temporarily illuminated the calming, bright blue of the enclosure.

She turned her head in the direction of the tarp wall and then back towards Gabe. "Looks like I screwed up again!" she exclaimed under her breath. Her eyes drifted down towards the hand that Gabe was still holding, and then back up to his face. "Why are you holding my hand?" She forced a smile, but didn't make any effort to pull her hand away.

"Oh, I'm, I mean, we're here to rescue you!" He suddenly felt embarrassed. He tried to release her hand but she reached out with her other hand and held his tightly between hers.

"Your hands are warm," she said.

He saw a similar scars on the lower side of her other wrist as well. "Ahh, yes... yours were cold."

She turned her head and looked around the shelter again. "We? Is there someone else here besides you and me?"

"Well, not exactly, they're up on the edge of the clearing," he stammered. "We're out here looking for you!"

"Looking? Clearing? So what you're saying is that were essentially alone! Where am I?" her voice suddenly seemed surprised. "Please, tell me my mother didn't send you!" Gabe noted the sarcastic concern in her voice.

She really doesn't know where she is!

"Your mom's back at camp. She's worried—" Gabe said.

"Right! Ah! My leg, it hurts." She let out a heavily disturbed sigh. "What's wrong with my leg?" She released his hands and attempted to sit up. She winced in pain. He saw the agony in her face. He guided her back to her original position.

"Easy... you got lost. Your mom sent us out to find you—"

"My mom... why would she even care?" She shook her head, suddenly becoming agitated.

"You probably fell from the cliff and injured who knows what else."

"How can that be? I don't climb!" she said, so matter-of-fact.

"It's the only way you could have gotten here," Gabe said.

She looked on, confused. "Maybe some bird dropped me off... where is here?"

"An island of rocks and trees in the middle of a landslide."

"What, an island?" she sounded confused.

"May I take a look at it?" he asked, trying to change the subject and calm her down.

"A look at what?" she gave him a funny look.

"Your leg... I need to treat your injury!" He felt even more embarrassed. "But first I will need to wash off the mud."

She looked down at her leg and raised an eyebrow. She nodded as if she had finally understood that he was actually trying to help. "That doesn't look or feel very good. Hey, where's my shoe and sock?" she asked as she looked away. "I liked that pair!"

"I don't know," Gabe shrugged. "You didn't have it on when I found you."

"You don't seem to know much do you?"

He ignored her sarcasm and pulled his water bottle and medical gauze from his pack.

He then attempted to wash the remnants of mud from her foot. "Your shoe could be just about anywhere."

She winced from the tenderness of her injury and coolness of the water. She brought up her hands defensively and balled up her fists to guard her leg. "Hey!" she yelled.

Gabe backed away and held out an open palm. "I'm just trying to clean it!" He held up the water bottle. She lowered her hands and nodded for him to continue.

"Take it easy, my leg hurts like a mother... that water's freezing! How would you like it if someone dumped cold water on your head?" her eyes scrutinizing.

He cautiously continued, watching her out of the corner of his eye as he gently poured water over the injured area of her foot and tried to clean off the dirt and debris.

"I didn't think so!" She frowned disapprovingly as she watched the water being poured onto the ground tarp. "You Gitt, you're wasting water!" She gritted her teeth in protest as she reached for the water bottle.

His eyes followed.

He fought through his annoyance. "There's no need to worry, I've got more, and besides, it has to be done!"

She snatched the water bottle out of his hand and started sloppily gulping it down.

"I guess that one is yours then."

She ignored him.

Gabe pulled another water bottle out of his pack and continued to wash the mud from her injured ankle and foot with a piece of gauze. She winced again but he kept on working.

When she was finished with the plastic water bottle she tossed it aside and gave out a heavy sigh. "You've got any more of those?"

Gabe gave her a strange look.

"What... I'm thirsty!" she shrugged.

"When was the last time you drank?"

"A while ago, I think... I don't know!"

Gabe nodded and attempted to give her the other half empty bottle that was in his hand.

She gave him a disapproving glare. "You're kidding, right!" her voice was aligned with sarcasm. "You've been holding that one to that filthy rag of yours! God knows what's in it."

"I thought you were thirsty?" Gabe reluctantly dug around for another.

Her eyes never leaving his.

"How long have I been out here?" she wrinkled her eyebrows. She appeared to be slowly softening up.

"All afternoon!" Gabe shrugged his shoulders. "Maybe, since last night."

He pulled another full bottle out of his pack.

"Since last night?" she shifted a surprised look to Gabe's face. "What's your name again?"

Gabe removed the cap and gave her a full bottle.

"It's Gabe, and yours is Alex, right?"

A bright flash followed by a bone chilling rumble caused them both to twitch and look around. Gabe spilled water on her but she didn't seem to notice.

She looked at the tarp wall with concern.

The downpour that immediately followed pounded the tarp even more violently.

"They told us at the briefing that it was going to rain," he yelled over the deluge.

"The what?"

He carefully tried to slide her pant leg up toward her knee to examine her lower legs.

She winced again in pain and grabbed his wrist.

"Sorry!" Gabe tried to explain. "I first thought you were a boy."

"A what?" she released his wrist and recoiled as she raised an eyebrow.

"I thought Alex was a boy's name."

She gave him a strange look and forced a smile. "A boy huh, Alex is short for Alexandra you dummy. Everyone knows that!"

"Right!" Gabe mumbled. "Well evidently not everyone!"

"I can't help that but I can assure you that I am *not* a boy!" she teased sarcastically.

Gabe's embarrassment was back. He looked away and occupied himself with his pack.

She studied him closely.

"Are you guna' look at my leg, or what?"

"Ahh, yeah. I'm going to need to cut your pant leg... to get at your injury," he pointed.

"You even think about cutting these pants and I'll kill you!" she threatened, "I love these pants!" She exclaimed protectively as she stared down at her leg, contemplating his request.

Gabe looked at her frustrated, and gave out a heavy sigh.

She squinted into his face. "Aren't you a little young to be pretending to be a rescue ranger?" she teased.

"Aren't you a little too old to be getting lost?" Gabe snapped back, he was getting tired of her sarcasm.

"Attitude!" She suddenly got quiet, her face drained of emotion. She turned away and crossed her arms.

Gabe immediately regretted his words.

"My uncle's... a ranger." Gabe continued, trying to keep the conversation moving. "Hey, my friend Erick and I, were just trying to help!"

What is wrong with her?

She silently studied him for a moment out of the corner of her eye. "Well then, cut away..."

"What?"

She looked directly at him and nodded, gestured with her hand. "You deaf little man with the attitude, the pant leg, cut away. I guess you have to do what you have to do! Right! You'll just have to buy me another favorite pair... and they're not cheap have you know!"

Gabe hesitated a moment before he retrieved his pocket knife from his pack. The beam of his headlamp flashed off the open blade.

She reacted nervously stopping him again. Her dark eyes grew in size. "Don't you have any scissors?"

"No, this is all I've got, I'll be careful, I promise!" he tried to reassure her.

"You know what you're doing right?" her voice concerned.

"Yeah!" he didn't sound very convincing.

She nodded, but her eyes never left the blade.

Strange.

Gabe suddenly remembered the slash marks about her wrists. His headlamp went from her knee to her hands, "How did you get those scars on your wrist?"

Embarrassed, she covered them with her hand. "I made some mistakes that I'm not proud of," she exclaimed, defensively. "I suppose you don't make mistakes?" she lashed out.

Gabe shook his head. "All the time... mistake is my middle name!"

"Right, now that's something I wouldn't be bragging about!"

Gabe let out a heavy sigh and gave her an odd look. "I'm not, I'm just saying..."

She watched him closely as he busied himself carefully cutting away at the hem of her pant leg, and then up towards her knee. When he reached the outline of a green and black tattoo on her lower leg, he abruptly stopped. His eyes traced the graceful curves of the thorny stem. A thorny vine of a rose wrapped its way around the backside of her calf and wound its way up toward her thigh.

A long stem rose!

"What's wrong?" her concern rang out. "Haven't you ever seen a tattoo before?"

He quickly diverted his eyes back to her lower leg.

Not this close!

He noted the deformity and the bruising. "Oh... looks like you fractured one of the bones of your lower leg." He gently pushed against the puffy side of her leg, starting at her ankle and working his way up to her knee. "I'm going to touch it... this might hurt a bit—"

"Ouch... son of a...!" she screamed out, as she tried to pull away. "What do you think you're doing?"

Gabe flinched even though he expected her to react.

"Are you doing that on purpose?" she continued to scream, her expressive eyes burning right threw him.

He quickly loosened his grip. "Yep, I'm thinking it's broken!"

"You think now it is!" she scolded as she guarded her leg with her hands. "Hey, you did that on purpose!" she wined. "I'm guna' sue you for malpractice!"

"Yes... I'm supposed to!"

"Supposed to...? What kind of quack are you?"

"I'll need to splint it, to keep it from moving!" He reached for his pack.

"To do what?" Her dark eyes followed the beam of the head lamp to his pack.

"To stabilize it... to keep it from moving so it doesn't get worse!" He had finally lost it. "I don't have to do any of this you know. I can just go back to my friends and leave you here all alone! Is that what you want?"

Her frown melted to concern.

Gabe regretted the harsh words as soon as they left his lips.

But she deserved them.

"I'm sorry!" her voice was much calmer. "It's just that..." she shook her head, gave out a heavy sigh and diverted her eyes.

He could tell there were emotional secrets.

"Will it hurt?" her voice was calm, concerned.

"It will hurt *less* if you let me stabilize it!" His voice still reflected his annoyance. He had learned basic first aid in the Boy Scouts, complements of his mom. She had wanted him to be around other father figures. It seemed like a silly reason back then, but now the skills were coming in handy.

"Will I be able to walk out of this place?" her voice rang with true concern for the second time.

"Not without help." Gabe shook his head, his voice calm, understanding, and hopeful. "They're coming to get us!" His headlamp illuminated her worried face.

"Who?" she looked concerned.

Another flash, then a deafening clap rang in his ears. He flinched, and jerked his shoulder in the direction of the sound. It startled Alex as well.

"If you haven't noticed," she spat out, "things don't seem to be getting much better."

Another flash back-lit a human silhouette outside, just beyond the tarp.

Alex gave out a startled scream.

"Erick?" Gabe quietly whispered. He slowly rose to his feet and yelled out into the storm. "Erick, we're over here!"

"What are you doing?" she whispered loudly, her voice laden with frightful concerned.

"It's got to be my friend, Erick, he must be looking for us." Gabe said as he moved to exit their shelter.

She grabbed his arm. "Don't... it's not—"

Gabe pulled loose from her grip. "It's him, has to be! Who else could it be?"

"It's not... hey, where are you going?" Panic was starting to settle in.

Gabe stopped at the entrance and turned to face her. "Relax, I'm getting my friend like I told you, I'll be right back. He's just outside!"

"And I'm telling you, that's... not... him!" she spoke softly, her expression worried. "I know what I'm talking about."

"Of course it's him, who else could it be?" he sounded so matter of fact. Despite her protest, Gabe turned, pushed open the tarp, stepped out and followed his light beam into the storm.

"Gabe, trust me... there are no humans out there!" she let out a frightened scream into the storm from behind him. "Don't leave me alone here..." her worried, muffled tone set back his confidence.

He spun around, flashing his headlamp in every direction. "Erick? Dan?" he yelled. The rain pelted his face, splattered his parka, and pulled at the tarp. The raindrops streaked almost sideways in the beam of his light in the steady torrent. Shadows stretched and bent in the ambient light. Every one of them seemed to move on its own. As far as he could tell there wasn't a single person anywhere to be seen. He glanced back in the direction of the darkened tarp. He suddenly realized that he had left her in the dark, alone. He had the only source of light. He refocused on what was in front of him.

The ledge is only so big, maybe Erick's on the back side of the boulders.

"Erick... Dan!" he yelled again into the wind and darkness.

He started to move forward into the storm to have a look around, but suddenly changed his mind. It was like his instincts told him, *no!* Without another thought, he slowly backed up toward the protected warmth of the tarped shelter. He took one last long look before he slipped back inside and pulled the entrance shut.

"I told you so?" she spoke nervously. The beam of Gabe's headlamp found her sitting up with the emergency blanket pulled snugly around her neck, a thankful expression on her face. "You didn't see anyone out there, did you?" her voice crackled with worry. She was shivering.

"No! It's miserable out there!" He dared not tell her about his sudden change of heart. It was then that he remembered one of the hazards of outdoor survival, wet clothes sucked away vital body heat. At this point, her shivering could be either good or bad. The body shivered to stay warm... the body shivered when it was frightened.

Hypothermia is a factor to contend with.

"Gabe, don't do that again! Promise me you won't leave me alone, again!" She sounded worried. "Promise me!" she screamed.

"I promise... I promise!"

She studied his eyes for a moment before she gave a sigh of relief. "So now what, we keep waiting for these so called friends of yours to show up?"

"I guess." he shrugged.

"They better hurry soon, we haven't much time."

"Are you warm enough?" Gabe changed the subject.

"Enough!" She returned an unconvincingly shrug.

"Well, they say," he cleared his throat, "in order to stay warm, you should remove your wet clothes." He diverted his eyes.

She wrinkled her nose and raised her eyebrows as she glared at him. "Did you just tell me to take off my clothes?"

"In survival situations we're supposed to—"

She cut him off. "I like you and all, Gabe, is it, but... the clothes are... staying on! Taking off cloths to stay warm... that makes no sense what so ever!"

"Like I was saying, taking off *wet* clothes in order to..." He threw up his hands apologetically. "Fine, I was only suggesting that, in order to—"

"Yeah, sure, but... still, I don't know you!"

Gabe nodded, gave out a heavy sigh and changing the subject. He still needed to find something to splint her leg with, but that would have meant going back out there into the forbidding darkness, breaking a promise. First, he needed to get back to the basics. "Still thirsty?"

She'd already guzzled two water bottles.

Her eyes brightened, "Yeah!"

"I'll get you some more." He knelt down to open his pack and felt a piece of metal, in his front pocket, press uncomfortably against his thigh.

The medallion!

He handed her the last water bottle. "Drink as much as you like. Evidently, we've got plenty!" he smiled as he gestured towards the darkness. "If it keeps raining like this, we'll be able to refill our bottles from the run off from the tarp."

"Great, an optimist!" she mumbled under her breath as she returned the smile. She quickly unscrewed the top of the water bottle, tossed the lid aside with the others, and guzzled down the water only stopping once for air.

He looked on with great interest, watching her delicate hands, face and neck, as she pulled the space blanket tighter around herself. He nervously fumbled with the medallion in his front pocket.

Could this be hers? How did she manage to hang it on that root?

She gave him a satisfied look when she finished the last drop and sucked in a breath. "I guess I was thirstier than I thought!"

"Would you like some more?"

She shook her head no. "I couldn't drink *all* of your water...."

You almost already did!

"I brought extra!" he lied, "and when that's gone...." He pointed his thumb over his shoulder to the storm outside, "we've got all of that."

She stared at him a moment, as if making sure he was serious.

She caught Gabe smiling at her.

"What's so funny?" she smiled back.

"You!" Gabe shrugged his shoulders.

She gave him a confused look.

The medallion?

The very one he had found on the side of the mountain only a short distance away. He pulled it out of his pocket and studied it closely, flipping it over to view the back for the first time.

Staring back at him was an engraving that he had missed the first time in his haste to put it in his pocket.

'TO NATURE BOY WITH LOVE, LYDIA.'

What?
He read it to himself again.

TO NATURE BOY... WITH LOVE, LYDIA...

Hey, my mom's name is Lydia!
"What've you got there?" Alex quizzed, as she leaned forward trying to sneak a peek at the medallion.

She grunted in pain and discomfort as she struggled to move around.

The question caught him by surprise. "A medallion," he held it up for her to see. "I found it near the edge of the slide." He thumbed over his shoulder in the direction, "it was hanging from one of the roots of a huge redwood stump." He offered it to her to look at. "Do you know anything about it... is it yours?"

"No!" She winced in pain as she reached out to touch it. "I wouldn't be caught dead wearing gold," she struggled with her words. "It impedes my energy flow, silver on the other hand..." She held out the both of her hands to show off her rings.

Gabe laid the medallion in the palm of her delicate hand, the metal clicked lightly against her rings. The scars on her wrist were more noticeable in the beam of his headlamp. For a moment, her hands appeared as if they had been sown on. The strange thought made the enclosure feel smaller and a few degrees cooler.

Those are suicide marks? How could she do it... why would she do it?

As she held the medallion in her hands, he noticed a sudden change in her demeanor. Her smile faded, her eyes narrowed, and her skin looked even paler in the wash of light. Then her hands began to tremble even more. The sound of whispers hissed from beyond the enclosure, over the pounding rain. The chill now ran the length of his spine. He found himself moving, just out of arms reach of her and away from the entrance of the enclosure.

"What's happening to me?" she whispered, her eyes searching Gabe's for answers. Her face was filled with panic.

Another flash of lightning was immediately followed by a bone jarring rumble. Out of the corner of his eye, he thought he saw the silhouette of a deformed man, standing just outside of their shelter. It was closer this time.

What the... are they back?

He felt his strength being drained. A numbing tingle ravaged his body, a strange panic overwhelmed him. The air smelled foul.

When Alex screamed he felt an electrical charge race through him. He felt as if his heart was trying to jump out of his chest. He watched Alex let the medallion slip through her fingers and fall onto the floor of the shelter near his knees. Without another word, Alex dragged herself away from it, cowering.

How can this be?

Gabe stared as the medallion began to glow a goldish-green color in the strange darkness. Alex screamed again and reached for her own wrist. The palm of her hand glowed red in the shape of the round medallion. Gabe stared, his eyes shifting between her and the medallion that lay on the floor before him. The enclosure immediately felt 20 degrees cooler. Their breaths hung mist-like around them. An uncomfortable presence filled the enclosure.

"Help me!" she cried, her voice was faint and sorrowful, her eyes pleading. "The medallion... take it away..."

It took Gabe a moment to reel in his emotions. Despite her injuries, Alex staggered to her knees. Her emergency blanket fell to the tarped floor.

Gabe stared in confusion and surprise.

How can this be happening? What's going on?

She frantically fumbled with the entrance and dragged herself, broken leg and all, out of the shelter, and into the darkness and rain. The lightning flashed again through the open tarp, blinding him for a moment. The dark silhouette of a deformed man stood just outside beyond her, its arms extended.

"Hey!" he yelled.

"Stay away!" she screamed back. "Keep... away! Please no! Not again!"

Another flash of lightning, and just like that, she was gone. The tarp flapped in the wind. The rain puddled by the entrance. His head lamp illuminated the empty interior. His instincts finally took over.

She has no light... the cliff!

He snatched up the medallion off the ground expecting to find it glowing hot, but, to his surprise, it was cold to the touch. A powerful, incense-like fragrance lingered in the air. Renewed strength prodded him along.

"Stop her... don't let her out of your sight!"

The whisper in the wind almost had the qualities of a human voice.

Not quite knowing what to do with the medallion, he threw it around his neck, shoved it under his coat and hurried out of the shelter and into the darkness, the beam of his headlamp slicing through the unknown.

CHAPTER THIRTY-FOUR
THE ULTIMATE SACRIFICE
MARCH 16TH 2000

It was starting to happen all over again. Alex felt it come on like an epileptic seizure. Then there were the voices, the unusual smells and noises, the black outs, and then the part about not remembering, not knowing. She hated that part. That was the worst.

How did I get here? What have I done this time?

She had fled the safety of the shelter and disappeared into the stormy darkness, a bewildered Gabe in pursuit.

A one-man rescue team waiting for the rest of his team to arrive, a kid just like me!

She couldn't take it anymore.

"They said the medicine would fix everything," she screamed into the night, "side effects they call it! I'll be able to live a normal life just like everyone else they said! Bull shit, all of it! Bull shit, bull shit, bull shit! How can I spend the rest of my life living like this?"

Her anger began to build as she stumbled into the darkness.

She fell to the ground. Her broken leg failing to support her weight. She screamed at the excruciating pain that almost rendered her unconscious.

The bone jarring, ear piercing thunder answered her back.

I couldn't keep friends if I tried!

"You couldn't if you tried... your broken, had been since the day you were born!"

The tainted voice whispered coldly into her ears.

"No one wants anything to do with a loser like me!" she screamed into the darkness.

The thought of Gabe gave her momentary comfort.

"That's only because he doesn't know."

The deep, sarcastic voice echoed in her ears.

"It's only a matter of time before he sees the darkness shine through showing him who and what you really are. Yes, I'm sure he'll understand! Just like all the others who'd made a quick exit once they found out that you're a freak!"

The words pressed painfully against her neck.

A freak!

The thoughts angered her more.

"Even your mom's too embarrassed to be with you!"

"But Dad... at least you understood. Why did you have to *die*?" she screamed into the storm.

Another flash of lightning momentarily showed her the way through the boulder field. The stinging rain pelted off her face. The sound of the thunder hurt her ears.

The abyss... It's time to finally end this!

She pulled herself along in the dark through the mud and towards the abyss.

It's so very close now!

Her angry, heartless thoughts no longer drew tears, they gave birth to disdain and sarcasm. They gave her strength.

Could Gabe have ever been a friend?

The thought slammed her brain again. For the first time in a long while, she found herself wanting it to be true.

But then again, we'll never know! Will we?

She felt hesitation in the darkness that was awakening within her, drawn out by the shadows that haunted this dark places around her ... the dark place within her.

They're here, Gabe saw them, he said so himself. They've found me! They've found us!

She felt them closing in. So much she wished they would just go away for good. She wanted it all to end.

The medallion?

She felt the warmth of its presence, still burning into her hand, bleeding up her arm and towards her shoulder.

How could it? It's just a medallion... wasn't it?

At first it had felt weightless, warm to the touch, but then it had suddenly become heavy. The burden pulled on her arm, pulled at her heart. It had tried to pull her away from the darkness, but she held on.

She reached up and fingered the silver chain around her own neck that held a silver medallion of her own, a gift from her late father. Squeezing it tightly helped her through the tough times. She had squeezed it many times until her knuckles turned white.

No, this one was the polar opposite.

Much like hers, the golden medallion was gifted from the heart of its previous owner, holding a power that surpassed her comprehension. She could feel it. It mirrored the kindness of those who touched it. She had dropped it because she couldn't hold the gold medallion any longer. It made her feel strange. An energy built from within, a pressure squeezed her chest, burned at her hand. She had no longer felt safe. She needed to get away from that medallion, away from those who were stalking her in the darkness. She needed to get away from Gabe. She couldn't trust herself.

The incense, the whispers, and then the young man's smiling face that suddenly appeared in the corner of their shelter as I stumbled out of it. The medallion, how did it glow in the dark!

Her arm now tingled as she continued to painfully crawl across the rocks and into the overwhelming darkness. The farther from the shelter she pulled herself, the more nauseating she felt. She couldn't handle a second more of it. A blood curdling scream slipped through her lips.

Who is that boy? What has he done to me?

"Help me!" her pleading words were absorbed into the storm.

She crawled to her knees and grabbed her wrist before she tumbled along in the darkness, painfully landing face first into the rocks and debris. She felt her flesh tear. The rain pelt her tender, bruised, bleeding, pitiful face. She tasted blood.

She cried out in agony.

The angry thunder shook the ground around her. The flashes of lightning illuminated her path.

The abyss was closer, she felt it.

A darkness trickled through her thoughts and then flowed through her mind. Her muscles tensed, a strange energy overwhelmed her entire body. She knew she was losing control, again.

"That's right, flee! Flee like the cowardly twit that you truly are!"

The mysterious voice rang loudly in her thoughts.

"Jump! Jump you pitiful excuse for a human!"

"Stay, away, from, me!" she screamed. The pain in her leg temporarily halted by an unknown force. The pain on her arm now radiated in towards her chest.

The lightning flashed again, blinding her and silhouetting a human figure off in the darkness. It was different than the deformed one she had seen at the shelter. Hatred pulsed in the darkness all around her.

It's them, they've found me again!

An eerie warmness rippled through her every muscle.

"Like an unwanted child in a crib."

The confident voice overpowered the wind.

She staggered to her feet. The pain in her leg temporarily forgotten.

They've come to control me again, to make me do things against my will!

She wanted to tell Gabe that she was sorry that she could not control what was about to happen next. She wanted to ask for his forgiveness for what she was about to do. She turned towards the distant shelter.

"You shouldn't have followed me! I left for a reason!" she whispered.

"It's destiny sweetheart, yours... his... theirs... ours!"

His? Oh no!

She took a couple of staggering steps backwards and then turned and stumbled forward toward the darkness. "No!" The growing pain in her leg temporarily numbed the discomfort growing in her heart. She tripped and staggered forward into the powerful wind, fighting to regain her balance as she moved blindly into the darkness. The ground seemed to spin. Words echoed in her mind from every direction.

"Where do you think you are going? He is the one, he is the very reason you are here... this moment in time is the very reason you exist... take him... take him now... finish him off!"

The shadow hissed.

The deep voice resonated in her bones. The cold rain pelted and chilled as the wind raked her hair across her battered, bloodied face, tangling it on her piercing.

"Alex!" Gabe's familiar voice echoed faintly off the rocks.

The wind ruthlessly shoved her from side to side, it angrily shoved her backwards towards the distant, rapidly approaching voice. She fought to keep her balance. She could not allow herself to fall down, not just yet, not before she reached her goal.

"Do as I bid... do as I command!"

The words stung painfully from within.

She needed to get away from Gabe. She didn't want to hurt him, but they were going to make her do it, just like they made her do it to all of the others.

"No, I... will... not!" she screamed as she held her battered face in her hands. The excruciating pressure in her brain was building within, and it would continue until she did the voices' bidding. She spun in dizzy circles in the darkness, fighting the disorienting energy.

"Do it... do it now, I command you!"

The voice increased, along with the excruciating pain.

She pressed her hands against her ears in an unsuccessful attempt to keep out the words. She screamed.

The pressure tried to move into her chest but something stopped it.

The voices, the hate that suddenly welled up from within, all came crashing inward. She balled up her fists and beat herself about her chest and face. The pain was excruciating.

"No, go, away!" she cried out. "Make them go, away!" she screamed. Blood dripped from her piercings.

"Good show, much better, very attractive sweetheart!"

The tarp shelter glowed white. The dark sky flashed with blue. The earth trembled. The scolding voices seemed to ebb and flow. Pockets of incense and sulfur took their turns swirling past her in the changing winds.

She struggled between choices, stranded between two worlds.

"Hurt the boy..."
"Let him go..."
"His life for yours...Yours for his!"
Rattled in her thoughts.
"You must leave..."
"You must stay..."
"You must choose!"

The voices swirled in the wind. One of the voices sounded different.

She stopped spinning and looked down at her throbbing palm. The mark of the medallion still burned red. A man in a robe was now clearly visible near the boulders.

"Gabe, what have you done to me?" she screamed. She looked back towards the shelter.

The glowing tarp was no longer white, a bright halogen light moved quickly in her direction.

"Alex?" Her name desperately slammed into the wind.

She turned away from the blinding light to defend her eyes from the brightness, to create distance from its source. The faint voice sounded familiar, but her mind couldn't place it. She watched her shadow stretch before her and then shrink in size as the light approached.

"Alex?" The voice was louder.

An angry gust of warm, sulfurous smelling wind pushed her toward the approaching light, away from the darkness that she sought. She stumbled to regain her balance. The fear that welled from within her drew a different kind of tears for the first time in a while.

Finally!

She almost forgot how good it felt to really cry.

"Do my bidding!"

The voice echoed so loudly and angrily that it pulsed in her temples like an intense migraine.

"Do it now!"

She pressed both of her hands harder against her ears. The hand that had been burned felt warm and soothing against her face.

"Finish him!"

The angry voice blared.

A warm gust slammed painfully into her chest knocking her on her but. She quickly rolled to her feet and clawed her way towards the edge of the cliff. She suddenly knew what to do. She staggered to regain her balance.

"No, it's wrong!" she screamed into the darkness. "I... will... not... do... it!" a gust of cold air slammed her again, this time from the side spinning her around towards the light. She scrambled to keep her balance. "You... leave him... alone!" she screamed.

"You have no choice!"

The harsh evil whisper chilled her to her core.

"Remember your promise!"

"Alex, stay where you are!" The concerned voice sounded as if it were almost right there in front of her. When she squinted into the bright light, the voice was now only a couple of arm lengths away.

"I don't care anymore!" she gestured her hands angrily towards the darkness. She screamed as loud as she could. "I'm tired of being scolded, prodded, belittled, abused, lied to, mistreated, mislead... forced to do things against my will. You will *never* be able to do those things to me *ever* again!" Her words were controlled, fearless, from the heart. "I will see to it!" her last words were calm, methodical and final. She meant every word.

"Alex, I care!" The reassuring voice acknowledged as it moved to within an arm's length.

She saw the silhouette of the boy wearing a headlamp materialize right there in front of her. She felt a strange energy growing within. She felt the fear dissipating, her willpower growing with every rapid breath.

"Get away from me Gabe... save yourself! Goodby!"

She turned towards the darkness and let her feelings go. "I denounce you. I denounce your evil ways!" she screamed into the wind and rain. "You can go to hell and stay there where you belong! Asshole!" She felt powerful, it felt good. She had been waiting forever for this moment to say the words.

"Then you will both die, together... as planned!"

Whispered the chilling voice so matter of fact.

Those words brought her a deep chill.

"Gabe, stay, away!" she threw her hands up into the air as she yelled into the darkness.

"Alex, it's me, Gabe!" the voice was closer yet.

He reached for her hand, she stepped backwards as she pulled it away. She was not going to be controlled again!

Her foot slipped, her knees buckled, and she felt the ground beneath her give way. The moment seemed to move in slow motion. She gasped for breath, she scrambled for her footing and instinctively grabbed for anything to hang onto. Her heart and lungs felt as if they were pressed upward towards her throat. For a second, she felt weightless.

It's finally over. Never again.

There was no time to scream, at this point, it didn't seem to matter. The deed was done, she would finally be at peace.

But then a firm hand snagged her wrist. Her arm went taut. A pain shot through her arm to her legs.

"No!" she screamed. She felt her petite body whip in the air like a rag doll, and then painfully slam into the side of the rocky cliff in the darkness. She abruptly stopped but her body swayed back and forth. The searing pain in her leg once again made itself known. The new ones in her shoulder and chest burned like fire. She cried out in agony. "No!"

Her legs swung free, dangling over an abyss she could not see.

The abyss.

She screamed angrily as she flailed with her free arm and legs, reaching and stretching for anything solid to hook her fingers and toes into, but nothing caught. Rocks and debris broke loose and cascaded loudly down to the bottom. Rain and wind pelted and pulled. A jagged pain ripped through her leg, shoulder and face.

She felt fingernails biting into her wrist just as a second hand dug in alongside the first and squeezed. After that, everything seemed to move even slower. She looked up into a bright light. The elements beat down on her. She kicked and tried to swing her arm and legs from the vice grip that held her in place. She felt her body being hoisted back up to the light. Her chance of being free were quickly fading, they would be all but gone in moments. No matter what it took, she was going to be free of this tyranny that had plagued her for as long as she could remember.

"No, I'm ending this once and for all!"

CHAPTER THIRTY-FIVE
INNER STRENGTH
MARCH 16TH 2000

Gabe wedged his legs in between the jagged rocks and pulled with all his might.

"I have you!" he screamed. He strained against her movements as he watched her face inch closer to his with every painful pull. "Only a little bit more... pull!"

Then it happened. The rocks he had wedged his legs against moved. His knees shifted, and hope slipped away right before his eyes. He fell face first into her, bumping heads with an audible clunk and they slid arm in arm several more feet down the cliff side, stopping abruptly with an agonizing grunt as he once again managed to painfully wedge himself in between a couple more boulders. His climbing harness had caught on the edges of the rocks. He felt it, his safety equipment had once again saved them both.

When he reopened his eyes, his ears were filled with bone chilling screams. His ribs throbbed as if he had been struck with a baseball bat. The world around him seemed darker. Light no longer preceded his gaze.

My head lamp!

The dark silhouette that swung like a pendulum below him would have been indistinguishable from the ground if it weren't for the distant light that cast shadows from below. It took Gabe a moment to process the urgent screams of terror. He gripped the arm tighter and forced his thoughts from pain to necessity.

Alex still dangled below him, her arm in his grip, her good leg kicking for freedom. Her free arm thrashed around in an attempt to peel his fingers free of his straining grip around her wrist. There were painful strikes against his arm. Things had gone from bad to worse in a matter of seconds.

This place!

Alex was more hysterical now than ever.

"Alex, it's me, Gabe! Stop kicking! Stop hitting!" he screamed at the top of his lungs. "You're going... to get us both... killed!" he panted.

"Leave... me... alone!" she screamed hysterically as she swung at him a couple more times, repeatedly striking him about his head and shoulders with the clenched fist of her free arm.

When he pulled up on his elbow to guard his bruised ribs, he painfully elbowed the boulder he was wedged against.

"Ahhhh... Alex... stop it! You're hurting me!"

She continued to struggle. He fought to maintain the hold on one of her wrists. Despite the discomfort, he pressed his legs harder against the rocks. He couldn't believe he was still in place!

God help us!

"Look at me! Look at me! It's me, Gabe! Let me help you!" he pleaded.

She stopped flailing her arms and legs, and slowly turned her dirty and bloodied face up toward his.

A scary sight met his gaze. Her wild matted hair covered most of her battered face.

He struggled to read the recognition in her dark, confused eyes. He couldn't, she was swallowed by the eerie darkness. Above them lay the darkest of skies; below them was an obscure light glowing against the bottom of a rock face an estimated 50 feet beneath them. It was then that he realized that his headlamp lay at the base of a boulder field. He felt so helpless, so very alone. If he let go, or if his legs slipped free, either one of them would surely fall to their death.

Now this after finally starting to get through! Focus... focus!
"I want... to help you! Do... you... understand?" he spoke slowly, his voice shook with fear and pain. "I want to help you!" His legs and arms now trembled under the strain of almost twice his body weight. He found his grip beginning to loosen. He was losing the battle against gravity. "No... just a little longer!"

"Why?" she screamed. "I don't deserve to be saved!" she whispered. "If you only knew... what I have done, you would Just let me... die."

A flash of lightning illuminated the cliff side below and her frightened expression of indifference. Spots filled his vision, sweat and dirt stung his eyes. A sweet smell of incense filled his lungs. Now he knew what it was like to be blind, to be at the mercy of fate, but he knew he wasn't alone.

"Gabe... save yourself!" Her sorrowful voice rang up from below before the thunder shook his core. She sounded so distant. "I am broken and I can't be fixed... they've tried. You see... it's for the better."

He gripped her arm more tightly, but he still felt her slip another fraction of an inch closer to being lost. The rain, the dirt, the sweat, they were making it impossible.

"I... will... not! I... can... not let... you... go!"

"Why?"

Cold disbelief rang in the darkness.

"Save yourself! You heard it from her own lips. She can't be fixed! She can't be saved!"

"It's not... meant... to be!" Gabe forced his voice. Dirty water dripped over the edge of the cliff, down their necks, onto their heads and into their eyes and around his nose and mouth.

He spit out the dirty water to clear his throat. It tasted like mud and something bitter. He struggled for breath. He felt his rapid pulse pound along his neck, shoulder and arms, it echoed in his head. His respiration increased, his vision blurred.

The wind distorted his hearing, confusions grew in his mind. Despite all of the rain, he was dying of thirst.

It was the strong aroma of incense that made him cough, irritated his throat.

He diverted his eyes from the direction of the ground below. The vertigo was making him dizzy. The ground below was where he didn't want to be.

"You can save me, and yourself, by letting me go!" she pleaded." Her voice was calm, sounded exhausted. "Save yourself by…"

The smell of incense grew stronger. The blackness above no longer seemed dark.

How could that be?

A light seemed to be building on the bluff above them. An excitement grew, an energy renewed.

"Erick?" he whispered into the darkness. The light grew brighter. It was approaching the edge of the bluff. It reminded him of that night in the alley when a bright light had chased those three guys away!

Had it only been two weeks ago? Seems like months.

His thoughts raced.

"Erick… we're down here!" he yelled up the bluff to whomever was up there in the waning darkness.

The smell of sweet herbs became more pronounced. The light grew soothingly warm and intense until the brightness was blinding, his fear melted away with it. He wanted to turn away, to shelter his eyes, but the desire to know held his gaze fast.

"Erick, we're down here!" he yelled again into the storm. He realized that his radio wasn't with him, it no longer pressed against his side. He had left it with his pack in the shelter. "Erick!" He turned his head and screamed again up toward the bluff. The movement strained his neck.

The outline of a human form peered down at him from over the side. He felt a new wave of strength and endurance surge through him and begin to build. Rescue had arrived without a moment to spare. That thought alone filled him with a renewed strength.

"If I could only push myself up a few inches more…."

"Hang in there son, help is on the way!"

The deep, gentle voice echoed in his ears.

Son? That voice… Erick? No, it's a man's voice.

"Dan?" Gabe's body reacted with a bone numbing tingle.

"Dan!" he screamed as he turned and strained his neck for a better view. The pain was unbearable. "Down here!"
"Breath... relax... focus on me, focus on my voice."
The gentle words rang out against the storm.
"Focus on me... nothing else is more important than this moment."
"But... who...?" Gabe whispered.
"Gabe, focus on your breathing."
The voice was calm, confident and reassuring.
"Remember what you have learned."
Remember what I have learned?
Gabe's thoughts flashed to his karate class, the breathing exercises, and the meditation. It was then that he realized how deep and quickly he was panting. How every rapid, breath was stealing from his oxygen starved muscles. At this rate, muscle fatigue was imminent.
"Kick loose the girl... she isn't worth it... save yourself!"
A deep, sarcastic voice echoed over his shoulder.
That voice? It's different!
It vibrated from within, brought a sudden fear and hatred to his soul. He struggled to look into the darkness. A foul smell of rotting meat hit him fully in the face and chest. He coughed and gagged and almost released his grip of Alex's wrist. He felt her stir beneath him. She no longer spoke.
Did she smell and feel it too?
"Focus, Gabe!"
The calm voice returned.
"Remember, you have a choice!"
He felt his body tingle in the sudden cold. There were two separate voices, two opposites.
Which one am I to listen to?
"Gabe, me of course... she's spoiled goods! You know that! I know that!"
The heavy, matter of fact voice returned.
"She's not worth saving. Trust me on this one. Given the chance, would she risk her neck to save yours?"
The knowing voice festered with sarcasm.

"*I think not. Has she not tried to kill you already? She would have succeeded, too, if I hadn't intervened, if I hadn't positioned you between those two rocks that you now hang from for the second time.*"

The sarcastic voice prideful.

"*How do you people say it... keeping your friends close and your enemies closer?*"

The smell of rotting meat and sulfur reappeared on the winds, its stench was gagging. The whispers, the voices in the wind, they were all back. His body trembled. His energy was draining away quickly! He felt dizzy. He could hardly breathe the heavy air. He felt his grip weakening again. There was very little left.

"*Yes, that's right, do the right thing, save yourself. You are more important than...*"

The voice cleared its throat.

"*That!*"

The words were cruel and pointed.

Gabe looked down at Alex's motionless figure.

The hatred in the voice ran deeply. It reverberated in Gabe's chest. His fingers tingled.

"*Yes, look how helpless she is. Look how strong you are! You're a survivor. Yes, you will do well, I shall see to it!*"

The heavy voice suddenly became calm and casual.

"*Drop the girl, and you will not only live, I will give you whatever it is that you want. It's as easy as separating your fingers. Either one, at, a, time and... I do enjoy the suspense, or all of them at once in a single gesture. You do want to be warm and dry, don't you? I'll bet you're pretty thirsty by now. Giving her all of your water, such a gentleman. I will see to it that you will be gifted with powers many will envy. You will never be thirsty again.*"

The last words put tears in Gabe's eyes, and a sad loneliness in his heart.

"*Focus Gabe!*"

The calm voice returned.

"*If all of what was said were true... would you be here now? Some decisions are right, and some decisions are wrong, but we have to live with our own choices. Do you think she is living with hers?"*

The sweet scent of incense overpowered the smell of rot and decay. He could breathe again. The tightness in his chest, the crushing pressure, was gone! He tightened and readjusted his grip. He felt Alex's eyes staring up at him from the shadows. She no longer spoke. She no longer moved. Her steady breath was the only indication that she was still with him.

"If she were trying to kill you..."

The soothing voice exclaimed.

"Wouldn't she have done so already? She had ample opportunity, ample time, yet all she did was try to flee! Are those the acts of a would-be assassin?"

"Not so!"

The deep voice bellowed.

"You ignore the obvious!"

"She was fleeing you when you stopped her."

Stated the soothing voice from the light.

"She was drawing you to the edge if you recall!"

The deep voice from the darkness countered, with less confidence.

"Your actions backed her toward the cliff."

"She was waiting for the right moment. Look, she still clings to you as we speak. She is controlling your destiny with a shift of her weight, a turn of her pathetic body. She waits, she can still do, the deed!"

Gabe's glance returned to Alex's lifeless silhouette.

"She is saving her strength. She is biding her time—"

"Gabe, trust your heart, not your thoughts! She pulled away from you. She was willing to lay down her life for yours! That, is true love! Those are not the actions of a person trying to take your life. Those are the actions of a person attempting to take their own, in lieu of taking yours!"

The thought put a little fear into Gabe's heart. He had seen the slash marks about her wrists. She had tried to take her life before.

Was she going to do it again?

The thoughts echoed around in his head. He thought of his mom, how she had never really recovered from the passing of his father. He thought about how much she cared for him, how his uncle and aunt had dropped everything to be with him. He thought about how his best friend Erick had joined him to find closure despite the outcome, and how he ended up here with Alex. Her life now depended on his trust, love and understanding. He envisioned their faces smiling at him, every one of them whispering words of encouragement, first one of them at a time, and then all of them at once.

Gabe felt the strength returning to his shaking grip. His breathing was now more steady and controlled. He struggled to look back up over his shoulder into the silhouette of what looked like two faces smiling down at him. One was of a young man in a white translucent robe he did not recognize, the other was of a man whose features were familiar.

The curly hair, mustache... his demeanor.

"Dad?" the words squeezed out of his parched throat. "Is that you? But, you're, dead!"

A delicate smile graced the peering face.

"My body indeed, but my spirit and soul are free. I was granted time with my son in which I am so proud."

Gabe felt tears pouring down his face.

How could this all be?

"But... you're dead!" Gabe was on the verge of panic, "Does this mean that I'm dead too?"

"A family reunion, how wonderful!"

The pathetic voice continued,

"Now, can we get back to business at hand! Let's recap... You have damaged goods in your weakened grip. I don't think your dad here is in the best position to give advice. Look what good it did him!"

"You are strong in more ways than you know!" the young man's caring voice continued.

"You have stood by your convictions. You have seen beyond judgment, and have looked into people's hearts."

The older man continued,

"*That my son, is a gift, given by the grace of God, and wielded by his devout servants.*"

"*You are indeed a chosen one! You are the reason we are all here. By God's grace!*"

The young man's soothing voice was interrupted by the sound of slow clapping.

"*Such a romantic...*"

The sarcastic voice was back.

"*As we all know, time is irrelevant!*"

The sarcastic voice sounded louder, as if it moved closer. It whispered in his ear. The smell of decay was overwhelming.

"*This moment will pass like the others. Gabe, your time is running out. You or the girl? Like he said... the clock is ticking. Freedom of choice... got to love it!*"

Gabe was stunned. He was exhausted. His vision was beginning to blur even more. His hands trembled, and his body convulsed in a rhythmic motion as his muscles gave their every last bit to hold tight.

How could all of this be? Is this what happens to people before they die?

"*Oh, you are not dead, yet my stubborn little boy! You still have your God given ability to choose! So choose!*"

The sarcastic voice was firm.

His thoughts were now sporadic.

"*This will all be over soon. All you have to do now is open your hand, and let go. It's really that easy.*"

Weaseled the sarcastic voice.

"I can't do that?" Gabe was beyond the point of no return.

"*Can't or won't?*"

Gabe couldn't even move to pull himself up. This was it. Gabe squeezed Alex's arm even harder, but he still felt her delicate hand slipping through his grip. "I... won't... let... you... go!" Gabe's voice echoed loudly in the storm.

"*Yes, I know!*"

The gentle voice retorted.

"*That is why you have been chosen. You have found the strength to find love and understanding in some, and jealousy and deceit in others.*"

Gabe felt a gentle hand against his shoulder and back. It was warm and comforting, it seemed to give him a sudden burst of strength. The smell of incense filled his lungs. A welcoming joy filled his heart.
I can still do this!
The thought gave him strength. He felt the renewed energy, and pulled even harder on Alex's arm. The attempt to readjust his numb legs almost caused them both to slip and fall to oblivion. The attempt caused him to gasp for breath, and to focus on slowing his thundering heart.
"No..."
The gentle hand with a familiar touch squeezed his shoulder.
"Save your strength. Help is coming."
The numbness in his shoulder disappeared with the touch. Gabe wanted to scream, but the calm voice soothed him again. For a moment, he thought there were other arms alongside his. Alex felt light as a feather.
"I see you found the medallion..."
The older man's voice continued.
"Think of me when you wear it. I will always be with you, in here."
The figure touched its own chest.
"Did mom give it to you?" Gabe struggled to speak.
The figure of his father nodded.
"I do not need it anymore. It belongs to you now! You have earned the right to wear it."
Gabe felt a pressure in his chest. His father's features glowed with joy and understanding.
"Whatever happens, however abandoned you may feel, always trust, always believe. God will never forsake you!"
The sound of slow clapping interrupted his thoughts. A deep sarcastic voice chime in.
"Oh, how touching, I beg to differ. You're still hanging around I see. What, you haven't dropped her yet?"
The voice sounded surprised.
Gabe diverted his eyes down towards Alex. She still hadn't moved a muscle. Now wasn't the time to worry.

"You can go ahead and believe that if you would like! Or what these clowns are going to tell you."

The odor of sulfur and rotting meat returned.

"He has nothing to offer you but a mere simple medallion that you already possess!"

The sound of the deep voice set Gabe ill at ease. He thought he saw shadows moving about the darkness around him.

How could that be... were hanging off a cliff!

The gentle, comforting squeeze that Gabe had felt on his shoulder helped him feel more at ease, filled him with courage and strength, but now, it was gone.

"I will not... let her go. You can't have her!" he projected his exhausted voice out into the darkness.

"I can introduce you to thousands who will disagree..."

The deep voice continued.

"I believe your mother, is one of those!"

He laughed sarcastically.

"You leave my mother alone!"

"Oh, has spirit this one, But, no matter... it is never really over. I am never really gone. You deserve each other..."

He snarled.

"You may regret your decision, freedom of choice, a blessing and a curse, all wrapped up in one nice little package. No matter. When it comes right down to it, so many souls, so little time. How do you young people say that? You choose, you lose!"

"I choose to hang-on!" he screamed.

"So be it, for now. Until next time!"

An evil laugh followed.

Within seconds the odor of rotting meat and the whiffs of sulfur were replaced with the powerful sweet scent of incense. The darkness no longer seemed so dark and ominous. The presence of the deep voice was finally gone. Gabe felt his hope and courage rebuilding. The bright light still glared in his eyes.

"Gabe, trust your heart!" the echo of the gentle voice said as it was absorbed into the rain.

Gabe momentarily felt the gentle pressure of a hand on his shoulder one last time. "Dad!" he screamed. Tears ran freely down his dirty face. He was overwhelmed with the sudden fear of being alone again. "Don't leave me!"

"He will never leave your side."

The young comforting voice whispered.

Gabe watched his dad's smiling face fade with the dimming light.

"Dad, don't leave me again. Dad!" he screamed at the top of his lungs, tears filled his eyes. He tugged again at Alex's arm, straining to pull her up, but nothing. He couldn't budge her. He could hardly feel his arms and legs. His strength was quickly fading away, soon there would be nothing.

The light became dimmer, the air colder. He burst into a heavy cry. "Dad, come back!" His words now were only harsh whispers. Just before the reflection of light totally disappeared, it began to build again. Much fainter this time, the beam of light spread back and forth as if searching, coming closer with every pass. He thought he heard the whispers of multiple voices in the wind taunting him again; but no, unlike those, these words were clear, the voice familiar.

I know that voice!

The spark of joy within began to burn more brightly. His dad was right.

"Erick... down here!" Gabe screamed with every ounce of his breath, his desperate calls piercing into the storm. "Erick, we're down here. Hurry!" His lungs hurt.

"Gabe?" came the astonished reply. "Gabe!" echoed even more loudly. A headlamp peered over the edge. "Oh my God!"

The silhouette of his friend wasted no time closing the distance. He heard rocks shift, and felt the debris slide down past him. Some bounced off his body. He felt his warm tears run down the side of his face as his body convulsed with every sob. This time, they were truly tears of joy. His guardian angel had arrived.

CHAPTER THIRTY-SIX
LOVING STRENGTH
MARCH 16TH 2000

It was the light that drew Erick's attention toward the edge of the bluff like a moth to a flame. A strange urgency prodded him along. With his pack strapped to his back and his climbing harness secured to his waist, he followed the beam of his L.E.D. headlamp, willed his exhausted, mud-soaked legs forward, moving with grace and speed through the saturated, uneven, impassable terrain.

***

At first he clipped into Gabe's discarded climbing rope with his harness and carabiner and followed the portions of it that hadn't been fully engulfed by the veracious mud slides. He connected and disconnected the rope as he went. When he ran out of rope to trace, he followed the voices in the wind that screamed into his ears. His sweat mixed with the mud and rain.

No way was this a coincidence. Without the guidance of the legion, he knew he would have been disoriented in the chaos of the late winter storm, swallowed up in the mud or buried beneath debris. The torrential rain carved gullies to block his path, ate its way through the loose soil, attempted to destroy all the evidence of Gabe's passing. The flashes of the blue lightening meant to frighten and discourage him acted as flood lights, illuminating the whole mountainside. The loud thunder meant to deafen, disorient, and intimidate worked more like a motivator.

He sank knee-deep into the ooze with every step, fighting its attempts to suck off his boots and bury him alive in the quicksand-like mud. After he put on his makeshift snowshoes, he became lighter, he moved along quicker, becoming more agile on his feet. In some places he felt as if he drifted over the worst of the terrain, bounded over obstacles almost twice his size. He knew he wasn't alone. Several times out of the corner of his eye he saw them, the young men in white robes and shiny armor holding off the shadows around him, directing him through the gauntlet of obstacles. At times he felt them lifting him up, pushing him forward.

Carried or floated?

When he looked back, several times, half expecting to find a second and third sets of foot prints alongside his own, he saw none other. He was astonished to find, in some places amongst the worst of the muck and mire, no footprints at all. There was no time to ask how. The young man had said he would never be alone, and after today he would never doubt him again.

Helping hands.

His fear and uncertainty was gone.

He felt the presence of the legion of angels as he leaped over logs and scurried up and over boulders like a flying squirrel on steroids.

They guide my every step, my every foot placement!

Erick had closely followed his friend through the last two grueling weeks, now he was following a remnant of his passing through a devastated landscape. The mere thought filled him with an incomprehensible fear, energizing his willpower to push onward. His need to be with his friend was urgent. He hoped he wasn't too late.

***

To Erick's left, hidden among the boulders, his head lamp illuminated the blue tarp shelter, but he pushed on toward the strange, faint light that wrapped itself like an aura around the edge of the boulder field. He felt his adrenaline kick into overdrive when he looked back in the direction of the bluffs and, to his bewilderment, the light was gone!

Erick slid to a stop and screamed his friend's name into the wind and rain. Only the wind howled back from the darkness. A fear surged through his every muscle.

The cliff!

The words rang in his thoughts. "Gabe!" he hollered again. He moved closer to the edge and frantically searched within the beam of his headlamp. Then he heard it, a voice calling his name, Gabe's distant voice, crying out in desperation and anguish. The cry became louder as he homed in on its origin. "Gabe!" he hollered back. He ran the rest of the way to the ledge, and skidded to a stop within inches of the drop off. His heart pounded in his chest as he caught his balance, his fingers tingled with another shot of adrenaline.

That was close!

The beam of light illuminated the back of his friend's prone legs. They were wedged between rocks about five feet below the ledge. Below his waist the cliff side dropped out of sight and into the dark void. At the bottom was a faint source of light, his friend's headlamp.

The brighter beam of Erick's head lamp was absorbed into the storm.

"Oh my God... Gabe, hold on!" Without another thought, he kicked off his make ship snowshoes, scrambled over the ledge, and down the five feet of challenging terrain to his friend. Once within reach, he grabbed Gabe's lower torso and pulled with all of his might. He slipped in the mud and fell to the ground out of breath.

His friend wouldn't budge.

"Please, I need your help!" Erick's voice sounded desperate.

"And Help you shall receive"

The voice whispered into his ear, the smell of incense filled his lungs.

Young men in translucent white robes and shiny armor materialized around him. He leaned farther over the edge and re-grabbed his friend again, one hand firmly on his leg the other on the back of his climbing harness. In the corner of his eye he saw others standing next to him, their hands right there alongside his own.

"On the count of three."

The others nodded.

"One... two... three!" he screamed. Turning fear into strength he dug his heels into the ground, leaned back, and pulled with everything he had left.

His arms went taut as he felt the weight of gravity against his shoulder. He felt Gabe's body budge a little at first and then a few inches more exposing his friend's lower back. Without any time to waste, he quickly grabbed another fist full of his friend and wrenched him backwards some more.

"He's moving!"

But, he couldn't figure out why Gabe suddenly weighed so much! It was like a tug-o-war contest was taking place.

"Hang on, we've got you!" he yelled into the wind. "Keep pulling!" he screamed.

His friend moved a few more inches farther up the boulder field.

It was then he noticed that his friend's arms held another dark silhouette tightly within his grasp. A human form hung limp, suspended above the dark void, its long dark hair concealed its face and draped the narrow shoulders.

"A girl?" the words rippled through his thoughts as he stared, stunned. A flash of lightning and the rumble of distant thunder brought him back.

"God help us. Pull... pull!" Gabe's voice called into the darkness.

His heart warmed, his body tingled and shook with nervous energy. He felt his strength growing, starting from within and then building, moving down into his arms and legs. He wiggled and wedged his feet into the mud and rock alongside the others. He pressed his feet into the ground until they caught. With that, Erick released a barrage of his strength.

"Pull!"

It was then that he lost track of what happened next, everything moved in slow motion, sounds blended together. A loving gentle presence materialized out of the darkness.

He felt strange, lightheaded, as if he were floating on air. His arms and legs tingled, his chest filled with tender warmth. He remembered the skyline before him lighten to the east, a dark cumulonimbus clouds was backlit by a building source of light. A sliver of moon was rising in the east. The curving shapes and shifting edges of the thunderheads that drifting by moved like liquid. The night was no longer shapeless and ominous. The light rain dribbled across his face, a gentle breeze played with his hair. And then there was the sweet-smelling incense.

The incense is back!

He remembered the gentle beautiful voices. They started with one lonely tenor, but soon the baritone and soprano voices joined together in acapella harmony. Their tone rose and fell, building to crescendo after each verse, and then blending into a gentle whisper amongst the light rain. The song, he recognized the song.

"The prayer of Saint Frances?"

It was like the whole sky was singing in harmony, as if celebrating....

He opened his eyes wide. He lay there on his back, his headlamp shining straight into the darkness above him, his pack pushing uncomfortably against his neck. Droplets of rain splattered against his face. His arms were wrapped around a heavy object laying on his chest. Another dark object a human form laid next to him, facing away. They all lay in a tangled mess fifteen feet from the edge of the drop off. A blue tarp shelter lay partially hidden off in the distance between boulders.

The boy in his arms looked familiar.

"Gabe!" he whispered, gasping for breath as he squeezed his arms tightly around his friend's torso that laid motionless, face up on his chest.

The dark human form grunted painfully.

For a moment, a panic immediately welled up from within. "Gabe! Gabe!" he released his grip and slid out from under his friend. He turned his face towards him. Erick's head lamp illuminated an exhausted young man who could barely keep his eyes open. A smile stretched across his face.

"Erick..." Gabe's exhausted voice replied with a smile, "Get that light out of my face!"

"You're alive!" Erick felt an immediate relief; he hadn't killed his friend after all. A mischievous grin spread across Gabe's dirty face. Erick hugged him tightly again.

Gabe winced in pain a second time. "My ribs... take it easy. I think there broken... I think I'm broken." When he tried to laugh he winced in pain a third time.

"Are you alright?"

"I don't know... my body... I'm... so, so freakin' tired, I can...hardly move...." A sudden panic overwhelmed Gabe as if he had forgotten something. He swiveled his head in every direction and tried to sit up. "Where's, Alex?"

"Alex?" Erick responded. He suddenly remembered the other human form lying next to them. He turned to see Gabe's hand still gripping the figures wrist like a vice. He last remembered that Gabe was hanging onto the arm of the person below him as they were hoisting them up the cliff.

"The others...!"

He franticly swung the beam of his headlamp along the terrace. His beam reflected off the face of the blue tarp, the terrace and then back to them.

Where did they go?

"What the... how did we?"

"Alex!" Gabe's voice echoed in the clearing.

Erick's eyes caught the movement of the third person, their long hair, petit size. He heard the sobbing. He saw the soiled clothes. Their face was turned away.

Gabe pulled on the arm. The subject moaned, it sounded female.

Erick hesitantly reached towards the person and placed a hand on the shoulder.

"Are you okay?" Erick asked, his voice a few octaves higher then he would have liked.

A girl's bloodied face turned towards and looked up at him from beneath her matted, dirty hair. Her delicate features were hidden beneath a mask of emotions, dirt, blood and tangled facial piercings. Her smudged mascara gave her a demented expression. She looked confused.

Her sudden movement surprised Erick. He leaned backwards and sucked in a quick breath.

Her body shook as she sobbed, "I'm finally free!" Her words were accompanied with tears of joyful relief and satisfaction. Her eyes found Gabe's as he was trying to pull himself closer. "It's because of you!"

"You're a girl!" Erick exclaimed, the surprise in his voice and on his face was obvious. His words echoed loudly.

"And so I've been told!" her voice sounded exhausted.

Gabe wrapped an arm around her. "Are you okay!" his voice was nervous and excited.

"I'll survive..." she painfully struggled to sit up and return the embrace. She was on the verge of tears. "How about you?" Her whole body trembled uncontrollably. She rubbed her eyes.

"I'll be alright... Erick, get Alex to the shelter." Gabe barked as he pointed towards the blue tarp. "Sorry, I'm too exhausted to help you!" His voice sounded urgent.

"So the mysterious boy is really a girl." Erick exclaimed. He nodded and shifted his focus to the girl. "I'm Erick, a friend of Gabe's." he spoke slowly as he forced a smile. "He wants me, to take you to the shelter, over there!" He pointed.

"So Erick is it?" she continued to wipe her eyes, she cleared her throat.

Erick nodded.

"You don't have to talk to me like I'm stupid or something! Just get me over to the damn shelter like he said!" she lectured. Her sarcasm was back. She winked at Gabe.

He smiled in return.

"Well, alright then!" he responded, not quite knowing what to think. Her directness had caught him off guard.

Gabe gave him a nod. "Erick's a friend of mine, he's my guardian angel." Gabe's voice boomed proudly,

"Really!" she gave him a quick once over, "Where are his wings?"

"Evidently, they don't always have wings," Gabe said, "he'll take good care of you. I'll join you." He turned to Erick, "watch out for her injured leg!"

A rumble of distant thunder echoed across the clearing just as Gabe had finished.

She glanced between Erick and Gabe as the tears began to flow freely from her eyes. She mouthed the words Thank You in Gabe's direction.

He nodded.

Erick gently scooped her up in his arms, she seemed so light and delicate. Gabe finally let her hand go as Erick pulled her from his grasp.

"Gabe has set me free..." she whispered again. "I owe him my life!" she exclaimed, her voice ringing with passion and a new understanding. "I owe you my life."

Erick was speechless. He looked on curiously. He had hundreds of questions, but he knew there would be plenty of time to ask his friend later. It was all just a matter of faith, believing in his friends, the existence of angels and ultimately, the belief and trust in God. At that moment, based on everything he had seen, heard and felt he believed there was no other explanation, no other answer. He couldn't explain what he went through to get there or how they had gotten Gabe and Alex up the side of the cliff and over the edge of the ledge to safety.

It was now his job to be there for his friend. They were a good team. He had been chosen to do something special. He was sure of it now!

Another distant flash lit up the sky. Moments later it was followed by a bone-shaking rumble.

Erick stopped, turned and yelled over his shoulder. "I'll come back for you next."

He saw Gabe give him a thumbs up, in the beam of his headlamp, before he slipped into the shelter. He gently laid her down on the space blanket and wrapped another foil emergency blanket around her. She smiled and finished securing herself in the insulated cocoon.

"My guardian angels!" she mumbled. She carefully rolled to her side and then quickly fell asleep.

***

Gabe narrowed his eyes as he silently watched the beam of the headlamp fade away. He watched Erick carry Alex off towards the blue tarp, illuminating it in the distance. Once there, he watched their shadows danced behind the blue screen before they settled down. Their voices absorbed by the storm. The rains began to pick up, the wind was beginning to build up again.

There was another bright blue flash, Gabe counted the seconds. He got to six before the ground shaking rumble reached him. He smiled.

He lay there exhausted, cold, and tired, taking it all in. He had asked his body to do the impossible. Only moments ago he hung from the edge of drop off, fighting gravity and the demons of the darkness that haunted the moment. He had no idea how long she had hung from his arm.

Was that really my dad? An angel? Then what was that other horrid thing?

The thought made him shiver. He couldn't say the words, to speak of it would be to admit that *he* was out there.

But *he* was! And if this thing was truly out there, there was a chance that he would run into it again. The thought made him shiver even more.

It was time to be off the mountain.

Gabe forced himself to take a quick glance into the darkness. His eyes lingered, searching, hoping that it was all over, for the shadows to move on, for his father to come back. That's if it really was his father.

Was it a ghost?

The thought gave him the chills. He shivered, that was good, his core temperature was probably still normal. Alex was safe and he no longer felt alone. All thanks to the bravery of his best friend and the legion of angels that came to their aide.

He watched a wave of cold rain hammer the ground around him. The droplets splashed the mud onto his soaked and dirty clothes.

His muscles throbbed in his arms and legs, he rolled onto his back and tried to massage his limbs. It didn't seem to help. He felt his energy fade. He forced a pathetic laugh as he looked up into the falling rain.

"Maybe I'm worse off than I thought. How did I hang onto Alex that whole time?" he whispered into the sky. The thought made him shiver again. After a few more shivers he realized it wasn't just the thoughts that caused his reaction, he was freezing to death, his body core was dropping. It was time for him to make his way to the warmth of the shelter.

He staggered to his feet and looked back towards in the cliff and into the stinging rain. His eyes were adjusting to the darkness. The silhouetted horizon no longer seemed so dark and ominous. The monstrous clouds that drifted past were backlit from the east by the rising sliver of a moon.

"How beautiful!"

A strange thing was happening to him. He no longer saw the darkness as something to fear. He watched the rising columns of clouds mesh and mix together like boiling steam. Their edges distinct, their shadows stretched and danced. The occasional flash of bluish white light and distant rumble only added to the wonder of the night.

He smiled and took a deep breath, hoping for the fragrant aroma of sweet smelling incense to fill his lungs. He had to settle for the fresh aromatic aftermath of a late winter storm.

"He said we are never truly alone," his voice crackled with emotion.

He turned toward the shelter and slowly stumbled along. He laughed at his clumsiness, his exhaustion.

"Defying gravity... defying the devil? Like father like son!"

Hearing the words made him laugh. He fingered the medallion that still hung loose around his neck. It felt comforting. "The medallion? A gift from my father? How could the medallion have hung untouched there by people or animals for all these years? How could they have all missed it? How did my dad's journal get to my mom's study?"

"Nature Boy!" He couldn't stop his nervous laughter. He wrapped his fist around the medallion and squeezed it as he gazed up into the moon light. His grip was weak. "Thank you," he whispered, "thanks for letting me see my daddy... for taking care of my mom and friends. I will keep this close. Daddy, I will keep you in my heart and in my prayers. God, I will do as you ask. Please protect my friend Erick, my uncle Dan, my aunt Betty, and my mom Lydia. May she finally forgive and understand. Please take care of my daddy, Gabriel, may he find his new home away from this scar. And can you please help Alex? She really needs your love and understanding. She really needs a friend, someone who'll love and understand her."

For a brief moment a few of the brightest stars dotted the darker western sky. The dark and light clouds moved and blended like a living, breathing organism.

The storm was showing signs of clearing.

The breeze sounded like soothing voices, singing together in harmony. For a moment, he thought he recognized the tune. "The prayer of Saint Frances?"

He began to cry.

CHAPTER THIRTY-SEVEN
REPRIEVE
MARCH 16TH 2000

Dan tripped, rolled and caught his balance, just before he tripped again. He let his momentum carry him down the trail. His thoughts focused on his every step. His instincts guided his gut reactions. Bud's words of warning echoed in his thoughts. He used them to motivate himself. He used them to take his mind off things that outright frightened the hell out of him.

The trail began to level off, and he followed the flagging. He recognized the landmarks in the beam of his headlamp. The clearing was just around the next bend.

"God, I hope I'm not too late!"

He increased the length of his stride and with that came speed. Exhaustion, numbness, neither mattered. He had to get back. He had to tell them how potentially dangerous Alex really was. He was so sick inside that he could taste the bile from his stomach. He wanted to vomit, but that would only take away precious time, time he no longer had to spend. He cursed the fact that history had a way of repeating itself.

The shadows opened into the edge of the clearing.

"Twenty yards!"

His words echoed loudly in his mind. He could almost smell the adrenaline in his sweat. The forest to his left dropped away into oblivion. The wall of ancient trees on his right reflected back the light. The moon was finally making its presence known.

"Erick, I'm here!"

Before him there were the packs, the shelter, but, not Erick. He skidded to a stop and slipped onto his butt just outside the entrance to Erick's tarp. His thighs and calves burned with fatigue.

"Erick!" he panted as he rolled to his side. He gripped the edge of the tarped enclosure and yanked it open. To his horror and dismay, his headlamp illuminated an empty interior. "Erick!" his desperate voice echoed again. "Where are you?"

For a moment, he felt as if his heart had stopped beating. If he had been attached to a monitor, it would have been confirmed. He opened his mouth to scream Erick's name, but nothing came out of his lungs. His fingers tingled and he felt the blood drain from his face and hands.

Psychological shock, brought on by a traumatic event. He knew it all too well. Until recently, he had written off post traumatic shock as just another excuse for those who couldn't cope. Shock kills, he kept telling himself. He was no stranger to shock; it was a factor to consider.

> Total system failure, the feeling of impending doom, helplessness, nausea, vomiting, the loss of control, the willingness to quit. Triggered by the loss or increase of body heat to the core functions, the loss of bodily fluids, and then the outright shutting down of the bodily systems... reduced oxygen to the brain... the result, total system failure... inevitably, death.

He calmed himself and searched the interior of the shelter with his eyes again.

"Did I just miss him?"

There in front of him, by the door, propped up against a sleeping bag, sat the portable radio, with a note. He crawled in and snatched both of them up in his hand. He forced himself to read the note first. The note shook in his trembling hand.

> ***Dan,***
> ***Sorry! Don't get mad, I know you said to stay put, but I had to go! Gabe needs my***

help! The angel said there wasn't any time to wait!
I know crossing the mud is dangerous, but don't worry. We have a plan.
Remember what you said, we have the angels on our side... that were never alone. Well, you were right!

Erick... 8:53 p.m.

"Angels?" he mumbled to himself.

He wasn't so sure that was good or bad. The devil had his angels too!

God wouldn't have sent Erick into that mess, would he?

If he hadn't been worried before, he was more than enough now!

He looked down at his watch and crumpled up the note in the palm of his hand and let it fall to the ground. It was 9:25 p.m. He had only been gone for about an hour and a half and the plans seemed to have changed again. He turned on the portable radio as he backed out of the shelter.

"Erick! Gabe!" he yelled frantically into the microphone. He was on the verge of panic. "Erick, Gabe! Come on, answer me!"

"God, not again... why again? Isn't once enough? What will this prove?" he screamed into the night. His thoughts raced. He fought the building anger that began to ravage his soul. He closed his eyes and looked up towards the sky.

The radio came to life. There was static at first, but soon the words began to make themselves clear.

"Can you boys hear me?"

"---, we're safe!" the excited voice echoed into the night.

Dan found himself sighing deeply in relief as tears mixed with sweat streamed down the sides of his cheeks. He wiped them away as he looked up toward the heavens and whispered, "Thank You!" A soothing strength flowed back into his core. He scrambled to his feet, and staggered toward the edge of the clearing to improve his radio reception. Sometimes it was amazing what a few steps in either direction could do for the reception of a radio. His legs screamed in protest as they were forced to do even more work.

"Gabe? Erick? This is Dan. Do you copy?"

"Dan!" the excited voice filled his ears. "This -- Erick, sorry - didn't stay like --- told me."

"Erick, it's okay, it's okay! Where's Gabe? Is he alright?"

"He --- sore ribs, tired. Found Alex, --- a girl!" Erick exclaimed.

Dan looked up into the sky and closed his eyes as he gave a sigh of relief. The reception was getting better. Now if he could only just hold on and not lose the reception and his patience. "I copy. You've found Alex. Where is she? Is she injured?"

"She -- with me in --- shelter, --- --- - broken leg, minor bruises."

"Great!" he mumbled out loud to himself. He got back on the radio, "Where's Gabe right now?" his voice sounded concerned.

"Outside!" seemed to echo louder than all of the other words.

"Outside?" Dan exclaimed. He didn't like the sound of that. He could tell that Erick was holding something back. "Are you clear to copy?" he spoke clearly.

"What?"

"Are you by yourself?"

"Well, she -- asleep and Gabe -- outside."

"Good. I want to talk with Gabe right away." No matter how hard he tried, he couldn't hide the concern in his voice.

"What's wrong?"

"Just do it, alright! I'll explain later." Dan held his breath.

How can we get Gabe through this one unscathed?

There was a moment of silence before Gabe's familiar voice filled the air ways.

"Dan?"

The sound of Gabe's voice warmed his heart. "Yeah, it's me, big guy. Are you okay?"

"I'm - ------ sore – ribs, -- very tired!"

Erick's voice cut in on the background, "You should ---- seen him...hanging off -- --- cliff -- --- legs—."

"No, --- should ---- seen Erick," countered Gabe's. "-- jerked us fifteen feet ---- up the side -- --- cliff!"

Their excitement was contagious.

Dan gave out a deep sigh as he paced nervously from side to side, wiping the tears from his eyes. He needed to warn them about Alex. "Sounds like you boys did really good. I'm proud of the both of you. But boys, you need to listen to me! What I'm going to tell you is very important!" Dan stopped pacing and gave another heavy sigh.

"What's -----?" both of the boys asked together.

An immediate silence followed.

"How do I say this? Alex is dangerous. I repeat, Alex, is dangerous! She needs medication. She will hurt you if given a chance! Do not trust her." Dan slurred his words, "Do not take any chances with her! I repeat, do not let her out of your sight! Do not trust her. Do you understand?" There was a strange silence over the airways. "Boys, do you understand?" Dan repeated.

"Yeah, but—" Erick started to explain.

Gabe interrupted. "Alex isn't dangerous...," his voice dominated the radio, "You're wrong! How -- --- supposed to be dangerous? What --- you talking about?"

"Look, listen to me... listen to me! You've got to trust me on this one." Dan yelled out in frustration. He had to get Gabe to understand. His safety depended on it. When he spoke again it was in a strained calm, he spoke slowly. "Gabe, I have just received radio confirmation from Incident Command. They want us to take care of ourselves. Bud wants us to be safe!" Dan looked down onto the muddy slope that separated him from the boys, his light bringing the shadows to life. The ground between the forest and the boulder field creaked and groaned under the weight of the water. He heard the constant rumble of the distant creek. Sections of the soil were slowly slumping away downhill.

It was obvious that there was no safe way for him to get across. It was a frustrating, hopeless feeling.

To be so close, but yet so far.

"Gabe, I can't get to you right now." Dan felt the strain in his own voice. "No one can... I'm the closest help available for miles. Talking to you on the radio is the best I can do!" It sounded like an excuse, but it was true. "I'm surprised Erick was even able to get to you! This is some pretty serious stuff out there. You guys are on your own until they get a helicopter out to you. That will be at first light, at the earliest." he rattled on, almost without taking a breath. He had to trust them. He had to trust their judgment. He had to put his trust in God's hands as well, on this one.

He closed his eyes, and took a slow, deep breath.

"Hear me out. You can explain it all to me later. I realize there are things going on out there that I don't know anything about, things I don't... understand, but...."

The airwave remained silent. He didn't know if they could hear him or not, but this all needed to be said, then and there. "I loved your father, Gabe..." Dan continued. His voice crackled with emotion as he spoke from his heart. His eyes began to water. "I love you. We're all here at this place, at the right time because we were meant to be. The both of you, me, Alex, your dad! We were all meant to be here. For some reason, destiny has brought us all together. Your father...," he gave out a heavy sigh, and looked up into the sky, "is still here as we speak. I know you feel him! I feel him!" He looked back towards the boulder field. "His spirit permeates this whole hillside. He was chosen to do God's work, and he responded to the call. I don't quite know if you understand that or not."

The winds seem to temporarily die down. There was a big delay between the distant flashes of lightning and the rumble of thunder.

"You've been chosen to be your father's successor." Dan fought the tears building in his eyes. "There... I've said it!"

***

Both boys gave each other a confused look as they listened to Dan rattled on.

"The war between good and evil goes on as we speak, good choices... bad choices." Dan's voice on the radio echoed amongst the boulders, "A handful of men and women like yourself have

been chosen to help change the balance. Evidently, Gabe, you are one of those. There are some who will try to put a stop to that, to put a stop to you!" Dan spoke faster.
Erick stared at Gabe while he stared at the radio.

***

Dan nervously ran his fingers, from his free hand, across his head as he continued to talk on the radio. Tears streamed down the sides of his cheeks as he nervously paced back and forth.
"They've chosen a handful of their own men and women to carry out their actions. You need to ask yourself, is Alex one of the good guys or is she one of those, biding time, gaining your trust, waiting for opportunities? If not now, maybe later, after you've turned your back and let down your guard?"

***

Both Erick and Gabe turn towards the shelter and exchange a confused glance.
"I'm not... turning my... back!" Gabe yelled into the microphone, his body shook from the cold.
An eerie silence drifted through the air. The rain was now a light mist. The faint flashes were no longer followed by distant rumbles. The moonlight was turning night into day.

***

Dan stopped pacing.
"Should I have said anything? It just came out!" he whispered to himself.
The radio crackled to life.

***

Gabe's thoughts were clear, calm, and concise. He almost didn't recognize his own voice. "To forgive... to help others in need... isn't that what he... has asked us to do? Don't you feel it? Tonight... we're safe!" Gabe calmly exclaimed.

He looked back towards Erick.

Erick draped one of the space blankets over Gabe's shoulder and nodded.

***

Dan wiped the tears from his eyes as he dropped to his knees. It was beyond his control. There was a strange energy in the air.

"Yes, I can feel it!"

His body shook with every sobbing breath. He let the radio fall to the mud. He felt the exhaustion kick in. All he wanted to do was sleep, to escape the burden. His little nephew had changed. The process had begun, there was nothing he could do to stop it. The journey had started.

"Brother," he looked around, his entire body shook as he sobbed, "Like father, like son!" He turned his head up towards the heavens. "God, take care of Gabe. Take care of his friend, Erick. Please, release my brother! Don't forsake 'em!" Dan burst again into tears as he collapsed, face down into the mud. He let his emotions flow. He held nothing back. He felt a gentle hand caress both of his shoulders. He smelled the incense in the air. He didn't need to look around to know that it was his brother standing there by his side one last time, brother and brother, arm in arm.

The sweet sound of singing had filled his ears, drifting in on a gentle, gusty breeze. A single harmonic voice blended into an acapella choir. Their distant rhythm grew in power and strength as they filtered in from the building moon-light from the east. His shadow stretched towards the canyon below. Strange comforting warmth suppressed his chill. Euphoria caused him to cry even louder. The angelic choir morphed into what sounded like the thundering rotor beats of an approaching helicopter.

***

A steady choir hummed in beautiful harmony as the moonlight cast its silver-white sheen through the gaps in the dark clouds and across the battered clearing. The rain was reduced to a mist-like drizzle, the winds had died down to almost nothing. The lightning was only a distant memory. The clouds traded their height for length, their intimidating shapes now comforting, pulled along by upper winds, hustling them off to some other place in time. The coolness had been replaced with warmth. A settling peace had now filled the void. The ground had quenched its thirst, the storm had run its course.

***

A young man in a white, translucent robe stood perfectly still as he balanced on the highest point of the rocky pinnacle. Beneath him lay the landslide that altered the mountain and people's lives around him. The forested outcropping was like an oasis in the middle of a great desert, like a spark of hope amid tragedy.

The light sound of an acapella choir echoed through the mountains.

He surveyed the scene that lay before him, his robe moving in a breeze of its own.

"Releasing beauty from ugliness, happiness from depression, love from hate, trust from abandonment, understanding from confusion." His words flowed like prayers.

"Oh, by the grace of God does love and beauty exist in some of the most unexpected places. The healing has begun!"

The young man smiled as he looked affectionately down upon four humans whose lives had been touched by the grace of God; two boys wrapped in a comforting embrace near a makeshift shelter that held the re-born soul of a young woman who had made a life-changing choice, a man collapsed in joyful sorrow in the mud at the edge of the clearing. Their journeys were by no means over. In fact, they had only begun.

The young man closed his eyes and tilted his head back, an action he had seen humans do numerous times before. He extended his arms, palms up out away from his body to let the droplets of mist bead against his face and pool in the palms of his hands. They rolled off as if he were made of wax.

Oh, what he would give to feel the coolness against his skin, to have the droplets trickle down the side of his face, and gently roll down its smooth, graceful curves. To fear the heights from which he stood would have been human.

To fall from heaven; that would be to fall from the grace of God, to fall for eternity, never to reach your destination.

That was the curse of immortality. Some of his brothers had fallen. Fallen angels, the humans call them. Irish legend called them fairies and mermaids-merman. If only they knew how close to the truth they actually were. Much like humans, the angels had also made their choices. Angels were more human-like than they ever knew!

"Enjoying the view, Boy Scout?"

Hissed the deep, sarcastic voice, interrupting his thoughts. The angel didn't turn towards the voice, he knew he was there, he felt the dark angel's presence and sensed his disenchantment.

"Is it wrong to bathe in the glory of a well-fought-for victory? Yes, Lusif, the work of our father is flawless, isn't it?"

He slowly opened his eyes and turned towards the voice. His pleasant smile appeared even more so.

On the rocky cropping next to him stood a tall, attractive, muscular man with long, dark hair that hung motionless, French-braided down the middle of his back and broad shoulders. His dark immaculate beard was in great contrast with a large, silver-looped earring that hung from the bottom lobe of each of his ears. A small flickering flame glowed suspended in the middle of the loops. His black and gray pinstriped shirt and dark slacks gave him a businessman flair. His feet were obscured in a heavy, odorous mist that smelled of brimstone and rotting meat.

"If you say so..."

The dark angel sounded unimpressed.

"I suppose I can't talk you into jumping! I hear the journey is delightful and invigorating this time of year..."

The voice said, reeking with sarcasm.

"It's the sudden stop that seems to put a damper on the whole experience!"

The dark angel stared down towards the two boys and the tarped enclosure, a moment before he refocused his demented gaze back to the young man.

"So, Steven, what do you think about my new tattoo?"

His face deformed into one of a horned demon. Red and black Maori indigenous-patterned tattooed lines suddenly took on a life of their own and coiled down the side of his face, disappearing beneath the collar of his shirt. They expanded and contracted with every breath.

"To help put the fear of the Devil into them with every glance and recurring dream?"

Lusif chanted and stomped his feet, pounded his chest and arms rhythmically as he aggressively flexed his muscles in a Maori Haka form. He extended his long, dark, forked tong and wiggled it around. He bulged his snake-like eyes and contorted his intimidating facial expression. Massive goat horn protuberances slowly un-furrowed from the sides of his head.

The angel Steven stared at him, his smile unaltered, demeanor unfazed.

"It's good to see you again, too, brother."

"No matter."

Lusif shrugged his shoulders as his facial features returned to normal. His eyes scanned the area until they fell upon the man crying in the mud along the edge of the forest.

"You never had much of a sense of style or originality."

"Or a means to carry out self-punishment!" Steven raised a curious well-groomed eyebrow.

"Thank you brother…"

Lusif laughed as he nodded towards the man in the mud.

"What do we have here? Touching! Actually, more like weak and pathetic. I thought he was a bit tougher than that. Just when you think you know someone…!"

A pleasant smile graced the angel's face.

"Father's grace, the power of redemption!"

Steven gestured towards the repenting man.

Lusif gave out a heavy sigh and shook his head in disgust.

"I've got some redemption for him..."

He pulled back his sleeves and began to cross his arms.

The sky rumbled, and they both momentarily turned their attention upward. So did the other humans below.

"Well, maybe not today!"

Lusif recanted, shrugged his shoulders turned his hands palms up and bowed his head. He uncrossed and lowered his arms as he leaned his head towards Steven. He smiled, whispered softly into his ear.

"I have that effect on people. They either run in fear or want to be my best friend..."

He raised an eyebrow.

"I appreciate much more the first, the running gets the fear and adrenaline coursing through their arteries and veins!"

He closed his eyes, looked up into the sky, took in a deep breath and smiled.

The sky rumbled again.

Lusif opened his eyes and held out his hands apologetically.

The angel stared into his brother's eyes, unaffected.

Lusif raised the other dark eyebrow, tilted his head back.

"I like the challenge. It makes the soul...."

He took another deep breath, held it in his lungs for a moment as if he took a hit off a cigarette and then slowly let it out as a putrid smelling dark smoke rolled free from his mouth. He licked his lips with a serpent-like tongue then looked back towards the angel before he continued.

"That much more, desirable."

His crooked fang-like teeth flashed black and yellow before they returned to their perfect shape and white shade.

The angel nodded, unmoved by his brother's theatric trick and looked back towards the humans.

"Freedom of choice... who knew that it held so much power!"

Steven raised an eyebrow.

Lusif shrugged his shoulders.

"It's what keeps me in business. You win some, you lose some!"

Lusif wiggled his thumb toward the tarped enclosure and the two boys.

"*In the end, it makes victory all that much sweeter. Now that, you can't deny.*"

He gave a demented laugh.

"*You can be s-s-sure I will be keeping my eyes, ears, and minions on that one. Yes-s-s...*"

He held his "S" a bit longer to emphasize his point.

"*Freedom of choice is a powerful thing, a mighty s-s-sweet and powerful thing!*"

His sarcastic laughter faded off into the sound of the approaching thunder and light.

"*You can't win them all brother Steven... you can't win them all...*"

Lusif bowed gracefully and slowly blended into the shadows.

Steven respectfully returned the nod.

"*I can't win them all!*"

The angel returned his gaze to the humans, and then to the heavens. He watched them simultaneously look up into the sky. This time even he felt the difference in the air.

Then, as if on cue, the sweet voices grew louder, the instruments began to sound. The moon seemed so much brighter, the air seemed so much fresher. This time he also felt something so very different.

He slowly reached up and slid his narrow finger along the sides of his face. His skin was no longer smooth, there were creases about the sides of his mouth and cheeks.

Was that a smile!

ACT: FOUR
THE AFTERMATH

CHAPTER THIRTY-EIGHT
THE BEGINNING

ST. PATRICK'S DAY MARCH 17TH 2000

Dan scolded himself for driving too fast and carelessly down the crooked, muddy, gravel road. But when he got to the paved, blacktop portion of the park road, all was quickly forgotten, and he let his International Scout get a feel for the road. By the time he reached the ranger office, he was at one with his four-wheel drive International Scout.

He entered the full parking lot and skidded to a stop about mid center. Instead of finding an open parking stall, he turned off his engine, kicked open the door, and ran from his vehicle, carelessly blocking several others.

Frankly, he didn't care. He figured no one else was going anywhere soon with the search and rescue operation still winding down. He trotted the fifteen or so yards across the parking lot, and barged through the front door of the office. His sore, tired legs screamed at him. He panted as he wiped the perspiration from his drenched face. His thoughts raced through the last few hours as he turned and looked for the two boys.

"Where are they?"

***

As planned, within four hours, four other rescue team members arrived at the edge of the devastation, medication in hand. However, the unstable slope that separated the boys and victim was much too dangerous to safely cross. So the team waited for the helicopter to arrive before first light. He couldn't sleep a wink knowing that Erick and Gabe were stranded alone with Alex. They were so close, yet separated by a formidable barrier. In the predawn hours the weather had cleared, and everything went like clockwork. The helicopter had snatched the three of them off the rocky island ledge by first light. They dropped the two boys off at the park headquarters, Dan off at his scout along the shoulder of the road by his vehicle, and flew Alex north to the hospital in Springville.

***

He could hardly wait to see the boys. They were halfway across the reception area when his eyes met their smiling faces. They embraced, but Dan eased back on the hugging when he felt Gabe wince in pain.
"Oh, sorry... forgot about the ribs!"
"It's alright! It's not the bruised ribs. It's the smell," teased Gabe as he leaned back. "They've got showers here you know!"
"Funny!" Dan reached over and ruffed up the hair on Gabe's head.
He winced again in pain trying to push his hand away.
"I'm fine," said Gabe, "bruised ribs and all! Not bruised enough to go to the hospital though!" He looked over to his friend and nodded. "It would have been worse if it weren't for Erick."
"The dynamic duo!" Dan grinned ear to ear.
Erick shrugged his shoulders and smiled.
Dan extended his hand to Erick and pulled him closer for a hug.
"I see you didn't waste any time getting down here!" the familiar voice rang out with a chuckle.
A firm hand squeezed Dan's shoulder. He turned around to greet both the Chief Ranger Eddie and Deputy Bud with a firm hand shake. Their eyes sparkled with satisfaction. Bud's handshake lingered for a moment.

"I took the liberty of havin' the boys dropped off here. I think they were a bit disappointed, and would have liked to have flown all the way back to the hospital in town. I especially had a little trouble getting' your nephew here out of the aircraft an' away from Alex." Bud raised an eyebrow and smiled as he released his grip.

Erick looked over and smiled while Gabe looked bashfully towards the floor.

"I hear he did a fine job with patient care. Hell, they both did. Mighty proud of 'em!" Bud slapped both boys on their backs, taking it easy on Gabe's.

"Well, you guys pulled it off, as expected!" remarked Eddie as he patted Dan on his shoulder. There was noticeable relief in his voice, night and day from twenty-four hours ago. "Have you given any thought to what we discussed earlier, you know, about maybe staying around a while? You know we've got an opening."

"It'll be a change of scenery for you, a slower pace than what you're probably used to!" Bud smiled. "Maybe even a bit stranger aroun' here at times than one would expect." He looked over to Eddie.

"Yes, a bit harder to explain why things happen the way they do around here," the Chief Ranger continued, "a memorable place none the less! The ancient forest has a way of warming your heart and stoking the imagination. I'll have you know, this place isn't all that it appears to be."

Dan nodded as he looked back over to the boys smiling faces. He could see it in their eyes, read it in their expressions. He had already made up his mind the day they arrived at the campground, but he hadn't let on.

Oh, that seemed so long ago!

"Did these guys put you up to this?" he nodded to the boys.

The boys grinned. Gabe shrugged his shoulders.

There was indeed a warm, comforting feel to the ancient redwood forests. Their cousins had been around since the time of the dinosaurs and, historically, their range had covered almost every continent. Now their range had been reduced to a narrow coastal strip along the upper two thirds of California and a tad bit into coastal Oregon. Relying on the fog from the ocean's summer influence, they lived to be thousands of years old. Some of the strangest tales have been generated from within their majestic shadows. It was hard to explain, but he felt as if he belonged, as if they belonged. His brother, Gabriel, had always been an important part of it.

He turned to the Chief Ranger and smiled, "So, when do I start?"

"You already have! Welcome to the team!" He reached out and pumped Dan's arm with a firm grip.

Bud caught Dan off guard as he thrust a rolled newspaper into Dan's chest. "There's somethin' you should read!"

Dan stared dumbfounded at the bundled newspaper for a moment, then looked over to Bud for an explanation.

"Check out section A-1." Bud said.

Dan narrowed his eyes. "What are you talking about?"

"The newspaper, Section A-1, the front page... headlines." Bud tapped his finger onto the front of the newspaper.

Dan slipped off the rubber band, unrolled the newspaper and searched the front page with his curious eyes. There was a large photograph of a young man in a white lab coat standing in the middle of what looked like a science lab. Dan pulled a pair of reading glasses out of his pocket.

"A doctor. What does that have to do with...?" Nothing registered for Dan. His eyes scanned up towards the words at the top. He looked at them but he couldn't pull them together to make any sense out of it. He shifted his gaze in between Bud and the Chief Ranger for help. He was exhausted.

"Don't tell me you've forgotten how to read already. Here's the Reader's Digest version..." Bud impatiently fired off, noting his confusion. "Ten years ago, the good doctor was visitin' the park, this park, only he wasn't a doctor then. He was a college student workin' on his PHD or somethin' like that. He got in trouble. A rangers saved his bacon at a place called *Falcon Canyon*," Bud nodded, "the same area you guys were at last night. The ranger that rescued him lost his life in the process. Does any of this ring a bell yet? "

Dan felt his whole insides wanting to be outside. His fingers began to tingle. The newspaper suddenly felt heavier than it should have. He gripped the paper tighter so it wouldn't slip out of his hands. He fought the sudden need to sit down.

"The young man grows up," Bud's voice crackled with emotion, "he gets good at what he went to school for. He uses the gift that the almighty has given him, an' does the impossible!"

Dan looked at the two boys as they stared at him in attentive wonder, and then back down at the newspaper. He forced his eyes to focus on the words, and his mind to understand them.

RESEARCHER SPECULATES THAT THE RISE IN CANCER ISN'T JUST GENETIC, MIGHT ALSO BE ENVIRONMENTAL AND DIET RELATED.

"The park visitor my brother saved... gives back by saving others?"

But, why did my brother have to give his life at all?

"The young man may have brought us that much closer to isolatin' the gene that causes cancer," Bud continued. "He talked about how he was indebted to the men who saved him, the men who, by the grace of God, gave him a secon' chance."

Bud cleared his throat.

"Your brother saved him so he could save thousands of others. Did you know that? Did you know what was goin' on out there?"

Bud pointed in the direction of the mountain,

"Did you have any idea?"

The tears were rolling down Dan's cheeks by now.

"Your brother was more than a God-given hero. Your brother was like, an angel, sent to save that young man's backside!"

If he only knew how close to the truth he really was!

Dan thought he saw Bud's hands tremble for a moment, before he shoved them into his pockets.

Bud's voice suddenly became serious, "Dan, I don't believe in coincidences, and I know that you don't either."

Bud shifted his gaze between Gabe and Dan. "I don't know what the heck is goin' on aroun' here, and I don't think I want to know. Gabriel's legacy is it?" Bud shook his head and broke into a joyous laugh. "Who would've ever thought?" His voice echoed loudly.

Dan found himself laughing lightly at first, but then his whole body shook in quivering trembles with every deep breath. He couldn't tell if his tears were from sorrow or joy. He felt a strange understanding of the last two weeks.

Why were we there? Why did we do what we did? Why did Gabe have to be the one chosen?

Dan no longer cursed the mountain. It was all part of him now, part of their legacy.

The two boys looked on with confusion.

The ringing of the Chief Ranger's phone interrupted the strangeness.

"Chief Ranger Eddie Mendoza here. Oh hello, Lydia. Yeah, he's right here," the Chief acknowledged. "Dan, it's for you! It's Lydia. She wanted me to notify her as soon as all of you boys made it off the mountain." He handed Dan the phone and gave him some space.

The others continued to talk.

"Lydia, we've done it!" He exclaimed. "No, hadn't doubted it for a minute."

He looked over to the boys and winked as he rubbed the tears from his eyes. He cleared his throat. His voice bubbled with confidence. "Thank you...! It was a team effort, really! Okay, put her on!"

He looked up to see if the others were watching. They weren't.

There was a moment of silence before his wife's voice rang out joyfully in his ear piece. He took a couple of steps away from the others, and turned his back towards them for privacy.

"You're in trouble now!" One of the men in the office teased.

The others laughed.

Dan waved them off.

"Honey, yes, I love you too! Am I sitting down?" He still stood up as he glanced back over to the others. "No, do I need to be? I'm in the office with the other *guys*!" He emphasized the word.

There was more silence on the other end of the phone. He thought he heard her crying.

"Honey, is everything okay?" Something was up; he felt the nausea growing in his gut. When she spoke again, he stood there still, froze in his tracks. The words had caught him by surprise. He felt all of the energy drain from his body, and then pour back in, twice as powerful, twice as strong.

"What?" his voice was louder than he wanted it to be. "You're kidding right? How... I mean...?"

He gripped the phone tighter as he staggered to regain his balance. A lump suddenly appeared in his throat. Tears of joy filled his eyes. He lowered the phone to his side and slowly turned to face the guys in the room.

Everyone was silently staring at him by now.

"Everythin' alright?" he barely heard Bud's voice over the confusing chaos that battered around between his ears and chest.

Did they hear all of that as well?

He looked up to the heavens and whispered, "Thank you!"

"Dan?" Bud yelled out again, concerned.

Dan turned to them and gave them a goofy smile. All of their concerned eyes were bearing down upon him. Their hearts filled with questions and concerns.

"I'm... I mean... we're pregnant!" his dumb founded expression broke into tears. "We're finally pregnant!" he yelled enthusiastically.

"Congratulations grandpa!" Bud's voice echoed in his ears.

Members of the group cheered.

"The saying is absolutely true." Dan's voice squeaked with emotion. "Good things also come in threes."

The legacy had yet another chapter to write for Saint Patrick's Day.

Somewhere in the ancient redwood forest there is another beginning brewing away.

About the Author
Illustrator
Father and Daughter Project.

Robert Leiterman and his daughter, **April Leiterman** are both Humboldt State University graduates. **Robert** with a BA degree in *Recreation Administration* and a minor in *Resource Management* (1986), and **April** with a BA in *Film Cum Laude* from Humboldt State (2020). They both live on California's North Coast behind the redwood curtain and enjoy spending time with their families, being in the outdoors, exploring, filming, and being creative.

Robert is a retired park ranger with a unique perspective. His experiences and vivid imagination has inspired him to share the richness of the North Coast environment in an educational and entertaining way. He is also the author of other books in print.

April an artist, writer and film maker with several projects under her belt. She has illustrated other books in print.

Books by:

ROBERT LEITERMAN

RECENT PUBLICATIONS (NON FICTION)

THE BLUFF CREEK PROJECT: THE PATTERSON-GIMLIN BIGFOOT FILM SITE
A JOURNEY OF REDISCOVERY
ISBN: 9798706738211 (SOFT)
(E-BOOK)

(FICTION)
THE BIGFOOT TRILOGY

The Bigfoot Mystery – The Adventure Begins
ISBN: 0-595-14175-7

Yeti or not, Here we come! –Bigfoot in the Redwoods
ISBN: 0-595-26561-8

Operation Redwood Quest – Search for Answers
ISBN: 0-595-30513-X

OTHER NATURAL HISTORY RELATED BOOKS: (FICTION)

Great Valley Grassland Adventure
ISBN: 0-595-20302-7

GOJU QUEST – A Martial Artist Journey
ISBN: 0-595-34185-3

Either One Way or the Otter
ISBN: 978-0-595-38218-7

Robert Leiterman

Ona Crainn – An Ancient Secret – From the Trees
Cover design and illustration by April Leiterman
ISBN: 978-1-4697-4469-8 (soft cover)
ISBN: 978-1-4697-4470-4 (e-book)

Made in the USA
Monee, IL
31 January 2022